DIFFERENT
FAMILIES

DIFFERENT FAMILIES

Alison Scott Skelton

Seaview Books

NEW YORK

Grateful acknowledgment is made for permission to reprint from "For Anne Gregory," "The Unappeasable Host," and "In Memory of Major Robert Gregory," by William Butler Yeats. Reprinted with permission of Macmillan Publishing Co., Inc., from *Collected Poems* by William Butler Yeats. Copyright 1924 by Macmillan Publishing Co., Inc., renewed 1952 by Bertha Georgie Yeats.

Manufactured in the United States of America.

FIRST EDITION

Designed by Tere LoPrete

Library of Congress Cataloging in Publication Data

Skelton, Alison Scott.
    Different families.

    I. Title.
PZ4.S61966Di   [PS3569.K39]   813'.54   79-4890
ISBN 0-87223-610-2

FOR CLEM

"Wish me luck as you wave me good-bye!"

DIFFERENT FAMILIES

I

"Once there was a farmer," said Robert, "on the banks of a river."

"Why should I go?" Mary Jo said again. She rubbed bare feet into the plush of the red Indian rug by the bed. She had wedged herself in that bedroom corner, between the bed and the green wicker chair and the amber vase of dusty yellow reeds. Her bikini, the same green as the chair, and salt-stained, had dried on her. She had looped her thumb through the lacquered metal ring that joined the two triangles on her left hip. The gesture was unconsciously aggressive, from the habitual wearing of jeans. It stretched the fabric away from her body, showing white untanned skin and a small puff of blond pubic hair.

"With a fox, and a goose, and a sack of grain. Don't ask me why."

"I damn well will." Mary Jo's eyes came up from the sandy rug, and her hips swung sideways, innocently widening the bikini gap. She said, "I damn well will. She's *your* wife."

Robert sliced carefully through the slab of beef fillet, cutting long, thin, cross-grained strips. The hot afternoon breathed through the screen onto his hands, dappling them, and the bloody cutting board, with sun. The window needed painting again, and the mildewed curtains were sun-rotten. If it were winter, there'd be time to repair, and mend, and work. Robert laid the meat strips out on the board like square worms, and dropped two bits of gristle onto the linoleum, automatically. The larger cat came at once, and the smaller lurked.

"Ex," he said. "Ex. I meant, don't ask why the fox." He put the knife down. His patience was upsetting her. He called it his middle-aged gift, but it was more accurately his English inheritance. David had it already. "The grain and the goose I can understand. He was after all a farmer. But the fox? Anyhow, he couldn't leave the fox with the goose because the fox would eat the goose. Or the goose with the grain, because the goose would eat the grain. And the ferry would only hold two, plus himself. Are you going dressed like that?"

"Robert. Please." But she went away to the oilcloth-covered table and lifted her sweatshirt from one of the straight-backed mismatched wooden chairs. The sweatshirt was gray, an unappealing, unflattering color. It said "Columbia" across it, but Mary Jo habitually wore it with the fleecy pile interior on the outside. It was a man's size, and anyhow Mary Jo had not gone to Columbia, and beyond that Robert did not ask. When he was in school they'd exchanged big, brassy senior rings. God knows what they exchanged now. Mary Jo scrabbled awkwardly into the sweatshirt.

He said, "The grain and the fox were all right, of course."

"Robert," Mary Jo said in a little voice. "I'm sorry. Honest to Jesus." She was now all brown long legs dividing endlessly to the sagging hem of the sweatshirt. She slid her feet into her sandals, coarse hand-sewn leather from the Village. Robert shrugged. He said, "Put the cats away before Paul comes. He has his thing."

"Asthma."

"Hysterics."

"No. It's really asthma, Robert." She picked up both black cats and opened the window and poured them out. They plopped heavily annoyed on the deck. "You don't care about people."

"That's what's wrong with me." He said it quickly, before

she could, and continued cutting meat. Once beside him, she made herself busy, rubbing half a clove of garlic about the rim of the wooden salad bowl until he had to say, "You'll be late."

"Send David."

Robert could see David through the open door of his bedroom, Robert's workroom, really, which he had contentedly given up at the start of the summer when David came. A corner of his typewriter glinted, gray-green and a little dustily, in the sun. So. It was summer. The sun was kinder on David's blond hair. He was lying on the bed, in his jeans and American T-shirt and sneakers, fully dressed, sound asleep. They had had wine with lunch. He'd lain in the sun all morning on the deck. But it was neither drink nor heat that he slept from, but emotion, Robert knew. The sight of the boy brought a tenderness in him that was physical, a passion. He looked from Mary Jo to David, one young body and another. His mind nudged them closer, a fingernail to a blackboard.

"Send the goose to the fox?" he said. "Oh, never."

"Then go yourself," Mary Jo said, pressing the garlic clove till it slithered and leaped like a frog.

"That, sweetheart, leaves the grain with the goose."

"Oh, for God's sake, Robert. I'm sorry, I'm sorry. How many times do I have to say it?" Then she said, "Why don't we both go and meet Philippa?"

Her casual, unthinking use of the Christian name sent his tongue seeking rapid reprimand, but at once he was entangled in such complexities of rights and conventions that he said only with a little smile, "Oh, sure, sweetheart. Hand in hand." Then he laughed and said, "Besides, I'm not leaving David alone when Paul arrives in his Daisy Mae outfit. And the Soldier of Fortune in tow. Christ, poor Goose."

"David's a grown man, Robert."

"Isn't he just," said Robert, laying the knife down beside the meat. She began to cry. "Sweetheart, if you must know, I am not going because I am terrified. I am terrified for reasons that have nothing to do with you, and surprisingly little to do with David. You are a young woman, and very few young people, and almost no women, can ever believe there are important scenes in life that don't include them. But it happens to be the case. And this is one of them."

Mary Jo was crying more openly. Robert looked from her wet brown face to David's, calm in sleep. Mary Jo would also never believe that David lying there, clothed and awkward, was stirring him inside more than all her smooth nakedness. No one without children of their own could understand. He felt like a juggler between the two. He washed his hands under the cold faucet. The water was sickly warm from the header tank on the sun-baked roof. The pump whirred. Through a corner of the dusty screened window he could see a white moving shape traversing the blue of the bay somewhere between the mainland and the Pines harbor off to the west. He dried his hands on the red-striped dish towel. "I can see the ferry," he said.

Mary Jo had curled miserably into the green wicker chair, but jumped up now with urgency and rushed to the sink. She splashed water on her eyes and rubbed them dry on the towel. They remained red, and now her hair was wet at the sides, and one long rope of it that had fallen into the sink dripped on the gray sweatshirt fleece. Still, it would all dry in half a minute in the sunny heat beyond the door. "It isn't fair, Robert," she cried childishly, and then added, "You bastard," to salvage adult dignity. "How do I know who she is? I'll walk right past her. I don't even know what she looks like."

Robert shoved his hands in the front pockets of his jeans. They were new jeans, dark blue and crunchy and stiff. Robert did not season his jeans. He bought them new, at Stein's in Sayville, and threw them out when they got faded. He could afford to do that now, and enjoyed it. Mary Jo did not like that, any more than she liked the way he was looking at his watch. It meant age to her. Not the good side of his age, his half-silvered wild hair, and his courageous, untalked-about past. But the other side: of petty illnesses, and stubborn links with a time before her birth.

"Oh, you'll know her. You'll know her," he said, still looking at the watch, an old watch with big numbers. "She's blond, like David, and blue-eyed. She'll stand out a mile," he added then, with illogical confidence. "You'll know her."

"But if I don't?"

"So what of it?" He stepped closer to her, but he was still looking out the window, at the ferry and the mainland, burnished red-brown over its greens, late summer color. It amused him that an island could become a mainland by virtue of another island's attentions. It was like himself and Mary Jo, he knew, but he was unsure how. "So what if you walk right by and don't know her? You're strangers, why should you know her?"

Mary Jo shook her head, biting annoyingly at a length of her own damp honey-blond hair.

"Go on," Robert said, and she picked up the boat key with its small red and white buoy and clattered out of the house in her flat sandals. The screen door banged sharply shut behind her. Robert glanced instinctively to David, at the sound, but he had not awakened. Then Robert went and stood at the door, looking out through the gray shading of screen. Mary Jo stood at the T-junction where his narrow walk met the main walk leading off to the shared bay-front docks where they tethered the speedboat and the Sunfish. She was half hidden by rampant beach plum and poison ivy, and the one low branch of the one scrub oak. When Robert was a shy, tiny child, and his mother would send him to the candy store for the Sunday papers, he would linger like that, where their paved walk joined the tarred road, with his feet scuffing around, like Mary Jo's, praying his mother would magically forget and spare him the burden. She never did, and he would trudge off, wary, to blush and stumble over the words, "Zolenski's papers—please," and the impossible complication of the change.

Kindness for the sad child arose, but yesterday had been a cruel day, and endowed him with a cruel power. "G'won, sweetheart," he said, from the gray shadow within, and then he laughed quietly and called, "You can't miss her, she looks just like Vera Lynn."

Mary Jo looked up sharply. She sensed somehow he was not precisely speaking to her. She shoved the keys into her other hand and balled a fist around them. Then she tugged the sweatshirt down snugly over her bikini bottom and turned away. Robert did not wait to see her go, to hear the boat engine burr, or to see her reappear beyond the lee of the island, heading west with a white angry wake behind. Instead he went back to his kitchen and dumped mushrooms into a colander and turned the faucet on. He said very quietly, to the girl in her absence, and a little to the boy still sleeping in the side room by his typewriter, "So what of it, sweetheart? Just suppose I went, and *I* didn't know her? Where would that leave us, little goose?"

Mary Jo's voice shouted suddenly defiant from the distance of the boardwalk, echoing shrilly over his neighbors' roofs, "So who the fuck is Vera Lynn?"

August, 1940
Yorkshire

"You'll know her," said Mike. "You can't miss her. She looks just like Vera Lynn."

"Sure."

"She does, pal."

"A dame's a dame."

"Not this one. Honest to God, Bob. You don't know a good thing when it's staring you in the face. She's beautiful."

"So what's she want me for?" Robert leaned the borrowed black bicycle against the salty wet stone balustrade. The sea was gray smooth and calm, the tide fully out, showing flat packed dark gold sand, cold and uninviting and strung with black coiling tangles of barbed wire.

"Who knows?" Mike said, laying his own cycle down flat on the paved promenade. The wheel spun and he kicked it still. "So she sees you at Quaglino's. She thinks you're a star. We all make mistakes."

"I bet she's a drip. I bet you've made it all up."

"Yeah. I made it all up. You got a cigarette?"

Robert reached automatically into the breast pocket of his tunic and pulled out his packet of Lucky Strikes. His mother sent them occasionally in little brown packages with one of her sad offended letters tucked inside. "So what's the matter with *your* mother? She doesn't send cigarettes?"

Mike shrugged and took one from the pack, returned the pack, and turned his back to the sea wind while he lit it, very carefully lest he waste the match. They were getting very hard to find, of late. "She's patriotic," he said. "She won't waste the shipping space." He measured a cigarette-packet length with his hands and raised one eyebrow. "Besides, she doesn't like me smoking. She says it's bad for my health." He laughed, shrugging easily. "So's Jerry," he said, "but she's willing to ignore that."

"Sometimes I think my mom's on the other side," Robert said, without a smile. He was slender, and dark, and beside the big stocky blond Canadian, he had a way of looking poetically sorrowful.

"Bullshit," said Mike.

"No. I mean it. You ought to see her letters. I wish to God the States would hurry up and get into the war. It would shut mom up, at least, if not Hitler."

"I bet that's them," Mike said, looking down off the sea-front, to where far distant on the near empty stone promenade three girls had appeared, running down the steep steps.

" 'Let the English fight their own battles. Let 'em send the Black and Tans, like they sent them after your granddad!' "

"Jesus, she doesn't say that." Mike was only half listening. He raised one arm and waved until the three girls saw and stood staring at the two far figures in airforce blue.

"Aw, she says it all right. Goddamn long Irish memory."

Watery thin sunlight crept out between two sodden banks of cloud. It shone white on the peeling salt-weathered stuccoed fronts of the tall Victorian houses bordering the promenade. Everything looked shabby and more worn, except the sea, which gathered a misty glory. Off to the north, the thin light hit the white chalk face of the Flamborough cliffs. Robert thought them like the Palisades across the Hudson. They could be seen far, far out to sea, like a beacon, by sunlight or moonlight. They had not succumbed yet to the blackout.

"Christ, look," Robert said. "Sunshine."

That brief brightness, already receding, was the first sun they'd seen since coming to Carnaby. Robert had an illogical conviction that sun, like sugar, and cigarettes, and bananas, was a war casualty. And that it would come back with peace, like in the songs. The squadron had been sent up a week ago, annoyed and reluctant, from the south, the Kent and Sussex coasts where the action was. They'd seen action, both of them, and grown a sense of magical survival by having survived their few, stretched-out weeks in the summer skies. And for all that it scared the pants off them on occasions, neither Robert nor Mike had come across the Atlantic for any reason other than action.

Now, for no reason but official nonsense, they were here, to hell and gone north, in Yorkshire, at a half-assed aerodrome on the moors overlooking the equally half-assed little Victorian town of Bridlington. For seven wet, rainy days they had hung about the place, in rotating periods of readiness, standby, and release, until dusk brought its usual stand-down. Midday, today, they were both sitting about in that odd state of bored tension, prepared for action, presented with none. They played gin rummy and poker, sitting on wooden chairs in their leather flying jackets, until in mid-afternoon they were released. It was the sought-after period, that late afternoon stand-down, with freedom extending on into the night.

They fled the aerodrome at once, whirring down the steep empty roads into town on old black bicycles, looking for something, anything offering excitement. And then Mike had come up with the story about the girl. He'd met her two nights before in a country pub, one of those small cottagey places with many rooms, some for mixed company, some male preserves, all hung with fairy lights and glittery horse brasses, and carefully blacked out against the Yorkshire night. She had come in with her aunt and they sat in a corner drinking ale. She lived nearby or had done so, before going into the forces. She was with the WAAF now, based near London, and was home on leave. Only she was not staying at home with her parents in the country, but down in Brid, as she called it, with the schoolteacher aunt, now a bastion of the WVS. And she knew Robert. Or knew of Robert.

"How did she know it was me?" he asked suddenly. Mike was lifting his cycle and wheeling it purposefully down the seafront toward the girls.

"Aw, who knows? She asked another dame. They were both in the audience. She found out the squadron number or something. Anyhow, it was me being Canadian and in the same squadron that made her speak up in the pub. She reckoned I'd know you, what with you being a Yank. You know how they are . . . 'Oh, you come from Toronto. I have a cousin in Montreal called Cuthbert, do you know him?' "

Robert laughed. "It isn't their fault. It's a little country. They can't picture big places. Hey, are those dames really going to swim?"

The three girls had been wearing belted raincoats, but they took them off now and laid them across the rounded stone of the balustrade. They were, all three, wearing trousers and blouses which they delicately unbuttoned, with their backs to the seafront houses of the town. As delicately they lowered their straight-legged trousers and stepped out of them, and, standing then, each in a black bathing suit, and with their shoes yet on, they folded their clothes, laid them on the wall, and gathered up their white towels and clattered, in high heels, down the flights of steps to the shore.

The gap in the coils of barbed wire was just fifty feet wide, and had been left there near the North Pier, jutting out into the sea, for just this purpose. At the foot of the steps, where the tide had curled the sand over them, the girls left their shoes in a neat line, and suddenly broke and ran, giggling, toward the sea.

"That's her," said Mike, "the blond. A bit of all right, eh?"

She ran down the long flat beach, ahead of the other two girls. They had stopped to primly tuck hair into kerchiefs and knot them up, on top of the frizzed pompadours on their foreheads. She had no pompadour, no kerchief, but a loose bob of honey-blond hair. It whipped up in the wind, and tangled as she ran on. There were eight people on the promenade, two soldiers, Robert and Mike, and four middle-aged ladies in coats and hats. Everyone stopped and everyone watched. The soldiers laughed, and everyone pretended to watch only because it was cold, and just off rain, and the girls were mad to be bathing there in the pathetic little channel between the barricades. But that was not the reason. Beauty was the reason; beauty, and freedom on a grim wartime strand. And impulse.

It was the impulsiveness, not the beauty, that caught in Robert's throat. She never broke stride, but hit the water with one, and then another long bright leg, and then plunged two more leg-lengths, and then flung herself, with wild faith, full length. The instant she touched the water, the sun broke through, striking gold sand and gold hair, and the gray-white froth of the North Sea. Robert brought his hands together and clapped, long, loud, theater applause. The beach was silent, the sound ringing. The two girls, her companions, turned around and paused, and then struck poses, swaying their hips and ducking their frizzy heads together like preening birds. They giggled, but the sound did not carry.

The girl in the water swam, long fine strokes, far out to sea.

"A bit of all right?" said Mike with a confident, self-satisfied grin.

"I'll say," said Robert. He was in love from that moment.

He was artistic, perceptive enough to know that impulse, that freedom meant something. And it did; that surety of the body possessed only by those who've given it. It meant she was not a virgin. Robert was not wise enough to know that.

She came up from the water after her swim, and while her companions giggled and splashed each other like Edwardian maidens, she walked slowly, intentionally up the damp sands. Mike and Robert were sitting on the bottom step of the stone flight, watching a formation of aircraft, their own, wheeling about the sky. They sat thus, with Robert concentrating on the distant planes with more and more difficulty as the girl approached. Then she stood in front of them, her towel in a roll about her shoulders, the ends flicking down over the ruched black top of the swimsuit. Salt water ran down her neck, and between her breasts, disappearing within the black ruching. Robert could not keep his eyes off her bare wetness. He had had only one woman, and female bodies were yet a foreign land.

"*Hel*lo, Mike," she said. The voice was rounded and ringing and the glance she cast sideways at Robert as she spoke was accidental. The introduction that Mike proferred then, of Miss Philippa Hallsworth, was so clearly secondary and casual that no one could imagine she had engineered it. Robert was certain it was Mike's doing, Mike's little game, for whatever reason of his own. But the girl was lovely, a strong, out-of-doors English blond, with high cheekbones and a wide kind mouth, sporty and friendly; and who was he to complain? She shook his hand and then Mike and the two kerchiefed girls just faded out of sight.

They climbed the steps to where he had left the bicycle. She rubbed herself with the towel, shivering. He offered his tunic; she refused, scrubbing briskly with the towel, like an athlete.

"Like a cup of tea, or something?"

"Splendid."

They began to walk, Robert pushing his cycle with her

raincoat across the bar. She slipped her blouse on and carried her trousers. "Wait, I must get dressed." She was not giggly, or shy, about clambering into the loose-legged trousers, right there on the promenade. Of course, it was deserted, watched by black-headed gulls and distant elephantine barrage balloons, and little else. Still, she was not shy. Robert thought then, that is their reserve, not refraining from doing things, but refraining from acknowledging them. He liked it. It was cool and alien. The wet bathing suit made damp patches at her breasts and hips.

"I asked Mike to introduce us," she said calmly. So she had. He withdrew inside. "I saw you at Quaglino's. You were terribly good."

"Thank you," Robert said, trying to be unaffected and cool as herself. But he grinned deprecatingly. It was his nature not to risk taking himself too seriously. "It was just a lark. I've quit now. I looked up one day and my CO was at the nearest table."

"Did he make trouble?"

Robert shrugged. "He's a good guy. But I had to quit, of course. I was just doing it for fun, anyway. And the money."

"You're a professional."

He shrugged again. "Well, they paid me."

"No. I mean before; you've done it before somewhere."

"Not cabaret."

"Then you're an actor, or a singer, something in theater." It sounded important to her, and yet she seemed too intelligent for a stage-door jenny. He nodded.

"At home in the States. I did some acting."

"You were good."

He shrugged again, bemused. "How are you so sure?"

She smiled. "So I'm right. I like theater. I like artists. Some people are afraid of them, but I'm not. I know they're frightened, too. Like horses."

"You're damned full of yourself," he said. But she was smiling, that wide, friendly smile.

"How about my cup of tea?" They were down near the harbor now, beside a small café snugged up against the southerly harbor wall. It was a small place with tatty windows, streaked white from gull droppings. Each window held a cardboard sign proclaiming tea, or scones, or pie and chips, and the price.

"It looks scruffy," he said.

She shrugged, an easy shrug, and a lingering toss of the honey-colored hair, thick hair, wet at the ends.

". . . those great honey-colored ramparts at your ear . . ." He thought it suddenly, and restrained the desire to speak it, and to touch. The one too theatrical, the other too crude.

"I like scruffy," she said. She was slumming. He realized at once, with a faint twinge of annoyance. A high-class girl, slumming.

They went in and sat down at a table at the window. But at once a soldier and two girls came in, and asked if they could have that larger table, and Robert and the girl relinquished it. It was a quiet kindliness which saved their lives, and cost the soldier and his two girls their own.

They settled again at another table, nearer the small wooden counter from which the sole waitress dispensed teas and plain scones and thin yellow slices of dried-egg cake. Philippa poured milk in her tea until it was pale, as one would serve it to children, and added the single lump of sugar provided. But she refused anything to eat, and Robert, feeling suddenly that eating was undignified, sat, a bit hungrily, with his hands around the bitter black brew in his own cup. He made a face as he drank it.

"Put sugar in it," she said, nudging his single lump across the table.

He shook his head. "It's worse that way; besides, I feel guilty."

"About a lump of sugar?" Her voice was ringing again, and incredulous. He wanted to say, hush, but no one looked up. "Don't be silly. Everyone gets their share. Take yours." She shoved the lump even closer, and he took it to shut her up, and crumbled it into the tea. It tasted worse then, as he'd said, the bitter black edge only half gone. She shoved the chipped white milk jug to him, triumphantly, but that would be worse yet, like watered-down coffee, translucent as dishwater. He shook his head and pushed it back.

"I feel guilty all the time. We get so much when we're flying. Bacon and eggs every morning. Two eggs."

"So? You're earning it," she said matter-of-factly.

He shrugged. "I keep thinking about the children."

She raised one finely plucked eyebrow. "We're not starving, you know. We're looking after ourselves quite nicely. Pity is not required yet."

"Give it time," he said sharply, because she'd been sharp. The other eyebrow joined the first, and the wide strong mouth settled into a solid displeased line. He noticed suddenly she had a very stubborn chin.

"Just what is that meant to mean?"

"Oh, nothing."

"Just what, Robert?"

"Only that things might get worse before they get better."

"Do you think we don't know that?"

"You've just said . . . aw, forget it."

She shook her thick hair with annoyance, and Robert longed again to tangle fingers in it, behind her ear, at the nape of that long fine neck. He did not wish to talk about Britain, nor his ambivalent faith in her. He wanted to talk about Philippa Hallsworth.

"No, Robert, we'll not just forget it. You think we are going to lose."

"To hell I do. Would I be here?"

"Why not? Artists love martyrdom."

"Not this one, sweetheart. Look. I think it's a grand little country. I also think it's going to need all the help it can get. That's why I'm here, okay?" There was a sudden distant rumbling sound, almost as metal on metal. Robert looked up, uneasy, and said, "What's that?"

Philippa remained looking into her teacup. "The sea," she said calmly. "The tide's coming in. The café's built into the seawall." She shrugged behind her. "The sea is out there." Robert stiffened, uncannily aware of the wet cold weight creeping in up the solid dark gold sands. He shook his head, ruffling his dark hair in an old nervous gesture. Since the hurricane, the sea and he had borne each other with a restless unease.

"Spreading alarm and despondency," Philippa said with her wide grin, once more. "It's an offense, you know. We could throw you in the Tower." Then she stopped laughing and said, "We're not going to lose, Robert. We are not. We cannot." He heard then another sound, a distant droning, wavering in pitch, a sound that raised each head in the café.

"Ours, surely," said Philippa.

"Theirs," said Robert.

It was theirs. Two thousand feet above their heads, Bruno Schroder was winning his Iron Cross.

Bruno would live to hear the raid on the shipyards of Tyneside acclaimed a great success, and their loss of thirty bombers discreetly glossed. The painful absence of their ME 109s; the weak fighter support of their longer-range but less maneuverable 110s would be forgotten. Bruno would be awarded his Iron Cross in a ceremony in Berlin. His mother would come with her country hands in gloves, and be very proud. But that was the future. Just now, Bruno wanted only one thing in the world: to get his ass back to the French coast in one piece.

The Heinkel was damaged. They did not know how badly. One engine was leaking oil, and sputtering like an angry little animal crouched on the wing. The dorsal gunner was dying, painfully, with much blood and ugly sounds. The pilot was fighting to keep the bomber's nose up. Still, if the Spits did not find them, they would get home, to Chartres. But when they did, they could not land. No, not until Bruno did something very clever, did something about the one of the Heinkel's eight massive bombs that was neatly hung up in the bomb bay. Its forked tail wobbled somewhere below, how far Bruno did not know. He had a pretty good idea, though. Far enough to spark fatally against the ground the instant they touched down.

"I will get it," said Bruno. He was nineteen, a decent lad, a good country Lutheran. He had four fair-haired brothers and sisters at home, all smaller than him, all lost in admiration. His voice shook a little. He said, "It will be no problem. I will get it." He began crawling, delicately, down the gangway between the vertical storage shafts. Below him the bomb doors gaped open to two thousand feet of air.

"I see the coast," cried the pilot, with a boy's relief. The chalk cliffs of Flamborough were in their view. It cheered Bruno. In no time they would be home. Just this little problem first. He lay down on the metal gangplank, peering into the cavernous cloudy space below. There was a town through the clouds with red-tiled roofs. Like a German town. The hooked bomb wobbled blackly over it. He must get the thing loose. Just loose, away.

He hooked one ankle around a metal strut, and crooked his knee, bending his body downward. Like he would swing in the tree above the river at home, by the rye field. With Hilda and Ellen. With Hilda and Ellen. The town whipped by dizzily, and the wind pulled at him, like the town's arms. It was caught, just there, the little clever ring that held it in place was cleverly caught, by a little twist in the hook. One in a million. Surely they could not make it do that if they tried. No one could. He drew in his breath, and stretched his arm. He could not reach, with the ankle so firmly wedged. Perhaps if he slid, a little further, and just the instep and the toe held that metal strut. Circus people did that, with just the instep and the toe. He released the strut, his foot slid carefully. Then the Heinkel shuddered and dropped, the air-stream giving way. Bruno lurched. "Holy Jesus!"

His hand slapped against the bomber casing. And like that,

just like that, it came free. He lurched again wildly, scrabbling with his legs, and then his boot toes lodged between the strut and the gangplank and his heavy leather flying jacket caught itself up, like a brake. He heard himself crying out, "Oh, help me, help me." But it was himself who helped himself. There was no one else. Then he sat on the gangplank, his legs dangling, holding on with his hands, like on a teeter-totter. Hilda and Ellen were on the other end. He was crying; the bomb was falling. The bomb was gone.

The white Flamborough cliffs flashed by, and they were safe.

"No siren," said Philippa.

"A stray," said Robert. Then the siren went. The bomb hit in almost the same instant. There was a white flash and an increased glare of daylight as the windows shattered. The two girls and the soldier took all of the impact, all of the glass, shattered and tattered instantly into strips of flesh and bone. Philippa was still sitting, though the tablecloth had been shredded away and she herself was dusted white in plaster dust.

"My cup's broken," she said. "It's broken my cup." Then the roof came down on them all.

There was blackness. Robert was aware first of the blackness, and then of the noise, a long, solitary horrendous female scream, and a man's voice shouting, almost petulantly, "Get these bodies off me, damn, get these bodies off." There was a child crying; he had not even been aware of a child in the café. Now one was crying weakly, "Daddy, daddy, daddy," over and over again, without emotion, like a child wakened in the night. Then he heard Philippa, in a clear voice, calling his name.

It shamed him. He had not thought of her, but only of himself, that he, Robert Zolenski, was in a bombed, crushed building, with a numb painful thing on his legs, and an aching dizziness in his head. Most of all, he was afraid, and mostly of fire. But it was not fire he had to worry about.

Then someone was calling, "Over here, I think, over here." It was Philippa again. He could not see anything, and blinked his eyes open and shut, wondering if he was blinded. His eyes did not hurt, but it remained black all around him. "We were sitting right here." Again it was Philippa's voice, and he realized dimly from the calm masculine voices replying that a rescue was in progress, far too quickly, surely. Then he knew he must have been unconscious. He became desperate to know how long, and wriggled to bring his right arm, and his watch, near to his eyes in the blackness. He never thought once to answer, to use his voice in any way, to guide his rescuers. He did not even think of rescue. Only the tremendous need to know what time had passed.

But his struggle for the watch shifted the layers of lathing and plaster, and stirred the settling dust. "There's someone here," said the calm voice. "Bring the light." Robert relaxed. He was shocked and felt sleepy. They were coming. It did not matter. He could sleep, even, while they came. Then the noise came, the grinding noise, like metal on metal, and above it, a noise of stone, shifting on stone.

"Hurry it up, mate," said the calm voice. "The tide's coming in."

The first water hit Robert's face like the tail of a snake. Somewhere, somehow below him, a human cry began, a deep-throated terrified cry. A man, crying. The calm rescuer's voice said distantly, again, "Hurry it up, mate. We'll shift this one and see where it gets us."

"We'll not get those down there," another voice, as calm, replied. But there was a frantic scuffling above, as if hands worked with all the urgency that voices lacked. There was a grayness about Robert now, and he knew he was not blind. Philippa was still calling his name, and he wondered why he did not answer, and wondered, uncaring, if he was one of those down there who could not be reached. The darkness over his head shifted suddenly, and the weight on his legs shuddered. Then the water hit him again, a long rippling splash at the end of a rumbling roar. The sea was coming in; through the broken seawall, into the wrecked café; in. It would fill everything, every nook and cranny between ruined brick, and plaster, and tin roof, every nook and cranny of his body, eyes, ears, lips, lungs. "Oh, God, Jesus, no." In an instant he was back home, on the bay shore, in the hurricane, watching the glass houses fall.

"I hear him," Philippa cried, and then the darkness was jerked away, and Philippa's face, plaster white, and with blood smudging her chin, was over him. She did not cry out, and ask if he was all right. She said calmly, "Chin up, darling," and began pawing efficiently at the rubble of plaster and lath that covered him. He could not believe she had said it.

Other, stronger hands were jostling the weightier debris that pinned his legs and he became suddenly aware of a great deal of pain, and intense cold. But it was all right; they would free him. He lay on his back, trying to raise his chin, and grinning stupidly through the plaster dust. "I can't get it up," he said, and giggled at his own astounding wit. Philippa said nothing; she kept looking over him, at something behind him. The rumbling noise came again, and the darkness returned momentarily. There was a great crashing and water was everywhere. He gasped for air and swallowed brine. Below him the voice that had cried was now gasping and choking.

"Poor bugger," said the calm male voice. And then, "Sorry, miss."

Robert saw that Philippa was soaking wet, and the water was making a paste, like a death mask, of the plaster dust. He cried out suddenly, "Take her out of here," because he knew then the whole place was going into the sea, like the glass houses. "Please, someone, take the girl away."

"Nonsense, silly goose," said Philippa. "We'll all go in just a minute. Be patient." He was aware then that she was directing and organizing his rescue. That she was giving orders to the men. And even more amazing, they were obeying. Then they moved the roof beam off his legs, and he fainted.

He was in daylight when he awoke, the sick sea daylight of a stormy evening. The wind was rising and somewhere far away someone was crying and there was the faint musical sound of falling glass. He was free of the fallen café, free of the ground, floating, being carried, lying flat, with blankets all around him. In spite of them, he was freezing. Somewhere, in the distant ruins of the café, or in his head, an equal chaos of splintered thoughts, a man was crying, choking. He was still there. Drowning. He was still there. They were leaving him behind.

"Wait," he cried. Someone patted his hair. "No, wait, he's still there. He's not here."

"No, no. Poor goose."

"Papa's not here," he cried suddenly, with the gray sea sky beginning to swirl above him. "Papa's not here."

"His father, was it, luv?" said the calm male voice.

"No, of course not. He's an American. His father's not here." Robert closed his eyes. His leg hurt, and his head, and they were being far too frighteningly kind.

He whispered again, plaintively, "Papa's not here."

He woke up in a hospital bed. He lay very still for a while and looked at the cream-painted world through interwoven lashes. He remembered everything, and was urgently trying to assess his own injuries. He did not feel particularly bad, but he had seen people desperately injured react without pain, or even concern. He had a headache, and the weight and thickness about one leg told him that something had happened to it. Perhaps a sprain or a break even. Perhaps an amputation. He could feel his toes. But you always could. Frank, the stage electrician from the Gateway, had lost both legs under a subway train and insisted years afterwards that he felt them yet, ghosting along beside the manufactured ones he walked on. Robert saw himself swinging along with that odd, hip-tilted emasculated gait, and closed the cream-painted world out with his eyelids.

Then he opened his eyes again, just the slit, feeling embarrassed. It was probably just a sprain. Probably nothing was wrong with him. He was a fraud. Philippa had been so brave and he, Robert Zolenski, fighter pilot, had been screaming for his papa. Still, maybe he was dying.

For the sake of the romance he thought it would be better. His mates would shrug and divide up his cigarettes and the Hershey bars his mother had sent, and be glad he hadn't taken his precious Spitfire with him into the Promised Land. Philippa would remember him, a wistful recollection . . . Rose of England—dah-de-*dah*-dah . . .

"I tink he's sayin' somethin' . . ." said a gentle Irish voice. Male, thank God, not his mother.

"He's trying to *sing*," said Philippa with incredulous English disdain. That was when Robert realized they'd given him drugs, a very great many drugs. He opened his eyes more fully. On his right there was a tall, good-looking WAAF officer in immaculate uniform, with a bruised cut on her chin: Philippa.

Beside her sat a priest, not a military chaplain, but an ordinary priest in a lint-marked dark clerical suit and dog collar. He had a wrinkled old face, and sandy gray hair, and green-yellow eyes that watered at the corners. He said, "Dere now, an' are you feelin' better now?"

"What's he doing here?" Robert asked Philippa.

"You asked for him."

"I did not."

"Sure an' you were callin' out for a priest when they brought you in. An' a very sensible thing to be doin'."

Robert turned his face the other way, mortified with embarrassment.

"An' we said a rosary, you an' me, are you forgettin' already?" said the priest, mildly, rubbing his eyes. Robert shut his own again. He could hear his mother saying, like she was sitting on the shoulder of the priest, like a small black Irish vulture, "Sure an' you'll find yourself running, little boy, back the way you come, for all your fine philosophies. Just you get a scare up your backside, and you'll be howling for a priest and the blessings of Holy Mother Church." She would slap the table at that point, so the painted statue of the Sacred Heart would reverberate gently on its shelf.

"Oh, damn it t' hell, my head hurts," Robert said. He would not look at the priest, even when he heard the shuffling of his feet and the creak of his chair, and the rustling of all that black cloth.

"I tink now he will be all right," said the priest gently, and patting Philippa's shoulder he went out the door.

"Is he gone?" said Robert, turning his head back slowly, so this time the pounding of blood did not sound in his ears.

"Yes," said Philippa. Innocently, he took her shortness to be reserve.

"Thank God," he sighed. "What's wrong with me, Philippa?" he asked seriously. "Did they tell you?"

She paused and tilted back in her chair. He saw she was wearing smooth, dusky blue silk stockings with her uniform, a prerogative of officers, and the seams were devastatingly straight. There was a carefully darned patch above one ankle. She was more beautiful, surely, even than on the beach. "Why should they tell me?" she said coolly. "It's patently obvious. You've a bump on your head, you've broken your ankle, and you're the snidest little twit the Boys in Blue can boast. And that's saying a very good deal, goose." She stood up.

"Philippa."

"I'm late."

"Late? Philippa? Where're you going? What've I done?"

"He sat up with you all night, you selfish sod. All night. He must be eighty if he's a day. Sod. I'm going to London. I'm late on duty and it has positively nothing to do with you."

She walked to the door, the seamed legs crossing deliciously.

"Philippa."

"Good-bye."

"When will I see you?"

She shrugged, a narrow, elegant shrug. "Who's to say? Maybe the next time someone drops a bomb on your head." Then she grinned suddenly, maliciously, made a little coy, cockney-girl wave of her hand and said, "Cheery-bye, ta-ta for now, and all the rest of that rubbish," and walked out the door.

He sat up straight in the bed, staring at the closed door, and suddenly shouted "Bitch!" at the top of his lungs. Then he was promptly dizzy, nauseous, and then elaborately sick all over the bed. A nurse came, cleaned up, and held his hand.

He left the hospital a fortnight later, on crutches, and spent three weeks in a convalescent home in Scarborough. By that time his squadron had been posted south to Hornchurch, where he rejoined them via a jammed wartime train. The whole thing could not be what one could call a fortuitous meeting.

He had not, of course, initiated it, and would have perhaps been wise to forget it. However, it had whetted his appetite and injured his pride, as amorous failures are inclined to do, and it played on his mind. Within a week of arriving in the south, he had launched a campaign to find her. It was not difficult, documented and listed as they all were by the bureaucracies of a military society. He knew already she was at Stanmore, and soon found she was in the Operations Room. Various compatriots provided information, and their society was extraordinarily close knit. Within two weeks he had her phone number.

It was another two weeks before he found the nerve to call her. When he did, the number rang interminably and was answered by an alien female who asked his name, and had clearly never heard of it before. He'd not made much impression on Philippa, if that was anything to go on. He almost rang off while the girl was searching their digs for the object of his quest. Perhaps she wouldn't come to the phone at all. Or worse, she'd come and finalize her lack of interest in him with a crushing bang of the receiver. Or even worse, have forgotten him completely.

The receiver rustled and clattered, as it was handed from

one pair of hands to another, and he found himself alarmingly short of breath. The sound of her voice was all he needed to collapse into a tailspin of infatuation. He stammered something inanely and awaited defeat.

"*Hel*lo, Robert," she said.

II

"He-*l-o-o*, Robert, c'est moi. Ro*behr*." The voice said it French, accent grave. There was a scratching at the screen, a little multiclawed scratching like one of the cats. But it was Paul. Robert sprinkled the bowl of sliced mushrooms with lemon juice, quickly, with his fingers, and laid a flat plate on top.

"It's open," he called. But Paul would not come in until Robert had dried his hands on the dish towel and crossed the wide square room to where he lurked, a shadow behind the screen. Robert tucked the tail of his shirt into his jeans, and braced his face into a smile. Paul was in his louder mood, effusive and theatrical, and Robert felt a need of additional strength. But it was his own fault; he had asked Paul himself, and deliberately, out of another weakness. He would always, when faced with conflict, or intimacy, screen himself in a crowd.

He saw Steve Deutsch when he reached the door. "I've brought a friend," said Paul shyly. That was why he had not come in. Robert said nothing as he opened the door. Steve Deutsch was standing a few paces behind Paul, his head tucked down in his usual slouch, blond hair and moustache, both dipping downward, a face of morose malevolence. His jaw was square, the chin dimpled like a film star's, but the mouth weakened by a sour turning. He had a big nose, somehow an older man's nose, with a bulbousness of age, and one of his eyelids drooped slightly, that eye forever skeptical. He was barefoot, in too-long blue jeans, and a shirt hanging open down the front. The cuffs of the jeans dipped to the sandy deck at the back and were frayed about the heels. He stood to the side of the door, seeming only partially willing to enter. With the same sideways posture he poised always on the edge of Paul's life, enjoying the money, the ambience, the profitable theatrical connections. Robert doubted he gave anything at all in return.

"Do you mind?" Paul said quickly and tense.

"No, of course not."

"I was sure there would be room. There *will* be room, Robert?"

"Of course."

"I'll send him home if there isn't room. Only I was sure there would be room."

"No, of course there's room."

"He won't be offended. Will you, Stephen?"

"There's *room*, Paul. Come in, the flies are getting in."

"Oh, dreadful. They're so bad this year; have you any of that spray? Only not by the plants, of course. Or the cats. Oh, Robèrt. The table!" Paul flung both hands in the air and tilted his hips sideways, and gazed adoringly at the set table. He wore white jeans, and a white turtleneck, too warm for the day, but extremely elegant, with a silver medallion on a chain around his neck. His hair was dry from too much washing, but softly black. He was capable of great beauty. "The *sil*ver. And that *gor*geous arrangement. Who did the arrangement, Robert, you? Don't tell me the *boy* did the arrangement. I mean, I'm sure he's artistic."

"Mary Jo did the arrangement, Paul," said Robert.

Paul was quiet for a moment, looking at the russet leaves of beach plum and the cut wild holly. He prodded it carefully, still silent, and then said suddenly, "Of course, you are *not* meant to cut this." He fingered the holly. "It *is* protected. But then, I don't suppose she'd know, would she?"

"*I* didn't know," said Robert, lying, and then there was nothing else Paul could say. Robert said, "Drink?"

Paul, who had been cruising in his curious cat way about the room, said, "So? Where is she?"

"Mary Jo?"

"No, silly." Paul waved that away, in his best, quick mock-British way. He had become so British since David came that David at times sounded American by comparison. "Her lady-ship. David's mamà. Your *wife*." It amused him no end that Robert had had a wife; he relished the subject, and dwelt on it at length. Sometimes Robert suspected that Paul had had hopes regarding himself, in the years before Mary Jo.

"Mary Jo's gone to meet the ferry."

"Mary *Jo? She* has? Oh, Robert. You are tact embodied."

"We have been divorced for thirteen years."

Paul shrugged, a ripply dancer's shrug. "Women don't for-get in thirteen *years*, Robert. *Wom*en are elephants."

"What in hell would you know about women?" Robert said mildly. He lifted the wilted, damp-paper-towel-wrapped lettuce from the lower compartment of the refrigerator and slung it in the sink.

"Gently, Robert. Lettuce is alive, it shocks. I've had women, Robert. I'm *capable*, you know. And *don't* cut it." He took the lettuce out of Robert's hand, shoved his vegetable knife disdainfully aside, and began tearing little strips off with his sunbrowned fingers. At the same time he glanced once quickly over his shoulder to the door of David's bedroom. But Robert had shut that door before he came. "Women *bore* me," he said then. "They're shrill. And they're messy. Body, mind, and soul. Messy." He shook the lettuce leaves, so the drops of water scattered off. "It's wet, Robert. There's water all over it."

"I've just had it under the faucet, damn," said Robert. "Do you want a drink, Steve?" He said it sharply, because Steve, who had lurked in a chair by the door since he entered, his bare feet on the canvas sack he had carried in, and his head buried in a Marvel comic drawn from within, had risen suddenly, crossed to the refrigerator, and was feeling about inside it with one big hand. It came out clutching a beer.

"It's okay. I've got one, Robert." He turned his back on them then, lifted the can opener from the sink, and opened the can with a quick wet snapping clunk. Then he flopped backward onto Robert's bed, all in one motion. His hand with the beer can came down neatly on the wicker bedside table. He raised his head, sipped from the can, and lay flat. "Fucking hot," he said.

Robert hated Steve Deutsch. He hated the way he spoke, assuming first names without introduction. He had read one of Robert's books, and announcing so on their first meeting, used that as a stepping stone to intimacy. Then he proceeded with accurate youthful malevolence to tear the thing apart. He hated that way he used his youth as a weapon; enticing Paul to make a fool of himself, enticing Robert to lose his much-prized liberality of nature. Most of all, enticing David into a dangerous romantic dream, not of love, or of sex, male or female, but of war.

Paul had had many young followers. It seemed to Robert they were getting, of late, younger, and the changeover more frequent and more stormy. He considered it a bad sign, and would have spoken to Paul, in some late night boozy commiseration, had not Mary Jo been just exactly Steve's age. Indeed, Mary Jo had brought Steve Deutsch here to the beach house, to the island, and to Paul, and around them he had circled all summer, like a whining persistent wasp. "I read your latest," said Steve. "I borrowed it from Mike at the fruit shop."

"I hope you're comfortable," Robert said quietly.

"Sit up, Stephen," Paul said at once, almost like a father. Steve did not sit up. He said, "It's better than the other."

"*Which* other?" Robert said. He was tossing the square

strips of meat in flour and black pepper. "Pour me a gin, please, Paul," he said then gently. "My hands are covered." Paul, soothed by the tone, went off and found the bottle and the ice, and said under his breath to the boy, "Stephen, please get up. It's rude. Oh, Robert, I do love the table," he said again, as if to make up for Stephen. Stephen swung his legs onto the floor and raised himself on one elbow.

"Oh. I forgot. You do churn them out. *I* don't know which one," he said. "You know, this one with the blond girl with the big tits that gets laid on page twelve. And page forty. And page forty-six, no, was it forty-seven. Forty-seven was it, Robert?"

"Do you turn down the page corners?" Robert said, smiling.

"I bet you get the hots when you write that stuff," Stephen said casually. "I bet you keep Mary Jo on the bed beside you. One hand on the keys and one on her pussy. Jeez. I'm gonna ask her some day."

Robert flung the meat into the sizzling oil and it hissed up a cloud of steam. "You do that, little boy," he said.

Paul said without preamble, "Go home, Stephen."

"Aw, I was joking. Robert doesn't mind. Do you mind, Robert?"

"Go for a swim and cool off," Robert said. "You've plenty of time." And as he stirred the frying meat, he said again, "Oh, plenty of time."

"Great." Stephen sat up suddenly like a kid with a good idea. He was such a kid sometimes, it was impossible to imagine him as soldier, and killer. "Where's David, anyhow, down at the beach?"

Robert could sense Paul's tightening tension, just at the mention of the name. Like a horse, twitching all its skin, with flies. He saw the involuntary glance at the door again. "David's sleeping," he said.

"Sleeping? Shit, it's the middle of the day. I'll wake him up." He started for the door, but Paul caught his arm.

"He was tired," said Robert.

"Leave the boy," said Paul dramatically. "*Don't* wake him whatever. Not for us. Let him have his rest."

"Bullshit," said Stephen, and pulled loose and slammed the door open. David sat up, in a muddle of tangled blond hair, and sleep-sticky eyes. There was sweat dabbling his forehead. "Howzit going?" said Stephen.

David did not say anything, but sat up, and then stood up, straightening his clothes, almost embarrassed, as if he'd been caught playing with himself. Robert thought he had not really said anything since yesterday afternoon. And even then Robert had done all the talking.

"Coming for a dip?" Stephen said.

"Is mother here yet?" David asked Robert. Robert could see he was really looking for Mary Jo as he said it, and his eyes swept over Paul without seeing him. Paul's very small smile quietly faded.

"She'll be half an hour yet. Go have your swim. And a shower. You look like hell."

They went off then, together, David and Steve, alone and secure in their youngness, and left Paul and Robert to do all the work. Robert did not mind. He had not had him nearly enough of his seventeen years to grow weary of parental indulgence. He glanced out the south window, over the deck on the ocean side. He saw them, towels over shoulders, disappearing over the arch in the boardwalk, where it crossed the dunes. Perhaps they would just swim, and not talk. Perhaps they would not talk. A small panic flickered in his stomach.

He went back to stirring the frying meat, trying not to think of Stephen, and Paul roamed about morosely, the house emptied of interest for him. He leaned on the draining board, holding his gin and tonic in two hands. He said, "That's not stroganoff, surely."

"It's roast turkey and cranberry sauce."

"You *don't* precook stroganoff, Robert."

Robert sprinkled the pan of meat with chopped tarragon. "I'm afraid when you are anticipating the sort of evening

I'm anticipating, you do. And if you've any sense, you finish it before anyone arrives, and go for a walk. A long walk," he added quietly.

"I'm sorry, Robert," Paul said. He could quite suddenly, on occasion, be immensely kind. "Is she coming to take him back?" The question was rimmed with unease.

Robert turned the heat off and covered the pan. "She can't take him back. She can't *take* him anywhere. He's not a baby."

"He's a minor."

"Barely. She's coming to suggest he go to Cambridge. A perfectly sensible suggestion, don't you think?"

"Then you don't mind?"

"Of course I mind." Robert measured out two cups of Uncle Ben's long grain rice and poured it into a sieve, ran the sieve under the faucet, and left it to drain. He peered out the west window, and toward the bay. It was pale blue and calming and there was no sign of Mary Jo, or his boat, or Philippa. He looked at his watch and decided it was too early, and was surprised at the nervousness in his stomach, the old ulcer feeling that the war had started, the theater nurtured, and writing had cured. Maybe it was Philippa all along, the cause of that. The thought startled him.

"Oh, Robert," Paul cried, from where he had retreated to a chair by the dining table, "we are silly, aren't we?" He jumped up and crossed to the door, to the small canvas bag Stephen had dropped there, which had caught his eye. He pounced on it and worked at the buckled straps. "We've both forgotten, can you imagine?"

"What?"

"Your prezzy!"

"My what?" Robert said tiredly.

"Stephen's brought you a present. And we've both forgotten. But never mind, here it is, when I find it." He continued rooting in the canvas.

"Steve has?" Robert said, mildly amazed. He anticipated wine, good wine, and knew very well that Paul would have

Alison Scott Skelton

chosen it and paid for it, and put the gift in the boy's name, like the quarter for the collection his mother once used to press in his palm. Paul was as sadly dedicated as she to winning favor for the undeserving.

But then Paul triumphed over the canvas, and brought something out, not wine-shaped, wrapped in red, satiny paper, and though Robert was sure the paper was Paul's, when he saw what it contained, he knew at once that the gift was indeed from Steve.

"There," Paul proclaimed as Robert held it cushioned yet in the pale furred inside of the paper. "Isn't it absolutely the most gorgeous thing?"

"Oh, it really is very beautiful," Robert said quietly, not because it was, but because Paul was beaming his own delight in the thing. It was a wood carving, a woman's head, and neck, and part of one shoulder, all ending in a flat base. The wood was honey-colored with a pale, indistinct grain, and the face was elongated with long pale wooden hair, sleeked around flat oriental cheeks. The eyes were so downcast as to appear closed.

"It's Vietnamese," said Paul.

"Yes," Robert said, without expression. "I know."

He turned it over and over in his hand, rubbing the smooth subtle wood. It was a Trojan horse of a gift, bellied out with silent statements. "Thank you," said Robert.

"Don't thank me." Paul waved his hand airily. "Thank Stephen, it's nothing to do with me."

"I realize that. I'll thank Stephen. When he comes in." He searched for a place to put the carving down, and in the end set it clumsily on the table, crowded between the twin candelabra and the silver bowl of leaves. Paul almost immediately picked it up again, turned it about, and set it down in a slightly different position. Robert felt a physical resentment that would have him shove the thing in a cupboard in the darkness. He hated ornaments, even innocuous ones. Besides, art, bad or good, was the voice of its owner, and Stephen was putting words in his mouth. He'd laid a conversation piece in Robert's house, like a snare.

"It's quite unique, you know," Paul said. He moved it once more on the table. And then lifted the bowl of beach plum leaves and finally set them aside on a windowsill. The carving now centered the table, between the two candelabra. "He went up into the hills and found this native wood-carver. He learned *all* their dialects. Remarkable, really, a very clever boy. He drew a sketch of what he wanted, sort of an ideal of female beauty. Abstract, of course. And the wood-carver did this"—he touched the sleek wooden hair—"from Stephen's design. Imagine, this Vietnamese, *Mont*agnard wood-carver, half *na*ked probably, sitting and carving *this* with Stephen's sketch before him. If that isn't 'the twain' meeting, then what is?"

Robert resisted the childish desire to switch again the positions of the silver bowl and the carving. It did not look unique to him. It looked like any number of wooden African-style madonnas, childless in this case, that were so fashionable at the moment. Abstracted out of all earthly reality, made airy and unbelievable like so much modern religion. He could see nothing individual about it at all, and suspected the wood-carver did dozens like it, with no sketch. But it didn't matter. David would believe every word.

"At least it wasn't Steve's machine gun before him," he said.

"The Montagnards are *peaceful*," Paul said at once.

Robert laughed, and pulled out a chair, and sat down at the table with his watery gin between two hands. He looked at the carving and said, "Yeah, but is Stephen?"

"That was uncalled for, Robert." Robert made no sound or gesture of apology and Paul stepped back hurt. Eventually he said, "Well, at least he's doing *something*."

"So. I'm doing something. You're doing something. Mary Jo is doing something. Doing something does not have to involve killing people."

"He's doing something for de*moc*racy."

"Oh, shit, Paul."

"Well, I only say, thank God somebody is." Paul put on the face he used to play soul-troubled young Catholic priests. "Thank God somebody has the foresight. *And* the courage. It takes courage, Robert. It takes courage," Paul intoned solemnly. "Ask not what your country can do for you; ask only . . ."

"Ask my ass," said Robert. Paul turned his back. Robert said, "Hey, what's happening? You were always a nice, decent East Coast pinko. What is this, middle-aged spread?"

"You've been listening to that stupid little bitch."

"I've been listening to my own head," Robert said mildly. "Mary Jo is a naive, gentle child. Stephen is a naive, vicious child. I'm with Mary Jo on this one."

"You don't understand," said Paul. He sat down as well, by the window, looking out at the faded deck chair beyond the dusty screen. "You don't understand the boy's needs." Robert ignored that, not worth an answer, but then Paul sniffed pathetically and said, his eyes half closed, "Robert, I'm so scared."

"Scared?"

"I'm so scared he'll go back. Oh, I'm so scared. He talks of nothing else. Another hitch. You don't understand."

"I understand all right," Robert said. "I wouldn't worry myself too much." He wanted to say, *he's got all he wants out of Vietnam. A few knick-knacks, a now defunct dose of the clap, and enough soldier-boy stories to charm the pants off all his tarts. And I don't give a fuck as long as he leaves my son out of it. Forget this one, Paul, he's not your kind. And get him the hell out of our lives.* Instead he said, "He's done his bit. He's got a good job. I don't think he means to go back."

"He's quit his job," said Paul. Robert looked up, surprised. Paul had found Steve the job. He had been working as lighting technician to a mobile theater group, touring the New York slums. The hours were erratic, and the women easy. It had seemed his perfect setup. "He's going back," Paul sniffed. "I'm sure of it. He's a soldier," he said then romantically. "What can we offer him to hold him here?"

"For the love of Christ," Robert said, and went back to the stove.

"A tail gunner on a helicopter," Paul mourned. "What chance has the boy got?"

"More chance than the wood-carver," Robert said under his breath, but Paul did not hear.

Paul said suddenly, "You of all people should understand. You had a war."

Robert paused, standing uselessly in front of the stove. There was nothing to do there but hide. He began slowly washing kitchen implements, one at a time, and laying them with great care in the stainless-steel drying rack. "All right," he said, "I had a war. It isn't a right, Paul. The world doesn't guarantee us all one. Thank God. Our generation happened to be stuck with one. That does not justify Steve's generation going looking for one. It's a different war, if you can call a half-ass squabble in a half-ass jungle a war."

"All wars are half-ass squabbles to begin with," Paul said shrewdly.

"Sure, and if bloodthirsty little bastards like Steve Deutsch would stay out of them, they might stay that way. This isn't an American war, Paul."

"American advisers have been requested to help in the cause of freedom. Any sheep can go to war when there's a draft, bleating all the way. It takes a man, an idealist, to volunteer."

"It takes an idiot."

"You volunteered."

There was a long silence in which Robert washed the vegetable knife, and the meat knife, and wiped the blood from the cutting board. Then he said, "How did you know that?"

"You volunteered when it wasn't an American war. You were hardly out of school. You had a marvelous career ahead of you, and you forsook it all. Gave it up. All for a cause." He waved his hand in the air. Robert knew he was really talking about Stephen, for all its being the details of his own life described. He said, "You've been talking to my mother."

"I had coffee and cake. After I bought the philodendron. Last Thursday. I brought it up, of course; she wasn't really bragging."

"Bragging?" Robert laughed delightedly. "Dear Christ. She's never forgiven me yet." He waved away Paul's confusion. "You wouldn't understand. It's something to do with something that happened in County Down a hundred years ago. Women are elephants."

"Why did you go to war, Robert?" said Paul, half solemn and half in challenge.

Robert wiped the meat knife dry, carefully, a little eerily, hating its razor edge. He said very softly,

The Danaan children laugh, in cradles of wrought gold,
And clap their hands together, and half close their eyes,
For they will ride the North when the ger-eagle flies.

"Robert," Paul cried delightedly, and clapped loudly, like in a theater. "Why ever did you leave the stage?"

"I saw which way the wind was blowing," Robert said mildly. Then he smiled, and said almost to himself, "In thirty-eight, it was not hard to see."

Autumn, 1938
Long Island

It was blowing from the northeast. A real nor'easter, Stanley Zolenski would call it, once it really got going. But it began gentle, more rain than wind, more rain than Robert had ever seen. And once it had really got going, there wasn't time to call it anything. But it began gentle. As rain.

For Robert it began simply as an inconvenience. He had a chance to fly that week. Mike had found a generous fool with an aging Puss Moth biplane which he had promised to lend. Robert had no license yet, but Mike, who had, was instructing him. It was planes that were hard to come by. But the weekend had been lost, washed out by the torrentially heavy rains, and Monday and Tuesday saw Robert back in the greenhouses, in the steamy heat, and ill-tempered.

The rain still thundered against the glass roofs, streaming down the multipaned walls and running in torrents from the edges of open panels. It splashed regularly through gaps in the rough wood roof of the dim potting shed where he now sat. Outside, he could hear the wind slamming against the big "houses," rattling the glass. It had been rising since morning. He sat, hunched over the bench, sweaty in the clammy air, patiently potting up geranium cuttings.

They were a sideline, the potted plants, a recent branching out. Roses were the heart of the place: Zolenski's Roses, World-Famed. Or so it said on the green-and-white painted sign by the flagpole at the cinder track entrance to his father's green empire.

It was a small empire, seven long glass houses, five lined in a row, at right angles to the maple-shaded street, and two on the opposite side of the cinder track, parallel to the road and set back behind a field. The field was autumn scrappy now, with yellowing stalks of corn blowing in the rain, a scattering of left-over zinnias, and tangles of pumpkin vine.

Behind the glass houses, by the furnace shed, were two huge mountains of bituminous coal, where in childhood Robert and his sister had submitted to the irresistible temptation to climb and slide among the slippery blackness, and earned thrashings. Beside the cinder track, right at the edge of the nearest greenhouse, was a small two-story wood-frame cottage, the Zolenski family home.

It was white painted with dark green trim, the reverse of the sign, and had a roofed porch at the front, with two wooden steps down to a flagstone path. The porch was closed in darkly by a waist-high shingled wall, with solid square pillars at each corner. It shadowed the house, making it dark and often cold for much of the year. But Robert's mother liked the porch and sat out on it on the glider in summer evenings, shelling peas, while inside his father played piano and joked through the open window between them.

Robert regarded the porch as the heart of the house, the heart of the family. Beneath it, reachable by a hole in the latticework skirting, had been the earthy hideaway of his young childhood.

A quarter of a mile down the road, beyond two empty fields and a reed-filled salt marsh, was the Great South Bay. Shallow, deceptively mild, and a strange benefactor.

It gave Stanley Zolenski his small, glass-walled empire. That was years ago now, and the time was Prohibition, and the means, a very special boat. She belonged to a friend, a garage owner, short on business in the old rural island of those days. Once he'd used her for fishing. Now he had wider nets. She was forty feet long and powered by Liberty engines and she earned them both a small fortune.

They kept her in a quiet creek, well hidden in marsh reeds, and they took her out only on moonless nights for the swift run to the beach, the night trade, and afterwards, the flashlight meetings on empty Long Island roads. They were young; it was exciting, and it was enough to take a Polish immigrant's son from head gardener on a Bellport summer estate to owner of the best rose houses on the South Shore.

Robert was seven years old the night when, for them, the rich smuggling trade came to its end.

It was a night like many throughout that summer, when his father, against his mother's protests, had taken him out on the black waters of the bay. There was as always the meeting on the barrier beach; the men without faces in the dark, high above his head, the heavy clinking cargo being loaded aboard as he followed his father's trouser legs and the tiny light of the shielded flashlight, down the sandy beach path; the comforting, familiar roar of the big inboards driving them smoothly away into the night. Then suddenly, the terror of plunging into a pool of light, the searchlights raking them, and the voices, angry, loud voices, shouting for them to halt. But the engines only roared louder as they tore forward instead.

The collision flung Robert flat on the deck, and then his father lifted him by one arm, half wrenching it from its socket, and tossed him like a peat sack into the bilge. He started to cry and there was a spluttery, spattering sound and a whistling in the air. Then they were away, tearing wild through the darkness for home.

In the morning, Robert went back to the creek and the reed-hidden boat, and traced a grubby finger around the round holes in the bow, beneath the name *Diana* painted there. It was a kind of farewell. At breakfast his father had said, "That's enough. I'm not going to push my luck."

Three weeks later he bought the wooden house with the porch and the empty fields stretching to the bay. That winter he left his gardener's job in Bellport, and one cold November day they moved to the new house and in all the chaos of moving, Robert remembered only creeping beneath the porch in his best long trousers, to hide from his sister in the dark.

In the spring, the first foundations were laid and the glass-house frames built skyward, skeletal things and spidery, and then the glass came, and the safe, secret tropical world of warm steam pipes and moist black earth took form within. That was the spring of 1928. Ahead lay the bleak, impossible years, but the Zolenski family rode the Depression like the brave *Diana* had ridden the waters. Their world of wheelbarrows and mud and rose cuttings, little thought of and less needed, survived when other worlds failed. Somehow, amidst all the misery and hunger and despair, there were still men on Long Island who would pay, every day, for red roses to set in silver bowls.

Now it was autumn of 1938, and on September twenty-first, the bay took back its gift.

All week the sky had been smooth and gray and still. Long

gray clouds hung in long silent lines above the water. The barrier beach was purply gray and looked flat and sullen, and the bay itself was still, gray and flat and full with the high autumn tides. It seemed brimming and restless. On the Friday, Robert's father took his arm outside the greenhouse door in the evening and said, "Listen."

There was a low far murmur, gentle and dreamy. It was the surf, four miles across the bay, pounding the ocean strand. The bay itself was yet as still as silk. Stanley Zolenski said there was a big blow coming and cursed it. It would mean broken panes and climbing the great slant roofs with flat ladders and putty and fragile sheets of glass.

On Saturday, the rains started. Robert had a rehearsal for *The Trial of Mary Dugan* with the South Shore Players, and rode to the high school auditorium on his bicycle. He got soaked through, and rehearsed in his drenched clothes, and came home chilled. His mother, certain always that he would inherit what she called her "Irish tendency" to weak lungs, was worried. Somehow, the week that was to come ended that kind of worrying forever. It was the last week of his childhood.

He was, granted, eighteen years old, but he'd only just graduated from high school that June, and uncertain of his future, he'd slipped easily into his ordinary summer work in the rose houses. His father always wanted him to come into the business, and was pleased. His mother had wanted him to go to college and become something laudable, but there was no money for that, even had he the grades, which he had not.

He had excelled at school at basketball, for which his lean, tall frame and sharp reflexes were obviously created; and at dramatics. He had played every school play lead since his debut, at seven, tap dancing and singing "Tea for Two" with his father's topper sitting down on his ears. His voice survived the break and settled into a fine tenor. With it he had also something approaching a real dramatic talent. It came from nowhere; there was not a trace of art in his family other than his father's gentle tinkling on the old upright piano. Indeed there was little other trace of it about himself, a common enough kid with cropped dark hair and rather striking dark eyes, but little else to note.

Still he had a singular ability to get up on a stage and become someone else. It was as simple as that. He was considered a phenomenon, and the local amateurs had graciously invited him to play his first adult part, the "Defense Attorney," in their current production. He was fifteen years younger than any of them, schoolteachers and housewives with a little talent and a lot more artsy pretense. They were doing their best to ruin him with dreadful advice, innocently enough given, and probably would have succeeded had the murmuring at the barrier beach, now audible over the driving rain, not intervened.

Beyond theater, which he had never once considered as a profession, and flying, which was a youthful obsession like tinkering with the family's old Chevy, he had no idea of his future. That last fleeting Long Island summer he had spent knocking about the candy store with Mike, cadging flights at the club airfield and drinking beer.

Mike was the son of the Canadian sister of another local phenomenon: Mrs. Middleton, an English woman of uncertain age and uncertain origin, whom a long-ago widowhood had left stranded, like a memsahib, in an unlikely suburban colony. She pedaled up and down the street on a tall black bicycle, baked shortbread on Sundays, and was rumored to keep on her living room wall a picture of the Prince of Wales. And by having her Canadian nephew to stay that summer, she completely changed Robert Zolenski's life.

At one-thirty Robert's mother came into the potting shed and brought him hot coffee and a scarf which she wrapped around his neck "against the weather." The wind was battering against the wooden walls, but the air inside was warm and clammy, as it had been for days. He protested and was reminded of his two uncles who had died of TB. Young, and a little callous, he was bored with the old Irish-Harlem saga. He said it was a wonder they hadn't died of potato blight. She grew angry because he mocked the dead.

He could see her lips moving as she left him.

He felt sorry then. She was superstitious. She was also lonely in her religion in their family. His father was the child of Polish Jews, but was not religious. Robert and his sister had been raised Catholics and went to Mass every Sunday until, at ten and twelve, respectively, they announced quite suddenly that they both had grown up and would not be going any longer.

Catherine Zolenski cried, but Stanley extended his always gentle tolerance another notch and refused to allow her to force them. Henceforth, she went alone, lace mantilla in hand, each Sunday, to the Church of Our Lady of the Snow. Stanley read the Sunday papers, and Robert and Dolores lay in bed and listened to the radio. So ended the first lesson.

At two o'clock Stanley Zolenski came into the potting shed, a gust of wind slamming the old door shut behind him. He was holding a folded *Daily News* and was pointing at something on the sports page at the back. He said, "So, is that a team, or is that not a team?" It was the last thing he ever said to Robert.

The wind that had risen steadily all morning suddenly changed its pitch from a roar to a scream. "Wait a minute, wait a minute," Robert muttered, to himself, or to the wind. The crash of the next crescendo shook all the wooden walls of the potting shed, and he saw, eerie, as in a dream, an illogical white space of sky between the eaves and the frame of the roof. It was going, the roof, they both knew, and they leaped up and out the door.

Outside, glass panes were falling like rain from the greenhouse roof. The wind speed had doubled in fifteen seconds, and before they were ten feet from the door it doubled again. They ran clear of the potting shed, struggling now to keep their footing, and Robert saw the big oak in front of the house lean to the horizontal. The next gust had it over in a shower of muddy roots and a great crash, and the potting-shed roof went fleeing over the fields in tatters.

Robert caught his father's sleeve, pulling at it, but his father was entranced by the rain of glass and would not move. He started to shout, and drag him away to the house, but happened to turn then toward the bay.

What he saw there made no proper shape in his mind. It was as if the world had bent, folded, right at the beach, and the bay now stood upright, right angles to the land, the silver gray of stormy water reaching up into the sky like a cloudy wall. And it was moving.

When he realized what it was, he was filled with such a sickening, childish terror, he wanted only to run to the house, to the solid porch and the latticework shelter beneath, and hide. But the child was in his mind alone and his body behaved with a man's cool calm. His father was hysterical, he knew, the frozen, still hysteria of shock. He guided him gently, trotting beside him, to the door of the old Chevy in the cinder drive, and then he flung himself up the steps and met his mother and sister, crying, at the door.

Without a word, he dragged them both down the stairs and forced them, confused and protesting, into the back seat of the car. He reached then again for his father's arm. But his father's eyes were suddenly alight with purpose, and he turned to the greenhouses, and broke free of Robert and began to run.

The gray wall hit the beach a quarter mile away and in seconds they were drenched with spray. Robert caught his father again, pinioned his arms, and fought with him, and the roar of the gray wall ate up their words. But his father tore free again, slipping on the soaking ground, and fled from him angrily, and he saw then the need that lit his eyes. Far off, on the farthest rose house, one door was standing open, flapping wildly in the gale, one wooden door that must ever be shut. The glass was falling in cascades all around and the terrible wind was ripping down the roof frames, but his father ran straight on into the wind, straight on toward the gray wall, to shut that door.

Robert screamed "Pop!" once more into the nothingness that was battering him off his feet. But there was no more time, and he turned then with the wind lifting his body, fanning his clothing out flat against him, and ran for the car. The gale was rocking it, broadside, and lifting it up, near overturning it. The engine started up and Robert's mother, numb in the back seat, suddenly cried out, "Wait, you're leaving papa, papa isn't here," as if he was not aware. Then the flagpole crashed down in front of them. Robert slammed the car into gear and heard the pole clunk beneath the wheels. In the mirror, through solid sheets of rain, he saw the wall hit the farthest greenhouse. It crumpled like paper. He could not see his father anywhere.

He tore away down the cinder track, the left side of the car lifting crazily. At the corner he swung wildly around a fallen tree and turned north, inland, in quest of high ground, and the first water hit his rear wheels.

Robert put his foot down and prayed for a clear road. One fallen tree and they were lost. He hit the mounded tracks of the Long Island Railroad at sixty, and the car, wind behind it, launched into the air for twenty feet. It slewed sideways on landing, but he didn't even slow. Behind him his mother was screaming and battering at him with her small fists, crying for papa, but Dolores, shocked but sane, held her pinned against the seat.

He zigzagged desperately down the crisscrossed maze of streets, trees falling on all sides, west and then north, east and then north, cutting across lawns and shrubbery, but always north. Once more the waters caught him, and foamed up around the running boards, but then he crossed the highway, and in the empty scrub beyond found a cross-island road, narrow and straight, and lined with scrub pine, too tough and too low to fall. Up that at a steady sixty they made their escape.

Five miles inland, on a small hill by a wind-battered farmhouse, he stopped. He was not even then sure he had outrun it, but he knew if the thing could reach this far, it would not stop before Connecticut, and he wasn't driving there.

They sheltered in the farmhouse. His mother grew quite calm and kept talking of papa as if he was right there with them. Dolores sat, dry-faced, and moaned softly like a hurt animal. They sat for an hour with the trees falling all around the farmhouse, and the occupants—strangers whose gray shocked faces slipped in and out of Robert's life that day without his ever learning their names—wondering aloud about their roof.

The roof held. An hour after the devastation, the wind dropped to nothing and the sky cleared, and outside in the shattered ruins of the farmyard, among the dead chickens and goats, was the clearest, purest summer day Robert had ever known. For the rest of his life he would not look at that dazzling blue sky unique to remote islands and the clean places of the world without a shudder.

He left his mother and sister and went out to the car. The farmer warned him that they were in the eye of the hurricane and the winds would return, in minutes, and stronger, from the opposite direction. He went anyhow.

He could not find his way at first. Every landmark was gone. Houses were smashed to heaps of timber, or turned crazily on their sides and strung with blue-sparking torn power lines. Trees and smashed cars lay across the roads. But he recreated the pattern of streets in his mind, and over heaps of rubble and through open fields brought the Chevy as close as possible to the place where the green-and-white house had been. He had to drive over his father's pumpkin field, absurdly swerving about to miss the bright, water-scattered fruit, gleaming in that marvelous star-white sun.

Then he got out and walked. The house had vanished, leaving nothing but foundations. Even the solid old porch was gone, and the lattice shelter beneath. He saw, shining in the sun, a small heap of bright-colored metal toy cars; a forgotten piece of his childhood, long ago hidden under the porch and exposed now brutally to an unimagined light. He stepped numbly into the rectangle of the foundation and picked up one small red car from the heap and put it in his pocket.

He walked then, slowly, to the greenhouses. In years ahead, and yet unconceived, he would recall them in the bomb sites of London. The great steel roof beams were bent and twisted and fallen into the rows of tattered, leafless rose stems. Every-where there was glass, in shards and splinters and great sheets. It crackled like ice beneath his feet.

Salt water lay in pools in the grass and among the roots of the broken roses, and trained instinct, like a stuck phonograph record, kept repeating he must wash the salt away or they would die. Beyond the wreck of the last glass house the bay had taken the last fields for itself, and tossed there now, bright green and blue, and veiled in creamy foam, in the sun.

He found his father beneath the roof girders. While it was drowning him, the bay had raked him through the five stiff hedges of long-stemmed red Avoca roses. They had taken most of the flesh from his face.

Robert wrapped his fingers around the toy car in his pocket and sat down in the salt pools by his father's body. The sun went out. Beyond the bright bay he heard the winds returning.

He stood up almost calmly. The wind was coming back, but the wave would not return. Even the Atlantic could not do that twice in a day. He covered his father's body with his jacket and walked back to the car. He turned it with difficulty in the waterlogged ground, and drove carefully back to the mid-island farm, picking his way through the debris, rattling about the road now in the rising winds. By the time he reached the battered farmhouse, the sky was black once more, the rains slashing down. Dolores was waiting at the door, her eyes frantic. But he walked in calmly, ignoring the wind and the bits of trees flinging before it. Nothing could hurt him today, he knew. Death didn't have any bigger weapons than that watery thing it had flung across Long Island. He was immune.

He told Dolores what she already knew, and then went to tell his mother. The farmer and his family retreated mouselike from their grief. Alone in the silent kitchen with the hurricane roaring outside, he told her again and again. She fought back. She fought with blank ignorance, with mocking laughter, with tears, with fury. She would not believe.

Four nights later, in the community shelter in the high

school, she sat up in the darkness and shrieked like a banshee for a full terrifying minute. In the morning, quite calmly, she sat on the edge of her canvas cot and discussed what Robert should do with the property, what Dolores should do, and what she should do. He had not told her the house was gone, but she had seen enough flattened devastation much further inland to guess. "I always wanted brick, Robert," she said. "Papa always said brick was cold, but I always wanted brick. I'll have brick now." She directed him then to sell the property and buy a building site. Papa was well insured; she would be fine.

When the trains were once more running, Robert took his mother and Dolores to her sister's home in Jamaica. There, among solid city buildings, there had been wind and rain and the occasional falling coping stone. Robert felt like a pioneer returning from a frontier.

He went back to the island. He arranged his father's funeral; no easy matter in the posthurricane chaos. He arranged the sale of the property, and the purchase of a corner building site, a quarter acre of abandoned farmland and shattered pine scrub in the adjacent town. The builder, hearing their story, was amazed they wanted to build anywhere on the island. But it was inland, a full mile. And the house would be brick, stucco and brick, heavy as stone. Catherine Zolenski stayed with her sister all that winter. Robert did not let her come back to the Blue Point property until months later when it was no longer theirs and when the ruins of the glass houses had been bull-dozed into the ground.

She only stayed ten minutes. She got out of the car, hesi-tantly, turning around and around, and walked slowly to the faded toppled ruin of the big oak that had stood before the house. It was settling into the earth, becoming natural in its new horizontal state, its roots weathering free of soil. She took one feathery end of a root in her hand. He stood watching her, she there like a child, holding the tree. He started to cry, but she only nodded, once and again, as if to someone speaking in her own head. He saw that she was reconstructing the place in her mind, the landscape of his childhood, tree and house and glass houses and coal heap and flagpole. She said then, "All right, Robert, let's go," and walked to the car, got in, and sat with her small misshapen feet together neatly on the worn mat, and her handbag sitting upright on her knees. She did not look as they drove away.

On the way back to Jamaica they stopped and looked at the hole in the ground on their corner building site. Fresh red bricks were heaped, waiting, and stacks of sappy, golden timber, shining in the late autumn sun, all paid for with the price of the rose farm. The air was rich with the tang of wet oak leaves and the piney scent of the cut wood.

They moved in in the late spring of thirty-nine, but it was never Robert's home, nor Dolores's. Dolores left that summer to set up house in Washington, with her new husband. She had been engaged for two years, against her mother's wishes. Her fiancé was a Catholic, which pleased Catherine, but Italian, which did not. Perhaps no one would have pleased Catherine. Whatever the reason, she never called Albert Conti anything other than "the wop" from the day he married her daughter until the day he died at Guadalcanal. Still, she had endless Masses said for him when he was dead.

That left Robert alone in the strange new house, paint-scented, with his mother, feeling out the fit of widowhood like a new coat. He had lost three things he'd grown up with, three things of which he was certain: his father, his livelihood, and his future. In a world still shaking itself out of the Depression, as from sleep, he did what countless other country youngsters did. He went to New York. Once there, or almost there, with his bed in Brooklyn, a sleeping bag on the couch in the fourth-floor walk-up where Mike had settled instead of returning to Canada, he did something almost no one did. He began a career in the theater.

He would never have done it if his father were alive. It was not sensible, and his father had a high regard for good sense. Robert would not have crossed him. But for the hurricane

he'd have gone on trundling barrows of manure and rose cuttings, and his hands would have grown wise as Stanley's to the
intricacies of roots and blooms and the delicate sensual art of
grafting. He would have lost Mike, too, for Mike found work
in a Brooklyn garage and his aunt in Blue Point saw little of
him. Still, the hurricane had come and cut Robert loose, and
now he was left to graft his own self, as best as possible, onto
the world. He left the new house in Bayport with three dollars
and fifty-three cents in his pocket, a letter of introduction to a
theatrical agent, courtesy of one of the more influential stars of
the South Shore Players, and something less than his mother's
blessing.

The agent, an elderly Lithuanian lady called Anna Beinhart,
ran her business from her apartment on West Eleventh Street.
She opened the door to him with little murmurings and sideways glances from behind her tortoise-shell glasses. She looked
dotty, and Robert sized it all up; she was nearing retirement,
approaching senility, and scraping around for clients. That was
why she had agreed to see him. As she led him into her small
living room, he found himself looking down on the top of
her tiny head with its braided, artistic bun of thick gray-black
hair, caught up with a filigree ivory comb. She turned quickly
as they entered the room and pinned him with a dark stare. The
eyes were large and nearly black, and old now; eyes that had
once, in the romantic Parisian eighties, caused a rather poetic
suicide.

She waved a short, square hand to a low, sagging sofa,
covered in fading dusky red velvet. Sun poured onto it from
the window overlooking a courtyard garden. He sat down
with his knees bent up to his chin. On the chromium and
smoked-glass coffee table were mounds of papers and pictures,
contracts and letters. Here and there his innocently curious
eyes struck, unavoidably, a name. Some of the names were
famous. He was surprised.

She went out and made coffee, herself, and he sat alone
among the many cats and jungly climbing plants, and the rows

of photographs on the walls of nineteen-twenties' stars. When she returned, she set good coffee before him, and pastries, and told him he had an elegant face, his haircut was lousy, and if he did not learn to look somewhere other than the floor, he might as well become a street cleaner. She did not refer again to his future career, or any business he might have with her, but told him a long, sad tale of her illegitimate daughter who had been brilliant, and had died young. As he was leaving she gave him a slip of paper with four addresses, and four dates, and times. They were theater addresses, the dates for auditions.

He went to all four and he found himself, within a week of coming to the city, with his first job. It was a tiny walk-on part in a small venturesome play that closed after three days. The next job took two months waiting for. But it was followed by others, and some were larger. Soon he was earning twice what his father had paid him. He left Mike's apartment in Brooklyn and took one of his own on West Seventy-sixth Street, a half block from Riverside Drive.

It was on the first floor of a converted brownstone mansion which had a quirky history and an eccentric Irish landlord who proudly did all his own repairs, plumbing and electrical circuits included. The result was an eerie mayhem in the cellar where blue current flickered gaily along the rafters. Robert did not mind. He was young, and knew, courtesy of the hurricane, he was meant for a long life. His new home was tiny, but all he needed, with minimal cockroaches; and it was private and peaceful. Below him in the garden apartment lived a writer of Western stories, and his wife. She was young and pretty with long curling dark hair, and on clear days in that autumn Robert could sit at his window and watch her hang her washing in the September sun. It was a very special time. He had all he wanted from life, some things he'd never dreamed of, and knew by instinct that it was a time that would come but once. Life was in its spring. Oddly he was not in love.

He worked nights, of course, as those in his profession generally do. And when he was working, and not seeking out auditions, he had his days free. He was, for all his having lived on the outskirts of the city all his life, still a stranger to it, with a country boy's permanent awe. He became a devotee, a lover, in a way that the homeborn do not, and spent his days gliding through the seas of Checker cabs in its chaotic streets on his ancient bicycle. He gravitated to the docks and the railroad stations with a boy's delight in the mighty machinery they were built for, and the constant suspended feeling of action about to begin, like the moment before the curtain rose.

That summer, the summer of thirty-nine, the docks were full of great ships from all of the world. Robert learned them, got to know them well, waited for their arrivals, and saw them away: the *Mary*, the grand old *Aquitania*, the *Normandie*, the *Ile de France*, the *Athenia*, the *Rex*, the *Europa*, and the *Bremen*. Then suddenly, in September, a great slice was cut away; a great slice of the seagoing world suddenly had other things to do.

But on that October day, when Robert Zolenski stood leaning on his bicycle and watching, Italy had not yet taken up that preoccupation, and the *Rex* was arriving in all her glory. People flowed from her, dark from a more kindly sun, with cases and hat boxes and armsful of welcoming flowers. Then suddenly the crowd parted and a young lady stepped from the canvas-covered gangplank and was met at once by a small man in a dark gray, fur-collared overcoat, quite dwarfed by a vast armful of red roses. He thrust them into the young lady's arms and faded away into a knot of raincoated, camera-clutching newsmen. Miss Rhonda Greenwood was back in New York.

Robert was enchanted. He had seen Rhonda Greenwood in four different films. In his senior year he had gazed with juicy young yearning over her vast screen face from the back row of the Sayville Playhouse. Now here she was, live and breathing, in a trim suit with blue pencil-slim skirt and a shining mass of fox fur. It seemed odd that she could be so small, the top of her white-blond head barely reaching the shoulder of the stocky little man in the gray coat. She looked older, too, and from twelve feet away Robert could see the wet, nervous tip of her tongue polishing her bright red lips. But her skin was cream perfect, as on the screen, and her hair, bobbed in a shining fold, shone unhumanly, like the coat of Anna Beinhart's Persian cat.

The man in the gray coat was an arm's length away and Robert heard him saying to three of the newsmen that Miss Greenwood was arriving back from two weeks' filming at Cinecittà, Mussolini's cinematic extravagance built to rival Hollywood, and would soon, after some much needed rest, be willing to consider another role. Robert was just experienced enough in the ways of his new profession to know the man with the roses was her agent. He was, however, too innocent yet, and too dazzled by glitter, to realize that the agent had bribed the raincoated gentlemen of the *News* and the *Tribune* with lunch and three stiff Scotches to be here at all. And that Miss Rhonda Greenwood, once Mary MacCrory of Reading, Pennsylvania, was out of work and running scared. Robert saw only the image that, in smudgy printer's ink, would grace the center of the *Daily News* tomorrow, a lovely young lady with long silk-stockinged legs, balancing on the dock railing like a school girl on a gate. She smiled and swung her legs, but the knuckles of her hand were white. The pale sun glistened on the mountains of cheap furs.

"A little higher, Miss Greenwood." A giggle. She raised her slim blue skirt almost to the knee.

"Cross your legs, Miss Greenwood."

"C'mon, baby, give us those gorgeous gams."

Miss Greenwood flicked the fox tails over her shoulders and pretended to be offended, with a red-lipped pout. The wind blew her skirt higher and the photographers cheered. "Atta girl, Rhonda."

Miss Greenwood tossed her head, showing that angle of jaw and throat that a columnist had once called Hellenic. Her bleached white bob flicked pathetically in the gathering wind. She smiled and smiled. The cameras clicked, stopped, and drifted away. Miss Rhonda Greenwood teetered uncertainly on the railing, hooking one high heel around for support. The agent slid off with his arms about the raincoated shoulders, his face and voice cajoling. The photographers returned, snap-snap, shrugged, and were gone. Miss Rhonda Greenwood climbed alone from the railing, and walked, a flat-footed tired country girl's walk, the roses forgotten on her arm, into the terminal. Robert stood alone as the thinning crowd drifted away, wishing he'd lent his hand to help her down. He had not the nerve. He turned away then, looking across the cold expanse of water and docks, and saw the refugees.

The ship, a British ship, morosely serious in gray camouflaging, crept into its berth half unnoticed, meek, like a neglected mistress. She off-loaded hurriedly, as if she must soon be gone. The little group of children came off like a small gray snake. Robert crossed the wide concrete stretch between the two terminals, curious. A small, anonymous crowd was watching the disembarking, drawn by the novelty of the ship's wartime dress. It was one of the few real visible contacts with the distant war they had.

"Evacuees," said a man at Robert's shoulder, shrugging a rain-coated sleeve toward the children.

"From the war," said another, wisely.

"They're the lucky ones," said the first. "Rich kids. Bunch of little Fauntleroys. Bet the poor kids don't get off so easy."

Robert watched for a while with his hands in his trouser pockets, his shoulders hunched in his tweed jacket. He did not think they looked lucky. The dock was so big. Even for rich kids it was big. And empty. And cold. They were all dressed nearly the same, neatly and staidly, in some school uniform or other, the boys and girls both in dark blazers, the boys in heavy flannel shorts that flapped around knees reddened by the crisp harbor wind. They shivered stoically. They did not look like American kids at all. He could not picture American kids ever standing so still. He went closer, compelled by their loneliness.

There was so much chaotic protection around them—ship

officials, immigration officials, charity officials, American relatives—that they were left in a sort of calm in the center, like the eye of the hurricane. Quite suddenly, Robert was with them. Before him was one tiny boy in enormous loose gray shorts and a stiff navy blue blazer with some battered gilt-trimmed badge on the pocket. He must have been seven at least, from the solemn face, but he was thin and slight as a five-year-old. His blond hair was long by American standards, but neatly cut in a bang over his bright blue eyes. His cheeks were red as his knees, and he wore serious glasses with sturdy gray rims. Beneath them tears were quietly coursing. The face did not change, or crumple. Even the chin was stiffly steady, but the tears flowed endlessly.

Robert crouched down, like he would before a lost mongrel, making himself reassuringly small. He was at eye level. The wet blue eyes stared. "Can I help?" he said.

The boy did not seem surprised at a stranger's intervention. He stared, calculating, and then a very tiny childish hope swelled and brightened the stained face.

"Please, sir."

"Yeah," Robert said, bemused by the usage. "Hey, don't cry." The eyes blinked, and the whole body tensed with polite but happy expectation.

"Please, sir, I should like my mother."

Robert smiled slowly, half rising from his crouch. The sorrow had been so monumental, as if England herself had been wept for. But no; just mom's skirt hem, loosed from a baby's hand, by the crush. He looked around the muddle of people and said, "I'll find her if I can." He kept one hand on the blond, smooth head. "Where should she be? What's she wearing?"

"White Fields Farm, sir."

Robert turned quickly, froze in his half crouch, still looking stupidly at the crowd. "Where?"

The boy replied in the smooth litany of a child's memorized patter, "White Fields Farm, near Lambourn, Berkshire. At the end of the lane."

"Oh, Jesus."

"Sir?"

Robert stood up. "I'm sorry," he muttered, not looking. "I'm sorry," and he began walking rapidly away, pushing through the crowd, ashamed and embarrassed. Beyond the port buildings he glimpsed the gray, oily Hudson, and beyond again, distant open sea, cold and hazy, and a very long way to Berkshire. He walked back to where he had left his bicycle near the Italian Line terminal. The *Rex* waited alone now, bedecked yet in pennants like cheap theatrical furs. "Shit," he said softly, as he mounted his bike, and rode away, head down, pedaling hard, and thinking of Mike.

He still saw Mike from time to time. They'd meet at Baldwin's on Broadway. Or else he'd take the subway to Brooklyn and they'd go to the ice cream parlor run by the garage owner's brother and have ice cream and drink egg creams, and talk about flying. On rare, rich weekends, they took the train out to the island, stayed with Catherine in the new house, and had a few turns about the sky. Once or twice they had double-dated, but neither had enough money for anything but the pictures, and neither had a special girl.

Robert was still the kid from the island, loose in the big city. His job was acting, but it might as well have been auto mechanics, like Mike's. No glamour had rubbed off on him in the tawdry rehearsal halls or autumn-chilled theaters. He was too shy to attempt to date the occasional pretty dancer or tense ingenue he met. The hours were all wrong for social life, anyhow, and his evenings ended generally at the brick wall outside the stage door, among the ash cans and New York's ubiquitous lonely cats. There was plenty of time, yet, for Mike, and the wedge that had inexorably grown between them had nothing whatever to do with profession, or money, or class.

Three weeks ago the wedge, quite suddenly, appeared. They were sitting on the steps of Robert's brownstone, with children scurrying in the dark entrance to the writer's basement apartment below. They were playing with peashooters, and dried peas littered the sidewalk like pale yellow-green hailstones. Robert and Mike hunched up their jacket collars and perversely ate the ice creams they had bought from the vendor. They'd passed him on his corner at West End and Seventy-fifth on their way from the subway station, and were drawn in by the flow of schoolkids clamoring for strawberry, vanilla, chocolate-inside-and-out. Robert had chocolate. Strawberry was a color, not a flavor, and he resented vanilla, no taste at all, merely an absence. He enjoyed eating it in the new cold of autumn without the haste of melting summer heat. He could see the Palisades and two tugboats down the divide of buildings.

"I'm leaving," said Mike.

"Leaving? Brooklyn?"

"The States."

"You're going back to Canada?" said Robert, incredulous, New York being so surely the center of humanity. "*Canada?*"

"For a while." Mike bit at the ice cream, and winced as his teeth pained. He put his hand over his mouth and spoke through it. "I'm joining the RAF. I'm signing up." Then he said with sudden force, "I'm going over, Robert."

"The *Ar Ay Eff?*" Robert whispered. "Over?" His eyes narrowed under his odd, turned-up brows, disbelieving.

"To England. Before it's too late."

"Aw, for the love of Pete."

"I mean it."

"Too late for what, will you tell me?" Robert said. "They've been at war for two months and what's happened?"

"Enough. Give it time, Robert. You roll a rock downhill, it doesn't suddenly start rolling back."

"But England? You got nobody in England still, have you?" Mike shrugged, shying away from the emotion that was creeping up on them. Below the kids scurried with their peashooters, oblivious.

"We all have somebody in England, Robert. It's ours. It's our mother country. We're not gonna let that bastard have it." He was calm and quiet, and passionate.

"Who's so sure he wants it?" Robert said, weakly, with a shrug. Then he said, "I'm half Irish, half Polish Jew. How's it my mother country? The nearest thing my family's got to English connections was my grandpa getting his butt out of Ireland before the black and tans shot it off." Robert looked back at the river. The tugboats were gone, replaced by a freighter. Far off on the New Jersey shore he saw a tiny toy freight train. Mike was leaning back on one elbow, his eyes half closed, with a funny smile. He began to sing, almost to himself,

London Bridge is falling down, falling down, falling down,
London Bridge is falling down . . .

Suddenly he swung about, half lying on the weathered red-brown steps, and pointed the ice-cream stick at Robert, and waited.

"Huh?"

"Finish it."

"Finish it?"

" 'London Bridge is falling down' . . . Finish it."

"Why?"

"Finish it, damn it. '*Lon*don Bridge is falling down . . .' " Mike swung the stick like a conductor's baton.

"Aw, shit. 'My *fair* lay-dee.' Okay?"

"My point."

"What point? It's a nursery rhyme." Robert shrugged, seeing themselves as the kids with the peashooters must, two grown men licking ice-cream sticks, singing nursery rhymes. The children had stopped to watch.

"A nursery rhyme. The language of the cradle, the language of our childhood. Our *mother* tongue. We're all England's children."

"The fuck we are," said Robert, softly because of the children. But Mike stood up, hiked up his trousers, stretched his arms, and flung the ice-cream stick cartwheeling toward the Hudson. He looked big and tough, with his bristly blond crew cut. Robert could imagine him fighting a war. Annoyed, he sat in mock complacency finishing his ice cream and warbling in a high falsetto, " 'Keep the home fires bur*ning*, while the hearts are *yearn*—' " Mike clouted him, a friendly back of the hand that had a sting of strength behind it. Then he would not talk about it anymore, which chilled Robert, and annoyed him more than bravado.

After Mike left, Robert sat alone on the step as early autumn dusk came down on the Hudson and lights came on down on Riverside Drive and high up on the apartment blocks across the street. The children drifted away, called by mothers in pincurls and kerchiefs. One remained, scuffing a new brown school shoe under the stairs in the debris of the pea fight and the dried yellow leaves. He disturbed Robert's thought until Robert said, quite suddenly, unfairly, "Hey, kid, go home. Your mom's got supper ready."

"No, she hasn't."

"Go home anyway."

"Will when I want to." Robert saw a dusk-brightening smile. The little bastard was enjoying it. "Hey, mister."

Robert ignored him.

"Mister?"

"Yeah, what the hell?"

"You going to fight the war?"

"What war?"

"The *war*," said the kid, annoyed. "Over there." He pointed to the dim Palisades, soaking the last of the light.

Robert looked, confused, and then said, "What you talking about, kid?" He was interested now.

"The *war*. My dad says there's a war over there."

"Over *there*?"

"*Yeah*." The kid put thin knuckles on his hips, mimicking parental exasperation. "Over there. In *Ger*many."

Robert blinked, and then grinned, and then laughed to himself with delight, lying back on the cold steps, with the tread of one sharp in the arch of his back.

"What's so funny?" the kid pouted uncertainly.

"New *Jer*sey. New *Jer*sey."

The kid shrugged, more uncertain, sensing his own confusion. Embarrassed, he kicked at the leaves. "So what's the difference?" he said with a buck-toothed smirk, and put his hands in his pockets and sauntered very carefully away. He cast a speculative eye at the Palisades and shrugged.

"Betcha won't fight," he shouted suddenly. "Betcha won't fight *any*how."

"Dry up," Robert said under his breath, but the damned dumb little bastard had won.

He saw Mike again, of course, but something was gone. They were no longer brothers in young insolence. Mike had become a zealot. And even though he hardly spoke of the matter of England again, his zeal fluttered between them, a crusader's banner on a wind of change. They had suddenly nothing to say to one another.

Had that not been the case, Robert would have told Mike about the evacuee children. They used to share that kind of thing. But there was no one to tell then. He rode home on his bike and met the writer's wife in front of the old brownstone. He would have liked to tell her, but could not find words, and only carried her two armfuls of brown paper bags to the black door behind which she lived; beyond which he could not go. So he got back on his bike and rode off, and he told Anna Beinhart instead.

He pedaled off down West End and Eleventh Avenues, turned east at Forty-second to Fifth, and all the way to West Eleventh Street, and the house with the geraniums on the front step, and two Persian cats in the window. She had said, Come see me Thursday. So. It was Wednesday. She did not seem surprised. The play, in which he had once nightly for three weeks carried a tray of filled glasses, stumbled across a human form, and said, "My God, it's Sir Albert," was closing next week. It had not been a great success, artistic or financial, but it had paid the rent. Now he, and Anna Beinhart, would need to find something else.

"Nervous, Robert?" she said with her sharp, old-woman smile as she opened the door. He shook his head.

"I had nothing else to do. I thought I'd come and see if anything had turned up. You did say come tomorrow."

"In our business, Robert, we always look as if we had something else to do. At ten in the morning, we look like we had something else to do. And we look successful." She went away, into her pokey kitchen, and began grinding coffee in her hand mill. It smelled wintry and beautiful. "And," she said, "we do not wear sweaters that our mothers have darned with the wrong color wool."

"*I* darned it," Robert said, relaxing into the vast soft settee, and hoisting a cat up onto his leg.

"So? Congratulations are in order?" He heard the coffee pot clunk onto the stove with a wet hiss. "You have a public, Robert. You owe them style."

"The hell I've a public. Who knows me?"

"Almost nobody," Anna Beinhart said, reappearing in the living room, hands on heavy hips. She wore a long skirt, nearly to her ankles, in some obscure rough fabric, printed with bright flowers. She dressed like no woman he had ever known. She smiled shrewdly at his uneasy pique, and added, "You're a two-bit half amateur with half a foot in the business. But somewhere, one little girl who spends her days counting pennies in the five-and-dime will have seen you and thought you Adonis. For her, Robert, you wear a new sweater."

"Yes, ma'am."

"Tony Aldgate is casting on Tuesday. I don't think he'll look twice at you, but it's worth a try."

"Thanks a lot," Robert said touchily.

"So?" said Anna Beinhart. "And who knows you?"

Still, she handed him one of her slips of oddly romantic paper with a delicate pen-and-ink unicorn in the corner. It was not a trademark of any kind, no business symbol, but a motif of her own self. It went with the mournful dark Semitic eyes, if not with the round old lady pouring coffee and heaping his plate with pastries. "Eat. You're too thin. Adonis isn't a scarecrow."

Robert ate and read the address written in her shaky old hand.

"Tuesday," she said. He nodded, and folded the unicorn paper and put it in his jacket pocket.

"I saw some evacuees today," he said. "Refugees. From the war."

"On West Seventy-sixth Street?"

"Down at the waterfront. Coming off a boat. I saw Rhonda Greenwood, too," he added with sudden verve. "She was coming off another boat, the *Rex*."

Anna Beinhart scooped one of her pale gray-blue cats out of a chair; it yowled, almost human, and rubbed its forehead against hers. She fondled it, turning it around in her plump arms as if it were a velvet cushion. "All fluff and claws, poor silly fool," she said.

Robert said, "I felt rotten."

"For fluff and claws? Don't be soft-hearted, Robert, you're too young to afford that. She's a silly girl, badly handled. She's peaked too young. In five years she'll be back in Reading, Pennsylvania, waiting on tables, or whoring. Or dead, perhaps."

Robert shuddered. "No. Not her. The children, the evacuees, they're from England."

"So who's evacuating? Germany?"

"I don't think it's funny."

"Am I laughing?" She shrugged with a little disdainful snort and said softly, "Refugees." She walked to the sunny window, still cradling the cat, and then dropped it, four-footed, to the carpet, like a forgotten thought. She turned back to Robert.

"So who fled Russia when she was fourteen? A fourteen-year-old girl. No parents. No relatives." Her voice softened, and she said, "With my lover, I fled. He was eighteen. Don't be shocked, Robert. We married young in those days. So, if we were bohemian, we had lovers young. There was a cable car. A cable car down the mountain. We must go down it. They were behind us, the czar's elegant soldiers. A girl and a boy on a cable car, eighteen and fourteen. But Jewish. They cut the cables. It ran, oh, it ran like the wind. There was a cliff. At the last moment, we jumped. I hurt something, something inside." She cupped her hands over her middle. "In my insides. It was never right again." She shrugged. "He was not hurt. You see, I flung my arms about him and cushioned his fall. Still, that morning, when I look at him, he is an old man. His hair is white. He had black, black hair. In the morning, it is white.

"So then, we run. We are refugees. No one wants us. In Paris we find friends. Intellectuals. They talk about God, and shelter us because they don't believe in Him. That way, they prove they are better men for it. So. We are refugees."

"Anna?"

She nodded.

"What happened to him?"

"My lover?" She shrugged her hands still folded over her middle. "He saw me kissing a painter one day in Paris. Once. I kiss him thank you for a loaf of bread." She picked up the cat again. "So he put his head in the gas oven. And he died." She shrugged again. "For that I break my young body cradling his beautiful head." She smiled to herself, rocking the cat like a child.

"Anna?"

"Mmm?"

"What do you think Hitler will do?"

She dropped the cat again and walked about the room, picking with her old hands at the heavy leaves of the rubber plants. "What will a madman do? Cut tramcar cables? Make refugees? Is this new, Robert? Has he invented it?"

"He hates the Jews."

"So? He is the first then? Once again it is not good to be a Jew. So when, Robert, *was* it good to be a Jew?" She turned her palms up, and then dropped them, and sanguinely poured more coffee and said, without looking up, as she stirred the sugar in her own, "Robert?"

"Yes?"

"Change your name," she said.

Robert did not see the man sitting alone in the back of the darkened theater until it was all over. He knew at once he would not get the part. He read well, but he was built wrong. The director leaned twice over to his slim secretary and said, "Too thin. Impossible." The part was that of a gardener on a grand estate. "Wheeling barrows of horseshit? Never." Robert smiled quietly, resigned, as he watched the others read. Anna Beinhart had taught him that neither irony nor truth had much weight in this business. She had also taught him when to keep his mouth shut. The part went to a young man with a limp smile, two years at a mediocre acting school, and shoulders like a baseball star.

Robert stood to leave. As he picked his way through the rows of empty, scruffy seats, a hand touched his shoulder. The man was about fifty, slender, with a pencil moustache and a narrow, beard-shadowed face. He said, "Have you an agent, Mr. Zolenski?"

"Anna Beinhart, sir."

"I'm casting *Saint Joan* next week. I would like you to play the Dauphin. I'll be in touch." Robert half lifted his hand, almost in protest, as if there was a mistake, but the man was already walking away. Then suddenly reviving his good sense, he cried out, "Don't you want her address? My agent . . ."

The man stopped, half turned with a distant smile. "Oh, I know Anna." He smiled again. "I know Anna," he said.

The doors swung open, letting bright light in from the

foyer, and then swung shut. Robert was alone in the dim quiet of the empty theater. It was the stuff dreams and bad films were made of. It never happened. Only it did, once. It happened to Robert Zolenski in the October of nineteen thirty-nine. He had that marvelous rarity called talent.

Robert was superstitious. He had inherited it from his mother and did not like to be told so. But it was true. Transmuted, of course, his superstition. She worried about hats on beds, candles with wax windings, and visions in the night. He worried about unlikely ease; he doubted good fortune. His fingers sought the mindless security of touched wood. It was too good; it couldn't last.

It did. The part was his. Rehearsals commenced. The director, that mysterious figure with the pencil moustache, liked him. He was pleased with himself, as well; given gold where he'd handled only dross, he worked with fervor and grew in ability. But the unease hung about him, like stale smoke. He needed a confidant and had none.

Mike was moving into another world. He dropped in, casually, at the apartment on Seventy-sixth, and casually said he had quit his job. He was leaving next week. The RAF would train him in Canada. He smiled politely at Robert's fantastic success, like a parent admiring a string of paper dolls.

The mood hung on. Anna Beinhart told him it was nerves. He met the writer's wife in front of the house again, and she asked him in for coffee and told him to have faith in himself. Opening night was a week away. His name would be in lights. He drank sherry with Anna Beinhart, toasting that success.

The following day he was leaving the theater, late afternoon, alone as always, and heard a voice call his name. It was an eerie echoing of the day of the audition when the director had spoken to him from the darkness. It was no slender, pencil-moustached saviour this time, but the small old man who soddenly pushed a brush back and forth through the long rows of seats, with a small armada of candy wrappers before it. He touched Robert's sleeve with tentative, fumbly fingers.

"Yes," Robert said uneasily, drawing back from the reek of stale wine.

"Listen, kid. Want to tell you something." The man rocked back on the handle of his broom. "Want to tell you. Heard how you got that part. You're a great kid. You've got a great break, but you're great. It's the chance of a lifetime. What you do with it is what counts. It'll be the making or the breaking of you. The making or the breaking." His voice cherished the phrase, rolling it, resonantly, and then he muttered again, "You're great, kid."

Robert nodded politely and thanked him, and started to move away, but the man kept speaking, a monologue, like a Greek chorus, moving the action. Politeness pinned Robert to his voice. "Mine was the breaking. Drank myself silly on opening night. Nerves. Or something." He shrugged. "Woke up on the floor of my dressing room. Everything dark. They'd just left me there. They were so disgusted. I don't blame them really." He paused, a little too long, pursuing the drama of the moment, and said, "My understudy did very well." He shuffled away, pushing the broom. "Big star now, my understudy. You remember that, kid. This is your big one. You won't get another. Nobody ever does."

Robert left the theater with his head down and his coat collar up, and his hands deep in his pockets, like a disconsolate schoolkid. Anna Beinhart would have given him hell had she seen him. He got his bicycle from the alley and wheeled it by the fading tawdry posters of old shows out onto the street. An old Italian man, his hands black from charcoal, was roasting chestnuts on a little smoky cart on the pavement. The air was wintry, and the smoke sweet and warm. Robert bought chestnuts in a paper cone and ate them, standing in front of the theater marquee, with his bicycle leaning on him like a friendly dog. He burned his fingers, licked them, and got charcoaled shell in his mouth. Had he asked anyone at all, even the chestnut roaster who made the theater corner his regular post, they would have told him that the drunken old fool with the broom had never been on a stage in his life. He had been born a broom pusher and would die a broom pusher, and was quite content. But he liked drama and its atmosphere, and it was that taste that made him a theater broom pusher, rather than, say, the department-store variety. And that same taste bred his ancient, richly embroidered, utterly imagined tale of vanished success. It was his one indulgence. Unfortunately, mixed with a superstitious Irish inheritance, it created in Robert an insane certainty. He would never play the Dauphin on that stage. He would never see the curtain go up. Every facet of the effort was doomed, fated to extinction by the whisperings of a wino, Banquo's ghost reincarnate. From that moment, Robert saw failure as the only natural outcome, and while half of himself worked bravely for success, the other half sat back smugly and awaited disaster. It was only a matter of time.

He finished the chestnuts, crumpled the paper and threw it in the gutter, fastened the clips about his trouser legs and rode off with a shrug and a clatter of loosened chain.

Three days later, the time came. Robert took a taxi from West Seventy-sixth Street to the theater. It was a rare extravagance, but he was short of time. He had a costume fitting, and he was in a hurry, too much of a hurry to go by bike. He had just four hours before he must be at Pennsylvania Station. Mike was taking a train to Montreal. Robert had promised to come and say good-bye.

The cab turned down the narrow street, where the theater fronted, just off Broadway. They had done the marquee, and the man with the broom was messily slapping paste on the billboards in preparation for the bright posters. The marquee said, in the third row of unlit globes, "Robert Zolan." He felt a twinge at his truncated name and tried to think it was a lack of light bulbs, not lack of conviction, that had shortened it so.

"Shame about that ship," said the cab driver.

"What ship?" Robert asked, still staring at the marquee.

"Don't you ever listen to the news?"

"Not today, I haven't. What ship?" He looked around now, from the marquee to the driver's bristly neck. The engine rumbled, bored.

"The Ben-gal-ee. British ship. Torpedoed in the North Atlantic. U-boat got her. The bastards. Seventy children. Little e-vac-u-ees. Seventy children. They saved one but he died later. All those kids. That shit Hitler. Seventy kids. Here's your theater, sir. Are you in the show?" He nodded at the marquee, sizing up the young man with the white silk neck scarf arriving at an illogical hour. "Hey, is one of them you?"

Robert looked up at the odd, dignified new name. The wintry sun shone palely on the glass of the bulbs. He half opened the door. The broom-pushing Banquo swung around with poster paste on his hands, his eyes squinting against the daylight. Then Robert shook his head and shut the door and said without looking up, "No. Not me. Look, take me back, please."

"Back?"

"West Seventy-sixth Street."

"You just come from there."

"Damn it all, I know that. Take me back."

The cab driver shrugged, got disgruntled because he didn't understand and he liked understanding things. Then he realized he had another fare coming, and nodded and acquiesced, cruising back through the city streets. Robert paid the driver and went inside. He sat at his bedside table and wrote two letters, one to the theater management, one to Anna Beinhart. He wrote a check addressed to the Irish landlord. Then he went downstairs and knocked at the writer's door. The writer's wife answered. She'd been baking and had flour on her hands and small wrists, and a smudge in her dark curling hair.

"I don't have any stamps," Robert said. "And I'm in a hurry. Will you mail my letters? Tomorrow?" She nodded, puzzled, and knowing nothing mattered any longer, he leaned suddenly forward and kissed her mouth. Then he went out before she could speak. He packed everything he owned into two suitcases, and left one addressed to his mother, standing in the middle of the floor. Then he took the other in his hand, and at the last moment crossed to the wooden mantel over the long-boarded-up fireplace and took a small red car, a child's toy, from its dusty place there. He put it in his pocket, and shifting the suitcase to the other hand, he went out the door, down the steps, and walked to West End Avenue. He hailed another cab, climbed in with the old leather case, once his father's, on the seat beside him.

"Where you going, kid?"

"Montreal."

"You a wise ass?"

"No. No. Penn Station."

He met Mike thirteen minutes before train time. Standing in the sun, by the old gray stone wall of the station, he scrawled a farewell note to his mother on a postcard of the Empire State Building. It was appropriate. Irish born, but raised a true New Yorker, Catherine had never set foot inside it.

She kept the postcard for years, by the statue of the Sacred Heart, until it grew dusty and colorless, immune always to questions regarding it. By proximity perhaps, it developed an almost religious grandeur there, faded and hallowed, a postcard of the Empire State Building.

III

A postcard of the Empire State Building, shining and icy against a blue winter sky. And, oh yes, an aerogram. We mustn't forget the aerogram, Philippa thought, with a wince of loneliness; four or five pale scrawled ball-pen lines, barely legible on the thin frail paper. "I'm all right. Pop's jolly super. He bought me a surfboard. Absolutely marvelous. Weather grand. Love to Uncle Andrew and Vicks. David." That was it. The sum total of Philippa Wardlaw's communication with her son since June. *Not* a good track record, David's grandfather would say.

The postcard had arrived within days of his departure. Bought at Idlewild Airport, it reported his arrival there, information that Philippa felt she could have deduced herself. She had driven him across from Lamlash and down to Prestwick and seen him securely aboard the aircraft. Barring disaster, there was hardly anywhere else he could have ended up. His next communication followed a full fortnight afterward, and the rest of the summer had been silence.

"Needs a proper hiding, that boy," Andrew had said. Philippa had said nothing. There was too much inverted relish in the words. He waited, eager as a tongue-lolling spaniel, for her response. She knew what he hoped for, a descent into acrimony and recrimination. Andrew always enjoyed her children's failings. (Except perhaps this last, devastating thing that Victoria had sprung on them.) Nothing pleased him more, generally, than a mutual session of lamentation over them. Then everything went his way: Philippa on his side, and a wedge of displeasure between them both and the off-spring of her first marriage. It made his ownership of his wife somehow more complete, his superior age for once an advantage. He could chastise her gently, a foolish child grown wise under his sensible guidance. Sometimes, when Philippa was truly exhausted, like now, she would let him, for the sake of peace.

The truth was he expected little of either David or Victoria. It was the mixed blood, he would say privately. Never any use, mixed blood. Old Hallsworth and he had agreed at once on that. Of course, they agreed on most things; as they'd both agreed at once on the basic premise of their relationship: that Andrew would make a splendid match for Hallsworth's unfortunately wayward daughter. Straighten her out, settle her down, get her back on the rails. Damn decent of him, Hallsworth had said from the start, shop-soiled goods, so to speak, ha ha. The port had been powerful that evening, all those years ago. Philippa had still been married to Robert, that's how *long* ago it was. And Philippa had known, from the start, the whole familial plan. She had been, like now, simply too weary to resist.

Damn the fool boy for letting her down. Damn him for proving them all, once more, right. A postcard, and not even the right stamps. She'd had to pay some stupid small sum to the postie outside the door of Lamlash House before she could even see the wretched thing. And the old sod had probably read it, anyhow, whizzing arrogantly up the long beech-lined drive on his damnable rattly red bicycle.

Philippa straightened self-consciously on the narrow wooden-slatted bench. She was so crammed in by people and luggage that any motion resulted in a flurry of apologies and a half-hearted shifting of some presumed offending object.

"No, please, it's quite all right," she said in her most conciliatory voice, but the clipped accent ensured that she would be misunderstood.

"I'm *sorry*," said the girl sitting beside her, and heaved a wicker basket full of scratching noises. She did not look sorry but annoyed. Philippa sighed and tried to lean back, but the curve in the side of the ferry made it impossible. It was like an oversized pleasure boat, a private cruiser; how they could consider it sufficient, she could not imagine. Ferry to Philippa meant the Brodick Ferry which plied the angry waters of the Firth of Clyde, crossing in appalling weathers between Ardrossan and the isle of Arran. It was, as those waters and weathers demanded, a proper steamship, a miniature liner, with steel hull, and smoking funnel with MacBraynes painted on it, and room for hundreds of people, and cattle and motorcars. Seventy-two hours before she had stood on its salty wet decks, Andrew behind her on Brodick Pier, already retreating to the Douglas Hotel and a gin and tonic. Ahead, Ardrossan, and the busy journey to Prestwick, and the irritating uneasiness of flying, and the greater uneasiness beyond. New York, Robert, David: three unknowns. The first she had never seen. The second two, intimates in their separate ways of her own body, were now as alien.

"Pop bought me a surfboard." That was it. That was the line that, unlike anything Andrew could say of him, drove between her and her own son, creating an Atlantic-sized rift. He was quite ecstatic about the gift, of course; not surprising, David, indulged by his wealthy stepfather and by her own father, liked and expected to be bought things. It was not that that had angered her, but the name. Pop. Not Father, as he had been taught, or Pater, as some of his friends, now only half-jokingly, still indulged themselves. Not even Papa. But Pop; childish, intimate, and utterly American. For the first time in years, Philippa was quite suddenly afraid of Robert again.

She had gone straight to her hotel room in Manhattan, and gone directly to bed, exhausted, and breathless with the August heat of the city. But she had slept badly, disoriented and chilled by the icy air conditioning. She had awakened at eleven in the evening, too late to do anything, call anyone, but unable to sleep. She called for room service, but in her weariness could not make clear to the Negro voice on the other end what she wanted. She felt as foreign as on the Continent. More foreign, for there she spoke good French, and if necessary could find an interpreter. Here the need of interpretation was dismissed, but lurked yet in the thick, blurring accents, as messy and overheated and shabby as the city she had dimly glimpsed through dusty taxicab windows.

Eventually her cup of tea arrived, or rather a cup of cooling water, with a tea bag crouching disconsolately on the saucer. There was a ham sandwich, too, as ordered, but a vast thing, with heaps of coleslaw and vile yellow mustard and dark tangy bread. She pushed it to the back of the tray with a shudder and dipped the tea bag into the water. It leaked a yellow stain, like a child peeing in the swimming baths.

She abandoned it, slept, awakened with terror at the humming of the air conditioning, dreaming she was in London with the bombers overhead. She sat up, patting her face with a handkerchief. She had not dreamed of that for years. In the morning, she telephoned Robert.

It was not easy. The telephones were difficult, and different, the hotel operator speaking the same thick-throated Negro tongue heavy with impatience. She felt like a small girl again, her own small self riding the train north from home to St. Catherine's, with her school trunk, and the awful felt hat, and her plaits banging on her embarrassing new chest, as she stumbled about the carriage, alone, crying, getting everything wrong. She got out at the wrong station, that first journey at age twelve, and waited hours on a north of England rail platform, until being found by some official and rerouted like a lost parcel for Edinburgh. Philippa's Journey to St. Catherine's became a family epic, much laughed over in years to come.

Philippa was not laughing now. She felt too old, and too weary, ever to see the humor of New York. Finally, she made her connection, and Robert's voice was on the other end. Dimly she recalled he had no phone of his own. "Don't worry," he had said, "it's a public phone booth number, but it's at the end of my walk. I always answer it first, if I'm expecting a call."

He did, thank God. Philippa relaxed a little, her fingers polishing the red leatherette surface of the Gideon Bible by the phone. Put there to bolster one against the phone system, she thought, and almost smiled. It was all right now. He would join her in the city, surely, with David. They would have dinner at her hotel, peaceful and civilized, both proud of their handsome son, the one good remnant of their marriage, and then Robert would see them safely to Idlewild and a plane for home.

But it had not happened like that at all. Calm, civilized, it was all that. Oh, very calm. "Me? Come in there? No, sorry, Phil. I never come in in the summer. David? Yes, he's here. Of course. No, he wasn't planning on going in. Look, come out to dinner. We'll talk it all over. You come here." And that was it, as casual as if she were his publisher or his agent, and had not just traveled three thousand miles, and the question was some trivial matter, the timing irrelevant. She could come to him. And she would, too, she knew with intense anger, the sort of anger she'd not felt for years: Robert anger. She set the phone down. She had conceded. If she did not, she would not see David. He would not come to her, nor would he write to her. For the first time in all the years she had known Robert, she was seeing him on his own home ground. Like all who fight on their own territory, as she well knew, he was possessed of a quite fathomless strength. She was the invader now, and David, her David, was in the enemy camp.

She lay down on the shiny synthetic damask bedspread and put her face on the backs of her hands. Solemnly she cried for a short while, deliberately, knowing she simply must have release. Then she straightened up, sat up, and went into the small, windowless bathroom. An extractor fan switched on when she flicked the light switch, and added a second hum to the permanent rumble of the air conditioner. She washed her face thoroughly, with a good scrubbing from the face cloth, as she had been taught years ago at St. Catherine's. She looked up at her own face in the wall mirror, no longer even surprised at the absence of the beauty that had once courted her from all mirrors. Where beauty went, everyone knew. But where, could anyone tell her, did the love of children go?

David had always been her child, not Robert's. He would have been even if there had been no divorce. Not Victoria, no; without Robert's absence she would have been different, father-centered, as daughters are, and no doubt happier than the willful, skittish, often spiteful creature she, as all father-neglected girls, had become. But David was Philippa's own. Even from babyhood. Children, like lovers, have their illogical favorites, all honest parents know.

In honesty, Philippa knew she was right. He had been a beautiful child, and although strangers instinctively connected his beauty to her own, he did not really resemble her, but Robert. He had Robert's elegant, verging on unmanly, delicate features, but her own English fairness. And he was bigger than Robert, broader, better built in every way. Grown into manhood, he could, caught in a sudden glance, take breath away. And his nature was as sweet as the face, the powerfully candid eyes, the soft, strong cheek.

As a tiny child he would for no reason come and lay that cheek against her own. Her mind went fluttering back, from cheek to cheek, the times he had done that, the small soft hand pressed into her own in crowded shops, at the oddest moment in church, at home, anywhere. The baby eyes that suddenly glowed at sight of her. The face that crumpled to grief if her own turned away. The small body wordlessly leaning against her knee and thigh. His school-holiday face, bright with reunion, or holidays past, dark with despair. How could children be so ruthless, sanguinely taking love from squally babyhood onward, right to manhood, and then suddenly simply forgetting? All that devotion, half of saint, half of lover, where did it go?

Perhaps it had gone to Robert. The thought was heady, sickening; mixed with the diesel fumes swirling in the hot air, it brought sudden nausea. Philippa struggled to her feet, clutching her leather overnight case. "I'm sorry, I must have some air. Please." They all looked at her as if she were mad. She struggled down the crowded aisle between the benches, making for the open deck aft. Her silk kerchief, abominably sticky in the humid heat, began to slip forward, shadowing her brow. She had not a free hand between handbag and case to push it back. The journey, all of it, was a nightmare.

Breakfast at the hotel had begun it. She ordered a boiled egg, creating a half-hearted consternation. Surely they ate boiled eggs. "Just when we're sick, ma'am," said the waitress. But it arrived, loose on a plate, with a cup beside it. Scantly looking at her, the waitress sliced the thing in half, and poured the soupy contents into the cup as Philippa watched astounded.

"Do you not have an egg cup?" she said wearily. The waitress shrugged at what was before her. An *egg cup*, obviously.

"You want toast, ma'am? Coffee?" Philippa shook her head, watching the disemboweled egg congealing gently in its slick china surround. She got up and left the table.

In Pennsylvania Station, overcome with shaky hunger, she braved the breakfast front again. She went into a packed, shiny-countered café within the underground labyrinth and climbed awkwardly onto one of the high chromium stools, between the rows of business-suited, newspaper-shielded breakfasters. She ordered coffee and a bun, and, bewitched by the heaps of same-colored paper, paid for it accidentally with a five-dollar note, calling it a one. No one corrected her. Once outside, she saw she had been cheated. She wanted to cry. She was not a poor woman, but since childhood she hated cheats, any blatant unfairness ruffling the fabric of decency. She went away and bought a newspaper, and missed hearing her train called, the accent blurring unrecognizably on the loudspeaker. The lighted place names and numbers on the electric board by the train gate flicked relentlessly over.

Tucking her newspaper under her arm, and hoisting her case again, she went to the Information window where a girl with an acne-spotted face said between twanging mouthfuls of gum that she would have to wait until eleven. Philippa made a little fortress on a bench, surrounding herself with her case, her handbag, a paper cup of orange squash, and her newspaper. She had bought it on impulse, finding with a great harsh loneliness that she was unfamiliar with any of the names. It was small and easily handled. She opened it out and realized at once it was the sort of blaring tabloid she would never read at home. But resignedly she turned down the name and attempted bravely to read the first story. It was about a woman who had heard voices from God proclaiming she must eat her baby. The roasted, bone-picked skeleton was pictured in bland printer's ink. Philippa put her hand to her throat and dropped the paper to the dirty tiled floor. It was a country of the mad.

The train, when she finally boarded it, was hot and crowded and dirty, the windows so grimed over that the weary landscape slid by green and dusky in a dirty green sun. The metal rim of the green leatherette seat prodded into Philippa's back. Overhead a huge black fan turned against the fly-speckled roof of the train. It was ominous and eerie, the sort of malevolent sharp machinery that had frightened her to tears as a child, all the more ghastly for the illogic of the fear. Today, in weary disorientation, such ancient fears rebirthed.

She withdrew into her mind, trying to imagine herself in her cool, clean, tended drawing room in Lamlash House or, even better, home at Greenshaws in Yorkshire, out on the cool, wet moor. The train and its burden of people followed, prodding in on her with its rattling and clanging and clatter of wheels and rails, and couplings and jangling chains between the carriages, whose doors stood open for the air. She glimpsed patches of dry weeds, and gravel, and the corners of dull gray wood ties whizzing by perilously close. Children played in the aisles, and a dog sat all but feet from that rocketing disaster without. The parents were so casual of safety, casual of everything. Did no one ever dress to travel in America?

Here and there Philippa found a lady with hair teased up into a great bouffant nest, and nail varnish and shoes and stockings, and a neat collarless boxy summer suit worn with the odd blaring ungrace of the nation. But for the rest, there were denim trousers and khaki shorts, and flower-printed cotton skirts and little blouses, knitted, cut like vests, scooped out to brassiere level, cut in at the sleeveless arms. Everyone was half naked. Across from her a huge man with dark, European features sat in grimy gray trousers and knitted vest and nothing else. His dark skin gleamed with sweat and glistening curling hair. Such intimate hair, matting his body, bedroom hair. Her eyes were assaulted by the hair, her nose by the thick smell of sweat.

The man brooded out the window, scratched himself, oblivious of his nudity, his middle-aged sexuality on display, like overripe fruit. Philippa's eyes shamed her, returning to him like her childhood's eyes seeking out the marble fig leaves in the museum in London. What was happening to her? Her eyes settled on the silver medallion gleaming on its chain about the man's sleek, sweaty throat. It lay rooted in a little bush of hair at the hollow of the throat. On it, St. Christopher carried the Holy Child, through a black jungle.

"Miss." Philippa flung about, gasping. There was a small dark-eyed man in a shabby dark suit standing in the aisle. He had a cake box in one hand, held by the string, and a newspaper, the same awful newspaper with its eaten baby, under his arm. The train was stopping. He said, "Your station, miss. I heard you tell the conductor. Sayville. Right?"

"Oh, yes. Oh, thank you. I didn't realize."

"It's all *right*," the man said, with a vague knowing shrug, almost annoyed with her though he'd volunteered his help. Philippa stood up bewildered, and when the man reached to help her with her case, she quite rudely snatched it back. She could not trust anyone suddenly.

"Suit yourself," he said, without feeling, and walked away down the aisle. Philippa followed, ashamed. Outside, the heat pounced on her with the bright, sea-white light of the sun.

On the concrete platform before the oddly pretty station, she shrank back from the thunder of the diesel engine pulling out, and waited until all the carriages had rumbled and clicked away, past the dinging bells of the road crossing, and disappeared beyond the lush green trees lining the curving rails. Then suddenly it was very quiet, and the low voices of the passengers who had descended with her from the train seemed muted on the hot air. She recognized several of them from the train, and one from the station in New York, that slim, long-haired girl in denim trousers and skinny black sleeveless sweater, that girl who reminded her, with her belligerent beautiful face, of Victoria.

The girl was clambering into a big blue van with dust-stained sides on which someone had scrawled "Clean Me" with an insolent finger. There was a man in a cowboy hat standing beside it. He announced, rather than asked, "Fire Island, miss." Philippa nodded, reluctant to enclose herself once more in the heat of a vehicle, but went forward, it being the only way to David. The man, rather kindly, helped her up, but her stiff alligator shoe betrayed her, and she stumbled into the vehicle.

None of the three men sitting on the bench made the slightest move to break her fall. The girl did, and as Philippa went to one knee, ripping her stockings on the rim of the van floor, a thin young hand caught her elbow. "You all right?" the voice asked, with a momentary flicker of interest rather than concern. Philippa said she was, and the hand released her.

She made her way to a bench on the right side of the big vehicle and sat down. She was angered; the shoes had betrayed her. She usually wore more cooperative shoes, but she had expected nothing but the airport and the city and had dressed accordingly. This adventuring into the hinterland had not been part of the plan. Still, she was embarrassed and felt herself to have looked old, which annoyed her. She was still comfortably capable of a day's stalking on the uplands of Mull or Arran, and frankly doubted that wispy thin girl who had helped her could herself keep the pace.

Humiliated, she sat with her torn stocking concealed by her other leg and looking across at the three men on the bench, saw at once why they had not helped her. They were that sort. Philippa withdrew inside a discreet emotional distance. She was not a prude, and not naive. But she could never overcome her distaste for them.

It took no surprising subtlety to see them for what they were, utterly blatant in their tight trousers and bloused shirts and strings of necklaces like teenage girls. Still, Philippa would have recognized them anyhow, from the set of lip, hip, shoulder, whatever subtle slants of the body turned man to woman, or man-woman. She'd met others. Last winter, in Victoria's appalling Edinburgh flat, there had been two.

Philippa had stopped in, unexpected, on her way from Arran to London, cherishing some foolish mother-and-daughter fantasy involving lunch at the North British (Victoria in tweed suit and nylons) and a cozy chat over coffee, even a brandy. Idiot, she thought now, looking back; Victoria did not even possess a tweed suit, probably did not even possess nylons. Somehow, in her absence, the image of the girl desired overcame that of the girl existent. The image vanished soon enough.

It was four flights of worn stone Scottish stairs up to that flat on Bristo Street. There were bicycles and battered prams at the foot. Philippa found the prams the most distasteful. Students, after all, were allowed a temporary squalor, a bit of mucking in with the world. But prams were permanent, lower-class tenement squalor. Victoria had no business in a place like that. Philippa clicked up flight after flight in her city heels. A woman was scrubbing the third flight, surrounded by a steaming pail and an atoll of soapy puddles. She bustled bottom first down a step, looked up with red energetic cheeks. "Tairrable day."

"Yes," Philippa had said without thought. "Shocking." She went on hurriedly. Victoria's door was painted bright green, a ghastly color, and someone had scrawled in felt pen, "Smashing show, Vicky, all best for the Festival." It was washable pen and the Festival was months ago. With a distant twinge of affection, Philippa knew that Victoria had cherished and preserved that sign of her theatrical pretensions. Philippa used the word with deliberation, too, because life with Robert had shown her enough of the theater that even she knew pretensions from ambitions. That thing that, even at this distant date, she would admit Robert had had, Victoria had not, and desiring it, no matter how strongly, made no difference.

The person who answered her knock on the door was a complete stranger, not Vicky's flatmate, not anybody identifiable. She was a big, broad girl in corduroy trousers and a big loose sweater, the sort of girl that, when Philippa was that age, would never wear trousers unless forced. The sort of girl who ended up in the Land Army, humping bales, and being seduced by everything that passed. She said, booming, "*He*llo, can I help?" as if Philippa were selling something. And then when Philippa did introduce herself, she swung her vast corduroy hips around and shouted into the dark interior of the flat, "*Ho*kay, you lot, bums off the floor. It's Vicky's mum." And that was her welcome to her daughter's university home.

There were people everywhere in that flat, sprawled about on the floor in the drawing room, as Philippa in a moment of hilarious unthinking anachronism termed it, cluttered about the kitchen table, lying on beds in the two bedrooms, sitting, standing, crouching cross-legged. Considering the hour, she was sure that at least some of them must have been there all night, for surely ten or twelve people don't call for coffee? It was like an orgy, though to be sure they were all completely clothed, indeed overclothed, in coats most of them, but that was no wonder, the flat was colder than the Edinburgh street outside.

She found Victoria in her bedroom, lying on the worn colorless rug, drying her long hair by the tiny gas fire. She lay quite flat on the floor, the ends of her hair and one reddening ear only inches from the small blue flames. The hair, once deep silky brown, was now so dried and tattered by over-washing and the Edinburgh winter that it fuzzed out in a pale, bleached buff halo.

Seeing her, Victoria half sat up. "Oh, hello mother," she said with a small smile. "I wasn't expecting you." Then she kissed Philippa's cheek shyly and lay down again, drying the other side now and with her back to her mother. "Off to London?" she said, her voice muffled by the hiss and plutter of the fire.

"Of course," Philippa said stiffly. There was a silence, and Victoria's friends went quite naturally back to whatever conversations and actions she had interrupted. Philippa thought to suggest lunch, but she could not think of anywhere in Edinburgh she could take Victoria the way she looked just now. Besides, good manners would have her ask all her friends as well, and there were so many.

"I'm sorry about the letter," Victoria said, from behind her hair.

"What letter, dear?"

"The one I didn't answer. I've got it on my desk somewhere. I was going to answer it tomorrow."

Philippa knelt uncomfortably on the grimy floor. "No bother, dear," she said with a small smile. There were so many, many unanswered letters, it seemed distinctly odd to lay a weight of remorse on any single one. Behind her, someone switched on the wireless, and a young, working-class voice bawled about love with a background of a great thumping of discords. The big heavy girl in corduroys began to stamp and sway, even while she was talking to a young man in glasses, her body unconcernedly making its own vast rhythm.

Philippa, still kneeling, half turned and looked about the room. The walls were covered with that cheap, textured paper that the landlords of student flats so favored. Someone, Victoria, or one of the flatmates, Fiona or Pat, had painted it all over with a single coat of buff emulsion, over which they had splashed huge murals, silly things, a great whale with a spout in one corner, and a vast St. Andrew's cross in another. High up, between the door and a handmade bookcase was a six-pointed star in the blue color of the Israeli flag. So Victoria was one-quarter Jewish. They'd all made no secret of it. But why flaunt it? she thought with sudden anger ricocheting back to Robert.

Victoria twisted around, tugging at her hair with her comb. It caught in split tangles below the teeth, and she wrenched at it angrily with a sharp gasp of pain. "Oh, my *hair*. It's shocking."

Philippa smiled again. Vicky's voice was so English, so ringingly English. For all Andrew's efforts, for all her Scottish schooling and Scottish university, Scotland had laid not one inch of a claim on her.

"It's far too dry, dear. Stop washing it."

"Oh, I can't *bear* it dirty. I just can't bear it."

Victoria swung around and sat cross-legged facing her, tugging despairingly at the dry buff tangles. She shrugged. "How's Andrew?" she said.

Philippa took the comb from her daughter and quietly began to work on the tangles, and Victoria slipped effortlessly back to girlhood and sat patient. "You'll just have to bear it, ducks, or it will all fall out, I dare say." She worked carefully at it, with the same certain fingers that had plaited it for school. "If you start at the bottom and work up, it will never tangle," she said. "Uncle Andrew's very well, except for his back, for which I have no sympathy. He insisted on doing the dahlias himself again, and set the old lumbago going, silly goose."

"Mmm." Victoria shrugged, uninterested, picking at the frayed hem of her trousers. Great cottony strings hung about her ankles. The trousers were worn to bare patches at the knees, and her sweater was grubby. How could she be so fussy about the hair, about her face which she scrubbed with skin-destroying mania, about her underwear which must be spotlessly clean, and was on occasion changed twice a day, and still show the world such a tattered, scruffy exterior? Like a mortifying saint with a hairshirt beneath his clothes, hidden from the world's eye. Cleanliness must be an invisible sacrifice.

"Oh, shit," Victoria suddenly cried, and then as her hand went to her mouth and her eyes to Philippa, she said, "Sorry, mother." The gas fire fizzled to nothing, died, and the cold kept at bay by its meager effort closed in clammily. "Hugh!" Victoria shrieked. "Where's Hugh? The meter's buggered again."

The hand came to the mouth again and Philippa said suddenly, "Oh yes, dear, you're sorry. Don't bother, pet," but there was more sarcasm than affection in the words.

"No, really, I *am* sorry. Only I simply *hate* the cold, and this meter's impossible. *Hugh!*"

"I've a shilling right here, dear," Philippa said, clicking into her alligator bag. "You needn't bother Hugh or whoever. Look, here's two."

Victoria looked at it as if she'd never seen a shilling before in her life. Then she nodded slowly, but did not take it. "Oh, mother, we don't use *those*," she said with a little knowing smile. There was a giggle from behind, from the big lewd girl in corduroys.

"Perhaps we really ought to give it just the oc*cas*ional one," she said, but then Hugh appeared. He was a small, neat young man, modest height made graceful by good proportioning.

His hair was golden brown, glossy and wavy as a collie's coat, and his face clean cut with clear, light blue eyes, and the sort of fully formed lips that really young girls found sensual, and older women saw as slightly effeminate. There was nothing about his face or form that could be called offensive, and when he slipped down on the floor beside Victoria and bent his smooth head over the meter, there was no visible physical evidence of any relationship between them. Still, Philippa was suddenly certain that this was Victoria's young man. He banged the meter sharply with one hand, retrieved the battered fake coin that fell from it, and fed it shamelessly back into the slot. The gas hissed into the room, and the young man, Hugh, quickly drew a box of matches from his tight trouser pocket, struck one with a smoker's ease, and held it to the bars of the fire. The flames puffed blue across it and glowed. Hugh held the match up suddenly in front of Victoria, and she with a smile blew it softly out. He laughed, got to his feet and walked, with an easy saunter, away.

"That's Hugh," said Victoria and casually turned aside. He was her lover, Philippa knew at once. Victoria slept with men. The knowledge rang so hard upon her that she struggled to her feet and left the room. Victoria thought she was going to speak to Hugh, but that was not possible. What could she say? He was a nice young man, surely. What could she say? Leave my little girl alone? Oh, really.

She stood in the battered doorway between the two rooms. That was when she saw the two men. They were sitting at either side of the big, broad kitchen table. One, the older with a round moon face and a balding head, was talking, the other listening, and the one talking was carefully stubbing out a cigarette as he explained something, turning the stub round and round in the broad glass ashtray. He seemed a very pleasant man, and the other's rapt, almost awed attention was pretty and touching, or would be if only they had been of different sex. But they were not, and their hands, lightly linked beneath the table, tightened as the conversation went on until, with a final gentle nod, they were loosed and dropped apart. Philippa knew then, as now on the ferry, what they were. They looked calmly, pleasantly happy. It was the failure to look even potentially suicidal that worried Philippa so.

She had turned around and gone back into the room where Victoria was now sitting cross-legged on the floor, chatting with the big Land Army girl.

"It's wrong," Philippa said.

"Pardon, mother?"

"It's wrong." Philippa gestured with one finger to the gas meter. "Feeding the meter. It's stealing, Victoria. It's stealing."

"Oh, *moth*er." Victoria stood up and shook out her dry, frizzy hair. Then she grinned, as if to make it light, and said, "The landlord's an absolute bastard, I assure you."

They were without shame, she, her lover, the lewd fat girl, the unnatural men. Shame was no longer in fashion.

The green door closed on Philippa, and the gray stairs smelling of carbolic soap led her away. She did not see Victoria again for half a year.

The afterdeck of the ferry, up an awkward four wooden steps, was crowded with weekenders. Dismayed, Philippa turned around in the two feet of free deck, and balancing herself against the weight of her case, and the slapping of the waves against the bow, she made for the upper deck. There was a double staircase leading to it, open, like on an old London bus. Philippa had managed enough of those with packages and babies, and she mounted the left side gamely, clambering over the two insolent teenagers sitting on the bottom step. The air that greeted her at the top was neither cool nor refreshing, a hot thick wind. But the diesel smell was gone. She gulped at it, feeling clammy sweat on her throat and a churning in her stomach. No. She would not be ill. That would not do.

She found a seat on one of the gray painted benches, settled herself with her case on the floor and her knees uncomfortably stretched over it. She untied the silk square and slipped it off her head, shaking her gray-blond hair free. She folded the kerchief carefully so the two Labrador faces portrayed on it were but eyes on a buff square, and placed it neatly in the alligator bag. She clicked it shut and reformed the damp, crushed waves of her hair with three fingers of one hand. Then, a little uneasily, she looked around.

The water and the flat alien land were swallowed up in a gray-white haze of heat and sun glare. There was so much light everywhere, and all of it so diffused, of little use to see by. Philippa wished she had the dark glasses she had left foolishly in the Rover at Lamlash, and wished she had something, anything light in her wardrobe, to have brought along. She was wearing, of course, her best summer suit. But summer, for the past ten years, had meant Arran during the parliamentary recess, and Arran had no summer worth discussing, certainly none justifying a separate wardrobe. The few bright June days, fleeting among the weeks of Western Isles wind and rain, they weathered in tweeds, panting like the unshorn sheep. Philippa had given up summer frocks as she had given up so much else when she surrendered the Sussex house.

So she had come with her good light summer tweed, and her lighter woolen skirts, and sweaters, and two good blouses. She leaned forward and slipped out of the jacket and folded it across her knees. The blue crepe blouse from Jenner's clung like plastic to her damp skin, its throat bow drooping. She untied it and let it hang open, conscious of her dishevelment and not caring. The girl sitting across from her had no shoes. A crepe bow could hardly matter.

It was the girl with long hair, she realized suddenly, who had reminded her of Victoria, the girl from Pennsylvania Station. She had clipped the long hair off her face, tightly, like a dancer, but her face, like Victoria's, was too narrow for such dramatics. She was knitting, with two broad white needles, an inch thick, and great piles of loose, loopy mohair wool.

Philippa watched with distaste. The needles clicked dully, and the garment, whatever it might be, flowed gray and shapeless like a spider's web. The sight of it alone made Philippa sticky with heat. The fat needles clicked on, the girl, mindless of all about her, bent over them, eyes behind dark glasses pinned upon them like the eyes of a hidden snake. There was something so smug about women who worked with their hands. Philippa detested the whole gamut: Yorkshire farmwives on buses with useful woollies growing from their stubby red fingers; middle-class women sewing endless Crimplene frocks; even some of her own friends at times smirked ostentatious contentment over needlepoint. Philippa, her memory yet fresh of nights of wartime woolly dedication, rebelled utterly. She had not lifted a knitting needle or a pin since the day clothes rationing ended. It was her own private V-E Day. Once, when Andrew had demanded, as he did often, rhetorically, "What did we fight the war for, anyhow?" Philippa had flipped back without a moment's thought, "Off-the-peg clothing, what else?" He had not found it funny in the slightest.

Anyhow, none of her aversions to handwork proved hereditary. Oh, David was sufficiently useless, but being male no one noticed. But Victoria; Victoria had let the side down, as Andrew would say, and rather badly at that. Knitting, sewing, oh yes, but not satisfied, she went on weaving, spinning, carding the wool, dyeing, teasing, shearing the ungodly sheep as well, milking, currying, hoeing, rooting, weeding, plowing; hands endlessly busy, self-satisfied, self-righteous, remending the old broken world. She lived now in two rooms of a collapsing stone croft house above Brodick Bay, with two men. Victoria, Hugh, and Peter, the blessed trinity of the New Jerusalem.

It *would* be on Arran, where everyone knew everyone and everyone saw everything. There was surely not that need to hurt Andrew so, whatever she thought of him. She had all the Hebrides, Inner and Outer, to choose from. Philippa would never accept that malice had not played as strong a part as convenience in the choice.

"But, mother, be reasonable. We're getting it *free*. Lindsay is *giving* it to us." That was Lindsay Baillie-Johnstone, twenty-three-year-old Cambridge failure, now studying hairdressing in London. He gave them TighnaMara. No great sacrifice; it was worthless, riddled with dry rot, the land strangling in bracken, and anyhow Lindsay was heir also to another six hundred acres scattered about Scotland, and a stately home in Wales. Last year he gave twenty-five acres of Glen Moriston to a leftover mistress, rather a consolation prize, from what Philippa had heard. The year before, forty-two acres in Aberdeenshire, and a disused manse, had gone to an American beat philosopher he'd met on the night sleeper to London. Socialism had some odd allies these days; at that rate he'd redress the old balance all on his own, Philippa had little doubt. But still, for Victoria's threesome on Arran, almost on her doorstep, she owed him no thanks.

Eventually, in spite of Andrew, she went to see them. By then, they had been in residence several months, and Lamlash was accustomed to them, three Welly-booted, public school tramps, in Peter's muddy Land Rover. Throughout Philippa's visit Victoria sat at her immense handloom, deep in beady-eyed intent, letting her fingers become the masters of conversation. The shuttle crossed, the treadles clattered, the comb coming down on each sentence, cutting it off. In the background, a woman's recorded voice wailed with an American accent about love and a snow-white turtledove. They had no water, no electricity; they cooked over the smoking peat and coal fire, and they used the back wall of their house as a lavatory; but the recorded music was splendidly reproduced on an expensive German machine.

"Stop doing that," Philippa said, irritated. "Please."

"It's quite all right, mother, I can do it while we talk. I can do it with my eyes closed."

Philippa shook her head but gave in. The treadles clacked on, the warp threads jumped and twitched, and the shuttle flung back and forth between Victoria's certain, pompous hands. Philippa was sure she was refusing to stand to conceal her bulk. The two men, both of them, were conspicuously absent. "You must at least think about it," Philippa said.

"There's nothing to think about." Victoria smiled soothingly.

"When I return from America."

"You're going, then?"

"Of course I'm going. David's due to go up to Cambridge in five weeks."

"Surely it's down, when you're as far north as this," Victoria said mildly, eyes firm on the loom. "I don't think he'll come back. I think he'll stay there. I don't think he wants to go to Cambridge."

"Oh, thank you very much, missy," Philippa said sharply. "I hardly think you know. You've not seen him since God knows when."

"I saw him in May. At Lindsay's party. Remember? I do get around, you know."

"Yes."

"Cambridge won't suit David. I know; we're very alike."

"Ridiculous. You're not alike at all. Besides, you've never even liked David and he's never liked you."

"Mother, what rubbish. How perfectly rotten."

"And perfectly true. Oh, come now, Vicks. What you mean is, you're afraid David will make a good job of university, and show you up. Right, missy?"

"Rubbish. I don't give a damn."

"You've two months before the autumn term. It could all be settled by then. A decent flat, a home help. We will help out financially, of course. Naturally you'll lose your grant, married girls do, but money will not prove a problem. We will see to that."

"Andrew?" Victoria laughed.

"I have considerable money of my own. As you know."

"Oh, my independent mother. No. No, mother, I am not going to marry Hugh. And no, I am not going back to Edinburgh, married or otherwise."

"Marriage is not the only solution," Philippa said. Victoria stopped, her hands still at last.

"Oh, really, mother, you do amaze me. Of *course* it's not. What have I been saying?"

Philippa got up from her chair and walked away and looked out the window at the spectacular view of sea and sky and the distant Scottish mainland. She cried out suddenly, "Vicky, darling, you just have no idea. You have no idea how *long* life is. You've *time* yet for all of this, but later, later." She whirled about, catching Victoria in mid-weave. "Listen, darling, I've made all the inquiries. I have the names, everything. A good home . . ."

"For God's sake, mother, it's not an eff-ing Labrador." Victoria stood up, her firm round front pushing out her sweater. Somehow she was still in her jeans, or someone's jeans. "No. It's my baby and it's not going to anyone's good home. I will have my baby. I will not have it adopted. And I will not have Andrew's Harley Street doctor 'do something' for me, either. So you can stuff that for a start."

Philippa shut her mouth and swallowed hard. She turned back to the mocking peace of the pastoral landscape. After a while when capable of dispassion, she said, "I never, never suggested such a thing, Vicky. Never."

"Andrew did," said Victoria with a smug cold smile. She did not allow even a decent interval for Philippa to absorb the thrust, but went on. "He wrote me a letter. Oh, you didn't know, did you? Well, he did. It was—" She paused, and pulled her sweater down so the bump was smoothly contained. "It was," and then, having found the word, she used that cold smile again and said, "insane."

"What do you mean, insane? What is this, Victoria?"

She leaned back, flaunting herself and her pregnancy, and half closed her eyes, summoning from memory. "Oh, I can't recall it all, it rambled so, but my favorite line was, 'Victoria, you have behaved like a trollop.' A trollop," she shrieked suddenly with shallow gaiety. "Dear *God*, mother, I thought the word went out with Dickens. 'Victoria, you have shamed your mother and myself. You may wish to be modērn, but you must understand that decent people will not stand for it. Damn it all, girl' "—she dropped her voice to an imitation of Andrew's best public school gruff—" 'you cahn't go around opening your legs to every man in sight and expect to come home, proud as punch, and flaunt your big fat belly around Lámlash House.' " Victoria finished with a flourish, her hand coming down on her stomach. She waved her narrow hips to and fro, so her firm swelling body danced back and forth. "Here I come flaunting my big, fat belly," she cried, delighting in her own anger. Then she cut off suddenly and said, looking down at herself, "Actually, I'm really not that big. Perhaps I should wait a month or two."

"Oh, Vicky, please. Do stop. You disgust me."

"Andrew disgusts *me*," Victoria cried suddenly. "The big, effeminate prat."

"Victoria," Philippa whispered, but she did not look up. Andrew had disgusted her as well. To use such words to her daughter. Her daughter. He could be such an insufferable bastard in his pinstripe, port, and Havanas way. What disgusted her most was the creeping knowledge that for Andrew the illegitimacy was a saving grace. A married pregnancy he could not banish from his sight, but that, too, would have disgusted him. It was the earthy damp swelling of fertility that he fled from. Philippa had ten years of his fastidious marriage bed as proof.

"I'm sorry, Victoria," she said. Victoria shrugged diffidently and flung her shuttle.

"He doesn't bother *me*," she said.

"Vicky?"

"Mmm?"

Philippa folded her hands on her lap, selecting her words.

"Vicky, I want you to understand that whatever happens, with you, with Andrew, with David, I still love you. I will always still love you."

Victoria looked up, blinking, her eyes refocusing from their concentration. She said, "I know, mother," without gratitude or surprise and went calmly back to work.

Philippa stood by, bemusedly hurt, almost made to leave, and said suddenly, "Has it never occurred to you you've caused us considerable distress?" But then she shook her head and waved away the answer. Of course it had not occurred to her. Had it, she would at least have apologized. She did apologize sometimes, for not writing, for using crude language, for showing up unexpectedly at Lamlash House with friends who smoked Andrew's cigars and drank Andrew's whisky. But for her central major sin, failing to in any way resemble the daughter they had invested blood, life, time, and a great deal of money in, for that she had not a word.

"I do not choose to cause you distress," Victoria said. "That is not why I am here, or pregnant, or in love with Hugh. I choose to live. Here, with Hugh. And Peter. And my baby."

"Whose baby?" Philippa said, feeling oddly malicious. "Do you know?"

"What?"

"You know what I mean."

"Mother. For fuck's sake. That's disgusting."

Philippa laughed, but Victoria dropped the shuttle so it tangled in among the reds and blues and browns of warp and weft, and stood up, her hands making a matronly firmness on her swollen body. "Really, I don't find that in the least funny. It's Hugh's baby."

"How should I know? They both live here. You seem every bit as affectionate with one as the other."

"We're friends, mother. You have friends."

"You kiss them both."

"*You* kiss practically everybody at your posh little parties. I don't expect you fuck them all. Oh, mother, I'm sorry."

Philippa was laughing, more delighted with Victoria's sudden burst of convention than angered by her language. She said, "Oh, never mind. Cheerio, pet, I must be going. Andrew's across with Mitzy at the vet. He'll be back soon now. Do send word if you need anything."

"Woolly booties, mother?"

"Oh, no, dear. Knit them yourself. You're far more capable than I, I assure you." She went out.

Years, years ago, she had had a friend, a Wren, during the war. She had gotten herself into what they called "an unfortunate condition" and had sought help in a shabby house in Earl's Court, the address of which circulated in the whispered exchanges of a kind of poisoned grapevine. It had worked, too, quite simply and with no dramatic, bloody death scene. She had come back, whole, fresh-faced, and devastated by guilt. Years, years, a lifetime of apology followed. She had been a Catholic, Irish, a stupid girl. But her guilt had been heroic. She was sorry for all the sins of the world, that girl. That was the way they were. Nobody, today, was ever sorry for anything.

Or grateful. Philippa stood quietly for a moment on the wooden porch of the croft house. Victoria had not bothered herself to see her out. She did not mind, welcoming solitude, after the claustrophobia of a blood relationship gone wrong. She looked around. Bright, cheap linoleum, well worn, covered the floor. The door was splintered raw with wet rot, and fungus grew along its edge, like on a dead tree. The paintwork, thick with the lazy layering on of coat after coat on unsanded wood, blistered and cracked open. It was the sort of house, so common here, held together for years by layers of wallpaper and crusts of paint. Strip that off and it would fall down.

Philippa had furnished Victoria's bedroom in Lamlash House with an antique rosewood suite, floor-length velvet drapes, and an oriental carpet that was a collector's piece. Then, there was her room in the flat in London, furnished all by her own choosing from Harrods. For her first term at Edinburgh,

Andrew had put a three-story Georgian house, one of his numerous Scottish properties, at her disposal. Well, Philippa thought, smiling slightly and pushing open the splintered door, Victoria had disposed of it. They found it sublet to five medical students. To be fair, they were serious, hardworking lads, and the place was tidy and well cared for. But Victoria was in that slum in Bristo Street.

And now this slum here. Victoria, apparently, liked slums. She reveled in them, in fact, and in all their peculiar gadgetry. When Philippa had arrived today, she had been dragged off to the lean-to scullery, black and dim with its minute window and soot-stained walls, and Victoria had showed her Peter or Hugh's latest discovery. A haybox.

"It keeps things warm."

"I know."

"But it works, mother."

"I know."

"I cooked soup in it yesterday. You boil it first, and then you pop the pan into the box and cover it over with the hay and . . ."

"And it cooks. I know. We used them during the war."

"But think of the money we're saving."

"You're not saving anything. You burn that ghastly peat fire night and day, so you might as well cook your soup on it."

"Well, of course. But if we had electricity, we'd be saving pounds."

"Victoria, you haven't got electricity."

"Mother. You've missed the point entirely."

So she had. Somewhere she had missed every point entirely. What was the point, for instance, of the twenty years that had passed since the day in the dark winter of nineteen forty-three that she gave birth to Robert Zolenski's daughter? The girl and all her young kind threw away everything she and her friends had built, defended, fought for, indeed, without melodrama, died for. (Philippa like all her generation carried a collection of gravestones among her mementoes.) They cheerfully now immersed themselves for no reason in the same drudgery she had borne, unbegrudged for a holy cause. They took the tools of that wartime desperation and played with them now like toys. And the treasures her friends had made their unique, remembered, and gallant stand for? Education was abandoned, politics forgotten (which of them ever voted?), grand houses forsaken for slums. Everything they had salvaged from the anti-Christ himself, their children took now in their smug little hands, distasteful as if it were excrement, and tossed away.

Andrew would fly into a quite wordless, insane rage at times over some tiny point that, like a flinted spark, set off the same sequence of thought. But Philippa felt no rage. She went, bemused yet, outside and shut the decaying door. Before her the ground was freshly turned, and marked with the prints of the muddy Wellington boots that all three young people lived in. New potato stalks were scattered about, their roots divested of fruit. Here and there, like a white marble, an occasional small potato remained forgotten. Philippa bent and picked one up in her clean manicured hands. She rubbed the dirt off slowly, and then more rapidly, feeling the slow pearly sheen of potato skin growing beneath her finger.

In the autumn of forty-three she had been home in Yorkshire, at Greenshaws, pregnant, like Victoria, pregnant with Victoria, indeed. She had helped lift the potato crop. Working foolishly, until her back ached and odd pains came around her stomach and down her thighs. They had all thought her brave, foolish, and noble. Were it not for the war, she'd have been forbidden the work. But for the war's sake, even her child was risked. Only Philippa knew quite how deliberate that risk had been.

Still, nothing had happened. The child risked in the potato field now stood, a woman, at her own window. Victoria tapped on the glass, and quite suddenly waved and blew her a kiss. Philippa watched for a long moment, and then, still rubbing the potato in the fingers of her left hand, she raised her right to her lips and returned the gesture. Victoria smiled, and the sun broke over the front of the house, suddenly, from behind Arran's dark mantle of cloud. It streaked out across the tattered barley crop, and down over the broken, bracken-ridden fields and onto the sea. White, like white fire, it lay across Brodick Bay and the Firth of Clyde and set black the low hills of Ayrshire.

Andrew would be home soon, crossing on the ferry with his petted, snappy Skye terrier on his knee, dopy with injections and smelling of medicine and pee. It was an old dog, with broken worn teeth, too old, mercy would have it put down, but Andrew was peculiarly soppy about it and would not concede to death. Andrew would carry it to its basket by the Adam hearth in the drawing room, where it would sit, licking itself with squelchy, intimate noises. He would say, "Well?"

She would say, "Well, what?"

And he would say, "Well, did she apologize at least?" No. She had not apologized. God bless, God keep her, she had not. "No matter, dear," Philippa said to herself as she walked down the rutted, twin tracks to the cattle grid, beyond which she had left the Land Rover. "Oh, no matter, I've apologized enough, surely, for us both."

The same sun streaked as white across the Great South Bay. Philippa leaned against the hard wood comfort of the ferry bench. The girl with Victoria's face rolled her knitting up like a woolen snake and put it away. Philippa closed her eyes against the glare. She had divorced Robert as apology to her parents. Philippa's bohemian fling, like Philippa's Journey to St. Catherine's, became an arch and prickly family password, secreting away emotion. Then she married Andrew as apology to her children. And since then she had done nothing but apologize to Andrew, for the error of her first marriage, for her children, and most of all, for being a woman and not whatever Oxford Adonis it was that had been the one, only entrant of his heart.

She was forty-two years old. Those apologies had, as with placating handkerchiefs, mopped up more than half of her life.

She was neither surprised nor particularly hurt that Robert did not meet her at the pier. He had withdrawn from her, physically and emotionally, thirteen years before, and would not take a willing step toward her. Since he had left her to make her own way from Manhattan, common decency was clearly not guiding him. And kindness he would not allow. She spotted the girl, Mary Jo, before the girl spotted her, and stood waiting, watching the confused stare of a stranger seeking a stranger until the dock was empty and they two were left with no alternative but each other.

"Mrs. Wardlaw?"

The broad American vowels and the uncertain treble tone made her name sound quite alien. But she nodded and said, "Yes?" She did not help, not with a smile, or an added word.

The girl, her voice still hovering between belligerence and wariness, said, "Robert sent me. I've got the dinghy."

"Jolly good," Philippa said, not really knowing what the dinghy had to do with anything.

"Oh, God," said the girl with a quick, mannerless grin, "you sound just like David."

"Oh," said Philippa. Somehow, she minded the girl's knowing David. She minded it more than anything, more than her rude familiarity, or her half-naked seaside dress. "Do I?" she said flatly.

"Yeah. C'mon. Everyone's waiting."

The girl ignored her in the rough, skimmed-stone journey in the dinghy across the bay flats. Really, from the moment of awkwardly shaking Philippa's hand, and helping her down the wooden ladder into the dinghy, tethered to a piling, she had ignored her. Her eyes had clicked shut of emotion, after her first, wary, careful surveillance. It was a dismissal. Philippa understood it completely, as indeed she understood the other fact that no doubt Robert assumed invisible: that this was Robert's mistress.

Young, pretty, clear-eyed with that undamageable clearness

that youth possessed, and could not of itself for all its sophisti-
cation rid itself. Only age took that look away. Odd how,
when young, and that same clear untried purity shone from her
own face, she had striven with makeup, near unobtainable
then, and expressions of mock despair, to banish it. Now age
had banished it of its own, and she would, like most women,
fondly have it back. She had been dismissed, with the cool
confidence of the young, secure in the knowledge of their clear
skin and firm bodies, and the restive power of the beautiful
over those whose beauty has passed. Hidden there, too, was
the modern young arrogance that all middle-aged women were
without sex; dried up or frozen in an era before freedom was
invented.

That might be almost true, Philippa admitted, and she would
not consider her face a rival to that of this thoughtless beauty
in her sloppy, dirty shirt. But she watched the bored, distant
face, jouncing with the vibration of the outboard motor beneath her sure arm, and watched it with a certain light disdain.

So often, so often when she was young, she had dismissed
older women like that. And other women, not older, one or
another imagined rival because her hair was mousy, or her legs
short, all things that women noticed, that meant nothing to
men if that sexual flame had struck from its peculiar, unpredictable flint. The woman who had taken Robert from her in
the end, she had dismissed on first seeing without a second
glance.

No, Robert had not surprised her, finding a young love, nor
hiding now behind her. And the girl did not surprise her,
mocking a middle-aged lady in tweeds. Philippa had run the
course, and this sun-spoiled creature with her insolent brown
toes hooked about the gunwale of the tiny boat had not yet
met the first jump.

Philippa looked ahead, across the evening water, to the odd,
lumpy shape of the island community, secure in its bushy little
trees. She glanced back at the girl. How long her legs were,

and how glistening. Her mind flicked to Robert and his long-fingered artist's hands, and there was a sharp pain at the top of her stomach, pressing against the breastbone.

October, 1940
Hornchurch, England

"She's so young," Mike said over his coffee. "That's what it is. She's so damned young."

"Everybody's young, mate," said Porky. Flight Sergeant Piggott, that was. Robert never knew his real Christian name. Porky sliced through his egg with finesse, eating every scrap and mopping the remnants with fingers of cut bread. It was eight o'clock. Briefing was at eight-thirty. The day stretched ahead, an interesting mystery.

"Too damned young to be all alone in a big city. Eighteen. Should be home with her mother. Going to work with houses falling down around you. Sleeping in shelters. Needs looking after, a kid like that."

"Watch it," Robert said, pushing his plate aside and reaching for his coffee. "That's the kind of talk gets a guy married."

"Could be worse," said Mike with a smile. The sun through the window, pale in the October morning, made a prickly halo of his crew cut. He lit a cigarette and sat, contented, with a private thought.

"Christ, he's got it bad, hasn't he?" said Porky.

"You don't want to get married," Robert said, suddenly serious. He felt a little responsible. He had urged that first double date with Maisie, after Mike had met her at an ENSA concert, so he'd have Mike along. Somehow he hadn't the nerve to take Philippa Hallsworth out alone.

"Nobody wants to get married," Porky said confidently.

He stood up and pulled on his cap. "Talk him out of it, Yank," he said.

"She's so young," Mike said again, to himself.

"Never too young," said Porky, on his way out the door. "But not marriage, that's another kettle of fish."

"She's not that kind of a girl."

"They're all that kind of a girl," Robert said, trying to look cynical, and older. "There isn't any other kind."

"Philippa?"

"Jesus, Mike, Philippa's *really* not that kind of a girl."

That didn't go down very well. And Robert apologized with a shrug and a gruff "I'm sorry," which didn't go down any better. In fact, that morning he and Mike were not all that friendly, and considering what followed, it was a goddamn shame.

But as they walked from the sergeants' mess to the briefing room, he argued his way out of it, half apologizing and half cajoling to get Mike to see sense. Sense was that Maisie Rudd was not really wife material, sweet as she was. And truth was that Philippa Hallsworth, whom Robert would not dare to consider wife material, was most certainly a different kind of girl. It was just facts. The facts that had been driven uncomfortably home to him several nights before, when, having scrounged his pay together, he had dined with her at the Savoy.

Thank God and the war strictures, it was not as devastating financially as it might have been two years ago. Even with its "special case" cover charge, the meal came to only eleven shillings. But the wine and the brandies threatened to clean him out.

They were chatting quietly over that second, severely ill-afforded brandy, with the soft sweet saxophone of the little orchestra seducing them with a tale about a nightingale in an unlikely place, and then, suddenly, they had company. He was a big, tall man, red-haired and dimple-chinned, in naval officer's uniform, with a face-splitting grin and a peace-shattering voice. "I *say*, surely it's Philippa."

Give her credit, she ducked behind the menu, but he pursued, across the room, disturbing diners with the cool aplomb of those highbred enough to dare, and ill-bred enough not to care. "It *is* Philippa."

"Hello, Archie."

She smiled politely, and extended her hand, but he leaned down and kissed her cheek, still beaming, and then straightened and crooked his arm in the direction of the door where the rest of his party, four young men in varying uniforms, and five ladies in prewar cocktail dresses, were entering. "Look what I've found," he bellowed. They were surrounded in seconds.

"We were just going," Philippa said.

"Nonsense. Have another brandy while we choose our starters. It's been simply *ages*. When *was* the last time? The West Riding Hunt Ball? Or was it the Northern Meeting?"

"I can't recall," Philippa said vaguely, her boredom with him apparent. He didn't see it, though, and the whole bright crowd gathered around, settling themselves at a nearby table, coming one by one to chat with Philippa and essentially ignore Robert. The brandies arrived and he hoped to God the loudmouth or somebody had paid for them. Philippa, seeing themselves trapped, suddenly became animated in a stiff, formal way and cried out, "Do meet Robert. Robert Zolan, the actor."

There were a couple of "Oh, do tells," and "Jolly pleased, I'm sures," and Robert half rose from his seat to the ladies and sat down again. He was angry with Philippa. He was not "the" anything yet. He was "an" actor, unknown, and probably futureless. His profession might demand flamboyant over-estimates, but his nature refuted them.

"I think we'd better go," he said, bewildered that the anger was turning to hurt. As he rose to leave he realized why. He was not good enough as he stood. Flight Sergeant Robert Zolenski, even with his DFM, yet needed some added glamour before he was quite presentable, at least to this crowd. Afterwards, he learned the loudmouth was an earl's son. He did not pay for the brandies.

Fortunately, as they prepared to leave, an elderly man at a

far table, dining alone, signaled something to the headwaiter, and when Robert reached for his wallet, there was only a discreet sideways motion of the waiter's head. His pilot's wings had earned him a reprieve.

That, anyhow, was the kind of girl Philippa was. And he, Lord help him, was, in the vernacular, bum over tits in love. In a way he'd have been better off with Maisie, to be honest, wife material or not.

But that did not stop him trying to rescue Mike.

They walked side by side, heads down against the stiff wind blowing off the emptiness of the aerodrome. It was cold and dank. At home the fall colors would be ending on the island, and yellow leaves drifting down the streets of Manhattan. It was a year since they had sat on the steps of the brownstone and argued about the war.

"You'd never think of it if you were home."

"I am home."

"What the hell."

"I'm staying. When the war's over. I'm staying. I'm going to marry Maisie and get a job. In London, somewhere. There'll be plenty of work, after the war, cleaning up this mess."

"Fine, fine. But not Maisie. She's not the kind of girl you'd marry at home."

"Look, you really want a punch in the nose that bad?"

"Mike, someone's got to say it. She's a sweet, two-bit broad. She hasn't a brain in her head, and she's not your type of girl. Sure you feel sorry for her. She's alone. Life is dangerous. But that's the war, and marrying Maisie isn't going to end it. It's twisting your vision of everything."

"Not of Maisie," Mike said stubbornly. He lit a cigarette and did not offer one to Robert. "English girls are different. You can't judge."

"No, pal. It's you who can't judge. She's the same as every gum-chewing, frizz-headed blond on the corner of Main Street and First Avenue, U.S.A. Only put her in a brave little home-made hat, and sling a gas mask over her shoulder, and she's

Miss British Heroine, nineteen forty. Wake up, pal, or you *will* wake up one day with no war and a ginger-headed cockney tart and a houseful of kids. You're too damned young if nothing else."

Mike puffed at his cigarette, and waited, and finally said quietly, with the same quiet that had frightened Robert that day on the brownstone steps, "You finished yet?"

"Yeah, I'm finished. Cut your own throat if you want."

"Right. Number one. Maisie isn't a tart. She's a decent kid from a working family. Like me. Number two. Main Street U.S.A. and streetcorner girls is *us*, pal. That's where we come from, and where we belong. At least it's where I belong. And where Robert Zolenski belongs. This guy Zolan I don't know so well. I kinda lost track of him. And number three, and you listen, pal, and don't start arguing already. Number three. It's not me who's in over his head. It's you. Maisie is my kind of girl. Near enough. What am I, anyhow? A mechanic from Toronto. Big deal. What's got you scared is you know I'm right. And if Maisie's right for me, then that just goes to show how wrong Miss Philippa Hallsworth is for you.

"The war's given you some damn funny notions. And one of them is thinking a gardener's son from Long Island can go traipsing to the Savoy with a bunch of stuck-up aristocrats and get away with it. You listen now, pal, and get it right. One day the war's going to end, all right. And me and Maisie, well, we'll be the kind of people me and Maisie are. We're just the same in England or Toronto or New York. But those pals of yours in the Savoy are going to take one look at you out of your Spitfire, whether or not you saved their blue-blooded precious necks, and they're gonna boot your backside out of their lives. Hitler may bomb London flat as a pancake, and push the whole lot of them into the sea, but you can be damned sure that even *there* there's going to be one place for Miss Philippa Hallsworth and Company. And another for you. Like I said, pal, in over your head."

"Are *you* finished?"

"Sure."

"Who's talking marriage? Me?"

"I know you, pal. I know what you're thinking and not letting yourself think. If it's not marriage, then what is it? You led me to believe Miss Philippa doesn't do the other thing."

"So Maisie does? You're bragging?"

"Maisie's a kid. A sweet, innocent kid."

"Oh, yeah. So where were you that night? Just answer that."

It was the night three weeks before, of that first double date. They went together, the most incongruous of foursomes, to the Windmill Theater in Soho. Well, Robert thought cruelly, you could hardly take Maisie to the Savoy, war strictures or no. She was a sweet enough kid, all right, with her funny lisping voice, and her way of always touching you, lightly like a sister, when she talked to you. Nice enough, and he'd have enjoyed her silly, kind company if she was not embarrassing him in front of Philippa. Not that Philippa said anything, but all those giggles and shrieks and "Cor, will you look" could not have passed unnoticed. The show at the Windmill had been Mike's idea, or maybe Maisie's, and Robert had little idea what to expect. Maybe Philippa knew more because when he'd mentioned it, she'd laughed her clear ringing laugh, and said, "Oh, Robert. Are we indeed. Jolly splendid." So he did not know if she was pleased or teasing.

So they sat, crowded into the old theater among rows of shouting servicemen, with the sirens wailing, dismal and ignored outside, and the dull thud of distant falling bombs, and a stage full of naked, white-powdered girls, posing archly in pretentious, hypocritical tableaux. Maisie shrieked and giggled some more and Mike grinned and patted her silk-stockinged knee, and Philippa sat looking calmly, with an amused quiet interest, at the stage, her wide mouth set in a gentle smile.

"Is that all?" said Robert.

"They mustn't move, you know," said Philippa. "It's the law. But don't worry. Later on, they put their clothes on, and sing." He wondered how she knew. He was sure she'd never seen anything like that before. *He'd* never seen anything like it before.

Outside, the all clear had not yet sounded, and they hurried through the blacked-out, oddly quiet streets, hoping the lull would last until they were all in their various homes. Maisie stayed in a flat in Earl's Court, and Philippa was stationed at Stanmore, and could take the underground, but Robert and Mike, both at Hornchurch, had the uncertain train ride ahead of them. "Right odd, weren't they?" said Maisie. "Hardly natural." She clamped her little veiled hat on her head with one hand. "Nuffink like real women at all."

"I can assure you," Philippa said with her distant laugh, "they are real women. The government insists."

"*Does* it?" Maisie cried. Robert imagined he could see her eyes widening. "But I didn't fink the government . . ."

"Never mind," Mike said gently. Then there was a scuffle in the darkness amid a crowd of soldiers pouring out of a pub, and when they were free of them, the two couples had lost each other in the night.

Robert was glad. By then he was painfully regretting the double date, and accident had provided him with what lack of courage had denied him; a chance to be alone with Philippa. They found a British Restaurant in Piccadilly near the underground, and had a late-night meal of rabbit pie and chips and tea.

"Sorry about the show," Robert said. "I'm sure it wasn't your kind of thing."

"It wasn't yours, either."

"It was Mike's idea."

"Whatever would you do without Mike?" she said.

"God knows," he said honestly. "He's the best pal I've ever had. The only one, really." Then he realized she was teasing him, and not too kindly, and he said, trying to sound sophisticated, "Oh, I've one or two ideas."

"Have you, indeed?" she cried, delighted. "Good-night, Robert, I must be off." She stood up, brisk and businesslike. "Early start tomorrow."

At the top of the concrete steps leading down to Piccadilly underground, she gave his hand a firm little shake. He started to lean forward to steal a kiss, but a bustling lady with two small children, and a roll of bedding, pushed by, down to the yet discouraged but still favorite of all London's varieties of shelters. "Hey, hey, none of that," she said good-naturedly. "This is my front door, this is." She grinned at them, a ghostly, barely visible grin under a crammed-on felt hat. The children, seemingly unaffected by either the late hour or the uneasy blackness, snickered.

"Sorry, ma'am," Robert said stupidly, and then Philippa was gone.

Mike did not get back to base until morning, just half an hour before his pass ran out. They shared a room, and Robert lay in his metal-framed bed, staring at the smooth emptiness of Mike's and the barren simplicity of chair and mirror and bed-side tables. The evening had left him chilled and dissatisfied, and he was jealous of Mike in the sensual warmth of Maisie's flat, with old firelit London rocking outside.

"What did happen to you two, anyhow?" he asked accusingly.

"She lost her shoe."

"Lost her knickers, most like."

"She lost her shoe," Mike said, in a stage whisper, for they had arrived at the long, one-storied wooden building that contained the briefing room and were surrounded by other airmen. "Then we lost our way in the blackout. Couldn't find you two at all."

"But you found her apartment all right."

"Hell we did. Took a taxi. *He* couldn't find it. Got lost down in Soho. All those doorways with flashlights and legs. Then there was a raid, and half the place was coming down on our heads. Spent the night in a street shelter."

"Romantic?"

"Our cabbie, and fifty London mums singing 'Knees Up, Mother Brown.' Maisie said I snored." He grinned, easy, happy, and Robert was envious of that shabby homeliness; like the well-trodden comfort that had underlain his own parents' marriage. Maybe Mike was right about Maisie. Maybe they should marry. But where in hell did that leave him?

The briefing room was crowded with the twenty-two young men who made up "A" and "B" flights, settling down in the uneven rows of wooden chairs. There was a murmur of voices, loud in the echoing, wood-walled room, and an eye-stinging haze of cigarette smoke. Robert pushed his way past Wielinski the Pole—"Whisky" the British called him, rather than grapple with his name—and Sandy MacDonald, both bulky in their leather Irving jackets and Mae Wests, and found an empty chair. Mike sat behind him. The room smelled of fresh varnish, and chalk dust, and the animal smell of their morning-damp leather boots, and woolen battle dress.

On the left, at the large, dusty blackboard, the meteorological officer was rapidly chalking up the forecast, wind velocity and direction, and cloud cover.

"Fairy tales," Mike said. "Yesterday it was one-tenth cloud, and the fog outside was thick enough to walk on."

Robert started to say that maybe that's what one-tenth cloud meant in England, but Group Captain Grieve, the "Stationmaster" as they called him, strode in, clipboard under his arm, small brown moustache flying chevron formation over his upper lip. "Your attention, gentlemen, please."

There was immediate silence, and they all stood, with a clatter and scraping of chair legs. "Sit down, gentlemen, please."

They sat. The intelligence officer, Flight Lieutenant Mac-Pherson, followed the Stationmaster in, and the armaments and navigation officers came behind. They took seats on the row of waiting chairs on the rostrum at the front of the long room. Group Captain Grieve introduced MacPherson and he began the main briefing. Robert forgot Mike and Philippa and Maisie. There was not any margin in the business at hand, no room for interrupted thought.

Business was the word. With the frenetic and desperate days

of September behind them, their war had settled down to being a job. Not easy, certainly not dull, and not particularly safe; but a job, with routine and pattern and time off. Those of them, like himself and Mike, who had survived thus far, were experienced and well prepared to look after themselves; nobody expected to die today. But then, nobody ever did.

MacPherson detailed a routine mission, providing fighter escort to a bomber force attacking a string of barges sheltering in the Pas de Calais. There would be two squadrons of Blenheims. He called upon the navigation officer, who gave them their course and their rendezvous point, twelve thousand feet over Maidstone in Kent. "You will climb to Angels fifteen, and maintain high cover across the Channel, over the target area, and if necessary on the return journey."

The met officer made his little ill-received speech about cloud cover, and wind speeds, and what weather they might expect over the Channel. There were snickers. His reputation hadn't been enhanced by yesterday's invisible fog. The armaments officer informed them that their guns were loaded with the usual one-in-ten tracers, and the navigation officer gave them their true course and then the course they would follow to compensate for wind drift. The Stationmaster took the floor again for his routine request for questions, followed immediately by his routine "No? That's all then. Report to dispersal now, please, and good luck, gentlemen," all in one calm smooth breath. They synchronized watches, drew maps from the map store, and went their separate ways. Robert wondered if half the reason for routine was not that its quiet dignity overrode even the potential of fear.

Yet as always, walking across the tarmac on his way to his dispersal point, he felt that tightening in the gut that worked its way through to his back, up to his neck, and down again. His Spitfire sat, outlined dark in its camouflage against the brightening sky. Sometimes when on the ground he would imagine what it would look like if he pranged it. Which parts would be bent, which shattered, which peeled right off like flayed skin. And where would he be? Imagination was his great gift, and for a long time he had wished it were not. If he could be thick like Porky, without soul enough to imagine past the next hour. Or ruthlessly courageous, like Mike, liking danger, at his happiest under threat, for all he pretended to share the fears of more ordinary men. Or even like Wielenski, the Pole, so vinegared with hatred that fear was bland as milk. Robert was not thick. Nor had he any love of danger. Nor any hatred. He had a quiet idealism which wore very thin at moments like this, and a love of flying which had never really included enemy fire as one of its attractions. But now it was a job, a role, like any role he had taken on, and he would play it. He kept the "final curtain" image out of his allegory. It embarrassed him.

Corporal Keith, his rigger, was standing on the wing of his machine, working over the Perspex canopy. He looked up and saw Robert and said, without introduction, "I've had a good work at it, sir, it should be better."

Robert nodded and thanked him, and climbed up onto the wing himself. "It" was a small scrape on the surface of the Perspex, shallow, indeed almost invisible. He rubbed his silk scarf along the satiny surface, careful not to touch it with his fingers. A smudge, or a fingerprint, or that small annoying scratch that had irritated him yesterday, though scarcely visible now, would up there with the sun behind it become a diffused blur, hiding precious, plane-sized patches of sky.

"I used jeweler's paste," Keith said. "It should be all right."

Robert nodded again, still examining it, the issue too serious for polite appreciation. He nodded a limited approval, and then swung his right leg into the cockpit, and then his left, lowering himself into the narrow space, and settling the bulk of his parachute into its housing beneath him. He did his cockpit check, methodically, resisting the urge to check everything twice for luck, like his mother reading a recipe again and again. He took the clipboard from his fitter and signed the Form 700, acknowledging his acceptance of the aircraft. He handed the clipboard back, the fitter reaching up for it, nodding briskly, and pushing the starter button on the battery trolley. The Merlin engine made its beautiful, comforting roar, and Robert relaxed, glancing to his left where Mike, in his own kite, was doing the same. The options were closed. He was going up, and he never worried in the air.

Mike was Blue Section leader of "B" flight. Robert flew in the number-two position to him and Porky number three. Robert was glad of Mike there. He was a good pilot, better than himself always, better than most. The sight of him off the port wing was secure. They warmed up their engines and taxied out onto the runway, and took off, the three sections of "B" flight flying in chevron formation, with Wielenski the Pole flying arse-end Charlie, above and behind, weaving back and forth for maximum cover. It was the guard position and it was vital. Fear in the sky, like in nightmares, was always at one's back.

They flew a reciprocal course to five thousand feet, turned back, and climbing yet, headed southwest, toward Maidstone. They found the bombers with no difficulty, two geese vees of twin-engined machines, and continued climbing, following their set course, with the Blenheims in sight, slightly ahead and below them, out over the Channel. The water, glimpsed through patches of low cloud, was gray and embroidered with flat wrinkles. A voice came over the radio, singing, heavy with static, accent, and sorrow. Wielenski the Pole had left his radio on send, by mistake, and as he tagged along behind he was singing "Loch Lomond."

> B'yun bunny bahnks
> En b'yun bunny brezz . . .

The words could not mean anything, but all the Poles were forever singing that song, as if the agony of exile carried by its creator went direct from Jacobite heart to Polish heart with no interpretation.

"Cut it, Whisky." The voice of Flight Lieutenant Anderson, Red Section leader, crackled through the song. The words cut off, mid-verse, as Wielenski switched back to receive, where he belonged. Robert was sorry. He had liked its sad romantic company.

With his left hand he felt inside the fleecy Irving jacket for the pocket of his battle-dress blouse, where the map was, and a chocolate bar, and felt the other familiar shape, square and metallic and hard, its sharp edges and the small circles of the tiny wheels blunted by the fabric. It was there; everything would be fine.

He looked left. He could see Mike, head forward, goggles firmly down, concentrating. There was never any nonsense from Mike, no singing, no horsing around. That was fine. That was the way it should be. That way you stayed alive. He glanced farther back. The spot was still there, diminished by Corporal Keith's efforts, but not gone. Light wavered around it, and blurred. It was all right, though, until he got the sun in that quarter. Damn the thing, intruding on his security.

For he felt secure, aside from that, almost cozy in the tight barren cockpit, the sun pouring in, the crackle of the airwaves for company. He reviewed the Good Things, in his mind, his own litany of safety, like a silent chant, half checklist, half prayer. There was Mike. There was the Merlin engine, powerful and trustworthy. The steel bullet shield behind his back. His faith in his fitter and rigger. *Honor thy fitter and thy rigger that thy days might be long upon the earth.* The Spitfire controls, marvelously light at full speed. Her blessed ability to turn inside her chief rival, the Messerschmitt 109. Her speed. Her innocent, early-flight willingness to put down in fields, on roadways, God knows where. Her sturdy, battle-tried framework around his much more delicate bones. He did not include either his eight Browning machine guns or the parachute tucked under his arse. They evoked conflict, tipped things into the realms of threat. And he placed on the plain negative the spot on the Perspex and his perennial devil, the

Channel. He was never fully happy flying over water, not even the waters of home. Surely, he could ditch. But then, like a spider in a web, there was awaiting him that old uneasy seducer, the sea.

He leaned his head back against the headrest and thought of Philippa Hallsworth, instead. At Stanmore where she worked in the control room, the WAAFs would have plotted their course and put the little cards saying "airborne" beside the squadron and flight numbers. Perhaps she thought about him, wondering if he were with them today. Maisie would have. Maisie would have said a prayer, or at least crossed her fingers, or something. But Maisie worked in a munitions factory and did some small, vital, inexplicable task, and would not know anybody was flying at all. And he could not picture Philippa indulging in such sentiment. "Chin up, darling," or maybe "Good show." But that was surely all.

They were within sight of the French coast when Anderson spotted them. An indulged youth of deer stalking and pheasant shooting served him ironically well; eyes trained to the moors were equally alert in the skies, and he was always first to see anything.

"Bandits, three o'clock, low."

Robert looked down off his starboard wing. They were there, two thousand feet below, nine Messerschmitts, flying in stepped-up threes, mean and dark with bright yellow noses. They were a thousand feet above their bombers and closing fast.

"Badger Leader," Anderson called, "line astern." They slipped in, one behind the other in a long line. "Tallyho." Anderson swung off, his number two and three falling in behind, and Mike, Blue Section leader, following. Robert saw Mike bank and go into his dive, and followed, pushing the stick forward and right and opening up the throttle. The machine roared into a power dive and Robert picked his target, the fifth Messerschmitt, number two in the second section, was his. His eyes flicked between his reflector sight and his mirror and his thumb and forefinger flicked the ring on the gun button to "fire." He rested his thumb over the button. The machine was one vast weapon, aimed with his whole body, an extraordinary extended power.

Just for a second his left arm brushed the lumpy shape in his pocket, pressing it against his body. The Messerschmitt was in his sights, at three hundred yards. When he moved his thumb he would probably kill someone. It rather astounded him, always, but it did not stop him. Two hundred yards. His thumb pressed, two seconds. The Spitfire shook with the recoil, braking in the air. The tracers homed neatly down the target fuselage. It was well done, actually, but he had not a moment to think about it.

He was through them all at once, two thousand feet below, and pulling out of his dive, the stick back to his gut, the kite climbing steeply, and with the gravity forces like heavy fingers against his eyes and cheeks, fighting the blackout that would send him looping the loop into eternity. In moments he was entirely alone in an empty blue French sky. That was it. That was war in the air.

He looked in his mirror and screwed around over his shoulder, trying to catch sight of the damaged Messerschmitt going down. But he saw nothing and would never know. There was no one at all in sight, nothing but sunlit gray hills of cloud and his own shadow racing far below. He looked around for the Blenheims, saw nothing, and continued climbing, seeking the safety and vision of height. For a moment the emptiness of blue sky, low cloud banks, and white-rimmed French coast, beautiful blue and green and gray below, beguiled the sense out of him. The moment was enough. He forgot his mirror.

"On your tail, Bob, on your tail." It was Mike, a crackly warning ghost on the airwaves. He jerked his head around, eyes first to his mirror, and then over his shoulder squinting into the sun. The spot, the scratch on the Perspex, diminished but not gone, blurred refracted light across his vision.

It came out of that white halo, near, fast, sweeping down and under him, diving and firing, its yellow nose glinting, a 109 like the nine they had attacked: one more had been flying high above. Jerry had his arse-end Charlies, too. Arse-end Gunter, surely, Robert thought, with mad fascination, watching the bullet holes silently ripping a line through his wing, one, two, three . . . God almighty.

He came brutally awake, and slammed the stick to the left, going into a flick half roll, and shoving the throttle forward and through the gate. The Spitfire flipped onto its back, shaking with the force of the overrevving engine. He had only a minute of that before she shook herself apart. He centralized the stick, and pulled it toward him, diving upside down, watching his airspeed indicator racing up. It hit four hundred fifty and he shoved the stick forward, easing the dive, and then pushed left to complete the roll. As she came up he kicked the rudder left, and threw the stick left again, whipping away in a split-arse turn to port. Ahead a bank of cloud loomed like a gray mountain. He flung himself and his machine into its woolly heart.

The sky beyond it was as innocently empty blue as the eyes of a child. He eased the throttle back and looked around, his eyes flicking to the mirror, all around him, wishing he had more eyes, and eyes below him as well. But he was alone. Safe. Thank *you*, Mike, he whispered. Thank *you*. Do the same for you some day.

He released his held breath with a shaky sigh and carefully checked his instruments, airspeed, turn and bank, artificial horizon, fuel, oil. Okay. Whatever damage the 109 did appeared to be merely cosmetic. He pulled the stick back and began a slow climb, seeking height and his errant Blenheims. He began to relax, though not to relax his eyes or his senses. Then he glanced again at the instruments, and saw the oil pressure dropping away like lost faith before his eyes. That low pass beneath the belly of his machine had not been for nothing.

"Jesus H. Christ," he said, but calmly. He switched the microphone switch on his face mask to transmit. "Badger Blue Two to Badger Leader. Returning to base." He repeated it and switched off and listened out. There was no answer, and he shrugged and banked left and turned for home. He checked his compass and set his course, and glanced uneasily at the oil pressure. It had dropped ten pounds. He throttled back until the airspeed read one hundred eighty to save his engine, and climbed as high as he could, up away from the long gray white-speckled wilderness of sea.

He almost made it. He was in sight of the Kent coast, the sea well below him, jubilation rising, when his eyes, flickering over the rectangle of the oil-pressure gauge and the circle of engine temperature, froze halfway to the rear-view mirror. He looked again.

"Oh, not now, baby. Just a little further. C'mon, sweetheart." Christ. Not now. Not in the sea.

The engine temperature swung alarmingly up, past safety into disaster. The gray wrinkled water far below grew intimate. He felt it, cold, heavy, swallowing his parachute, dragging at the lines, wallowing around him, drawing him down, into the dark. "Please, baby." The land seemed stationary, its white-rimmed border refusing to grow nearer. But it did, and the white sea rim was past, behind, and misty gray fields below.

"Okay, baby." He was over land. He must turn her, head her to sea before they parted company. There were people down there, houses and farms, and for all the hardware falling out of the skies these days she was still a lot of metal to drop on someone's head. If it could be avoided. And he reckoned it could. Just. For a moment he hesitated, looking longingly forward, landward. But he shrugged, touched the shape in his pocket for luck, and thrust the stick forward and right, giving a kick to right rudder and banking to starboard. She was slow, sluggish, the hot engine sputtering, threatening fire. God. Fire. He controlled panic, controlled the thought of all that waiting petrol and the crisped flesh of mates of his who had run afoul of it. The kite turned slowly, her reluctant nose seaward again, like a disgruntled horse turned back from the stable door. Releasing his Sutton harness, with quick practiced ease, he reached over his head and slid back the Perspex canopy. The roar of the air whipped in, pulling at him body and soul. He slammed the stick hard left and gave a brutal kick of left rudder, bracing himself as the ailing machine lumbered onto its back. Then he let go, and dropped quietly out into the sky.

Falling absorbed all his consciousness, falling and the need of restraint. Wait, count, one, two, oh never. He jerked the D-ring, ignoring the danger of entanglement with his own machine, now arching away, lonely and forgotten, into the sea. The chute deployed gladly, amazing Robert, whose human conviction of his own uniqueness had convinced him it would not. Surely he was the wrong shape, too heavy, too light, too unlucky. Too Irish. The parachute harness jerked him up by legs and shoulders into silence. Distantly an engine droned, and a voice, near, in his ear was shouting, "Holy Mary, Mother of God, pray for us sinners, now and . . ."

"Oh, screw it all, mom," he said to the clouds. Then there was real silence. The engine was gone. Below him, gray-green and dotted with green cauliflower heads of woodland, was England. Dogs barked, geese clamored, faraway children shouted in the fields. All the sounds of pastoral peace drifted clear and distinct up to his dangling feet. Safe, triumphant, cheered giddily by survival he shouted, "Don't you buggers know there's a war on?" and descended, an unkent prophet over Kent. In his right hand he still clutched the freed D-ring of the rip cord. He grinned at it and waved it about. He'd done it. Everyone said you couldn't, that you'd fling it away in the panic of pulling the cord and arrive on terra firma empty-handed. There was some kind of squadron-wide bet on about it, and a prize, no doubt alcoholic, for the first to break the curse of the D-ring. And he'd done it. Wait'll Mike saw *that*.

He landed in the brick-walled back garden of a farmhouse in Kent. A girl of about sixteen watched him growing out of the blue sky, all the while pegging clothes out on a washing line supported by a great pole. His feet touched the ground four yards from her. Their eyes were on a level and she stared solemnly over a line of tea cloths. Robert banged the release of his parachute harness by reflex and struggled free. His trained haste was unnecessary. In the still autumn air the canopy wallowed harmlessly down, enveloping a stand of gooseberry bushes in silk. The girl watched it, curious, and looked back to Robert, materialized on her drying green, and fastened another peg.

"I suppose you'll want tea," she said.

It was high tea, actually, served in a kitchen packed with children, the lady of the house, a dog, two cats, a live duck in a straw-lined crate, and two Land Army girls in their appallingly ill-fitted trousers sitting warily at one corner of the broad central table. They never said a word, either of them, but blushed and stared a lot. The two youngest of the children, a pair of mismatched evacuee four-year-olds with the watchful faces of London's East End, also were silent. Words were the prerogative of the native-born, the sixteen-year-old and her two younger brothers, broad-faced country boys with the confidence of belonging written all over them.

The sixteen-year-old kept moving about, fidgeting with things until her mother settled her with a sharp word. She went red and hurried to set the table, all the time stealing badly concealed glances at Robert. He was not at all sure whether she thought him heroic or insane, and decided not to play to the former, in case it was the latter.

The two little brothers were delightfully direct. They thought him heroic, and reverberated worshiping questions between them. Where was his Spitfire? (Where else?) How many Germans had shot him down? (Surely six.) How many Germans had *he* shot down?

"One and a half," Robert said honestly. They withdrew in slight but apparent disappointment. *They* would have had a dozen by now. Still Robert wasn't properly British, only Canadian. That explained some things.

"American," Robert corrected.

"*Oh.*" That explained everything.

Ken Roper, the master of the house, after apparent careful consideration rather suddenly signaled to Robert and led him from the kitchen down a long, seedy corridor smelling of dogs to a small room full of rubber boots and outdoor equipment, a pony saddle, two large metal milk churns, a garden rake, and a small battered sideboard from which he drew a half empty bottle of whisky. With solemnity he poured some for Robert and some for himself into two dusty glasses. "Cheers," he said with a great lack of cheerfulness. Robert grinned, got no grin back, and drank cautiously. "Damn hard to come by," said Ken Roper. Robert nodded, and then by inspiration remembered his chocolate and pulled the bar with a flourish from the inner pocket of the flying jacket. "Maybe the kids would like this?" For the first time since he arrived, Ken Roper smiled. He took the chocolate, a big grin spreading as he examined the bar.

"Yankee chocolate?" Robert nodded. "I say, you've not any more?"

"No. Sorry. I'd give it to you if I had."

"No matter. Here, I'll just tuck it away for my two lads." He slid it in beside the hoarded bottle. "Yon London scamps aren't getting this," he said with grim satisfaction. Robert knew he meant the evacuees. He could have wept. But Ken Roper hardly seemed a tyrant, only an ordinary father under extraordinary circumstances, who, loving his own children, wanted to save for them a treasure. He'd agreed to shelter evacuees, shown generosity in that; saintliness was a bit much to ask.

"Like another?" he said, nodding to Robert's empty glass. He sounded like he really meant it, but Robert thanked him and said no.

When they returned to the kitchen, the table was laid with high tea, that peculiar country combination of salad greenery and baked goods, uniquely English, now severely thinned by war's pinching hand. Mrs. Roper spread thin slices of brown bread with a translucent scraping of margarine for the family, and a generous layer for Robert. There was a small pot of homemade rowan and apple jam, and solemn small dollops were ladled out by Mr. Roper. The tea was thin, pale, and milky, with a small spoonful of sugar for each of the family, and a large one for Robert. The rest of the meal was made up of heaps of soft green lettuce and a minute slice of hard orange cheese. The evacuee children, glancing to left and right like watched puppies, fell on their plates at once, were halted sternly while Mr. Roper said grace, and then went back with scant pause to devouring every scrap provided.

But the two country boys watched Robert. They had stolen envious glances at his share of margarine. The extra sugar caused a wrinkling of each forehead. Robert realized that while their mother was warring within herself between rationed frugality and the hero's welcome she felt he deserved, the children had no such compunctions. Clearly one and a half Messerschmitts were insufficient to warrant extra sugar *and* margarine.

That was when the egg arrived.

The table had been cleared as if, in better times and better houses, for a fine port. Robert was presented with a knife and a small spoon, carefully set around a crocheted place mat. The egg, brown, large, and smooth, arrived, soft boiled, mounted in an egg cup, gilded but chipped, on a saucer, set on a plate. Each piece was good bone china, and none matched. Mrs. Roper set it down and straightened, and folded her hands on her apron and beamed. Her husband rubbed his moustache. All five children watched, the evacuees patiently, expecting nothing, but the two young native sons with clearly mixed emotions.

"But," said the youngest. Instantly his mother lifted him from his chair, turned him, brought her flat hand against his rump, and propelled him from the room. "But that's *my* egg!" he burst out in the doorway. Father's chair tipped, and his boots shuffled as he made to rise. The door slammed behind the sound of flying feet.

Robert looked at the egg, appalled, knowing he could not possibly eat it, and could not possibly not eat it.

"Please, really, ma'am, I mean the meal was wonderful."

"You can't possibly have had enough," said the woman.

"Come, come, lad. You've earned it," said Roper.

"It's a very nice egg," said the sixteen-year-old shyly.

"It's my brother's," said the loyal seven-year-old. In seconds, he, too, was out the door.

Robert ate, swallowing each mouthful like unabsolved sin. He had had two eggs that morning and four rashers of bacon. Tomorrow, if he was flying, he'd have the same. The civilian ration was one a month, just now, and it was obvious this patriotic farm household were turning all their produce over, as expected, to the nation. "It was great," he said to the three remaining pairs of eagerly watching eyes.

"There is one more . . ." said the wife, swallowing hard.

"No. No, I couldn't. Not possibly. Honestly." But they were clearing his place already with thankful sighs.

After tea, he was escorted by Mr. Roper and the two Land Girls, as a sort of honor guard, to a barren, unnamed train station and loaded on board with his bundled parachute tucked under his arm. As the train pulled away, the three solemnly waved as one would do to an honored, but not entirely enjoyable, weekend guest. It was only then that he realized he had no idea where he'd been. All the secrecy designed to confuse enemy paratroopers had had, not surprisingly, the identical effect on himself. He stared at the blank, half-weathered patches on the brick station wall where once there had been a place name. Somewhere in England he had been, no doubt, and no doubt would never return.

The journey back to Hornchurch took several hours of changing trains and asking directions and getting lost and asking again. He arrived at base in the late evening. The day seemed to have been unimaginably endless, several days long at least. He was exhausted, but still elated, clutching his tale of adventure like the D-ring, crammed into his pocket, a trophy that Mike would never top. Not the girl with her clothes pegs, or her brothers with their egg. No, never.

There was a light on in the room. It was oddly empty, and cold, even though Porky Piggott was sitting on Mike's bed, smoking one of Mike's cigarettes.

"Mike say you could?" said Robert.

"No."

"Greedy bastard. Give me one and I won't tell."

"Mike's bought it."

Robert took the pack of Lucky Strikes and had one halfway out before he understood. His index finger went on tapping the bottom of the pack, divorced from his mind.

"Over the Pas de Calais," said Porky.

"Mike?"

"One-oh-nine on his tail. Out of the sun. Just didn't see him."

"Mike?"

"Went up like a house afire."

"Bailed out maybe?"

"No."

"You're sure."

"Sure. I saw it all."

Robert sat down on his own bed. His hand found the D-ring in his pocket; it rubbed gratingly against the red metal car.

"Jesus," he said.

"Sorry, Rob. Like a beer?"

"Yeah." He stood up. He felt more lonely than ever in his life. More than after the hurricane. What was he doing here, among strangers? "Was it because of me?" he said quickly.

"How because of you?"

"He warned me. There was a Hun on my tail, too. He warned me."

Porky laughed. "Nothing so dramatic, mate. He just got careless. Nothing to do with you. But blame yourself if it feels nice." Porky stood and crossed to Mike's locker. He opened the metal door and felt around and came out with a black leather wallet.

"What you doing?"

"Fair's fair. If you're having a morbid session, Mike can pay. Beer money, mate." He drew a handful of bills from the wallet and tossed it on the bed.

Robert watched him go. The room was empty, exactly as this morning. He had an aching illogical feeling that he could simply step backwards, into yesterday, and Mike would be alive and they'd run through today again and make a better job of it.

"You coming, mate?" Porky called.

Robert chucked the D-ring on the bed and leaned over and lifted Mike's pack of Luckies from the bedside table. He shoved them into his pocket, but they pressed against the red car. Gently he lifted it out, ran the wheels round with the fingers of habit, and then tossed it on the bed as well with a strained shrug. Careless, he thought. Careless. He lit another of Mike's cigarettes and went out the door.

It fell to Robert to tell Maisie. Not being a wife, she earned no official notification. He found her flat, a third-floor walk-up in a converted white-fronted house in Earl's Court. It stood in a row of identical four-story buildings, all with pillared porticos at the front, all joined, end on end. Except the one next to Maisie's was missing, and one four doors away was also missing, leaving gaps like pulled teeth in the white jaded smile of the street.

Maisie had told them about the one next door. It was a fortnight ago, and already had been tidied away to neat piles of rubble. A mother had died there, clutching her two toddlers under the stairs. Maisie had cried about it, sniffing into a blue handkerchief.

Robert fingered the raw holes in the little stone wall in front of the house where the neat iron railings had been wrenched out for scrap. The masonry crumbled under his thumb. There was a list of names in small glass-enclosed plates beside the door. Miss Maisie Rudd, Flat Three A. The neatly printed "Miss" reminded him of her little hat with its dime-store veil.

He walked up the stairs and rang the bell. She answered at once, as if she'd been waiting. She was quite excruciatingly polite, the schoolgirl again, minding her p's and q's. It was only then that Robert realized quite how much she was in awe of him because of his profession, and because of Philippa. She had guessed his purpose the moment she had seen him alone in the doorway. Still, she waited for him to tell her, perhaps part of her politeness.

He said the necessary words, very fast and without any elaboration. Then he suggested she sit down, but she refused, standing, leaning over, her arms wrapped around herself, looking at the bare wood floor. She said, "Oh, God," once or twice, folding up into herself with grief.

Then, remembering him there she became self-conscious and offered him sherry. He refused at first, which was a mistake, because she began to close even tighter within herself. He remembered his mother with her numb incomprehension during the hurricane.

"Thanks very much. I'll have a sherry."

She poured from a dusty bottle on a lace doily on the sideboard into two pink glasses. " 'Fraid it's not much," she said. "I've 'ad it simply donkey's ages. Don't drink by myself, do I?"

"Who does?" Robert said pointlessly.

"Thank you," said Maisie. Robert shrugged uneasily, not at all sure for what, and said, "I'm sorry," for everything.

"You're so nice to me, you know? You're both. You were both so nice." Her shoulders began to shake and her head wag to and fro, but nothing else happened. "Mike was always so nice to me. Ever so nice. Nuffink was too much trouble, you know? He treated me so nice."

"He loved you."

She put her head down again, her fingers working around the sherry glass. "It's very good of you to say."

"I'm not just saying it, Maisie." There was no reaction and he burst out impulsively, "He was going to ask you to marry him." It was stretching it a bit, but what did it matter now if it gave her comfort. "He was talking about it this morning. Before he went up." The closeness of the morning with its irrevocably lost normality again closed in upon him.

She was not comforted but angry. "Don't tell me lies, Robert."

"No lie, Maisie, honest."

She set her glass down on the worn deal gate-leg table and then turned to face him; her soft little face firmed in the light of the tattered buff lampshade, and grew old. "Please, Robert. It was enough that 'e was nice to me. Don't spoil it."

"But he wanted to marry you. He told me this morning."

"Sure, and 'e said tell Maisie I love her over the bleedin' intercom when 'e was crashin' like." She turned her back on him and said calmly, "I'm not the kind of girl blokes like 'im marry."

"What do you mean?" Robert said with the forceless fervor of the actor in real doubt of his own performance. "What kind of talk is that?"

"You know," she said bluntly, and looked on him with mature disdain. Then she picked up the sherry glass again and gulped down the contents and said quickly, "It don't matter, Robert. I think you'd better go." Her shoulders were trembling again, and the wagging of the head resumed, and quite suddenly there were tears running down her face, unromantically and unprettily, smearing her cheap, cherished face rouge with sticky snail trails.

Robert set the sherry glass down and reached both arms out to comfort her, and just as he did, the siren sounded beyond the blacked-out windows, and the hollow crescendo swallowed his words.

"Go if you want to," she said coolly. "I'm not bothering."

Robert hesitated, thought of the heap of rubble next door, and took his hat in his hands and turned toward the door. He hesitated there, looking around the cold, shabby little room. "Maybe you'd better come down to the shelter," he said. Maisie said nothing, standing numb and tear-streaked. Then she made her mouth into the "we can take it" smile and said, "Bugger 'itler. I'm sleeping in me own bed."

Robert grinned and reached awkwardly to pat her shoulder, his hand brushing the curled soft edge of her frizzy red hair. "You're a brave girl, Maisie," he said.

"I'm a tart."

"Aw, Maisie."

"A popsy. A floozy. A tart."

"Mike didn't think so."

"Mike's dead, isn't 'e?" she snapped. Then she began to sob again and she cried, "Oh 'e did, 'e did. Only 'e didn't let it show. I'm nuffink, Robert. I was born nuffink an' now I'm going to die nuffink, now 'e's dead. I'm not like you all, you and Philippa an' Mike an' all. You're all grand an' brave an' important." She laughed suddenly. " 'Ere, you know what I am? I'm the girl who makes the thing that drills the hole that holds the spring that turns the knob that works the bloody damn thingamabob." She was laughing and crying at once. "That's me, mate."

He left her standing alone in the center of her little bare room, in her faded flowered, peter-pan-collared dress, holding her empty pink glass.

He went out hurriedly into the blacked-out night, walking swiftly away from the white-pillared portico and down the tatty broken street, heading for the underground. Four days later an exceptionally heavy raid pulled three more teeth from the block, and a direct hit tumbled Maisie's shabby little room into the street. It was assumed that Maisie tumbled with it, though there weren't enough connected pieces of anything to be sure. Robert was haunted, not by the vision of Maisie dismembered, or even of Mike charred in the wreck of his Spitfire, but of two pale pink sherry glasses, entombed but somehow unbroken in the rubble of a street in Earl's Court.

The week after the raid in which Maisie died, Robert Zolenski of Blue Point, Long Island, and Philippa Hallsworth of Greenshaws Hall, West Yorkshire, were engaged to be married, and a fortnight later they were wed in Caxton Hall. It was hardly the accepted interval, but, as was generally observed, there was a war on.

They were engaged at seven-fifteen in the morning at the entrance to the Leicester Square underground station, having spent a perfectly respectable night together on the platform of the Piccadilly line, with most of the rest of London for company. It was the grim end of a grim evening.

They had met the night before in a pub in Dean Street, the York Minster. Philippa had known it from before the war. It was their first meeting since Robert's adventurous flight across the Channel and his landing in Ken Roper's garden in Kent. Over his pint of weak wartime ale he told her about that, but it had paled terribly, faded into the background of that day. As always, Mike had eclipsed him.

"He was so young," Robert said, feeling there was a truth in that somewhere, a significance.

"We're all young, goose," said Philippa.

"But you don't understand. You see, I thought I was going to die. But it was him."

"It could have been you."

"It was him. And he warned *me*."

Philippa sipped at her own glass of ale, warily, handling him with caution. "And you'd have warned him," she said firmly, "if you could. You couldn't."

"It wasn't my fault. Porky said it wasn't."

"No one said it was."

"I was eating all that bread and margarine. He was dying. I was eating bread and margarine. And that fucking egg."

"Have a drink, Yank," said an anonymous face under a flat blue cloth cap. Robert realized his voice was growing loud and unsteady. "He was so goddamned young," he said with failing control. The man with the cloth cap handed him another half pint which he did not need. Philippa with a quick neat gesture intercepted, slipped it around her back, and onto the polished wood bar counter. He had had more than enough, and even the man in the cloth cap knew that, but it was the only kindness they could offer, other than a cigarette, and Robert was already holding one of those. It was their favorite pub, and they were well known there. So was Mike.

Outside, the hollow, sad wail of the siren began.

"Oy, oy. Here we go again," said the man in the cloth cap.

"Thank God," said Philippa, seizing Robert's elbow. "C'mon, love, drinking-up time."

A few faces turned away from the bar and some turned back. Others rose quietly, as if it really were drinking-up time, and walked calmly out the door. "We going or staying," said Robert dully.

"Going."

He shrugged, swallowed the last of his beer, and set the glass down with an uncertain slithering clunk. He fished in his pocket, as if to pay for the drinks, but a man next to him shook his head and said, "On me." Robert nodded, a little confused, and Philippa smiled to the man and steered Robert toward the door.

"They think I'm drunk," he muttered as she did. She said nothing, but smiled a little more strongly, more determinedly.

Robert was wondering numbly if he had any money. He couldn't remember, but he and Mike had found that anonymous generosity so often that they had guiltily come to rely on it, working up bills they hadn't a hope of paying, and waiting for some patriotic onlooker to help.

The siren wailed and wavered, and was joined by the first distant explosion, barely audible, which moved several more patrons out the door. Robert and Philippa, she shrugging into her short tailored jacket, prewar, newly dyed dark green, civvy clothes for her evening out, went with them.

Outside, in the impossible, impassable black of the street, Robert's mood suddenly changed. The cold air and the ale mixed alarmingly, making him alternately sick and invigorated. He grabbed Philippa's hand and made a little hop and a skip, attempting to click his heels. "Der Fuehrer ees kummink. Heil," he shouted to the black sky.

He looked up then and saw two thin beams of white light waver up as if in response. Another joined it, crossing back and forth over the dim gap between darkened buildings. Philippa began walking swiftly toward the Leicester Square underground station, but Robert was still gamboling about in the street.

"We haven't all day, love."

"Night. I know, I know. I want to see." He said, like a child, "It's so pretty." Philippa looked up at the searchlights sweeping the sky.

"Gorgeous," she said. "Come *on*, love."

"Look," someone shouted out of the darkness. "They've got him." There was a flash of silver in the beam, and around them a sudden roar as the ack-ack started up on every side. At the end of the street, the gun crew suddenly appeared in the glare of their own firing, vanished into blackness, and appeared again, flickering images in rhythm with the sound.

"Hey," Robert shouted. "Hey, cut it out. They're shooting at him!"

Someone laughed, softly from the night. "Damn for certain they are, Yank."

"But there's a guy up there," Robert cried out.

"Sure, mate, an' we're going to blast him up the Khyber." In the darkness a group of people had gathered around them, all watching the pulsing, droning thing caught in the beam like a moth. It banked sharply, twisting to free itself of the light, but two beams crossed and held it. The shells bursting around it boomed distantly.

"Damn the sly bastard," the man said behind them as the bomber twisted out of the beam. Robert laughed, drunkenly.

"Who's side are you on, mate?" growled a belligerent voice.

"He's drunk," said Philippa briskly. "Come along, goose."

"Pal of mine," Robert said, waving to the black air. "My mate up there. Pal. Gunter." Of course, he knew at once. That was it. "Arse-end Gunter. Old friend. Old buddy." Must have been his reward for shooting Robert down and ridding the Channel skies of the Yankee Menace. Gave him a new job, on bombers.

"Thought you'd get away with it, Gunter?" Robert shouted. The blackness pulsed with the sound of firing. A hand touched Robert's shoulder, and a voice came from under the dim outline of an ARP warden's hat, "C'mon, mate, move it along, move it along."

Philippa's hand was behind the opposite elbow, and in the distance there was a series of thudding crumps. The last was close enough to bring a rattling of windows and a tinkle of broken glass. Suddenly, the roar of the ack-ack stopped and abrupt stillness framed someone's voice, saying knowingly, "Night fighters."

"Attaway, baby," Robert shouted, not sure whether to Gunter, their own planes, or to Philippa and the ARP warden, hastening him to shelter. In the silence emptied of firing, the whistle of shell fragments and their tinkling crash filled the street. Philippa whipped off her small beret and plunked her tin hat on her head, and pushed Robert into a doorway. While the metal rain continued beyond the sheltering lintel, Robert struggled ineffectually with his own tin hat until Philippa with a motherly sigh crammed it over his ears.

"Thanks."

"Right you are, twit. Go fight 'em on the beaches." She strode off down the street and he followed, more afraid of losing her in the dark, the way he'd once lost Mike and Maisie, than of the bombs. They found the street blocked suddenly, and the light of the ARP warden's flashlight flickered across a large fruiterer's barrow. Behind it was a Scots soldier in kilt and tin hat, pushing it along, loaded with two tin-hatted, giggling Wrens, clutching their gas-mask cases and singing, "Roll out the barrel . . ." A long pause, and then the whistle, shriek, and solid crump of a bomb . . . "We'll have a barrel of fun."

"Dah dah dah . . ." sang the Scot.

"*Roll* out the barrel . . ."

Whistle, shriek, crump.

"Move it a*long*, you blithering idiots!"

"We'll have a barrel . . ."

The street shook with a solid, resounding crack and crash. Robert's ears were numb, his head ringing.

"Jesus," he said. Then all of them, he, Philippa, the Scot and the Wrens and the warden, were running for the underground. The whistle of the last of that stick of bombs followed them down the stone steps. They were well below ground when it hit, but it shook the stone walls and sent dust cascading down all over them, and the sound and concussion knocked Robert off his feet. In the dark, feeling for Philippa's hand, he touched a leg, inert, a masculine leg in heavy serge cloth. He gasped, and leaped back, somehow imagining it to be a dead body.

"Oy, oy, mate," said someone attached to the leg. "No need to slam the door." There was a lot of sleepy laughter, and in the dim platform lighting Robert saw faces, appearing through the dust, men and women, sleeping on the platform, children tucked in feet to feet between parents. There were wicker baskets with food, blankets, and a forest of knitting needles.

"You're all right now, son," said an old, old woman in a felt hat with two crumpled velvet roses on it. She was smiling so kindly, so reassuringly, that Robert was a little amazed. He was even more amazed, touching his dusty face, to find it was quite inexplicably covered with water.

"Go ahead, ducks," said Philippa very gently. "Have a good cry."

He did, and slept then, with his head on Philippa's lap, and woke to the all clear and the bustle of awakening strangers. Suddenly amongst them was the ARP warden from the night before. He was standing at the foot of the stairs, covered with dust and dirt, his face charcoal gray with grime. "We've had a bit of an incident up here. Any able-bodied blokes?"

Robert went, and Philippa, ignoring the request for men only, went also. The bomb that had dusted them down last night had landed on a pub half a block away. Of the thirty-odd people within, none had escaped uninjured, five had been dragged out alive, twenty more bodies had been recovered during the night, and at least seven more remained unaccounted for, including the landlord's family. The landlord himself had been hustling a drunk into the street at the moment of impact and had escaped without a scratch. He was sitting now, exhausted beyond feeling or thought, on a heap of bricks before the rubble that had been his building. From the fingers of one bruised, bloody hand dangled a small pink child's purse. It swung back and forth, garish in the glare of emergency lighting.

Robert stared, guilty and mesmerized. They had been laughing, they had been sleeping; for hours, he had lain with the warmth of Philippa's soft thighs beneath his head. All the while, half a street away, a man had been clawing at broken brick and shattered stone, seeking his entombed daughter.

"Wakey, wakey, love," Philippa said crisply. "It's work time." She was three yards ahead of him already, shifting bricks with her pretty, delicate hands. They worked through the rest of the night into the cold wet morning. The rain had begun with the first light and grown heavy. It streamed down Robert's face, and Philippa's hair had tightened into wet ringlets. He remembered thinking at some point, as he stepped back for the AFS men to remove the third body, an old woman, perhaps the grandmother of the as-yet-unfound child, that Philippa's hair was naturally curly. He had not known. But a set would have come out in the rain, and a perm would have frizzed. Naturally curly and yellow as the sun. It was Philippa who found the child.

She stepped back and turned away, her lips pressed together so that they were white, and her eyes firmly shut. It was the only emotion she had shown. Robert looked down compulsively and regretted he ever had. Somehow, all the adult bodies had been relatively unmarked, sheltered by a beam, a sheet of plasterboard, simply smothered. The child had been more vulnerable.

"Oh, Jesus, what a mess," Robert whispered.

"Take him away," Philippa said quietly to the ARP warden behind her, not meaning Robert, but the man who sat yet with his head in his hands over the pink purse. "Just take him far away."

Robert kept saying to himself that it made no difference what happened, dead was dead, the soul was not affected by the manner of death, the soul was free. "Oh, Jesus *Christ*, what a mess." Robert also went away, a small distance, unable to take any more.

But Philippa stayed, a guardian over the bloodied flesh, until someone came with blankets, wrapped it up, and took it away.

Then she said, "Let's go home, Robert. I think we've done our share."

They held hands and walked away, into the brightening morning and the awakening city. No one noticed them go. But then no one had noticed them come.

Robert had half a day of leave left and he did not know what to do with it. He did not want to go anywhere, but more than that, he did not want to go back home at all and remind himself of Mike. He did not want to stay in London either, and remind himself of the little girl, or Maisie, or the family-less pub owner. Most of all he did not want to be alone to think and to face the alarming, overwhelming guilt that was rising up inside him.

"Why not us?" he said to Philippa grimly. "Everyone else is getting the chop."

"Dear knows," she said in her brittle, tired voice.

"I can't stand it."

"What?"

"Being alive, when everyone's dead."

"A bit of an exaggeration, ducks."

"Philippa."

"Mmm."

"Philippa, I want to get married."

"How laudably conventional. To whom?"

"Oh, for Christ sake, Phil, stop being so damn British."

"Any suggestion what I should be instead?"

Robert was giddy with tiredness, grief, and a morning mania of detachment. "How about an American? By marriage, of course. To me." He turned away from her, like a child whose Christmas request has met a blank glare of disapproval, and missed Philippa's second display of emotion of the day. She had begun rather gently to cry. But she as quickly wiped the wetness from her eyes and grinned brightly and said, "Thank *God* I'm not entitled to white. It's so utterly impossible to find."

"You're not?" Robert said, a little stunned.

"Good God, Robert," she said crushingly, and then added with only half-mocking unease, "Are you?"

IV

"Well, are you?"

"What, man?" David said, holding both ends of his towel hung like a yoke about his neck. He was trying to sound American and being undone by his brisk English consonants.

"Are you screwing Mary Jo?" Steve said again.

"Fuck, man," David said. He kicked at the boardwalk, annoyed, and regretted it. The surface was shaggy with rough weathered slivers.

"What're you stopping for?" said Steve.

"Nothing. I've got a splinter." David folded himself up, all knees and elbows, sitting on the edge of the boardwalk with one long, bare leg dangling, and the other crossing it with the large dusty foot turned upwards. He picked at the callused sole with thumb and forefinger.

"Fucking wood, full of fucking splinters," said Steve sympathetically. He stood, making a shadow across David as David tried to capture the dark sliver between two fingernails. They were short and broken from the summer's work on the building site and of little use.

"Screw it," David said and stood up.

"You'd better not. You'd better get it out," Steve said, suddenly concerned. "It'll work in."

To the bone, David thought. *A splinter will work to the*

bone. Don't sniff flowers. The white flies will crawl up your nose and turn into caterpillars. They'll eat your brain. Don't touch it. You'll go blind. He laughed suddenly. "Righto, nanny."

"Huh?"

"Nothing. Remembering something. Somebody."

"*Who*, for fuck's sake?"

"My nanny."

"Your *nanny?* Come off it. You didn't have a nanny."

"I did. For two years. After mother and dad split up. At Greenshaws."

"*Green*shaws. Christ. I can never believe it."

The boardwalk arched up over the seafront dunes and ended in a long steep flight of wooden steps, down to the flat strand. David paused there, seeking a new subject. Stephen embarrassed him when he talked about money, particularly David's family's money, with the sour edge of envy in his voice. It demeaned him, made him seem young and hard to look up to, and David wanted to look up to everybody in America, this summer.

"It's just a house," he said.

"Sure."

The beach stretched out, empty and luxuriant in its relentless, glorious heat. In Bridlington and Scarborough, where David spent occasional summer weeks, the seafront was as often as not wrapped in North Sea fog, and families plodded faithfully down the sands in coats and woolen sweaters, with only the children, oblivious to the elements like all children, prancing about in shorts and swimming costumes. Sometimes it simply rained, pelting down for days on end on the white round pebbles of the beach and the long gray stone promenades. Little ones clung to red tin pails and wailed, and mothers grew fractious and played bingo in the arcades. David closed his eyes and saw his own mother, oh, not playing bingo, hardly that, but walking briskly, determinedly down the promenade with Rutherford, the golden Labrador, beside her, she wrapped up in a good handsome Burberry and silk scarf, and Andrew in his sheepskin complaining. He opened his eyes and squinted into the unbridled sun.

"How's work?" he asked Stephen.

"Great. I quit."

"Surely you didn't."

Steve had no ear for the English idiom. He said querulously, "What the fuck did I say so for?" and jumped the last three steps of the boardwalk stair into the hot gray-tinged sand at the foot. "Mother*fuck*er," he shouted, hopping. The sand was blackened with sun, scorched, and blistering hot. Steve took refuge on a heap of dry seaweed. David crossed the fiery dark stretch in three long bounds and stood on the cooler white sand beyond.

"But you liked it."

"Aah, that cunt bugged me." He meant his boss. David was shocked continually by Steve's language, though he made every effort to imitate it. "Doesn't know a Fresnel from his asshole." He shrugged, slapping his towel against his calf. "Besides, I got all the bread I need till I go back." David knew he meant really that Paul Botvin had all that he needed, whether or not he went back.

"You didn't answer," said Steve. He was looking off too nonchalantly at the white haze of the horizon, his fingers twitching the edge of the towel into a taut cone.

"You fancy her," David said suddenly, surprising himself.

"Shit, man," Steve said with energetic disdain.

"You're jealous of my father. And you fancy his mistress."

"*Mis*tress!" Steve shouted. "God, you're cute."

"That's the word we use," David said stiffly.

"At *Green*shaws?"

There was a pause while David, at the edge of the wet, smooth tide-washed sand at the foot of the beach, wriggled out of his tight American jeans. He laughed then, to himself, and said, "At Greenshaws they don't even talk about it. Well, they do talk about it, if it's horses and mares or dogs and bitches. But not men and women."

"Christ. How'd you get born?"

"They *do* it. They just don't talk about it."

"Do *you* do it?" Steve asked. He'd dropped his stretched baggy jeans and was standing in his surfer's trunks, the peculiar fashion of that summer, with their long, tight flowered leggings reaching almost to his knees, while the trouser top was cut so low that the root of his penis was visible in a little crest of blond hair. An erection, David was certain, would vault the thing entirely.

"Now what do you think," David said with immense cool. He was torn between pride in recent events, shame at their complications, and worse, a new-boy embarrassment at their being only so very recent.

"I think you don't," said Steve.

"Rubbish."

"I know you don't."

"Rubbish, I said."

Steve grinned and shrugged and waded into the breaking waves. David said suddenly, "I have, you know." Steve grinned more broadly and dove into the sea. He came up with the hair on his head and the hair on his chest plastered down and dripping. He was wiry and muscular and overtly sexual. "What was she like?" he said.

"Who?" David was standing nervously at the water's edge, with the brown-white foam creeping up to his toes and sliding away.

"Mary fucking Jo."

"It bloody well wasn't *her*."

Steve gave up and waded out further into the surf, jumping up, buoyant as each rolling crest slid under him. The surf was light, but David hung back. He was a good swimmer, and a yachtsman, but there was something intrinsically different between the gray North Sea waters of home and the vivid blue Atlantic here. It was, he knew, less subtle, less shallow, and thus less dangerous, and yet he was afraid of it. There was such icy, fierce vigor in the wave crests, sweeping north from Brazil.

"Actually," said Steve, his back to David, "it's your father

I fancy." He whipped his wet blond head around to catch David's embarrassment, and did. "Shock you?"

David waved his hands about, with no sound. He was shocked beyond words, and miserably uncomfortable. He said, "Look, man, let's just swim." But when Steve agreed and slid down into the cold sea, David still stood in the hot sun, the water, rising with the tide, rushing about his ankles, like liquid sandpaper, undermining his heels, pulling the solid sand from beneath them. He could not leave it, and said, "Hey, Steve?" There was a wet sound of acknowledgment. "I don't understand you. I mean, you keep going on about women."

"And I screw men?"

David went silent.

"Sex is my bag, man. Some people like tennis." He dove under and came up wet and cheerful. "I like to ball. Guys, chicks. I tried a dog once, but it got all stupid and I nearly had to break its fucking back to keep it still."

David's mouth was wide open.

"This guy I knew at school, he took pictures. It was his dog. Sex is great. Even by yourself. I suppose you do *that*, anyhow."

David ran into the sea and dove over the breakers, preferring their combing crests to conversation. But he had to come up for air, and when he did, Steve, like a cormorant, was waiting for him.

"Tell you something."

"Oh," said David, not wanting to hear anything.

"It's true what they say about oriental girls." Steve waited for the effect, but the phrase meant nothing to David and he had to go on. "You see, they have these beads, and they shove them up your ass, and then when . . ."

David cut him off by saying, as manly as he could, "Oh, *I* see why you're going back." But then Steve was quiet, suddenly solemn.

"Nah," he said eventually. Then he added, "Oh, women are all right, but, like, man. That's *serious*. I mean, all this sex shit, it's just to take up all the energy. Christ, man, I'm like a coiled spring all the time. I need *some* release." He glanced sideways and saw David watching him, sufficiently awed. He'd never have dared use that coiled spring bit on anyone even maybe a day older than David. Or on any American at all. David was so easy, so utterly free of conventional wisdom. He apparently never went to the movies or he wouldn't take any of the crap Steve was handing out, and Steve knew it.

"Once you've been under fire, man"—he shrugged, pushing wet hair off his eyes, looking off to the horizon as if not South America but Vietnam lay that way—"everything else, like it's all just tinsel crap after that. That's what tests men, and men out there, crap, man, they're the only humans worth knowing." He rubbed his long heavy nose. He had a childhood scar on his left cheek and his fingers reached for it, as if to ennoble it with war's ardor. He said dreamily,

> 'Beloved soldiers who love rough life and breath
> Not less for dying faithful to the last.'

David was impressed. "I hardly thought you read that sort of thing," he said. Steve smiled knowingly, seeing himself as David saw him. " 'Soldier, scholar, horseman he, and all he did, done perfectly!' " he said slickly. Actually his reading extended little past the Hulk and Spiderman, but Paul was forever casting a cold eye on life, death, and Stephen Deutsch and spewing reams of the stuff. At the moment, its usefulness as social ammunition outweighed his embarrassment about it.

They came out of the water and shook their towels out, letting the hot sea wind lift them and straighten them landward, then let them gently fall, stretched out on the beach. They lay down on top of them, not bothering to dry themselves, with knees and shins in the sand. The beach was empty, at the drinks hour, with the heat of the afternoon thickening into the gray haze of distant thunderheads. Steve slid his hand across the sand divide between his towel and David's and laid his fingers on the smooth brown skin of David's forearm. David leaped away so fast he rolled right off the towel and into the white sand and came up with his thigh and side glazed in small pale grains.

"Now look here," he said, exactly as his stepfather Andrew would. "*This is simply not on.*"

Steve lay back on his striped towel, unperturbed, the unacceptable hand withdrawn and folded with the other over the wet skin of his lower stomach. His thumbnail caressed his own navel. "Okay, okay, keep your cool." He smiled, his eyes closed. "Oh, for ecstasy a watermelon," he said eventually. "Motherfuck, I'm randy."

David was kneeling, half on his towel and half off, watching with narrow, unhappy eyes. Steve said quite gently, "Look, man, I'm sorry. I won't do anything. Just lie down and get dry." David did, mostly because the alternative was going back to the beach house, and God knows, maybe his mother. He wished he'd brought his board down and had that excuse to head back to the surf.

"Anyhow," said Steve, "I thought all you English guys . . . fucking boys' private schools . . . I mean it *is* called the fucking English disease."

St. Vincent's School, York

1961

"*Fucking English private schools,*" *Grant Holland muttered, flicking ash from his Gauloise with quick disdain. Still, it was beyond a doubt now that he'd come to the right place.*

He looked out across the autumn mist of the playing fields with a speculative eye. Small groups of senior boys were lounging about the cricket ground and farther in the distance another clump rested at the side of the tennis courts. The dim sun of an English October evening glinted reddy green off the fading sycamore trees. Beyond, the spire of the chapel was dwarfed by the background of York. A part of the ancient wall glowed sandy white in the late light, and a spire of the Minster showed a tip above the trees. Holland's ever alert eye dismissed the beauty without thought. It was not relevant to the present, merely a distraction, and in Holland's life, as in the life of any undercover detective, distractions could mean death. Still, things were going well. His cover appeared to be holding. There was not one among them, masters or boys, who even suspected he was anything other than what he pretended, the sixth-former David Wardlaw, a quiet, inoffensive loner, without enemy or friend.

Holland began walking casually across the sports ground, heading for the dormitories. The pretense of the loner was useful. Any unnecessary conversation was dangerous, an avenue for curiosity. Better by himself. He walked slowly, not wishing to attract attention. His handsome, naturally boyish looks and unruly tangle of blond hair, plus a little quick plastic surgery at headquarters, had suited admirably to the role. Here and there a more perceptive master, generally an older man with wartime experience, would glance with vague undefined suspicion, some doubt touched off perhaps by the trained lightning-quick reactions of Holland's hands or the brutal flash of steely blue eyes. But it had never progressed beyond doubts. His cover was secure yet, he was certain. Had he been any less certain, he would not have allowed himself to be drawn into the conversation with Wedderburn at all.

Jeremy Wedderburn stepped off the pitch, swinging his cricket bat casually back and forth, just nicking the creased edge of his flannels. He had all the assurance one would expect of a baronet's son in the lower sixth, a prefect already, who had somehow managed to reach six foot one at age sixteen and top that off with black hair that would grace an English poet and eyelashes that sent the girls at the mixers bonkers. *Damned show-off*, thought Grant Holland. But he smiled his cool, reserved smile to put Wedderburn off his guard.

Jeremy raised one hand just above elbow level. "I say, Wardlaw."

Holland hesitated. Hardly in the mood for schoolboy chatter. He needed time alone to think out the problem before him. Still, to be unnecessarily churlish might in itself draw attention.

"Yes," Holland said mildly, drawing casually on the Gauloise. He flicked the long ash onto the velvety green grass.

"I say," Jeremy said, distracted, "whatever are you doing?"

David's hands froze with the fingers yet extended about the imaginary Gauloise. They tightened into a fist. He thought frantically and cursed out, "Midges. Bloody midges everywhere." He slapped at his neck and waved a fending hand about his head.

"Oh, indeed," Jeremy said, brightening. "Actually, you'll never believe it, but just for a moment I thought you were smoking."

David laughed loudly. "Smoking? On the cricket ground? And old Pebblepate lurking behind the stumps, no doubt. You must be joking." Hebblethwaite, the sports master, unfortunately named for a man unfortunately balding, was a veritable devil on tobacco.

"Jolly certain," Jeremy agreed. "Anyhow, what say tennis after tea?"

David, still smarting from the discovered Gauloise, went silent with amazement. "Me?" he said dumbly. "And you?" Then he cried impulsively, "Oh, ra*ther*." Somewhere, far away, Grant Holland laughed his cynical little laugh of distrust.

Jeremy looked at his watch. Almost simultaneously the bell in the chapel tower began to ring. "Shall we go to tea together?" Jeremy said, smiling and crinkling the corners of his eyes. The black hair fell over them, over his smoothly defined brows, in a perfectly unbalanced wave.

David nodded, uncertain. As they walked away Jeremy slung a rough masculine arm over David's shoulders. David glowed with the kindness of it. Grant Holland suddenly had nothing to say at all.

"I really like you, David," Jeremy said suddenly. "I'm not like the others." David was afraid to say anything, afraid that he would destroy this sudden undreamed-of companionship. He felt he couldn't bear to lose that gentle arm about his shoulders. But Jeremy went on and said for him what he was thinking. "I know I act the same sometimes. I am most appallingly sorry, you know. It's dreadfully rotten of me, but you see, old boy, I'm so rotten scared."

It was to David like a peculiar dream, where everything runs backward and counter to expectation. Jeremy afraid?

"You?" David said. "Scared?"

"Bloody right I am," Jeremy declared vigorously.

"But why?" David asked. "You're a prefect, you're top of the form. Everyone looks up to you. Whoever would even think of ragging you?"

Jeremy stopped, but he kept his arm in place. "Look, Wardlaw. Let me enlighten you. This place is a jungle." He waved a dismissive slender hand toward the figures of distant boys before the delicately serene landscape of trees and ancient city. "They're jackals. I know they bully you. And frankly, old man, I can't abide it. But I always thought, well, damn it, man, if I stand up for you, I'll draw their fire, won't I?"

"But what about now? I mean, suppose they see us."

"You know," Jeremy said, world-wearily, "I feel just now I don't give a damn. I feel it's time I stood on my own feet. And it's time someone stood up for you. I've seen the way things have been for you. Bloody abominable. And that business yesterday, about the books . . . well, one really cannot go on, can one?"

David shook his head confusedly. He was terribly uncertain what to make of this new, confessional Jeremy. It was not just that Jeremy was always one of them, that relentless five who pursued him, physically and emotionally, day and night. Jeremy was, or had been anyhow, to all appearances, the ringleader.

"I wish they'd give my books back," David said hesitantly.

"Have you told anyone?" Jeremy said quietly. "After all, it *is* theft."

"No. Of course not," David said at once, covering himself quickly in case this new Jeremy was some kind of pretense, leading to more humiliation. An admission of squealing was the last thing he needed. "No. It's only that, what with them being my father's, and only published in America, I won't be able to get any more."

"Won't your father send you another lot?"

"Oh, surely. But what can I tell him?" David said miserably.

"Point taken," said Jeremy. "Jolly miserable show, that's all I can say."

A miserable show. The words were so thin for the weight of emotion. It was heart's pain. His books. His Grant Holland books. Two years' worth, four a year. Eight Grant Holland books. He knew each cover intimately, with its grim-jawed depiction of Grant Holland, and usually some incredibly beautiful woman, an heiress or a kidnapped woman scientist, clinging to his arm. They were all rather the same, actually, but far from bothering him, the sameness was their most pleasing quality, reflecting the parallel comforting familiarity of each of his father's stories. Grant Holland was always there, threatened but triumphant; the women, well, they might really be the same woman, but she was always saved, and won. Even some of the adventures, some of the villains, had a cozy similarity, so that David could recognize on page fourteen, when the smooth, slick, slightly effeminate blond diplomat entered, that he would emerge from a chrysalis of innocence as a malignant agent of terror and yet, in the end, would most assuredly succumb.

"How can you bear reading them again and again," his sister Victoria would proclaim in disgust, dropping a treasured volume at his feet. "They're all exactly alike." Exactly, they were reliable, and in David's world, little was.

Reading them again and again, however, was what led to disaster. His father sent them faithfully, instantly on publication, and had always done so since that strange day during David's one American summer, he had found David engrossed in his raw manuscript, surrounded by neat stacks of soft yellow paper, and had asked with infinite hesitance, "Do you like it, David?"

Then there had been a bit of delicate feeling about, and only later did David realize that his father was concerned about the sex in them. Not that there was much then; in the Eisenhower years writers like Robert Zolan relied rather heavily on the closing bedroom door and three lingering lascivious dots. Still, David's ten-year-old enthusiasm for the spies, the guns, and the helicopters and his flat dismissal of the boring bits with the girl set his father's moral conscience at ease. So no doubt did the knowledge that anything hotter than the traditional dot dot dot would result in the proferred book zinging back across the Atlantic by return post, marked with a row of disapproving E-II-R stamps and Philippa's firm pen-and-inkwell hand.

However, over the years, they passed familial censorship, and now, as the Kennedy era in America had brought in a new lightheartedness about the printed word, Robert sent them direct to David at school. Now David read the new sexy bits with a flashlight under the blankets and his right hand roaming around the vicinity of his pajama cord. And in just such a literary position was he caught, the night before, by Matthew James and Nigel Osborne, who were not about to let that pass.

"I say, look at Wardlaw, he's got a book."

"A book? Wardlaw? Gone scholarly, has he?"

"Wardlaw swatting?" said another voice as a little crowd gathered about David's besieged bed.

"What kind of a book?"

"I *say*." Osborne wrestled the book from David, who was busy tightening the drawstring of his pajamas with furtive fingers beneath the blanket. "Look at *that*." He waved it, bright dust jacket splayed out, aloft in the dorm. Matthew ran to flick on the bright overhead light.

"Doesn't look quite like Shakespeare to me," someone, David had been quite certain it was Jeremy Wedderburn actually, shouted. In the confusion, struggling with his pajamas, in his embarrassment and his desperation to reclaim the volume, he could not be positive.

"What ripping good fun," Osborne shouted gaily. "Here, listen to this." He held the book up to the light and began to read.

"Better post a guard," Matthew said knowingly. "Not the sort of thing one wants old Tiddles to hear." That was the housemaster, Tilbury, a rather pompous bearded young man with a resounding lack of humor. Hugh Stewart-Smith dashed to the door and opened it a crack, thrilled with the excitement of the role. "All clear, read on, old thing," he declared airily.

Osborne stood on his metal-framed bed, his head up near the exposed dusty rafters of the old stone building. " 'Holland lifted the girl's prone form, still wet from the sea, and carried it to his own bunk within the boat's cabin. He was acutely conscious of the warm, wet softness of her exposed breasts . . . ' "

"Hear, hear," Matthew shouted, and David squirmed in a misery of embarrassment.

" '. . . her exposed breasts against his arm,' " Nigel Osborne read again. " 'As he laid her deliciously curved form on the bunk, her eyelashes fluttered and she moaned softly, parting her full red lips. Holland suppressed the animal stirring within him,' " Nigel read with deep emphasis. "I say, it gets better."

"Give it back," David pleaded. "Please, Nigel."

"In good time, my man, in good time. Wait, we're all improving our . . . minds." There was laughter, and someone then shouted what David had been most dreading.

"Who's the author, pray tell? D. H. Lawrence, perchance?"

"I say, who *is* it by?"

Nigel turned the book around and looked again at the dust jacket. As always with David's father's books, the author's name was less obvious than that of the central series character. Nigel read aloud. " 'A Grant Holland novel, by the author of *Blood for Tears* and *The Blond Died Young.*' " Then he stopped and his thin brown face contorted in a wild grin. "None other, my young friends," he cried delightedly, "but the world-famous Robert Zolan."

"Who's that?" said Matthew.

But Hugh Stewart-Smith cried out, "But that's Wardlaw's father, isn't it? It is. It is." And he pranced up and down, forgetting his post by the door.

"The literary wonder of the Western world," announced Nigel.

"Oh, do tell, Wardlaw," Matthew cried. "Is it true?"

"Of course it's true," said Nigel Osborne. "And I'll tell you something else. Wardlaw's got a stack of these somewhere. They come in the post. No wonder he never shows them to anyone. My God, if my father wrote trash like this, I wouldn't show my face in public." He thumbed arrogantly through the volume, and then tossed it dismissively to Matthew. But by then Hugh Stewart-Smith had availed himself of David's locker and dug out the other volumes from under the heaps of shortbread boxes and chocolate wrappers.

"Look at *this* one, she's hardly any clothes on at *all*."

"Uh, Wardlaw, whatever does your mother say about papa's literary efforts, eh?"

"Where does he do his research, that's what I want to know," said Hugh.

"Below the belt, old man," Jeremy Wedderburn put in at once. "Wardlaw's parents are divorced and all that." Hugh shrugged.

David said, "Please, you've all seen them, can I have them back?"

"Why?"

"I like to have them. My father sent them."

"Ohhhh. Jolly touching, isn't it?" Nigel looked around him. "But surely you *have* read them?"

David nodded, uncertain if the admission would bring more teasing.

"But *we* haven't," Nigel said firmly. "Come on, chaps, one each." He began tossing David's precious hoard about the room. David sat, mesmerized, unable to stop what was happening. Then there was a shout from Hugh at the door.

"Cover, everyone, Tiddles at large!" And they all dived for beds and lights blacked out. In the darkness, David lay crying in rigid silence. Maybe in the morning. But in the morning, there was not a book to be seen.

"I say," Jeremy said as they came within the square of ivy-hung limestone three-story buildings that framed the central quad of St. Vincent's, "Do you think me awful, not facing them? Beastly cowardly, I know, but . . ." Jeremy looked pained, but he bravely kept his arm about David's shoulders. On the other hand, the quad was deserted in the late dusky sun.

"Oh, no," David said, eager to show friendship, "Not at all. On the contrary, I understand. I understand very well."

David did understand. There were six boys in the lower sixth form, he and Jeremy Wedderburn, and then the four others. Two had gone to Oakley Prep in Buckinghamshire before coming to St. Vincent's at age thirteen. The other two attended a preparatory school near Scarborough, the same indeed where Jeremy himself had gone. That left David.

David had commenced his education at an ordinary state primary school, in Bridlington, perhaps at his distant father's democratic insistence. But at the age of eight, with his father pretty much ousted from power and influence by Andrew Wardlaw, he had been bungled into a small Church of England establishment of little renown and less educational worth. Still, it was the best string his grandfather could pull at that late date. It really didn't matter about the quality of his prep school, actually. The fact was, it was the different one: he was the different one, the one odd boy out caught between two teams, who, with the ruthless tribal loyalty of their years, turned on the outsider with unabashed intent to destroy.

There had been one other, actually, and they had in effect succeeded in destroying him. He was a clergyman's son, Peter Crook, and after half a term of vigorous intimidation he had collapsed with glandular fever and been whisked away forever into the bosom of family and church.

David had tried collapsing, also, but could never summon up anything more dramatic than a head cold, and even when gripped miserably by one of those, always failed to arouse even a flicker of fever on matron's thermometer. And fever was the magical property that won oneself long days of luscious cool sheets and silence in the infirmary, and a telephone call to anxious parents. No fever, however, no sympathy, and a pile of grubby handkerchiefs was one's only solace.

David had tried other escape routes from St. Vincent's. David had tried everything. Letters home, hysterical fits on the Day of Return, even running away. The last had earned him a whipping with a riding crop by his grandfather upon his unheralded midnight arrival at Greenshaws, and then tears from his mother, which was worse. Hysterical fits were of course summarily ignored, and letters in their own way ignored as well. Answered of course, but the answers were smooth catalogues, in mother's lovely pale script, of the state of pets and family, prompt and bright and concise, and containing no reference to the one question that ended each of David's letters, like a benediction of misery: "Please will you come and take me home."

In the end, after months, he stopped asking. Philippa Wardlaw relaxed in immense relief and was pleased to tell anxious friends and family that David had settled down at last.

"Next thing, he'll not want to come home at all, my dear," they'd say. "That's always the upshot of it all. It's always those that are hard to settle that end up loving it most." It was half true; David did in the end stop wanting to come home, either to Greenshaws or to his mother and stepfather's flat in London, or their house in Sussex. But the reason was rather because the one message that did find its way through that checklist of ponies, gun dogs, tame sheep, and assorted aunties was clear enough: "Stay clear, stay clear. You're not welcome any more."

Anyhow, by then David had found his escape, an avenue of release, away from the tormenting, subtle hidden teasing, the unsubtle bashings, the threats, the ignorant smiles of parents, the "brace-up" chins of schoolmasters. Even an escape from the dreadful Fridays, with music in the mornings at which he failed miserably and had his knuckles repeatedly rapped with the music master's hard little black baton, and then in the evening the regulation boiled-fish-and-potato high tea, which appeared with the certainty of sunrise, every Friday of the year.

Grant Holland was his escape. At night he read his eight treasured volumes, in a set, self-disciplined order, one a week, saving *Death and the Redhead* for the last, always, like the cherry on a cake. That was the one with the kidnapped daughter of the American diplomat, like a redheaded Brigitte Bardot on the cover, and was the base of his most favored fantasies. The redhead, Clarissa she was called, though sometimes he changed it to Jennifer and made her a brunette, in memory of the only real girl he'd ever known, a Bridlington fisherman's daughter he'd bid a last farewell to eight years earlier when he left the primary school. Jennifer-Clarissa, anyhow, waited for him secretly, trustingly, and usually in dreadful distress behind every disaster of the day. A master's mockery, a classmate's deliberate sickening fart in the lavs, any of the rich ugliness of St. Vincent's could be turned back, like a turned page, and behind would be the Redhead. And Grant Holland. Only that was himself, of course, though no one

knew, Grant Holland, disguised, bearing the schoolboy nonsense patiently, for the sake of his Country, or the World, or
Jennifer-Clarissa; waiting, biding his time, tight, a coiled spring.
Grant Holland could do almost anything, bear almost anything, escape almost anything. Almost.

"Ripping news, Wardlaw," Nigel Osborne shouted as David
and Jeremy entered the dining hall. Only now Jeremy was
four paces behind, his face coolly disassociated from David.

"What's that?" David said, beguiled by Jeremy's recent
offer of friendship into believing it might be something nice.

"It's Friday, old chap," said Nigel with brute satisfaction.
David's throat closed.

The plates came down the refectory table, served up by the
prefect at either end. David could smell it coming and had to
endure rows of it passing beneath his eyes, as the dishes were
sent, hand to hand, down the row of boys. Then his own
arrived.

"Anyone can eat fish, dear," his mother would say in her
sensible, bear-up-now voice.

"You'd eat it all right if you were hungry." That would be
his stepfather. "Now during the war, we ate whale meat. Try
that to tickle your fancy, boy."

"What's the matter, Wardlaw, not to your taste?" said
Tilbury, the housemaster. "Come, come, boy. There's more
to life than your senses. Unpleasantries mastered are victories
of the spirit."

David looked down at it. The plate was mountainous with
dry haddock, crammed in beside the matte-white, dusty heap
of mashed potato. Salty haddock water soaked into the white
and stained itself blue-green with the small scattering of mar-
rowfat peas, dry also, and malignant, like blue-green eyeballs.
David lifted knife and fork and mashed some fish into the
potato, and dipped it into the green of the peas. He crammed
it into his mouth. His throat remained closed. Thirst arose,

frantic against the dry flaky fibers, and pepper heated the roof of his mouth, making it sticky as glue. Water was allowed after the plate was clean. He swallowed, but his throat would not open. The bile rose into the passages of his nose.

"Come, come, Wardlaw, no need for all that grimacing."

David closed his eyes. The master turned his back and Matthew, sitting beside David, suddenly whipped a vast piece of his own haddock onto David's plate.

"But . . ."

"My pleasure," Matthew smirked.

"But please."

"Silence, boys," said Tilbury without looking up from his place. David forced a forkful into his mouth. It roamed about above his shut throat.

"Fish eyes," whispered Matthew.

"Snail streaks," said Nigel Osborne.

"Farts."

"Green shit floating in the toilet bowl."

"Oh, God." David closed his eyes and the vomiting began.

When it ended, he sat on the grimy white tiled floor of the lavs, where he'd been hastened by a disgusted Tilbury, his body cold and trembling. Then rescue came.

"Bastards. Thought to poison me, did you?" Grant Holland, ace detective, was in a mood for blood. He got to his feet, and stood shakily gazing into the finger-smudged mirror over one of the sinks. The fruits of adolescent hair-combing decorated the cracked porcelain, wrapping the corroded plug chain in whispy knots of wet fuzz. Holland's stomach churned, but he forced himself to concentrate on his own image in the glass until his eyes regained focus. The lean boyish face beneath its casual tangle of blond hair, though showing now the strain of illness, still belied the fierceness of the icy blue eyes.

Holland had come to the boys' school, St. Vincent's, in

search of . . . David paused a moment, thinking . . . in search of, yes, the kidnapped daughter of an American diplomat, holidaying in London. Kidnapped in London, and spirited north to a hidden sanctuary beneath the chapel of St. Vincent's school. Yes, of course. Holland knew where she was; it was getting to her that was proving difficult. And he'd made a big mistake, dining with Tilbury, the housemaster. Hoped to glean some information, but of course the old bastard was in league with the kidnappers. "Thought that fish tasted funny," Holland mused. Still, he'd survived. A constitution hardened by years of lean living served him well. He swept the boyish mop of hair out of his face with one hard, callused hand.

"Wardlaw," a voice called.

Holland searched the sordid room for somewhere to hide. Fat chance. All the lav doors had been removed.

"Perverts," Holland said aloud.

"What's that, Wardlaw?" The housemaster, Tilbury, was standing in the doorway. His voice echoed thinly in the tiled room.

"Nothing, sir."

"What's taking you so long, Wardlaw?"

"Nothing, sir. I was ill."

"No nonsense in here, Wardlaw. Clean heart, clean head, clean body."

"Yes, sir."

Tilbury edged out, still suspicious, but repelled by the sour smell of vomit. "Shower," he shouted as he retreated down the hallway.

Shower, thought Holland. Freshen him up, clear his head.

David went back to the sixth-form dormitory, removed his clothes, wrapped himself tightly in his plaid wool dressing gown, and made for the showers. He tried to maintain Grant Holland, but he felt too tired, after being ill, and he couldn't think of anything to do about Jennifer-Clarissa, in her room under the chapel. Tonight, in bed, he'd sort it out.

After his shower he remembered Jeremy's invitation to tennis, and so, frantic not to be late, he scrambled into his flannels and pullover and, dragging his racket out of the trunk beneath his bed, ran the entire distance to the courts, undoing all the good work of the shower. He arrived sweating and red-faced and breathing in boyish puffs. Jeremy was leaning elegantly against one of the net posts, twirling his racket against his white canvas shoe, not a single black hair of his elegant head out of place.

"What's the bother, old chap?" he said.

"Sorry. Late. Thought you'd not wait," David puffed frantically.

"All the time in the world," said Jeremy with the most gracious of smiles. He won, of course. All the games and the match. David didn't care. Getting to play at all was winning for David.

"Better luck next time, David." Jeremy grinned, twirling his victorious racket. Next time. David clung to the words.

"Damn, but I'm hot," Jeremy said then. "What say a shower?"

David nodded happily. It was his day for showers. He'd have stood under the bloody Angel Falls for Jeremy's sake at the moment.

Jeremy's hand came down on David's shoulder with a hearty masculine clap. "Jolly well played, for all that," he said. David tried to wrestle his thrilled smile into an appropriately cool appreciation. It felt so good to have someone touch him in kindness. Physical contact at St. Vincent's had heretofore consisted almost entirely of thumps in the kidneys for some imagined insult, or failing to answer the demands of some boyish superior instantaneously, or else the sharp crack of a wooden ruler across the knuckles for equivalently displeasing a master. A kind hand, a kind masculine hand; he couldn't recall any other. His stepfather never touched him, as if touching was a sin, or would incline to contamination with the Zolenski bloodline. *That's* who had touched him, cuffed him, boxed with him, roughed and tumbled him and tossed him in the air: Robert Zolenski, his father. But that was baby stuff, so long ago.

Jeremy's dressing gown was dark blue printed silk, with maroon revers. He tied it around his lean waist with a deftness that David envied deeply. He didn't even double the knot. If David didn't double the knot, any knot, shoelace, dressing gown, string on a package, it fell apart instantly. Jeremy strode off to the showers, white fluffy towel over his left shoulder, assured of his handiwork. David followed, flinging his own towel over his own left shoulder. It fell off and landed on the scuffed wooden floor.

In the shower room Jeremy said, "Dreadfully sorry about tea. Rather took you back, didn't it?"

David nodded, miserably embarrassed at the recollection.

"Are you all right now?" Jeremy asked gently.

"I just can't eat fish. I can't eat it."

"I know. With me it's Wednesdays."

"Tripe and onions?" David said with a flicker of a sympathetic smile. Jeremy's eyes crinkled in delicious companionship of shared misery.

"Jolly right. It's such dreadful rubbery stuff, anyhow, like old boots, even when cook does it at home. And *here*."

David nodded.

"Osborne says they use leftovers from the hospital. You know, what's scraped off plates after the geriatrics have drooled over it."

David shuddered, his always weak stomach not needing that further disruption. He untied the double knot of his woolen dressing gown and turned on the taps of the shower. There were four showerheads, of old and crusted chrome in a communal row, with white tile and a drain below them, but Jeremy chose the one next to David and continued talking steadily as David dropped the dressing gown off his shoulders.

The hot water steamed over both of them, the clanking of the ancient pipes drowning out whatever it was Jeremy was saying. David was preoccupied, scrubbing the newly thickened hair in his underarms and groin, and did not notice that Jeremy was not washing or doing anything, not even talking anymore, but just watching him and breathing like he were still playing tennis. When David, with soap running down out of his hair, eyes closed, turned and groped for his towel, Jeremy's arms went about his waist. They did not do anything there. They just went around his waist, and Jeremy's puffy breathing sound was somewhere at the back of David's neck.

"What are you doing?"

"David."

"Let me go. Stop, Jeremy. Please."

"David."

"Leave me alone, Jeremy," David said agonizedly, and then Grant Holland suddenly shouted, "Get off, you bloody queer!" and hit Jeremy Wedderburn in the mouth.

There was an awful silence, a nonsilence, full of clanking pipes and running water and steam, and Jeremy crying, a gasping cry, half young man's anger, half girl's grief. David said, wiping his face with the towel and backing across the shower room, for he expected Jeremy to leap at him and thump him, "I'm sorry, I'm sorry."

Jeremy did not leap on him or thump him. Jeremy closed his eyes and rubbed his puffy lip and then turned off the shower heads, both of them. But the clanking continued as the antique plumbing only gradually got the message. David dressed quickly in his scratchy plaid dressing gown. He was agonizingly sorry. Jeremy had been so kind, so kind. An entire day, almost, he had been kind. But he couldn't, he couldn't. Whatever it was Jeremy wanted him to do. He couldn't. He was not even precisely sure what the thing was, really, that queers did. But it was that, the queer thing, he knew Jeremy was asking.

Still, he was not angry, because he really did understand. He understood, quite suddenly, the root truth of it: Jeremy was lonely. His father worked in the Foreign Office somewhere far and hot and steamy, Malaya, maybe. For two weeks of the year Jeremy went away there, and came back to St. Vincent's suntanned and reticent. For two more weeks of the year, his parents, suntanned and preoccupied, whisked him off to a family fortnight in London. That was it. Jeremy was one of the few boys who really did prefer St. Vincent's to the parent-less home of the holidays. He was lonely. David knew loneli-ness as if it were his brother, and he'd recognize it anywhere, even in the previously unbelievably assured person of Jeremy Wedderburn. He only wanted someone to be kind. For a moment David wavered. Just someone to touch him, kindly. He remembered that soul-warming arm on his shoulders. David understood. But try telling Grant Holland any of that.

Jeremy wrapped himself in a towel and made his face very calm and cheerful, and said, "Sorry, old chap. I say, you won't tell anyone, will you?"

David shrugged. He just wanted to get out of there.

"Please don't tell anyone, David." David was dressed and carrying his towel and his toothbrush toward the door.

"David?"

Perverts, Grant Holland thought, but he said nothing, grimly controlling the desire for violence, and left the room. Of course he should have finished the pervert Wedderburn, right there and then, but he had a revulsion for dirtying his hands, so to speak. Besides, he felt just a little sorry for the pathetic little worm.

He would live to regret it.

It was two days later, when his momentary weakness about Wedderburn caught up with him. It was Sunday, the one day of the week with no lessons, and after church parade, no real commitments. It was David's favorite day. He could be alone, roam about the city, or venture into the Yorkshire countryside, or, more frequently, drift about the grounds of St. Vincent's, apparently aimlessly, but in truth invigorated by one of two fantasies. The first, the safe one, was Grant Holland. The second, even more precious, but more dangerous, was at once more realistic and more impossible. He would be walking, just as he was now, and a car would pull up beside him. Sometimes, it was a familiar car, Andrew Wardlaw's big black Humber. His mother would step out and smile and say, "Surprise, David. We were just passing and thought we'd drop in for tea."

"But it's not a visiting day, mother," David would protest. "It's not allowed."

Mother would smile, secretively, but not say anything. Then they would take him to tea, at the Station Hotel in York, where plates of cakes and scones would roll by the gilded pillars on a rosewood trolley. After his fourth meringue, mother would lean forward and say, almost in a whisper, "Pack your things, David, you're coming home with us." That was where it always ended. There was never an explanation of this sudden, wonderful escape, probably because David could never think of an explanation. Had he been able to, he would no doubt have used it, long since, to fuel one of his real-life pleas for release.

There was, however, another, less common version of the same scene, a sort of second-string dream. In that episode, another car would pull up, a vague, undefined car, perhaps a rented car. The door would open and no one would come out, but a voice from inside would call his name. He would step closer, peer in, and there in the shadow within, barely visible, and dim (the dimness was necessary because David had not seen this car's occupant for six years now and the memory was fading) was his father.

"Come on, David," he'd say. "Time to go." Time to go. That was the last thing he'd said when he'd left David's stateroom on the *Queen Elizabeth* in New York harbor at the end of that American summer. And peculiarly, but David was sure of it, the last thing he'd said that day misty years ago when he'd last left Greenshaws Hall. A big, bony man, handsome and gentle, squatting on his haunches, supplely, like another child, and rubbing a child-David's blond head. Time to go. Time to go.

That dream ended even more simply than the first. David just got in the car. And the car drew away. That was it. God knows where it went. Perhaps they drove all the way to America, under the sea. Today, David dreamed neither dream. He lacked the courage. Today he clung to safety, Grant Holland and Jennifer-Clarissa. A wisp of smoke rose from his imaginary Gauloise.

Holland was deep in thought, mulling over the possibility of a secret passage running from beneath the chapel, where Jennifer was held prisoner, to the cellar of an old coaching inn on the banks of the River Ouse. Rumor held of its existence. Could that be the kidnapper's secret route? He flicked ash off the cigarette and, holding it from underneath, drew, savoringly, on the last remnant of it. Still lost in reverie, he tossed the butt away. For a moment, David Wardlaw resurfaced with a wince. Cigarette butts on the cricket pitch; Grant Holland should know better. No, he shouldn't; American and all that. David stepped aside and let Holland get on with it. A canal boat. That was it. A canal boat on the River Ouse. That's how they got her here, through all the police roadblocks. He lit another Gauloise, triumphantly, and made his big mistake.

He'd let himself be seen. He was in open ground and beyond, by the big sycamore beside the cricket pavilion, were the Five. And the Five had seen him. The big man in the battered raincoat strolled on, oblivious, but behind him, the Five, one by one, slipped onto his tail, like shadows, like wolves in the forest. When Holland looked up, sensing them there, it was already too late.

They were beyond the playing fields, out in the open waste ground, the stone buildings of St. Vincent's School gray and distant beyond the trees. Ahead was the emptiness of the motorway, with its impersonal river of metal-cased beings. You could commit murder in front of them and not one would stop. Holland was in trouble, big trouble, and he knew it.

The motorway slashed through the heart of the school common, a late intrusion, postwar, and in the distress it foisted upon the landscape, created a living symbol of the ugliness of postwar change. The English hated it, Holland knew, and conversely he rather liked it; it was forthright and rugged and practical. American, in other words. He often came to stand on the frail steel footbridge that linked the two halves of the severed common and kept alive the old common lane and muse on this ironic modern wonder in the heart of oldest England.

It was for the footbridge he made now, for his escape. He walked quickly, not wanting to be seen as afraid. They were like dogs, the Five; show them fear and they would give chase, slavering for violence. He glanced quickly over his shoulder. There were three. Just three. Where had the others gone?

He was midway across the footbridge, hanging suspended over the oncoming waves of thunderous metal, when he realized he'd been tricked. Two heads suddenly appeared, disembodied, at the far end of the bridge. They grew upward, gaining necks and chests and waists and then legs, as they climbed the concrete stairs. Then there were two at that far end and three at the end he'd come. The sly bastards had sprinted across the forbidden carriageway. He was surrounded by the Five.

Five to one. Pretty tough odds, even for Grant Holland. Suddenly he was infinitely weary. He stubbed out his Gauloise on the metal bridge railing and gauged its height with his eyes. He could fight it out, sure. But what was the point? He'd take a hell of a beating. They'd leave him in the end, bloody and bruised, to make his way and lick his wounds in solitude. He might survive. But in the end, they'd only find him again, another time, another place. There was no winning against the Five.

They were within five yards of him, on either side, grinning casually, hands in pockets, as if out for a quiet stroll; their eyes full of threat.

"Well, well, well," said Nigel Osborne.

"Communing with nature, old chap?" said Hugh Stewart-Smith, stretching up to be as tall as the others.

Grant Holland moved so lightning fast that for an instant they were all caught speechless. In that instant, he had vaulted the guard rail, and clung, wavering in the open beyond, his feet wedged through the uprights of metal, and both hands on the concrete center post. He teetered there, the rushing traffic flashing by, with wind claps of noise. A horn blared.

"I say," said Matthew, "he'll really do it."

"Rubbish. He's just trying it on."

"Oughtn't we to leave off?" Matthew said again. His voice had a weak, awed, small-boy quaver.

Holland closed his eyes, bracing himself for the agony of the next moment. He bent his knees, readying to jump, though his sweaty hands clung yet to the concrete pillar as if they loved it.

"Hold on there, Wardlaw," a suddenly adult boy's voice said, "we're only larking about." Holland looked around, a grim smile playing about his lips. Jeremy Wedderburn, the ringleader, a perverted sadist. He'd get no mercy from him. Damned if he wanted it from *him*. He let go with one hand, swaying, with the high bravery of not caring a damn.

"David, no!" The voice was high and shrill with sudden disbelieving panic. Jeremy jumped toward him, but the guard rail was between.

Grant Holland turned and gave his careless crooked grin for the last time, raised a nonchalant hand and leaped into space.

"David!" a voice shrieked into night.

When David awoke in hospital, there was still a voice saying "David." It was a calm voice, however, and a female voice. His mother's voice. But when he opened his eyes, he didn't see his mother. She was somewhere in the background, it seemed. What he saw was his stepfather, Andrew Wardlaw, MP, a big, tobacco-y brown shape, smelling of cigar smoke, and leaning claustrophobically over him. He felt he couldn't breathe and remembered all those film scenes in which nurses and doctors said imperiously, "Stand back, give him air." Only no one said anything, and there seemed to be neither nurses nor doctors about, and for that matter, he was in a private room, shut off from the ordinary bedded rows of a hospital ward. Andrew Wardlaw and his mother had him all to themselves.

"What's this then, m'boy?" demanded Andrew with the same voice he used for school reports.

David said instinctively, "I'm sorry," not quite knowing yet why he was there, but carrying a distant feeling of guilt into his awakening, as if of a wet dream. But that wasn't it; it was something more complicated and more awful.

"Well, it was a damned fool thing to do, is all I can say," Andrew Wardlaw grunted, seeing David wasn't going to be talkative. He grunted backwards out of sight, and a metal chair creaked as he sat. David's field of vision was narrowed severely by the fact that he could not turn his head. It was in a peculiarly padded brace and he'd seen such things.

"Have I broken my neck, mother?" he said calmly, but panic was rising and he tried desperately to wiggle his toes.

"No, silly," she said calmly. "Actually, you've not broken anything, which is really quite remarkable. Considering." Philippa didn't scare easily. She was used to children riding ponies and coming home from gymkhanas wrapped in bandages.

"A good rest will sort you out," she said. "In a week or so. You've had concussion and strained your back, they tell me. Nothing to worry about."

"Mebbe so," Andrew Wardlaw rumbled. "But it was bloody foolish, is all I can say. If that lorry driver hadn't pulled up when he did. Doesn't bear thinking about, does it?"

David remembered everything then, in a bright, clear rush, the footbridge, and Grant Holland, and the Five. He felt extraordinarily embarrassed that he'd done anything so melodramatic.

"Why, David?" his mother said with gentle command.

David loved her voice and it made him want to answer honestly, which was almost impossible. He shrugged as best one can, lying flat in a neck brace.

After a long pause, he said, "I haven't any friends."

"What absolute rot," Andrew Wardlaw said, instantly. "And what sort of ridiculous reason is that, anyhow? When I was at school, m'boy, if one didn't have friends one made friends. One didn't jump off ruddy bridges."

"I didn't."

"Ridiculous. You were seen. There were five boys watching you. You jumped. The lorry driver even was quite certain. You jumped. Oh, yes, m'boy, the police were called, don't you know? You made the *Yorkshire Post*, front page; I'm sure you're delighted with that. Insane schoolboy dramatics. Your mother was absolutely mortified with embarrassment. Mortified."

David paid no attention to that. He knew who was mortified, and it was not his mother. "I didn't jump," he said stubbornly; because he hadn't. It was Grant Holland. But that was the impossible bit, so he did not say anything more, not even when Andrew Wardlaw said, "This is not getting you out of school, boy. So if that was the idea, you've wasted a lot of people's time."

"I know."

"Surely you have *some* friends, David," Philippa said. David winced as he tried to shake his head. It hurt.

"Balderdash. There was that boy, who was that boy, Philippa, the one who kept coming to the hospital and asking after David?"

"Oh, yes. Oh, he's very nice, not at all like the others. Jeremy Wedderburn, David. He's come every day. Such a nice boy. He's come every day."

David never did go back to school. He used a sudden savage wisdom quite alien to him: his mother, for all her brisk calm, was frightened. She envisioned him as a suicide, which was hardly the case at all. But he let her believe it; cruelly, out of desperation. Andrew Wardlaw had neither time nor sympathy for him, but he'd struck a pivotal weak link in Philippa. They left him alone in the hospital room, and when Philippa returned half an hour later, she returned alone. That was when he learned about the private tutor at Greenshaws, and all the mechanics of his final years' schooling were laid in order.

Delighted, he did not question. Nor did he question why his stepfather did not return, even to say good-bye. He accepted the fact that, when he returned to Greenshaws in a fortnight's time, his mother remained there for some weeks. He was convalescing, and there were necessary arrangements about his new solitary schooling to be made. What he never knew then, and learned by chance only very recently, was that his parents had separated, and Philippa had filed for divorce.

Nothing came of it. Greenshaws was not a healthy sanctuary for Philippa. Her own father was there, and once more he browbeat her back into her marriage. And it all passed blissfully over David's head. He was free.

In ten months he grew five inches. It was as if a physical constriction, like some human cheese press, had been removed. He expanded in body and mind and spirit. Adolescence slipped from him, gradually, but distinctly, and young manhood hardened about him, like his own hardening, lengthening body. He noticed women, real women, and sex became an impossible delicious obsession. He took up sailing and got very good at it. He learned to drive. But Grant Holland died in the hospital in York, and Jennifer-Clarissa died, too.

When, some weeks later, his father's latest book arrived, he read a few pages, found it bland and dull, and laid it, with little thought, aside. But as he did so, he found a strange stirring image in his mind, an image that would likely have never been revived had he not been standing in the dim entrance hall of Greenshaws at the time. It was of a man he hardly knew, a tall, bony, handsome man, squatting on his haunches beside a small boy in the same entrance hall. He was playing with a small red car, rolling the wheels over and over on his long fingers. It was David's car; the man, his father, had given it to him two days before.

"Don't you like the car, David?"

"It's very nice, father."

"But don't you *like* it?"

The boy, David, squirmed restlessly, not knowing what was expected of him. He had so many cars and the red one was rather small and chipped. He liked things new and unchipped, with the excitement of the shop still gleaming on them. He had taken it from his father and smiled dutifully, and put it aside.

V

"Time to go, David," said Stephen.

David sat up in a panic. He'd been nearly asleep with the sun glaring through the thin skin of his eyelids, making a red haze. Now the brilliant white sand looked blue-black, in negative. He waited for his vision to return, rubbing his eyes. The wind had risen, evening strong, but as hot as ever.

"Oh, God. What's the time? Is it late, do you think?"

"Who cares?" Stephen said, but he got up and shook out his towel and then tied it around his waist, low down, like a sarong. David threw his own towel over his shoulder with a quick, flipping ease, and it stayed there, secure on the sweaty skin.

"My mother's coming," he said, to himself really.

"So? Big shit."

David turned around very slowly. He looked very carefully at Stephen Deutsch's big crooked nose, and his moustache, and the two white tips of teeth that showed when he talked, barely moving his mouth. Then David Wardlaw hit Stephen in the mouth between moustache and teeth on his sunburned upper lip.

Unlike Jeremy, Stephen swung right back, glancing his fist across David's ducking cheek. Then they were punching and brawling, slipping barefoot on the soft sand. But it was hot and they were sun-drained and tired.

"What the motherfuck, man?" Stephen said, stepping back querulously, and David lost all momentum. He too stepped back, palms upwards, shaking his head. But he had learned something. He was stronger than Stephen, and better co-ordinated. And he did not have to say sorry, and did not say it. They just began to walk, quietly, back toward the boardwalk stair, their jeans and towels looped over their arms. Stephen rubbed his puffy lip, and sucked at it. He grinned then and suddenly slapped David's shoulder.

"Wait'll we get to 'Nam," he said with his old bravado. "The Yankee Beast and the English Terror. Poor slant-eyed shits won't know where to hide their asses." He slapped David's shoulder again and said, "How about it?"

"I don't know. Wait until I've seen my mother. Then I'll tell you."

"What the fuck? You going to ask permission? Please, mommy, may I join the marines? Fucking *hell*, man."

"No," David said calmly, with the new assurance that came from knowing he could handle Stephen. "But I do wish to tell her first."

Autumn, 1940

Hornchurch

"I simply wish to tell them first. Is that so extraordinarily diffi-cult to comprehend?"

Robert linked his hands about Philippa's waist from behind her back, and felt a rigidity of uncooperation. He did not understand, but he did not want to argue about it, either.

Philippa's nightdress, home-dyed parachute silk, a gift from mysterious sources, was rumpled up above her middle. What Robert wanted was sex, but even were there time he sensed there'd be no willingness.

Anyhow, there was no time. Robert knew that, even in the unlit, blacked-out blackness of the room, even without reaching an arm out to the rickety bedside table and pulling the broken chain of the lamp. He had grown vividly sensitive about time; he had an immense awareness of it always, and could always readily account for any cluster of minutes passed. There just wasn't that much of it about, and he found he'd grown fond of it.

"They'll think I'm a coward," he said finally.

"Nonsense. You're in the RAF."

Robert reached for the light-pull. Brightness circled the bed. Philippa's eyes squinted puffily against it and her mouth quirked at the corners in a tiny smile. She was, even tousled and narrow-eyed, very beautiful.

"Ha, ha," he said. He pushed the dark red eiderdown off and swung his legs over the edge of the bed. It was an old-fashioned bed, high, with wooden slats along the sides and a dark, over-stained headboard carved with two perfunctory roses. He remained sitting there, his bare feet just scraping the cold, pale blue linoleum, weighted down with an immense desire to return to the snug body warmth of bed. It was less weariness than fear.

The bed-sit room was so intensely cozy with familiarity, every object in it—the blue linoleum, the raucous red fake Indian rug, the cracked, peeling window frames with their antiblast latticework of tape behind the panels of blackout cloth, the minuscule two-ring gas cooker on which Philippa would cook their breakfast—reeked with security. As long as they were here they were safe.

Oh, not really, of course, and as proof, Robert could offer the two nights spent in the shelter that week. But they were together, even in the shelter. And as long as they were together, the *they*, the unitedness of them, was safe. They were sure to share the same fate, and both be alive, or both dead, he with his arms yet wrapped around her, and his face in the feathery hair at the nape of her neck, no doubt, but together. It was not death that terrified them both, but separation.

Morning, every morning brought separation. They garlanded each parting with kisses and kindness, lest they make unaware a final farewell in anger. It seemed as if they had lived like this, clinging at night and longing all day, forever. Time was bent and twisted, and telescoped by tension. Just as it seemed there had never been a world without droning engines, sirens and blackouts and a shortage of everything they might desire, especially time, so it seemed there was never a time before now, as if he had always lived with Philippa Hallsworth in the bed-sit on Lime Street, within spitting distance of the aerodrome, hymned night and day by the rumble and roar of the aircraft.

The knowledge of the race of time conversely extended each moment, each hour and each day, and laid an unfair weight on trivialities. They were full of premonitions, and rituals, and luck signs, country Yorkshire and old Ireland rising together from the grave of rationality to hold hands about them in a circle of superstition. Philippa would never wear green nor have it in the flat, even though it meant rejecting her useful prewar civvy jacket, and exiling a perfectly good pair of irreplaceable slipcovers, and simply doing without. Robert walked halfway around the room to place his hat carefully on the mirrored dresser in front of the window, and not on the bed. Nor would he allow a lamppost to inveigle its way between them on the street. Robert worried about Philippa all day, mentally tracing her route by underground and bus through the risky streets, while she worried about Robert in the equally risky air. They worried constantly, to excess, so that, exhausted by it, neither had strength to worry about themselves.

It was a terrible strain on young people, and the strain showed. They were not free ever to express natural anger, natural disagreement even, and as those early emotions sheltered underground, they began their life together resting on a silent disaster, like one of the unexploded bombs that littered the streets of London. They never talked nor planned of the future, which was probably just as well. Foresight would have gotten in the way of happiness.

The war had covered gaps in everybody's lives, papered over with youthful camaraderie all sorts of mundane realities. How would they live? And where? For although Mike, before his death, had charted out a perfectly navigable future for himself and Maisie, Robert in his deeper waters had marked no course. He didn't even have a map. Philippa's home, her parents, her world, were all prewar shadows, dimmed by the frenetic intensity of their vulnerable now. His own life, his truncated career, his severed connections with family, country, and work, had grown insubstantial, remembered ghosts.

Somewhere, he knew, there was still a theater. Indeed, even in London, after that first September scare, the shows had rapidly reopened. Someone was playing in them, someone not in uniform. And in New York there were plenty of someones, who, without any drive for martyred idealism, were walking in the steps he might have taken. He knew because his mother, always his harshest critic, disapproving irrationally of his stage career, now about-faced and used it as a weapon, sending him without comment neatly folded cuttings from the *Times* and *Tribune* cataloguing the growing success of friends and rivals left behind. Her favorites were always those lauding a certain Michael Martin who had, in November of nineteen thirty-nine, made a quite unexpected splash as the Dauphin in a riveting production of *Saint Joan*. "She ought to be his goddamn agent," Robert had cursed recently to Philippa, dropping a crumpled sheet of newsprint to the floor.

"Salvage," she said at once, sharply, and ignoring his temper, watched as he, seething yet, retrieved the paper and rudely flattened it out once more. She took it from him and completed the job with mild concentration, adding it to a neat heap maintained for the WVS collectors.

"You've just saved one billionth of a tree."

"For want of a nail the kingdom was lost," said Philippa firmly. Heaven help the blacksmith, Robert thought, were Philippa Hallsworth king.

But he loved her. Oh, he loved her. He looked about their morning room, shadowy in the corners in the dusty yellow lamplight, strewn with the chaos of last night's lovemaking. Their hoarded half bottle of Scotch whisky sat on the oilcloth-covered table, with two smudged, empty glasses in attendance. His blue tunic was slung across one chair, Philippa's tailored uniform jacket across another. On the pink chintz armchair her regulation WAAF bloomers waved bravely. Passion killers, they were called, but they'd hardly had that effect. Then, hardly anything could.

Every guarded emotion in them—excitement, love, anger, fear—mingled into a river of expression, and the expression was sex. Even Philippa, most firm mistress of herself and situation, bowed before it. On the floor beside the chintz armchair were her shoes, neatly aligned. And in one was the rolled, cherished silk stocking that had accompanied it. But the other stocking trailed across the floor, free and forgotten, like good intentions abandoned. Robert saw it as the ultimate sign of womanly liberation; stockings were more precious than anything, more than chocolate, more than cigarettes, more even than the warm golden whisky. She'd flung it down, and flung herself down, and enjoyed him and herself immensely. She was quite a different woman in bed. No one, no one would ever guess.

Robert least of all. He had gone to their first bedding with apprehensive and high-strung nerves, expecting the barrier of repression that all the cool control must surely reflect. After a tempestuous, exhausting hour, he had lain wet with his sweat and hers, his arms yet around her, watching her calm face asleep. He decided that he did not understand women, or the British, or perhaps British women, half as well as he'd thought. What's more, the learning process was utterly delightful.

After a week he was no wiser nor in any way satiated. He was so aware of the concentrated sexuality of their nights that he spent the whole day acutely conscious of his own private parts and forever visualizing hers.

In short, he was obsessed, and he thought therefore, naturally enough, that he was in love. Love sprang from fear, and love birthed fear. His days were a torment, peaking at the moment he turned the corner of the shabby terraced street of houses and looked with one quick stare, ready to shut his eyes forever. No, it stood, it still stood, she was yet there to return to, and not yet, like Maisie, crushed with all her frail belongings in the cobbled street. The silk stocking recalled Maisie's pink sherry glasses, equal in delicate, treasured absurdity.

It was not unreasonable fear. A mate of his had been married for just nine days before a direct hit on his flat left him widower to an utter emptiness of air, not even a grave to visit, only a vanishment in fire and dust. It happened. It happened all around them. Why should they, either of them, be spared? Maisie was dead. Mike was dead. Porky Piggott lay now in a London hospital. He'd had a bit of a prang, they all said. It was a curiously light little word to describe the fiery chaos that had left Porky burnt to a black golliwog face, noseless, with neither lips nor lids, and pain-filled lizards' eyes staring into air. It happened. And now, with love as a measure of the worth of life, Robert knew solidly the one fact that made living almost impossible, the fact that the younger, freer, more innocent, indeed his own previous self, could ignore. It could happen to him.

It could happen today. In half an hour he would leave the bed-sit, as would Philippa, and they would go their own ways, she to Stanmore, and he, from his breakfast table to the front line. It was, he considered, at least a most civilized way of waging war.

He looked down where Philippa still lay on the bed, her both arms now outstretched in luxuriating comfort.

"I think it's a mistake, Phil," he said.

She smiled to herself without opening her eyes and extended the fingers on each outstretched hand with a half-stifled, private yawn.

"If it's a mistake, we'll make it," she said. Her rich fair hair spread itself in a smudgy fan on the pillow, looking more golden than it was in the yellow light. Her skin was golden, too, and golden also the tiny delicate St. Christopher on its thread-thin chain. It lay, pulse light, in the hollow of her throat. Dignified, delicately enchased, it said clearly, in tones of Anglican refinement: this is no Irish Catholic bauble.

Robert touched her collarbone just below it, and she sat up quickly, and then leaped up from bed and began dressing with brisk efficiency. She made tea, ladling out two level spoons and none for the pot, and stirred semolina porridge for breakfast.

When he sat down to eat, she said with a rather forced smile, "Come along, Robert, be a good chap. You just toddle up to Hovringham on Saturday and we'll meet there. You will see them, and soon enough. Only I just prefer to see them first, alone."

"Prepare them for the shock?"

"Please, Robert, let's not be childish."

"You're treating me like a child," he said, adding unnecessarily, "Like the kid Miss Fauntleroy brings home from the wrong side of the tracks. 'Wait outside and I'll ask nanny if you can come into the kitchen and play.'"

"If you're going to take that tack, Robert, we've nothing more to discuss." It was the last sentence before argument, and Robert, conscious of the day's dangers, capitulated. Philippa accepted victory with a quick smile and a glance at her watch.

"Right. Worsley Arms, Hovringham. Three-thirty. Saturday."

"Scramble," he said.

"Don't be sarcastic, Robert," she said mildly, stuffing lipstick and compact into her handbag. "I was only setting you straight."

Setting him straight seemed, Robert thought, to cover an immense territory, and from anyone else he might call it bossiness. But it seemed to suit Philippa, regardless.

"And, Robert?"

"Yes."

"Keep off religion."

"Aw, come on, now. When have you ever heard me talk about religion?"

"Never. But don't start now. And no politics, either. And whatever you do, don't mention your ambassador."

"I don't often."

"*Or* FDR."

"He's *for* the war."

"And against everything else daddy believes in."

"How about sex?" he said with a large grin.

"Daddy?" Philippa's eyes widened over her tea. She set the cup down with a humorless clatter on its saucer.

"Never mind," Robert said sourly. "Sex, religion, politics. Joke, ha, ha. Get it?"

Philippa still simply looked at him. Then she slipped into her jacket and rinsed her cup under the tap without a word. Robert shrugged. "What do we talk about? The weather?"

"Precisely." She meant it.

"Jesus," said Robert. "I hope it's an awfully nice day."

It wasn't.

Mary Varley, kitchen maid at the Worsley Arms, first saw the young airman when she came from the kitchen to do the blackout. It was only half past four and the paper this week said five-thirty-three, but Mary had to be sure to be done before the afternoon teas. Both blackout and teas were her responsibility, and the warden was very strict.

The November air was gray and damp, the limestone of the village houses furred with wet mist, and the blue slates dripping. The street was scattered with children coming home from school, but even their shouting was muffled by the clammy air. They came in bunches, the Gray children from Hazel Cottage, the Haddeleys from the farm by Greenshaws. There were three of them, swinging satchels like weapons.

Behind them walked the two small evacuees with their pinched East London faces and satchels solemnly still, tucked beneath duffle-coated arms. Mary felt sorry for them; safe but miserable.

The airman was standing by the door, his blue uniform gray in the dimming light. He must have come off the Malton bus that she had heard pass a minute before. She looked up now when a motor vehicle passed; the rationing was thinning them out and Hovringham had grown quieter than ever. Mary came to do the curtains on the glass panes of the door, and he, catching sight of her, clicked the door open and half leaned in.

"May I help you?" Mary said. He kept one eye on the street of the village and said, "I don't know. I mean, I'm not sure." He had a foreign accent, blunt and heavy, but not Polish or Czech like so many around, but transatlantic, which was unusual. Mary saw then, as he stepped fully inside, the RCAF on his shoulder. He was a Canadian, then. She'd never met one before. She saw too that he wore wings and left his top button undone, which, in the new sign language, meant fighter pilot, and she was impressed.

"Are you waiting for someone?"

"A Miss Hallsworth . . . she hasn't telephoned?"

"I'm terribly sorry, sir, we haven't a phone." He looked worried and she said impulsively, "It's Miss Philippa, isn't it?"

"Yes. Yes, it is." He was glad, and surprised, and said, "Do you know her?"

"Hovringham isn't very large," Mary said.

"You haven't seen her? She was supposed to meet me, with her parents. I came out on the bus."

Mary shook her head and said with offhanded calm, "Oh, she'll come, I'm sure." She half turned to go and then stopped and added gently, "Would you like a cup of tea?"

He shook his head and ruffled his short, dark brown hair into spikes. He was handsome enough, with those deep brown eyes and the funny devilish upturnings of the brows, for all his foreign awkwardness. Lucky Miss Philippa.

Mary was not jealous. She and Miss Philippa would never be

rivals over men. There was a certain invisible line through the Hovringham vale that began at the doorstep of Greenshaws Hall and went roughly over the chimney of the cowman's cottage where Mary had been born. The boys who courted Miss Philippa Hallsworth and those who courted Mary Varley didn't cross that line.

Anyhow, Mary had a boy of her own. He wasn't a fighter pilot, though. He was out in the North Atlantic somewhere, on a destroyer. Only he couldn't tell her which.

There was a crunch of tires on the cobbled road beyond. Mary lifted the black curtaining and peered through the glass pane. "See, yon's Mr. Hallsworth now, in the motor."

"Oh, God," the young man said, and joined her at the door, peering over the shoulder of her black dress. A black Bentley was rumbling past the winding crooked row of gray-brown limestone houses. He stood straight and tugged at his tie and said, "Look, miss, do I look all right? I mean, I've never met them."

Mary turned back to face him, dropping the curtain across the glass. At once the airman, Miss Philippa, the meeting, and its purpose were all clear to her. He looked terrified. She stepped closer and gently straightened his collar and patted his ruffled hair down with a young motherly hand. "Oh, aye, right gradely," she said softly. "Never you worry. They'll think you just grand."

Then she whisked off to her windows about the inn, blackening the evening out, and not believing her own words. She'd lived her whole life in the same sturdy Yorkshire vale as the Hallsworths of Greenshaws. She knew, as well as any, the kind of man the Hallsworth women wed.

Philippa came first through the door. She still wore her WAAF uniform, and her fair hair fluffed out on either side of the shiny-peaked cap. Her face shone with the latening light, and her stride was strong. She looked like a poster girl, so pretty and brave he wanted to cry. She crossed the hallway in two long strides and kissed his cheek lightly, looking half over her shoulder the while.

"Quick, darling, daddy's fussing with the car." She ducked into the lounge, dimly lit only by the smoking wood fire, hurrying him with her. She turned then to face him. Her mouth was set in too delicately held a smile. Her eyes were narrow and uncertain. Robert said quietly, "You haven't told them."

"I tried, Robert, I did try. Daddy was so . . . oh, the gardener was giving him trouble and he's utterly impossible when any of the servants . . . there are so few now."

"Phil, we only have half an hour. You've got to tell them . . . they have to know. And we've got to be on that last bus back to Malton or we'll miss . . ."

"We'll tell them, Robert," she said sharply. "I told you we would. We will tell them together. That will be better anyhow." She looked again over his shoulder and there was the crunch of a footstep on the gravel and the sound of a heavy boot on the scraper at the door. "One thing, Robert . . . your name . . . I've told them Zolan . . ."

"But it's not my real name, Phil. It's just my stage name and God knows when I'll use it again."

"But you do use it, Robert, sometimes." She sounded a little desperate. "Be a brick. Use it now."

"But why?" he said with that querulous tone that precedes argument, and Philippa said sharply again, "Oh, Robert. See sense. Zolenski's so . . . oh, you know, what with all the Poles about and daddy . . ."

"The Poles are our allies," Robert said stiffly.

"Oh, don't be such a prig, darling. Zolan sounds better. That's all."

The door rattled open and they were both suddenly silent.

"Philippa? Where the devil is she now?"

"I'm here, daddy. We're in the lounge."

"Harold. Please." The second voice was female and hushed

rather than soft. It was the first exchange Robert ever heard
between Philippa's parents and it was prophetic. A marching
army and a buffer state: that was the Hallsworths, man and
wife.

Robert's mother always said, "Beware of a man who leads
with his chin; his head's bound to be following far behind."
Harold Hallsworth was a chin leader. It was a big, broad chin
that jutted its way into the room. He was a big man, too, the
kind of big man whose weight is all in the top quarter, in heavy
shoulders and thickened neck, and massive forward-swung
arms. The head was massive, too, and what hair there was
was stubbled short into an anonymity of color. His legs seemed
stumpy, the whole off-balance, as if pitched forward and
about to fall. But he wasn't about to fall anywhere, not Harold
Bradley Hallsworth.

He was tall for all that heavy width, too, and his small
and very sharp blue eyes met Robert's exactly level.

"Mummy, daddy, please meet Robert Zolan," Philippa said
like a sweet, well-mannered child. Mr. Hallsworth leaned
farther forward and shook Robert's hand and mumbled something quite indecipherable ending in a short loud nervous
laugh. Mrs. Hallsworth shook Robert's hand with one strong
downward stroke and said, "Philippa has told us so much
about you." But Robert knew it was only a phrase; no doubt
all Philippa's young men had been received with the same
rumor of acclaim.

She was a bony, homely person in a gray tweed suit and
heavy ribbed brown stockings, with a silk square tied triangu-
larly over her hair. Her face was weather-burned leathery by
a fondness for the hunt.

Robert found the tie of blood bewildering; this fair and
supple girl, daughter to so stolid a gray Yorkshire pair. He
did not, then, see that mother and daughter had eyes and cheekbones exactly alike, and the gay lifted chin of Philippa, so
challenging and bold, was direct descendant of the battleship

prow of her father. And that only age, and attitude, stood between.

Mrs. Hallsworth said, "Oh, splendid, dear. Shall we have tea and then we can all talk." She was looking at her husband the while, a nervous look, as bright and brittle as a butterfly on a pin.

"Jolly good idea," Philippa said, distractedly, and she led Robert off, behind her parents, through the long hallway with its graceful stair and carved oak benches. Robert's eyes were drawn bemusedly to the ugly black silk horse on Mrs. Hallsworth's head square. It leered at him with chocolate brown eyes, white-specked in the center, and flared silk nostrils. He thought it god-awful. It had cost three guineas in Harrods. Not that Mrs. Hallsworth would ever mention such a thing, or indeed that the knowledge would have meant much to Robert.

He could not make sense of Mrs. Hallsworth. Philippa's father in his tweed hacking jacket and plus fours was precisely what he expected. But her mother? He had expected something there, too, God knows what, but something different. Perhaps a lady like those he had glimpsed on yacht club lawns in black crepe dresses and diamond ear clips and little hats perched like bird's wings on their heads. But this?

Perhaps it was the war. After all, it was a time for austerity. But following the broad flat shoes of Philippa's parents, he sensed that austerity was no wartime sufferance for them. They were rich, all right, but somehow austerity was still their native state.

He tried to envision them in their home, the home they had pointedly not opened to him. He thought of them sitting at breakfast, or supper, or listening to the radio, like his parents when pop was still alive. But he could not see them at all.

His eyes caught the red-carpeted stair with its white balustrade, beckoning upward. Beyond were bedrooms with quiet fires and high coverleted beds.

If only they were alone, Phil and he. No parents, and no

weekend pass running short, and most of all no war. Just long days to walk on the gray rainy moors and long nights in the coverleted bed. And peace, and love. He felt so lonely and so angry, time slipping, flying, fleeing, and Philippa there and he here and that solid, dumpy, arch-voiced pair between them. He cast the black silk horse a bitter look, as if it were the cause of it all.

The dining room was long and low-ceilinged, the walls decorated with an elegant green Regency stripe. The windows were many-paned and the girl, Mary Varley, was busy closing out the last light with black curtains before lighting the wall lamps. Small, intimate prints were dotted about the walls, and except for the number of white-linen-covered tables, one would think oneself in a private house. They seated themselves at a round table of Mr. Hallsworth's choice and then promptly moved, upon his discovery of a draft across his neck.

"Can't be too careful of drafts," he said sharply, settling again at the second table. "Worst thing in the world, drafts."

Mary Varley brought tea, and a cake stand of silver and flowered china. But there was just scones on it and margarine. Mrs. Hallsworth poured tea while they spread margarine on scones and Philippa smiled distantly, like she was with another party entirely.

"Harry's in Singapore," Mrs. Hallsworth said.

"My brother Harry," Philippa said to Robert.

"Royal Navy," said Mr. Hallsworth.

"Have you any brothers, Robert?" Mrs. Hallsworth said. Robert shook his head.

"No. A sister; she's married. She lives in Washington."

"How nice," said Mrs. Hallsworth.

Robert sipped his tea slowly, declining to put milk in it in the English way and finding it consequently far too strong and bitter. His eyes were on Philippa, but she seemed always to be looking the other way.

"Mrs. Hallsworth," he said finally, "Philippa and I . . ."

"Oh, do tell me, mummy," Philippa cried suddenly, "how is Dinky?"

"Oh, splendid, splendid." That was Mr. Hallsworth. "In foal, you know."

"Oh, jolly grand. And Ruffles?"

"Philippa," Robert said, "we've no time . . ."

"Do tell me about Ruffles."

"Oh, feeling rather sorry for himself, you know. Poor wretched Ruffles." Mrs. Hallsworth spread another scone as she talked. "Chickenpox."

Philippa said, "Poor old Ruffs."

Robert cut in quite sharply, "What *is* Ruffles?"

"My cousin, silly."

"But Dinky?"

"My pony. Oh, *Rob*ert. Oh, such a pet she is, too. Miles too small for me, of course."

"Pony had six legs for years," Mr. Hallsworth laughed with the most animation he'd yet shown, his short, half-swallowed laugh. "Couldn't pry her off it."

"I couldn't bear to give her up for years after I'd grown out of her. Bumble has her now."

"Bumble?"

"Bumble. Amanda, my little sister."

"She used to buzz," Mr. Hallsworth said. "When she was younger. Of course."

Robert swallowed his tea in a gulp. "Mr. Hallsworth, there is something . . ."

"Oh, dear," Mrs. Hallsworth cried, "do look at the time. We promised Mrs. Gray we'd be back for early dins. She's on fire watch or something. Must fly, pet. Anyhow, your bus will be along in another minute."

Robert stood up suddenly. He had to do something. God knows when they'd get all this way north again. "I'm afraid we . . ."

"Just a moment, m'boy," Mr. Hallsworth said suddenly, and

his voice was subtly changed; so much so that Robert abruptly imagined their purpose had been revealed, after all.

"Of course, sir," he said quietly.

Mr. Hallsworth led him out the dining room door and down the long corridor, past the lounge with its darkened windows, soft lamplight now gentling the flicker of the fire. The corridor continued to a French window at its far end, that too now blacked out with curtaining. On the wall were a series of old photographs, all of groups of men lined up solemnly in long-distant summer sun.

Mr. Hallsworth pointed to one and said, "Perfectly splendid, these old photographs, thought you'd like to see them. That's the Yorkshire team of nineteen twenty-three. That's Wilf Rhodes there, m'boy."

Robert peered politely in the dim light at the faded line of men in cricket flannels.

"Of course, that won't mean so much to you, I don't suppose."

"I'm afraid not."

"No," Mr. Hallsworth said, almost to himself. Then he said aloud, "My family have lived in Greenshaws Hall for six hundred years."

"That's amazing, sir."

"Umm. You know I do think it's absolutely splendid, a young fellow like yourself volunteering to help out with this scrap of ours."

"You mean the war?"

"Umm. The war. Not your war at all yet. Not ever if that bastard Kennedy . . . but that's another matter."

"Was there something you wanted . . ."

"Only this. Philippa's a fine girl, well-bred, intelligent. Good sense of duty. No nonsense in her. Not impulsive or flighty. But well, it's wartime, you know, women get . . . you know. Decent of you to escort her about and all. And I do respect you, m'boy, the job you're doing. But you must understand. There are, after all, chasms between you. There is no question, absolutely no question, of anything serious . . . no question at all of you marrying Philippa. Understood?"

Robert drew his breath in, idly touching the faded photograph. He closed his eyes and then opened them and said softly, "This is going to be tricky, Mr. Hallsworth. You see, Philippa and I, well, we *are* married. We were married last week, at the Registry Office in Caxton Hall."

There was a long silent pause, in which Mr. Hallsworth's chin worked and his eyes half shut in a grimace. His hand, remaining still with its forefinger caressing the portrait of Wilf Rhodes, seemed to have ceased to be part of his presence, a stray into another time. Then he said, still without turning, "You damned oversexed Yankee bastard."

Robert drew back with tightened mouth and whispered, "Mr. Hallsworth, we're *married*. We didn't do anything wrong."

"What right? What right? Sniveling little son of some Yankee greengrocer, or whatever . . . what right had you to propose to a girl like Philippa? My daughter? How dare you?"

"She loves me. We love each other. Mr. Hallsworth, dammit, we've tried to tell you . . . we've been trying all afternoon."

"And why now? Like this? Why not before? Before you tricked the girl . . ."

"*She* wanted to get married down there; she said it would be"—his voice grated suddenly—"'a jolly lark' to elope and to come and tell you after. Christ."

"Watch your tongue, boy. This is no Yankee whorehouse."

"Mr. Hallsworth, I'm . . ."

"Not a word to her mother, boy. The shock will . . . she has a weak heart."

"For Christ's sake, we're only married."

"Only." Mr. Hallsworth grew very calm and then said evenly, "You will separate at once from my daughter. If you've not, God forbid, got her pregnant. An annulment will be arranged."

"No. No, it will not, Mr. Hallsworth."

"Don't worry. I'm a wealthy man. We will make it worth your while." He turned away with surety, the conversation complete.

"You bastard," Robert said. "You pompous damned snob."

Mr. Hallsworth whirled about with a hand raising and tightening into a fist. There was a sharp, tense silence up and down the corridor, still as the browned old cricketers in their long-ago rows. Then the dining room door clicked and swung open.

"Harold, I do really think it is time to go."

"Yes. Of course." Mr. Hallsworth was at once of amiable voice, waving a big airy hand. "We were just coming, m'dear." He turned his back toward the corridor and whispered to Robert, "I'll settle this with you, one way or another. I'll be on to your CO for a start."

Robert said coolly, "I had his permission. Of course. Philippa is over the age of consent. It is a private matter. I am really sorry, sir, really sorry it couldn't have been a happier one. We are living in a bed-sit in Hornchurch. You may visit, if you wish. I don't think we will be back here."

He walked away from Mr. Hallsworth to the door of the inn. There, Mrs. Hallsworth, making no comment of what anger clearly showed on his face, shook his hand again and said how absolutely splendid it had been to meet him. Mary Varley flicked out the lights in the hallway and opened the door for him. He went out and stood alone. She could see only dim outlines in the dusk, but his posture alone, stiff, hunched into his jacket, told her the outcome of that meeting over tea. Oh, she could have told him herself, Harold Hallsworth was a hard, cold man. But what good would it have done him? She was sorry, though, he had seemed so very nice.

Mr. Hallsworth kissed his daughter stiffly on the cheek, and Mrs. Hallsworth did the same, a brushing peck.

"Bye, mummy."

"Cheerio, bunny. Be good." They turned away and walked

without another word to the black Bentley, waiting in the evening by the vine-colored limestone wall. Robert wanted to shout, "For God's sake, kiss her, cry, she's your daughter and she's going to war . . ." But the cool Yorkshire evening swallowed them, and they kept walking, as calm and as cool as the sky.

They stood up all night on the train to London. The Malton train had been delayed, late into York, and they'd only just made their connection. The York-London train was crammed full of young men and women, a good half in uniform and most of the rest, though yet in civvies, with that uncertain transient air of the newly called up. Here and there among them was an apparent oddity, some businessman in pinstriped suit, a matron in a prewar hat, going about prewar affairs. But even they clunked along the corridors with civilian gas masks, cardboard-boxed, swinging from their shoulders.

Corridors and compartments too, where third-class passengers sat four to the three-abreast seats, were jumbled with canvas kit bags, pale in the dim light. Beside Robert, a young sailor sat on his, playing cards with a mate.

Philippa stood in front of Robert, and he leaned with his back against the brass handrail across the blacked-out windows. Beyond, nameless dark places rushed by with the clattering of steel on steel and the occasional high lonely shriek of the whistle. Philippa's hair was soft against his face, and pale blue in the dim blue light.

She said, not for the first time, "Really it will be all right. Daddy's a pet, actually. He'll come around when he's calmed down." She steadfastly refused to cry and Robert grew angry.

"You knew. I can see it now. You knew just how he'd react. You were afraid to face him. That's why we got married first, isn't it? Because you knew he wouldn't give you permission, if you'd asked."

"Oh, Robert. Of course I didn't know." Her voice was very

hollow. She shifted in front of him, and her gas mask nudged uncomfortably against his thigh.

He ignored her answer and said, "It was wrong, Phil. It was wrong to trick him, and spring it on him. And it was wrong of you to lie to me."

"I didn't *lie*, Robert. I didn't *lie*. How was I to know?"

"For God's sake, Phil. You could tell, just looking at him. You can see a mile away he's an impossible snob."

"No. That's not fair. That's terribly American, you know. Americans all think we're snobs. Just because they don't understand how we do things."

"Now you're sounding like your father."

"Really, Robert. I don't think there's any need to talk about this further." She turned her face away, though he couldn't see it in the dim light. But suddenly he could imagine her chin jutting out, like her father's. He didn't like thinking of her looking like that.

"You're ashamed of me," he said pettily.

"Don't be ridiculous."

"You're ashamed of my name."

"You're being a dreadful bore, Robert. I am not ashamed of your name. Any more than you are. But you've changed it, yourself, and you know that."

"For my work. So have Claudette Colbert, and Judy Garland, and . . ."

"Why?"

Robert hesitated, and then said quickly, "It just sounds better."

"Have you ever thought why it sounds better?" Robert was quiet, and Philippa continued sharply, "The trouble with you Americans is you're so impossibly self-righteous. You talk as if names and titles and all meant nothing to you, and the truth is it means more to you than to anybody. You're the worst snobs in the world. Look at that dreadful Mrs. Simpson."

"Your king married her."

"More fool he."

The sailor on the kit bag looked up suddenly, shrewdly, and half grinned. "Enjoying your 'oneymoon, sarge?" he said. But he laughed, and then Robert had to laugh, and Philippa softened and giggled, and then the corridor was convulsed as a soldier, kit bag over his shoulder, began to struggle through as the train slowed for yet another unnamed station.

After he'd passed, they resumed their places and shifted the suitcase from one side of Robert's legs to the other, and re-arranged the gas masks to poke into different parts. Robert said, laughing, and kissing her hair, "How's the dreadful Mrs. Zolenski?"

Philippa stiffened for only a second or two and then relaxed and sighed and stretched herself almost sensually against him, and said, "Oh, wizard."

Then she twisted around and kissed him, passionately, and said in a whisper so that the cockney sailor would not hear, "I don't give a damn about daddy. I love you, there's nothing he can do to stop that."

"He can cut you off without a penny, sweetheart, and I kind of reckon he will."

"I don't care." She shrugged, then turned again, leaning comfortably against him. "We don't need his money. I don't care about money. I never have. It hardly matters, does it?"

Robert laughed softly, bemused.

"You've never been without it, sweetheart. How can you possibly know?"

VI

"How can you possibly know?" Robert said lightly. He put down his drink, a second gin, and then moved the sweating glass onto a folded newspaper. He was annoyed and did not want it to show.

"How can I *know*?" Paul said. "It's so obvious. The boy is utterly transparent."

"I don't think so," he said.

"Oh, not to you. You're too involved. I can see because I'm not involved. I mean, what's it to me what the boy does?" Paul turned his glass around, studying the droplets of condensed water mercilessly. Robert said nothing. Paul said, "Of course he'll give up Cambridge. Of course he will. The boy adores you. He'll make any sacrifice to please you, and if you don't want him at Cambridge—which is *pa*tently obvious, by the way—then he'll do without. He's utterly devoted to you."

"A moment ago you were telling me he was utterly devoted to his 'English antecedents,' as you put it, and shouldn't be separated from them."

"Well, of course," said Paul. He fished around in his gin and tonic with a transparent plastic mixer, freeing his lemon slice from a log jam of ice cubes. "You mustn't be selfish. You have to share the boy, after all."

"Share him?" Robert said. "*Share* him. What have I been doing for the last seventeen years? One weekend while he was still in diapers and his grandparents were putting his name down for one stuck-up school after another. Then one seven-week summer vacation when he was ten. And at last, hallelujah, I've had my son for two whole months. And now his mother's come clear across the Atlantic to fetch him. That's sharing. It's like sharing the swimming pool with a school of piranha."

Robert stood up, kicking the green wicker magazine rack out of his way. "Love shares," he said. "Those people don't share. They can't. They can't reach up or down to people. Or sideways, either. You're either *of* them and they'll stand by you, no matter what goddamn thing you do, or you're not of them and they'll not open up to you if you're Jesus Christ. Fine. Fuck them. But they've got no right to my children." Robert crossed the room to the bottle of Gordon's on the drainboard. "They've got my daughter already." He leaned over the stove and lifted the lid of the rice pan automatically, putting it back without properly looking at the contents. "You know what she said to me on the phone? You know?"

Paul shook his head, looking downward at the silver medallion resting on his white sweater.

"She said, 'You still churning them out, daddy?' You know that voice they use, like they were all thirty-five years old. Still churning them out. My work. She's twenty years old. Dammit. She says that to me." He poured another gin and found a flattening half bottle of tonic, and captured two slippery melting ice cubes from the sink. "You want another?"

Paul shook his head again. "You're not exactly Boris Pasternak," he said.

Robert got angry and waved his glass, spilling cold gin on his hand and wrist. "I know that. I know I'm not damned Boris Pasternak. Or anyone else she reads at her damned university. I'm not looking for flattery, for God's sake. But, Paul, listen, she's twenty years old. A little goddamned respect, maybe?"

"Why are you so hard on young people?" said Paul.

"You *can't* say that. You can't *say* that. Mary *Jo's* twenty," he said, regarding that the clear clincher.

But then Paul said, "Does Mary Jo respect you?"

"Sure," Robert said, a little weakly. "Sure she does. Anyhow, she's not my daughter."

"She's somebody's daughter. Does she respect them? Do you think they're happy about her? What would you do if your daughter was living with some forty-year-old writer?"

Robert thought that a small, unnecessary malice, and said, "We're older than that now, aren't we?"

"Speak for yourself."

There was a petty silence. Robert sat down again. He said, retrieving adulthood, "They have my wife. They have my daughter. I want my son. Is one out of three so much to ask?"

"So you're going to keep him. No matter what the cost."

"What cost, for God's sake? What cost?" Sometimes Paul's delight in melodrama was a genuine irritant.

"His education."

"So. He can go to college here. I'll pay. I'm still churning them out, remember?"

"You'll *pay*. You'll *pay*. Sometimes, Robert, you are the total philistine. You'll pay for what? It's *Cambridge* they're talking about."

"I've noticed."

"They can give him *Cambridge*, don't you understand?"

"All right. So I can give him Columbia, maybe. Or at least the state university, if that's all he's up to. At least it will be on his own merit. And he'll still get an education."

"Oh, of course. An education. But the tradition, the elegance, *Cambridge*." Paul expanded emotionally about ivy and dreaming spires.

"That's Oxford," Robert said with his back turned. He was standing looking out the fly-specked window, watching the boys, David and Steve, returning. Their heads were close together. They were talking. Paul seemed not to hear.

"Customs and traditions everywhere. 'Oh, how but in custom and in ceremony are innocence and beauty born?' " He
raised a rhetorical eyebrow, squinting then into the late sun
sifting through the dusty air.

Robert turned around, went to sit down and then, remembering something, he went into the bedroom and rummaged
a while in a chest of drawers. He came out, unsatisfied, and
began poking into cupboards and investigating corners of
bookshelves. When he answered Paul looked up in surprise,
having thought the conversation closed.

"It would be fine," he said, "if it ended there." He thought
a moment more and said, "Custom and ceremony might very
well father a certain kind of refined innocence, but from the
moment of its birth it is ever afterward nannied by smugness
and self-satisfaction. Sure, tradition is beautiful; if it only
stopped at dressing for dinner and passing the port. [*The port
is red and goes to the left*, Harold Hallsworth rumbled across
the distant Greenshaws mahogany.] But it doesn't stop there.
It never stops. It invades every aspect of their life and it ends
up completely stultifying."

Robert was on his hands and knees poking into the dark
depths of shelving at the floor of a home-built cupboard by the
door. "They all seem to be suffering an overdose of toilet training," he said. He stood up, not having found the thing yet.
He stood in the middle of the room, remembering.

"You've been there," he said. "Didn't you notice? Didn't
you notice how they all have a time for everything? A strict
time. Morning tea time. Breakfast time. Lunch time. *Afternoon*
tea time. Drinks time. [*Drinkies, everyone*, Mrs. Hallsworth
brayed from afar.] Walkies for the dog time. They only
perform at goddamn potty time."

Robert got agitated with sudden unlikely anger and waved
his hands in the air. "I'll tell you a story. I was driving once,
from Bridlington up to Edinburgh. Early morning. And I
stopped somewhere in the Borders, at a hotel. I wanted some
coffee. It was twenty to ten. There was a sign on the door:

MORNING COFFEE SERVED IN THE LOUNGE. Fine. I went in. The place was deserted up front. And *that's* typical. They don't care if they do business or not. You want to stay in their hotel? Well, you work for it. Find the receptionist. Persuade her to talk to you. Still, that's another thing. Anyway, I wandered into the dining room. I could *smell* the goddamn coffee. There were, like, twelve tables, and maybe two of them filled. People finishing breakfast. And there was a waitress, in a black dress, white frills, the whole works, pouring coffee. You know, going around the tables, offering.

"She said, 'Can I help you?'

"I said, 'Yes, I'd like some coffee.'

"She said, 'No.' "

"No?" said Paul.

"No. 'Why not?' I said.

" 'It's not coffee time.'

" 'You're pouring coffee.'

" 'Yes. But I'm doing breakfasts.' It was a full pot. You know, a glass thing. No one at the tables wanted any anyhow. They'd all just said no.

" 'Coffee's in the lounge,' she said. 'At ten.'

"She was holding the goddamn pot in her hand. There were twenty cups on the sideboard. But the leap of faith it took to actually pour it twenty minutes before coffee time was beyond the reaches of her soul." He shrugged. "England, their England."

Then he remembered where it was and went straight to the shelf behind the wood stove where the kerosene lamp sat on a pile of nautical charts. It was there, underneath. Pleased, he lifted it out carefully, still neatly folded. He said in a conciliatory tone, "Now, isn't he better since he came here? Isn't he? You know what I mean? He looks like a kid now, not Noel Coward shipwrecked in Brighton."

Paul smiled, a fond reminiscent smile. "He did look funny that day on the ferry. Those trousers! And the crease. One sort of expected a *pith* helmet or something."

"Right," said Robert. He had laid the thing beside his drink on the table and sat for a moment on the edge of his chair. "And what do you think will happen if he goes back? And make no mistake, this is my last chance with him. Four or five years and he'll be irrevocably theirs. Cambridge, law probably, a City job; ten years, a Tory short list (if his stepfather has his way); fifteen years, he'll be braying about the countryside in a sheepskin coat with a sheepskin wife with angle irons for hips and a voice like a constipated seagull. Children with a nanny, or at least a Swedish au pair, Harrow for the boys, Roedean for the girls. He'll end up a young edition of damned Wardlaw; summers in the Highlands a-chasing the deer, and winters somewhere in England, a-chasing the votes."

"David in Parliament," Paul exclaimed delightedly. "Wouldn't he be gorgeous!"

"I won't have my son hear-hearing in a pinstripe suit," Robert shouted. He got up suddenly, wanting to avoid the boys whose voices drifted from the boardwalk. He picked up the folded thing and went out the door. He didn't answer when Paul called, "Where are you going?" and Paul got up as well, drink yet in hand, and followed. Robert darted around the corner of the deck, out of sight of the boys. He began climbing the wooden slat stairs to the flat roof. He heard Paul's footsteps, slapping in Mexican basket-weave sandals, behind him, and the light clink of the diminished ice cubes in his glass.

The wind blew, strong and hot, across the asphalted roof and the roar and hiss of the surf was louder. Below, the boys' voices came up, cheery and foolish with the slang of two countries. David was chanting football slogans, a working-class thing, an affectation. Robert said, experimentally, "How come you want him to go back so much, anyhow?" And when Paul stayed stubbornly silent, he added meanly, "I thought you were rather fond of him."

"Of course I'm fond of him. He's your son. Isn't he? I don't *want* him to go back, to *go* anywhere. I want him to stay right here. I want everyone to stay right here," he burst out with sudden emotion. "I hate everyone going away." He sounded suddenly on the edge of tears.

"You all right?" Robert said, deliberately not looking at Paul too quickly. He stopped fiddling with the rope and its metal dog-leash catch on the flagpole.

"Yes, I'm all right." Then he burst out again, his voice rising and wavering, "It's this damn business about Steve and the marines."

Robert put his palms flat on the hot wood of the railing. He was a little exasperated and a little scared. The silly dangerous topic was alive again. He should have guessed, heard it coming in the cresting of Paul's voice, and steered the conversation away. "What's that got to do with David?" he said at last.

"It *is* David. Don't you see? David's the whole cause of it. Steve only started in talking about it again after David came. He's been so disturbed since David came. He's trying to prove something all the time. All this talk about women and violence." Paul screwed up his eyes, squinting at the sun.

Robert ran the rope around the pulley on the flagpole and found the clips. He unfolded a flap of the cloth and began working them, stiff and salt corroded, into the dull silver eyes of the fabric.

"He's very impressed by David," Paul said finally. "David's very impressive."

"He's a kid," Robert said sourly. The first clip clicked into place. Below he heard the pump whir and the reverberation of stirring water in the header tank on the roof.

"Are they in the shower?" Paul said suddenly. Robert nodded, struggling with the second clip.

"Together?"

Robert dropped the rope. It clanked, musically, windblown against the pole, a heart-familiar summer sound, conjuring his childhood and the tall rust-spotted pole before the Zolenski greenhouses. He said eventually, "I damn well hope so. My pump's on its last legs." He had gathered up his rope and made his hands busy before he said, as casually as he could, "Are you and Steve—is it physical?" He left it there lamely; liberality had not yet reached his tongue.

"Of course not," Paul said, sounding both hurt and shocked. "He's just a boy. An innocent."

When Robert said the next thing on his mind, he was reminded even more strongly that Paul was a tight moral conservative who on frequent occasions put on a blue suit and a narrow striped tie and drove to Great Barrington for dinner with his father and mother. It did well to remember that from time to time. Robert, for the moment, had forgotten.

He spoke suddenly, boldly, as if a shocked corner of his own self resided within the tense white figure hunched over the seaward railing. He said, "I don't think that's the reason David wants to stay. I don't think Steve is, or the marines. I don't think I am. I think Mary Jo is the reason."

Robert shook the tangled ropes and the cloth snapped free, unfolding quickly on the hot sea wind.

"Oh, impossible," Paul said. "He can't be. It isn't decent, is it? He wouldn't. Not David. I know him. He wouldn't. It's practically incest. Not David." He saw the flag behind Robert, but was too intent to comment.

"You seem to know him better than I do," Robert said.

"I think I do," Paul said honestly; then with gathering conviction, "I do. We understand each other. We're artists. Of course we understand each other."

"Bullshit," said Robert calmly. "If you're an artist, then even I'm an artist. But what the hell artistic has David ever done?"

"He doesn't have to *do* anything," Paul said at once. "He's just a boy. He'll *be* an artist. Later." He grew stubborn with illogical emotion and said again, "*We* understand. We've understood each other perfectly from the moment he sat down beside me on the ferry. We're kindred souls."

June, 1963
Long Island

The man beside David wore denim jeans, rolled up to his knees, and what David would call a vest, an undergarment. Only the vest was dark red and had a little border of purple around the neck and armholes. The man was handsome, with a dark, movie-star face, and short, curling black hair, shiny in the fierce sun. The end of his nose was sunburned red, and he was rubbing cream on it, smoothing over the white curls of peeling skin.

He had looked at David when David came up the wooden steps from the lower deck, incongruous in long sports trousers and a long-sleeved white shirt and his face untanned. The man put away the cream and covered his head with a yellow straw hat with fringes on the brim. He looked at David again as David walked, sideways, down the narrow aisle between the rows of benches, with his leather suitcase bumping awkwardly between.

It was a Friday afternoon in June and the *Fire Island Princess* was crowded with weekenders. The sun was white hot, and the sky white-hazy, like the sky in France, David thought. His eyes were weak against it, from his sleepless night flight. The man with the straw hat moved aside so that David might sit down.

"Thank you very much," David said, settling the suitcase behind his knees.

"Oh. You're English, aren't you?" The man spoke beautifully, like an actor.

"Yes. Yes, I am." David looked up, surprised. He was not yet long enough abroad to realize how markedly his voice set him apart. The man in the hat smiled and reached to shake David's hand. David thought that sudden, but accepted the gesture, and then the man said, "Paul Botvin."

David said, "David Wardlaw," hesitating slightly. Somehow, on his own father's native soil, or native seas—for now the ferry was slapping against the bay chop at the mouth of the river—it seemed a little wrong to use that other, newer name.

"Do tell, how *is* Merry England?"

David shrugged, a seventeen-year-old's embarrassment at any style other than the prosaic. "About the same, I suppose." Self-consciously he unbuttoned the cuffs of his shirt and rolled the sleeves up to elbow height. He had, already, the Englishman's aversion to public undressing, but the heat on the sunbaked deck was unbearable.

"Ah, England. So long. So long." The man sighed and stretched his legs out, long, slim, sunbrowned legs. David saw he was barefoot. His left foot just brushed the bare calf of the man across from him. He did not apologize, as David would have done. That man, who had sat steadfastly silent throughout their conversation, suddenly emerged from behind his *New Yorker* magazine, as not a stranger but a companion, small and middle-aged, with fair thinning hair and a tired, soft-wrinkled face. He said without preface, "It rained every day. You had bronchitis and coughed and wheezed the whole time."

"I didn't *wheeze*," the black-haired man said sharply. "I did *not* wheeze. I was really quite ill, actually." That much was said suddenly to David, as an aside. "I was ill when I *went*. I had been working *terribly* hard, of course. One does." David, his ear yet innocent, did not hear the slight English accent affected for his benefit. The companion said, "Oh. One does. *One* always does. One is becoming too, too Noel Coward."

The black-haired man crossed his legs, withdrawing the left one carefully so that this time it did not brush the other's calf. He half turned in the seat, away from the companion, and more intimately facing David.

"Of course, you'll simply not be accustomed to the sort of

rudeness one finds . . . some places. I do fear you are in for some terrible shocks. England is so civilized."

David shrugged again. He sat a little straighter, trying to narrow his broad shoulders so they did not, with the rocking of the boat, brush now and again against those of the black-haired man.

"I suppose so," he said. "Rather boring, also."

"Oh," a small laugh. "The young. The young. Always looking for excitement."

"They seem to know where to find it, too," said the companion with a sharp obliqueness.

"Michael," the black-haired man said suddenly, "I'm really getting quite fed up. Quite fed up." Michael whipped up his magazine with a crack of opening pages. The dark-haired man smiled, a smile of gentle apology. A smile for David.

"Tell me, what brings you to the provinces?"

"I'm going to stay with my father. In Water Island. I'm going to work, actually." David was not sure he wished to continue the conversation, but there was no way out, short of rudeness. Neither his mother nor St. Vincent's had ever tolerated rudeness to his elders.

"Water *Is*land," Paul said. "Really?" David could not comprehend the enthusiasm. "All summer?" Paul continued smoothly with a white, handsome smile.

David nodded.

"How splendid," said Paul. "Perhaps we shall see something of you." It was casually said, and yet David became aware of the smaller man's eyes upon him, with a hard glitter above the drooping, sun-glossed pages.

"That would be very nice," David said politely.

Paul laughed lightly. Then he said, mimicking David's accent, "Oh, very nice, very nice. How sweet." It was a word for a child, condescending from a woman, unnatural from a man. It repelled David.

When he was ten and spent a summer in Bayport with his paternal grandmother, there had been a boy in a house across the shady suburban street, a boy called Tommy who talked a lot in a loud, bossy way. He had said Fire Island was full of crazy people and it stuck with David. So much so that when his father had written to say he'd taken up residence in the family's old beach house, David had felt odd. He did not, at ten, understand why the crazy people of Fire Island were allowed free run of the bright beach while other crazy people, according to the same knowledgeable Tommy, were locked away in a place called C.I. People giggled though, in something of the same way, about both.

"Pardon if I intrude, but who is your father, pray?" The black-haired man was smiling, that gentle, handsome smile.

"Oh. His name is Zolan. Robert Zolan," David said uncertainly, then added, "My mother remarried." He felt foolish saying that.

"Oh, *Rob*ert Zolan. The mystery writer."

"Yes. Yes. Do you know him?"

"Oh, Michael. This is Robert Z*ol*an's son."

"How very nice for Robert Zolan," Michael said primly without looking up. But then he brightened with a new thought and said slyly, "Imagine Robert Zolan with such a big, grown-up son. Robert's quite exactly your age, isn't he, Paul?"

"He's *years* older than me. You know that. Wherever did you get such an idea? Michael confuses *every*thing," he said, aside to David. "It's all those dull days in the tax office. Little busy bourgeois minds, buzzing away." Paul made a little fluttery bee shape with both hands.

"Paul," Michael said stiffly, sitting up very straight with his hands on the white, bare knees poking palely from his madras print Bermuda shorts, "I thought from the beginning this weekend was a complete mistake. I am now only *too* sure of it. I think I will stay right on the dock and wait for the next ferry."

"Please yourself," Paul said, taking off his hat and throwing back his sleek, black head. He stretched like a languorous and happy cat, a long, brown-skinned, glossy animal stretch. David looked up and saw, behind the shiny pages of *The New Yorker*, Michael's small eyes were watery in the sun, and squeezed up into tight, creased lines. David wished the ferry would bloody well hurry up.

They were midway between the two islands, with the water blue and warm, and where the sun hit it, too bright to look upon. Long Island was blue-gray and hazy hot, marked here and there with spidery water towers. In the far distance an unexpected low line of hills had emerged. The barrier beach was rapidly defining itself into a thing of shape and color rather than the familiar low hummocky line. Small squares of houses grew roofs and windows, and the dunes broke up into stretches of white sand and low, furry green backs of beach plum and pine.

There were boats everywhere, yachts and clammers and a preponderance of noisy, skithering speedboats, ripping around and around like unmanageable puppies. One zipped across the ferry's bow, full of shouting boys, children; the pilot mastering two huge outboard engines appeared about twelve.

David thought of Bridlington harbor and the yacht club, and the gracious order of the regatta in the bay, Bridlington Bay, and felt powerfully homesick, driven in upon himself, and already erecting the resourceful English shell of indifference and disdain.

Paul showed him Water Island, off to the left, marked at its western edge by two white half-moons of sand. Then he stretched his long bare brown arm behind David's back to point out the Captree Bridge, an arch bewitched by refracted light into a fat cigar shape, blue on the western horizon. He left his arm resting there, on the warm wood of the plank back of the bench, even after they were both again looking forward.

David pulled his shoulders in tight. He thought of Jeremy Wedderburn. He glanced nervously to his left. Paul had stretched back, the hat tipped forward over his face, his eyes half-closed, thick furred with black long lashes, a sensual delight. The low scooped-out neck of his shirt gave his chest the look of a woman's breasts. David's white shirt was clinging to his shoulders, sweat damp, in the beating sun.

"However will you get there?" Paul said as the *Fire Island Princess* thudded softly against the rubber-tire-cushioned pier at Fire Island Pines. The crowd on both decks of the ferry was getting to its feet and gathering weekend cases, and sacks of laundry and crates of bottles, and vegetables. On the dock, another crowd of people was waving, lazily in the hot sun, and shouting private jokes and first names. It was like a first day at school, with reunions and intimacy and an awful loneliness for the new boy.

David felt lost and said quickly, "I imagine I'll walk. It doesn't look far."

"But the *heat*," Paul said with concern. "You won't be used to it. And you're *so* fair-skinned. The English can't take the sun, can they, Michael?"

"I wouldn't know," said Michael.

"Here," Paul said with impulsive suddenness. "Have my hat. You should cover your head. Blonds must, of course. *I'm* all right." He stroked his black hair.

"But *I* gave you that hat." Michael was standing, his soft leather case slung over his shoulder, his face grown crumpled like the leather, his small soft body radiating unhappiness.

"No. Thank you," David said suddenly. "I don't need it, honestly." He felt so sorry for the little man in his misery. And also for Paul, in his disarming concern. The creeping revulsion that had armed him across the bay had vanished. Still, he hurried forward, following a heavy woman in a Hawaiian cotton dress, whose black, gray-streaked hair hung in a loose braid down her back.

She had a large tortoise-shell cat stuffed into a canvas bag, and as they climbed down the stairs, she stopped again and again to reassure it. David kept falling over her in his haste to be away. The cat sank deeper into the canvas and closed its eyes smoothly, like Paul had done on the deck.

Once on the solid dock, David picked his way awkwardly, the suitcase banging against small children, and small red wagons with house names painted on them, and the bare legs of the half-dressed people meeting the ferry. Paul followed behind, and a little behind him, Michael.

At a clear spot, away from the crowd, Paul stopped David with a hand on his shoulder where it was damp from the heat. They stood together while Paul pointed over the rows of tethered yachts and cruisers in the harbor, eastward, to show him the way.

"You might as well just take him to Water Island. You might as well," said Michael.

Paul ignored that and, as David pulled away, his fingers slightly tightened their grip.

"Well, I'm going," said Michael.

"Thank you," David said, stepping a further step, and Paul's fingers slipped lightly from his shoulder.

"I do hope . . ." Paul's beautiful deep blue eyes, narrow as a cat's in the glittery light, went stagily wistful.

"Hey, kid!" David half-turned; a strange voice and yet instinct told him it was aimed from somewhere below at him.

A small speedboat was idling toward the dock, and a man and a woman, middle aged, were sitting comfortably in the back. The man was big and heavy, with a red face and a bald head and tufts of sandy-gray hair above his ears. He wore a vest, also, but his was white, with a large hole under the armpit, and quite definitely the kind that men at home in England wore under their clothes. His Bermuda shorts were like Michael's, but his knees were massive and tanned, and he had shoes on, and socks. The woman wore the same kind of shorts, and white socks and canvas tennis shoes and a pink blouse cut low enough to show the top of a worn pink brassiere. A gold safety pin anchored one to the other. Her skin was the freckly red-brown of sun-baked redheads. Her hair might have been red, too, but David couldn't see it under the canvas hat. She had a beer can in one hand. David had never seen a woman drinking from a beer can, not even in private.

The man said, "I hear you want to go to Water Island?"

"Yes," David said uncertainly.

"Hop in. I'll give you a lift."

David looked at Paul, but Paul had turned away, his handsome face quite still and impassive. David hesitated and then said, "Yes. Thank you very much." He grinned suddenly, a boyish grin. He would not, he realized, have grinned a moment earlier at Paul.

"Gimme your suitcase," the man said.

David handed it down and then lowered himself with grace into the small boat.

"Goddamn queers," the man said.

"Sir?" said David.

"Goddamn queers." He gestured over his shoulder at the dock. David turned and looked, and then looked quickly back, over the boat's small prow at the blue water in the sun. Paul and Michael were walking away, quickly, hand in hand.

"Oughta be shot, all of 'em. Going after decent kids."

"He didn't do anything," said David.

"Oh, sure."

"Shut up, Ben, the kid doesn't know what you're talkin' about."

"Oughta be shot," Ben said again, complacently. "Like a beer, kid?"

"Oh, ra*ther*," David said, suddenly aware of the thirst grown on him in the heat of the crossing. The boat reeked sourly of stale beer, and there was an empty can rolling back and forth in the bilge, dribbling foam into the puddles of salt water.

The man pulled a can out of a crate beside him, with one hand, steering the small craft expertly in and out of the harbor clutter with the other.

"Martha, where's the church key?"

"I'll do it," the woman said. She had a kind, patient voice, and a mouth creased upward in a permanent smile. She was infinitely vulgar, and infinitely comforting, like a provincial English barmaid. She opened the can and handed it to David and said to the man, "You want another, Ben?"

He grunted and slurped the dregs of the can he was holding, and tossed it, empty, into the water. "Which house you going to, kid? So's I know where to drop you."

"Robert Zolan's house," David said uncertainly. "It's not got a name, I don't believe."

"You talk kinda funny," said the woman. "Are you foreign?"

"No. I mean, yes," David said. "I'm English."

"Ohhh. I love England. Westminster *Ab*bey and the Queen and those marvelous guards, watcha call 'em?"

"Hey, kid, you *know* Robert Zolan? The writer? You know him?"

"Watcha call 'em, Ben?"

"He's my father, actually."

"Your dad? No kiddin'? Hey, terrific!"

"What's he doin' with an English son?" said the woman.

"What's it matter?" said Ben, as if it was something to be a little ashamed of, and bypassed. "He's still some great writer. That Grant Holland, some character. I read 'em all. Must be terrific for you, being his son."

"I suppose so," said David, distantly, his eyes on the hot hazy beach slipping by, a quarter of a mile to his right. He said quickly, "Can you show me the house? I don't know how to find it."

"You'd of thought he'd of met the kid," said the woman under her breath.

Ben pointed out a red corner of flat roof, tucked away behind another, larger green roof. "That's it, kid, the funny square red one at the back. Looks like an overgrown privy, Martha always says."

Martha laughed easily and said, "Well, bejesus, it does."

It did. It emerged from behind its slant-roofed green neighbor as David sweatily climbed the boardwalk "highway" mounting up the narrow back of the island. Ben and Martha had dropped him a hundred yards from shore. The tide was out and there was too little water for the prop shaft.

"Sorry, kid, but I'll shear the goddamned pin if I go in any closer." David grinned from the water, knee deep, lapping about the rolled legs of his neatly creased beige trousers. He held his suitcase in one hand, just skimming the small green waves, and his shoes and socks in the other. His bare feet, soft and white and unused, curled unpleasantly against the stony, shell-strewn bottom.

The beer, gulped down, had gone to his head. He'd had no food since a five A.M. breakfast on the plane approaching Idlewild. Also, he was not used to drink. He felt giddy and over-cheerful and shouted thank you, and plodded away toward the shore.

He had sat at once on the beach and pulled socks on over wet resisting feet, and stuffed them into his shoes. They felt grainy and uncomfortable now, and his trousers, rolled down and wrinkly, were damp and sticking to his salty skin. The weathered boards echoed hollowly under his feet, and the walk undulated over the dunes, skimming the sand by a foot at one point, and vaulting twelve feet above a gully of little trees at another.

The whole community, houses and walks, stood on high feet, stilted up against the threat of flood from its twin seas. David hazily recalled his father's story of the hurricane of thirty-eight, the Big Blow he called it, that had swept right over the whole of this narrow, sun-baked island, over all of it, and on and over the big main island itself, and smashed his grandfather to death among his roses.

The air was still stifling away from both shores, but the residual roar of the ferry engines and the speedboat outboard and the water sound of the last hour hung about in his head, like the memory of the Big Blow. In the invisible distance, across the island, there was an almost imperceptible hushed sighing of the surf.

The house sat, a plain ugly red square, faded from the classic barn color to a sun-washed rust, on top of its own small dune. It had a railing all around the square roof and, at one corner, a flagpole from which an old American flag hung limp in the hot air. It was not well-placed, which was precisely why his father's family had afforded it. It glimpsed a blue triangle of Atlantic through a gap in the dunes at one point (and slightly more Atlantic from the roof) and had a fair view of yacht-scattered bay flats to the north. But its prime panorama was the rooftops of its neighbors and its own wilderness of holly, beach plum, and undecorated sand.

Still it was private enough, with its scrub pine and poison ivy hedges making green walls about it. If its indistinction had brought it to the Zolenskis in the first place, it was that remaining privacy that had kept it in the last Zolenski's hands.

At the juncture of the main boardwalk and the narrow private one to the red house, David put the suitcase down. He stretched his hand, rubbing it, creased white with the weight and sweaty, and then picked the case up with the other hand. The narrow walk was yet further narrowed by green encroachment, small scrub oaks and pines, and bushy beach plum leaning in from each side. Low down the wood was bordered lushly by glistening green and purple leaves. David remembered their shiny glory of color, and their trifoliate shape, from his distant Long Island summer.

Tommy had pushed him into a great mass of it in the woods behind his grandmother's house. Poison ivy, his father had told him, and painted him with pink cool calamine. He'd itched for weeks. His father had belted Tommy without a word. Now the ivy grew all around his father's house, launching itself up through the gray boards, bushing in from the sides. He had to pick his way, sideways, through hedges of glistening leaves, wondering why his father left it to so boldly dominate the way to his door.

The door itself was only a screen one, on the shady side of the house. Around it, decking stretched in both directions, so the house sat on flat planking like a cup on a plate. David put the case down again and knocked softly on the worn red edging of the screen.

There was silence, and then a scuffling noise and then a shout in a female voice. David saw a flutter of movement in the shady dark behind the screen and it swung open and two black cats streaked past him. A blond girl in cut-off denim jeans and a red cotton shirt was standing in front of him. She pushed long strands of hair from her face and said, "Yes?"

"Is this Robert Zolan's house?" he said, uncertain now, in spite of the neat lettering of his father's name on the crossbar of the screen.

"You from a paper?"

"No. I'm David . . ."

"Hey, are you? Hi!" she smiled, a wide, American-girl smile, and reached out a brown hand. "Look, he's out, but he'll be back soon. Come in and I'll get you a beer or something. I'm just cleaning up."

She led him into the box of a house, hot and sandy floored, and thick with the sourness of leftover wine. There were glasses everywhere, used, half filled. "He had a party yesterday," the girl said. She went directly to a small round-shouldered fridge in one corner of the living room which, with a bottled-gas cooking stove, and a sink, comprised a kitchen. David said no, really, to the beer, but she reached without looking and her right hand came out with a can while the left searched blindly in a small cupboard, evidently for a glass. She crouched down and peered into the dark interior and said then, "Do you mind drinking it out of the can? I can't find anything clean."

She opened the can with a smooth hand, without waiting for an answer, and set it on a small table by a wicker chair at one wide window. David sat and sipped at the beer and looked out the window below the half-lowered blind. The window was dusty and the sill covered with dry moths. Outside, on a long garden lounge chair on the deck, the upholstery faded almost white by the sun, a bright green bikini bathing suit was drying on a white towel.

David knew it belonged to the girl. One side of his mind

was thinking what a cushy job she had and imagining his mother's daily, Jean, prancing about in denim shorts. The other side was dozily picturing the girl in her green swimsuit.

She was standing at the sink, patiently washing glass after glass and turning them upside down on the scuffed enamel drainboard. Her short jeans were faded and tucked in snug under her tight rounded bottom. The knitted red shirt was worn and short, and he saw a strip of brown skin when she bent forward, and saw also, with an uneasy quiver, that she was not even wearing a bra. At school, devoid of any female companionship at all, he'd become adept at mentally tracing those shadows under women's clothing. It was silly, but it was better than rubbing against blokes in the shower.

He was suddenly ungodly randy and the beer and lack of sleep made his tongue easy. He said, "You've got beautiful hair."

The girl did not ignore him as Jean might have done (though Jean did not have beautiful hair, but a crimped clump. of manufactured curls). She turned instead, and shook the honey-brown mass of it, so much of it, so thick and tawny, half piled up and half fallen down again. Like Brigitte Bardot.

"Do you like it?" she said disarmingly.

"Yes." David was thickly nervous. "It's absolutely gorgeous."

"Oh, I love your accent," she said, softly. She smiled again, that wide smile. Her skin was so creamy dark from the sun, she looked Indian. "My name's Mary Jo," she said. David, caution lost to that last beer, asked for another.

She gave it to him, and his hand brushed hers as she did. She ignored that, pointedly, and returned to the sink, but David concentrated on that lush hair, and the glistening tanned stretch of thigh below the tight shorts, and what his hands felt like doing with both. He said, quite drunk and almost inaudibly, "Mary Jo, this is going to be a splendid summer."

The screen door banged, and there was a scuttling of two black cats and David looked up, lazily, and then leaped to his feet. His father was standing in the doorway.

He held a paper bag full of groceries and had a white sack slung over his shoulder. He was leaner and browner and oddly younger than David remembered him, even though his dark hair had grown gray-streaked and he now wore a small, neat beard.

He dropped the sack and the groceries to the floor and crossed the sand-strewn space in one strong bound and caught David up and hugged him, like a child, embarrassingly long, and stepped back and looked all over him with embarrassing tears streaking his face. He was laughing aloud and David was a little too drunk to be properly embarrassed. He felt joyously welcome, a welcome like he'd ached for in the lonely, calendar-counting weeks at school, and yet somehow, in his various homes, never quite attained.

He could not meld this man with that defeated stranger who had walked alone, all those years gone, from the closed door of Greenshaws Hall.

His father was saying his name, again and again, like a litany, still with the bright, unashamed tears running down his lean cheeks; unashamed, even in front of the casual help. David half turned, remembering the girl there.

But his father had released him and bounded a second time across the room to where Mary Jo stood in her little shorts and her tight red shirt. "Aw, sweetheart, forgive me, I haven't even said hello." Then he bent, with his arm around her brown-skinned waist, and kissed the girl long and richly on her wide-smiling sun-brown mouth.

VII

Philippa Wardlaw's wide, weathered mouth crept so gradually into its tempered smile that one had to watch carefully to see that it was happening at all. Mary Jo was not watching, and therefore did not see, nor did she see the reason. She was standing with the tongue of the red wagon held behind her back by both hands, like a small child scuffing bare feet at the end of the walk, the approach of the house in abeyance.

"It's that one," she said, staring fixedly at the faded door with its cat-pocked screen. The shadow behind hid any occupants. She heard the pump laboring and the weak trickle of the outside shower. "The red square one, that looks like a paper carton." She turned around then and saw Mrs. Wardlaw smiling. If she were in a better mood or less dedicated to the synonymity of youth and beauty, she might have thought it added prettiness. At the moment, it added confusion.

"I know," Mrs. Wardlaw added dryly. She was looking up and Mary Jo's eyes followed to the roof, to Robert and Paul leaning on the far railing with their backs toward them, and to, beside them, the flagpole.

The bold blue, red, and white of the Union Jack splayed and snapped from above the bleached, red railing, its multi-crosses intermingling, St. George, St. David, St. Andrew, Robert had taught her. She liked learning. "What the hell did he do that for?" Mary Jo said querulously now.

"Robert," Mrs. Wardlaw said in a voice scarcely above conversational. Robert turned around, leaving his hands clasped to the railing as long as possible, but in the end released the grip. His hands then joined each other, folded, waist level, seeming to want to hold on to something.

"Hello, Philippa," he said.

"How very nice, Robert," she said, smiling and gesturing with one crepe-cuffed hand to the flag.

"Thank you."

"It's upside down."

Robert knew it. Of course he knew it. The instant she said it he knew it. He knew the whole thing, the white strip that was broad on one side, narrow on the other, which went on top. He knew it. He knew the port went to the left, that grouse only came in braces, that foxhounds (which were never dogs) had sterns instead of tails. He knew that black tie was a Prince Charlie, and white tie, a Montrose. He knew that fish knives were a Victorian invention, and champagne a middle-class pretension. He knew one did not wear tweeds after six or drink cocktails much before it, and *no one* put ice in malt. He knew it. He knew it all. So why, if he knew it, did the sight of Philippa, just the sight of her, always make him forget?

And why in hell did God always let her remember?

He unclipped the flag. Philippa climbed the stairs, fourteen wooden steps, twenty-eight dull clicks of her alligator heels. Philippa was nervous of open treads since falling off a ladder during basic training, in the WAAF. Robert remembered that as he struggled with the flag. It gave him time to turn it over and reclip it, and run it up to a petulant half mast.

Philippa stepped onto the roof, the asphalt and gravel crunching grittily as she walked with a yet wary step. She looked at Robert, at Paul, and at the half risen flag. "Expecting a death?" she said.

She stepped beside him, not yet having touched him, as if they had never, or conversely always, shared a bed. She slipped the rope, hoisted the flag and fastened the line with swift naval panache. The flag fluttered happily. She kissed Robert, shook Paul's hand, and patted the rope cleat. Then she gave him the sweet, friendly old Vera Lynn smile, with just a trace of malicious delight. "Forever England yet, my dear?"

"England for*ev*er, Scotland for *nev*er." Mary Jo heard David chanting behind the slatted door of the shower. There was a lot of masculine laughter and then he varied it, "England forever, U.S. for never."

Mary Jo lifted Mrs. Wardlaw's worn leather canvas-strapped suitcase out of the red wagon and set it by the door. Robert hadn't called to her or spoken to her or even noticed that she had not, like Mrs. Wardlaw, climbed to the roof. They were all up there now, joking in low, dry voices about the flag. Robert was being both distant and theatrically expansive, a trick of his which she associated with any gathering of his older friends. She felt ignored and placeless and longed for the company of the boys.

But when they flung open the shower-room door and came out, combing their hair and punching each other, they ignored her as well. As they brushed by her, toward the house, she said sharply, "Will you take that suitcase in?"

David stopped short and said, "Is mother here? Have you brought mother?" His voice was urgent, and Mary Jo suddenly had no desire to talk about it.

"I'm going to take a shower," she said, as suddenly deciding it, and left the suitcase and ducked away, into the wood-walled outdoor shower room. It was a place of simultaneous pleasure and distaste; a double room with a chipped old toilet boxed in at one end, and the corroded shower head over its slatted decking at the other. There was a bench by the shower of splintery wet wood, and cupboards on the walls, homemade with plastic handles and ill-fitting doors. Mary Jo entered the shower room with slight revulsion, feeling hot and sticky, with the unpleasant tackiness of ocean salt on her legs and arms, and the dry roughness of sandy feet, and yet dreading the shock of the unheated water. It was tepid, from the roof tank, rather than cold, but still stunning against the sun-scorched out-of-doors.

She stepped warily over the wet boards. It was always damp, almost moldy, and the floor was mounded with little packed heaps of sand and streaked with brown seaweed. The boys had left their swimming trunks on the floor, and their salt-crusty masculine interiors and the recent wetness of their own shower offered unwanted physical intimacies. Mary Jo kicked the two heaps of stiff cloth aside with one foot, resisting the housekeeper's urge to hang them up. She was suddenly sick of cleaning up after people and being ignored for it.

The whole place smelled faintly uncertain, as if the plumbing were not to be trusted. Coming out would feel marvelous, clean and fresh in dry soft clothes, out into the hot soft air, freed from a small purgatory. Mary Jo pulled her sweatshirt over her head and folded it neatly before laying it delicately on the bench. She waited to the last minute always, with the water running already, to remove her bikini. She had a passionate distaste for displaying nakedness to uncertain surroundings, a distaste birthed in the pampered cleanliness of postwar American youth.

Mary Jo had never really lived anywhere old before coming to Robert Zolan's beach house, unless one could count the Shack, and that was more like a camp, or her baby years in Manhattan before her parents made the great suburban jump. Her childhood home was in Bayport, on the mainland, and only a few tree-shaded streets from the brick and stucco solidity of Catherine Zolenski's new house. Catherine's new house was over ten years old, though, when Mary Jo's rose up, a skeleton of golden beams in the boom of the early fifties.

Mary Jo Walsh was born in early 1944, when, from the relative comfort of the New World the war was going well, peace was in sight, and there were good times just around the corner. The corner, however, wasn't quite there yet, nor the street on which she would live. She was born into a world about to be rebuilt in her honor, and the honor of her peers, the many cherished children of survival celebrated.

Survival did not precisely apply to the Walshes since Mary Jo's father was fifteen years older than her mother, another generation, the itchy, Depression-haunted, heroics-neglected, between-the-wars generation. Her father never fought in the war her friends' fathers talked of, or any war at all. Still, she was, like her friends, the offspring of simple values, simply held.

Her parents built a new house in which to rear her, on one of those streets freshly cut out of the overgrown memories of island farms, hacked out and cleared, and then given some fanciful name of rural remembrance. It was a clean, fresh-cut place, surrounded by sunny crabgrass, treeless in the un-compromising landscaping of the day, untouched by the cob-webby corners of history. Even the attic was shining and clean, with gleaming droplets of fresh sap on the beams of the roof. As a girl she had escaped occasionally into the viny mysteries of the remaining patches of wood and salt meadow, but the yellow bulldozers rumbled relentlessly through most of those refuges of childhood, effectively clearing the magic of the country away.

When Mary Jo was six, the community built a new ele-mentary school for her, and when she was twelve a new junior high was provided. A high school followed, and except for occasional sorties into the nostalgic Old Building, a brick struc-ture dating back to the thirties, her growing years were co-cooned in linoleum and plastic, fresh plaster and aluminum.

Detached from the city she was born in by the suburban

diaspora, detached from the island she was raised on by a severance from all its history, detached by her father's age even from the war that was a springboard to her entire generation, Mary Jo was born and bred to be homeless. Finding her way into Robert Zolan's bed was so obvious a nostalgic Freudian connection that no one ever noticed it. No one in her family had ever read Freud, anyhow. They did not think in such terms, and if they did, they would never apply them to themselves. That sort of stuff belonged in the city, and the city they had left far behind.

Mary Jo pushed the door of the shower room closed, and then the light came in dim, and barred, where it crept through the shuttering. She could yet hear voices on the roof, but heard none of the extravagances of welcome she had expected, and wondered if the boys had simply gone into the house and not seen Mrs. Wardlaw at all.

She went to the handmade cupboard on the wall. The door, swollen with summer humidity, resisted, and then opened slowly with a scraping of damp wood. Many things in the beach house were handmade; many made by Robert. It was that sort of place, a spare-time house, cheaply concocted with leftover materials. It was outclassed utterly by Paul Botvin's architect-designed extravaganza in the Pines, and even by some of the new-era Water Island structures. It was prehurricane, Robert said, but Mary Jo was only vaguely aware which hurricane he meant.

The cupboard was not Robert's handiwork, but that of his father; it was that old. Mary Jo liked the cupboard. It was hers, and she opened it now looking for her own private things. Her unbreakable tube of Prell shampoo, her hair clip, her Tampax, a pair of clean, folded jeans, a spare pair of sandy white sneakers. It pleased her especially that she had a special corner of Robert Zolan's house, a private family corner. It pleased the part of her that liked using his boat, and the red

wagon with his name painted clearly on it in white letters.
That was the part of her still star-struck, not so much by the
man he was, but by the man he had been.

Mary Jo peered under the folded jeans, in the dim light,
hoping to find a clean T-shirt on the shelf beneath it. She did
not, but then did find an old white shirt of Robert's, pressed
and folded, and clean, if slightly salt-damp. She was pleased,
and dropped her sweatshirt off the bench and onto the floor
by the boys' wet swimming trunks. She began then to untie
her bikini top, and then stopped, and very self-consciously
went to the door and reached up, finding the almost forgotten
hook, high up the door frame, and swung it up and over and
through the eye in the door itself.

"Be sure and lock up when you come in."

"Lock up before you go to bed."

"Hadn't we better lock the door?"

Autumn, 1961

Long Island

"You've locked the door, you know."

"I know."

"He won't have you back."

"I know."

"Where will you go?"

"I don't know."

"It's your own fault, you know." Her mother was crying.

"I know."

Mary Jo shrugged and lit another cigarette. She thrust her
hand with the pack deep in her raincoat pocket, and tightened
the belt. She was in the doorway, the winter-bare doorway

newly divested of its screen. Her mother said again, "Where will you go?" She shrugged again in youthful cruelty and pulled on the black hat. Actually, she knew precisely where she was going, but she was hurting her mother to get back at her father—illogically but successfully.

"It's raining."

"So what?"

"You'll get wet."

"Yeah. I guess I will." She went out and began walking purposefully down the wet autumn streets shining in maple-shadowed lamplight. It was nineteen sixty-one and Mary Jo was leaving home.

Of course all of her friends were leaving home as well. They were all eighteen. It was the year for that sort of thing. But most of them were going farther and most of them with more honor. Most of them, in fact, were going to college.

Practically everyone was going to college. It suddenly seemed the only acceptable thing to be doing, the only thing parents could be really proud of. Which was interesting, considering that almost nobody's parents had gone to college. Still, they had all had the Depression and then the war. There weren't any really good excuses like that left. The only way out with any honor was being stupid and doing hairdressing (Mary Jo was not stupid) or being sweet and getting married (Mary Jo was not at the moment sweet). There was another sure exit, of course; Michelle Cochran had tried that, or rather an astute combination of all three. Michelle had been a little sweet, a little more stupid, and was now as a result a whole lot pregnant; which had everything to do with why Michelle was not going to Syracuse University after all, and had in a convoluted way quite a bit to do with why Mary Jo was not going, either.

Mary Jo Walsh was, at least until very recently, a sexual innocent. So much so that at age fourteen she had only just learned that the "w" in "whore" was silent. It was a small lack in her education, but significant: she had never heard the word pronounced, though she had read it often enough. She had read *The World of Suzy Wong*. She had also read *Lady Chatterley's Lover*. More recently she had read *The Story of O*. (She was mystified by most of it.) Her innocence was a virtue of omission, unintentioned, and her approach to its correction was purely intellectual. Her interest in the subject was avid. It was also unexpressed. She was an intelligent girl, but shy, without confidants, and with a family who had never talked about anything below the waist. Even menstruation she had met first in a book.

When she was older, she neither gave nor received intimacies, and the activities of the adventurers in car seats, on beaches, and in the back rows of movie houses were high holy mysteries only part revealed in a liturgy of whispers.

"And so they were up on this dune, and Tony had the blanket, and they were making out up there . . ."

". . . then someone snatched the blanket . . ."

". . . naked from the waist up . . ."

". . . *down* . . . around her ankles . . ."

". . . then Rick's mother came in . . ."

". . . on the *bed* . . ."

". . . Nude. Michelle was nude."

"Well, not nude exactly . . ."

"They *would* have been. In another moment."

". . . a compromising position, Rick's mother said . . ."

Mary Jo sat on spring afternoons in her seventeenth year, in the hot glassed-in air of the physics classroom, looking at Michelle. Michelle had smooth legs and wore seamless stockings, honey-beige, and sometimes even charcoal. Michelle wore a blue wool skirt, pencil-thin, with a slit at the back. She wore her hair in a French twist, and her blouse buttoned demurely to the collar. There was a neat navy Orlon vest over that. *Michelle was nude.* In there, underneath somewhere, under the blue skirt and the white lace-edged slip that showed in the slit at the back. In there somewhere was Michelle, the nude part of her that had *done it*. It was unbelievable.

Mary Jo tried to see Michelle nude. Not naked, like herself in the shower, wet and clean and rather young. But nude. Nude was special. Nude was dangerous. Nude was what happened to secretaries who got murdered in the *Daily News*.

She mentally removed Michelle from the molded metal frame of the desk-chair unit and transferred her to the bed in Rick de Villeneuve's bedroom. She had no idea what his bedroom would look like so she furnished it with the trappings of her brother's: sports gear and books and the record player, and a slippery stack of shiny-sleeved Kingston Trio LPs. She added Rick to the picture, a rangy, crew-cut basketball player in a cream varsity sweater. Then she put them together, in a compromising position. In all their clothes, even the honey-beige stockings and the varsity sweater. She daren't take their clothes off after all. Even with a brother of her own, she was not exactly sure what a boy looked like.

So in their clothes, in her created bedroom, they remained. They didn't do anything because Mary Jo did not know what was done. She looked back, at Michelle's tight blue bottom in the molded physics-class chair. Michelle had done it. Mary Jo failed physics and graduated in June without yet understanding fully how *it* was done. *It* had, however, gotten Michelle pregnant by then, and an obsession with it, in the hot dreamy spring, had reduced Mary Jo's grades to a low B average, and neither of them in the end went to college.

Mary Jo applied. She applied to a local two-year community college, in response to parental insistence. Despite the B average, Mary Jo was possessed of a snobbish and essentially correct conviction that the place was beneath her abilities. She applied halfheartedly, out of disdain. In the meantime, anyhow, she had discovered bohemia, or what passed for it in the modest years of her coming of age. She attended her college interview in a black skirt and black tights, and a green sweater that reached her knees. She had taken to carrying a copy of the *Communist Manifesto* on top of her armload of school books, and brought that recent affectation along as well, glaring over it at the interviewer through a belligerent curtain of honey-beige hair. It all had the predictable desired effect.

Freed of academia, Mary Jo put on her jeans, her black turtleneck sweater, and her silver earrings, taped a list of thirty-five Appalachian laments to the back of her guitar, and sallied forth to Greenwich Village to seek her fortune. Her parents, who still had hopes of her going to college to seek someone else's fortune, were unhappy about it, but they decided to give her until fall to find herself. Mary Jo spent the rest of the summer with her feet in the cool fountains of Washington Square, and in the fall she found Matthew Gittelson.

He was a Columbia student. He was seventeen, an only child, precocious, spoiled, gentle, slovenly, and handsome with the black-eyed devilish look of a cossack. He was an intellectual show-off and an emotional bully, and even his parents were afraid of him, rather as if they'd hatched some boisterous Marxist cuckoo in their nest. They were Communists as well, but old-fashioned, nineteen-thirties Communists, with dignity and manners, and money in the bank. They were everything calculated to offend Mary Jo's parents: Jewish, metropolitan, atheistic. They kept wine on the table and French cheese in the refrigerator, and played tennis in the Catskills on the weekends. It was virtually anarchy.

And if that were not enough, they believed in free love. Or rather, Matthew's father believed in free love and Matthew's mother went along because there was nowhere else to ride. Mary Jo went home to the Gittelsons for dinner. Matthew and his father grinned at each other across the table, drank their wine and ate their cheeses and raised eyebrows at each other. Mr. Gittelson goaded her with intellectual games she did not understand, and called her the Strindberg woman when she did not answer. Mrs. Gittelson cowered under the dark clever eyes of her husband and her son, and looked sorry for Mary Jo.

After supper, Matthew took her to his bedroom and made love to her amongst his Columbia notebooks, while his parents played chess in the living room. Afterwards they showered together and Mary Jo looked with surprise at the virginal blood on her thighs. She had imagined virginity to be, like her books, an abstract intellectual matter.

After that, they had coffee with the family, and then went back to bed. In the night they argued, and he stalked out and she lay crying, alone in his alien bed listening to the alien sound of the elevated trains, and wanted to flee the awful approval of the place, cool as the air conditioning. She wanted her own bed at home, not simply her borrowed bed at her cousin's in Brooklyn Heights, but her own, in the country quiet of the island, with the August crickets in the night, and her mother making coffee in the morning. It was her first meeting with nostalgia and it pointed the way, significantly, homeward.

Still, they made up their fight and went out together in the hot sticky Brooklyn daylight and were lovers. There followed three weeks totally dominated by bed. They crept out from time to time to gather sustenance, large wax cartons of milk and packets of Oreo cookies, intermingled with California wines and Mexican marijuana. At the end of the three weeks, Mary Jo was mistress of her own body and surprisingly, of his. He no longer made jokes at her expense, and he would not meet his father's eyes. He was a good halfway to being quite unexpectedly in love.

The idyll ended in mid-September. Word of Mary Jo's absences from the Brooklyn Heights apartment reached parental ears, and a dialogue began which resulted in Matthew's only visit home. Actually, she realized it was over the moment he stepped off the train. It was like seeing an actor step on stage before a misplaced backdrop, miscostumed and miscast. He seemed, with his tight jeans and long black hair and drooping moustache, a kind of city troll before the gentle maples and shingled houses of home—an object of revulsion. Mary Jo felt the revulsion, and she read it at once in the dismayed fading smiles of welcome.

Still, they did their best, they made allowances, they were hospitable. But Matthew's idea of hospitality, bred in his home, was Mary Jo's bed. When the house was quiet, her parents asleep, her little sister tucked under her frilly quilt, Matthew knocked at her door.

"Here?" Mary Jo's eyes opened wide with shock. She was wearing a floating negligee, pale blue and white, a birthday present from her mother. Behind her was her childhood bed, as blue and frilly as her sister's, and her dressing table with its organza skirt, and her long-disused bottles of perfume and tubes of lipstick. Matthew pushed by her into the room. She expected him to mock and laugh, and tried to hide her pretty, childish things. But he did not. He was fascinated. He touched everything, and put everything down again. She wanted to stop him, as if he were some bitter Russian elf who would blacken all her pretty things and her pretty self as well.

He was most intrigued by her negligee. "Hey, it's pretty. I didn't know you had . . . shit, it's softer than you are."

"Matthew, go away. Go back to your room."

"Why?" He put his hand inside her negligee.

"Not here," Mary Jo cried.

"Why the fuck not?" he said. He was smiling, but belligerent. And then she could not say no, because to say no would be to say, I hate you, you make me dirty, and she could not say such a thing. So she let him do it there, and hated it, fearing discovery and feeling violated in a way she had never felt before.

In the morning he went away, and she did not care. In the evening her parents called her to them. They had found out. She did not know how; she never knew how. They had surely not seen or heard. They simply knew.

"I don't want you here any more," her father said. "You're a tramp. You got no right here, around your sister. She's a decent girl. Go back to Brooklyn. Go back to that boy. I don't care. You can't stay here."

He said it as calmly as if he were sending her to the grocery for a loaf of bread. He was not angry, or even apparently sad. He was simply done with her.

Mary Jo cried. Her mother cried. Mary Jo followed her father around all next day, a Sunday, the worst day of her life. She followed him all day, like a small child, crying. He did not relent. She had totally, unwittingly, stepped backward off the cliff of adulthood, and he never allowed her to return. Her parents still lived five miles from where she slept now, and she had not spoken to them for two years.

When she left their door that rainy evening, she walked with lemming determination to the bayfront of the small wet town as an earlier example of soiled American womanhood might have made for some midwestern river to drown herself. In a way she did drown herself, submerging her whole being in the cloying rebellion of a group of young bohemians called the Clan. There were five of them, after Mary Jo joined them, six later when Stephen Deutsch came, with his hair yet crisped short from his hitch with the marines. When Mary Jo first took up her residence in the Shack, there were two other girls, Chrissie and Marjorie, and two other boys, Jeff and Marvin. They were not couples. Chrissie painted and kept to herself. Jeff and Marvin dug clams, and Marjorie went to bed with both boys. She was a soft, vast, fat girl with wispy brown hair, and both Chrissie and Mary Jo were far prettier. But Marjorie loved sex as much as the boys did, and they returned her compliments by giving her all their company.

Mary Jo's parents, like every one of the parents of the Clan, considered the Shack a whorehouse, a place of drunkenness and sexual abandon, and worse. But in truth, Mary Jo never slept with anyone the whole while she was there. She and Chrissie lived as celibate as nuns.

They were refugees, escaped from the country of schoolbooks and hopes of success, hiding out from the real land of jobs and marriages. The Shack—abandoned property of Marjorie's parents, who, roaming between Florida and New York, had rather forgotten its existence, as indeed they had rather forgotten Marjorie's—was a halfway house between childhood and adulthood. They were flung in together with nothing in common but homelessness, mishatched birds scraping together a driftwood nest.

When Steve Deutsch came, there was, at least sometimes, a certain amount of money, which they shared with innocent charity. Chrissie was able to buy a new supply of paints, and when Mary Jo, dressed habitually in frayed jeans shorts, Matthew's Columbia sweatshirt, and her familiar black felt wide-brimmed hat, cycled about the town on her childhood bicycle, she returned now usually with a bottle of wine or a six-pack.

She had collected the bicycle without warning, from the family garage; it was her property. She left a note so they would not call the police. She saw all her hometown from a refracted viewpoint, a stranger in the landscape of her own childhood, like the unrecognized journeyer in a dream. Once she saw her mother in the supermarket, and was swept with vivid homesickness at the sight of the familiar family sustenance being piled into the wire shopping cart. But they did not speak.

Then one day she came out of the liquor store with two bottles of mountain red and found that a middle-aged man had just run over the bicycle with his car. The loss was the biggest of her life. She had no hope, no hope ever, it seemed, of replacing it. At once the town through which she had glided, sadly free, became vast and unreachable, her only pleasure as crushed as its irrevocably flattened frame. It was her own fault. She had left it, in laziness, lying flat in the driveway. But she had, always, a quick temper, and was about to fly into it, and about to call the gray-haired, stoop-shouldered man the kind of things Steve Deutsch called all older people. But then something strange happened. Her anger suddenly turned into a kind of shaking, and the shaking turned to tears.

"My mother gave it to me," she said, looking at the mangled bicycle. "It was my birthday present when I was twelve." She had no idea why she was saying it, or even why she was crying, and worse, allowing herself, Mary Jo of the black hat and the tough frayed jeans, to be seen crying by some middle-aged stranger.

The man was sorry. He was really terribly sorry. He got sorrier all the time, the more she cried, but her misery was genuine, as was her embarrassment, and she was not playing on his kindness in any clever, womanly way. And he was a kind man. He offered to drive her home, and she, not able to face the long walk back to Blue Point with the corpse of the bicycle, accepted. On the way, they stopped at Flo's café, and leaned on the outdoor gray wooden counter, drinking coffee in paper cups. She had stopped crying, and laughed a bit, and even made a small attempt to swagger, to regain her lost maturity, but he was so quietly unimpressed that she gave up.

"I'll replace the bicycle," he said.

"No," she said suddenly, as suddenly taking charge of her own foolishness. "No. I left it in a stupid place. Why should you pay for it?"

"Because I can afford it," he said simply.

"Yeah, well, I can afford it, too," she said with a slight offhand belligerence. He started to protest, but then suddenly he stopped and said, all right, if that was how she wanted it. It was a quick turnabout. Later, Steve Deutsch said she was a fool, she should have taken the money, he could use it, if she couldn't, anyhow. But Mary Jo was pleased with herself and her decision. She was an honest person, and she knew she'd acted honestly. Also she knew something else, which pleased her, something more subtle. He had meant it, the offer of money, and had he given it, he could not ever see her again. There would have been an embarrassment of obligation. He had been glad she refused, she knew, not because he was mean, but because he did not want that embarrassment. He had wanted to see her again. It was flattering, although she did not particularly want to see him; he was older, alien, complicated. She assumed he was married, though she really did not think much about that. But he was also handsome in a craggy way, and he was different. She could tell by the voice. He was not a banker or a shopkeeper, like her father, or a teacher, even. He was something special and different; and difference, uniqueness, was in Mary Jo's narrowed world the highest attribute. He drove her home, unloaded the crushed bicycle beside the Shack, and said good-bye.

It was Chrissie who told her that he was Robert Zolan, the writer. Mary Jo had never heard of him. But out of curiosity, she went the next day to the candy store on Maple Avenue and scanned a rack of paperbacks. She found six with his name on them (a bit of local interest) and one with his picture. She had a vague feeling of a missed opportunity, though what the opportunity might have offered she did not really know. Still, he was the first person she had ever met who could possibly be called famous. For a day or two she tried out a small embryo fantasy in which she stumbled again across him; this time she would be dressed mysteriously in black, as a fellow writer should be, and would accidentally spill out a sheaf of paper carrying her longhand collection of poems. He would reach to read them. She would say, no, please, they're private. But he would override her, with a definitive curt writery wave of the hand. "But these are really *good*, Mary Jo. I have a friend, a publisher . . ." She thought about it a day or two, and then she forgot him, completely.

A week later, Marjorie called to her, with curiosity brightening her voice, "Mary Jo, there's some old guy at the door for you."

She ran through the dusty room, expecting at last her father and reprieve. It was Robert.

He began taking her out on weekends. He'd cross on the ferry to Sayville, and borrow his mother's car, the car that had crushed her old green English racer. The use of the car appeared to be a kind of apology on his mother's part. Mary Jo never fully understood; they seemed to do nothing but goad each other in quiet, half-humorous voices when she, rarely, saw them together. But there was an inherent sympathy between them which Mary Jo eventually understood to have something to do with her early widowhood, to which he often referred, and his failed English marriage, which she never mentioned. "Divorce is to widowhood what AWOL is to an honorable discharge," Robert said once, and then added with his grimacing little smile, "Either way you're out of the army."

In that car, a battered old Chevrolet (she only drives it to church, Robert would say, but she goes four times a day), he drove her about the island, safely cocooned in its warmth with the dark comfort of his calm profile beside her. He took her to interesting places, old island bars that none of her friends had ever heard of. Or into the city, to solid old theatrical haunts. He took her to the theater as well, which she only half enjoyed. He was hard to please, and nervous, there, sitting on the edge of his seat, easily disturbed, easily disappointed, and most of those evenings ended in disillusionment.

"But, Robert, they tried hard."

"It's not enough, it's not enough."

"You're so demanding."

"They're professionals, damn it." He would get angry, like a child with a new and broken toy. Once he took her to West Eleventh Street, to a house where an old friend once lived. But there was no old friend any longer, and they only looked at the house and went away.

She liked being with him. He took care of things, and took care of her. It was like being home again, but better. He paid her much attention, and seemed always pleased with her, as if her willingness to be with him was always a pleasant surprise. He was both polite and full of humor, and if his lined face and time-worn body did not excite her, his history and social mastery did. She soon saw that women, all women, sought him out at parties, and found their way to his side. She took her lessons from them, and fell into the easy adult habit of desiring what was already desired.

Their first lovemaking arrived with fall, in late sixty-two. They fell into it like the season fell into winter, a relinquishment of the easy, untenable days of summer. There was nothing coquettish about it; nothing even spontaneous. Geography determined that. When Robert came to the mainland to court her, he slept in his mother's house, there being nowhere else. Mary Jo had nothing to offer but a curtained-off corner of the Shack, and although Marjorie entertained each of the boys there, Mary Jo would not have brought herself to such public intimacies even with them. With Robert it was unimaginable. There was for them simply no convenient bed, and in suburban Long Island no banks where the wild thyme grew.

They were obliged to deliberate; something lovers should never do. It was October. Robert invited Mary Jo to Water Island. He was not coy and there was no talk of a spare bedroom. Mary Jo considered carefully, not morality, but motivation. She liked Robert, but she did not desire him. She neither loved him with the virginal passions showered on schoolboy heads nor yearned with the lust she'd learned for Matthew. She simply liked him. When she boarded the *Island Princess* one Saturday morning in late October with her haversack on her back and a very large doubt in her mind, it was because she had acknowledged both her need of his company and the essential inevitability of sex in any adult companionship.

That night, they took off their clothes together in the light of the kerosene lamp on the oilcloth-covered table, with the October surf muttering uncertainly outside. They were embarrassed friends, faced with mutual awkwardness. Robert's white, unfit, adult body was a small shock, and their first coupling, shielded beneath blankets, a fevered, nervous disaster. Robert apologized. It had been a long time, he said, disarmingly. Mary Jo said, no, really it had been fine, and thought about tomorrow when she could go home. They sat drinking coffee that Robert had made (he did all the cooking in those days) and talked for hours, she in Matthew's Columbia sweatshirt, and he in an old silk dressing gown Philippa had bought him in Harrods. Then, as an afterthought, they made love again, with great success.

Mary Jo glimpsed an adult lesson, that it was not the actors but their changing lines that made that particular human play work. Instead of going home, she stayed until Monday, and a week and a half later she loaded her two suitcases of belongings onto the *Island Princess* and moved in with Robert Zolan, for good.

For Mary Jo, it was love, but never lust she felt for Robert, and she decided that was enough. It was a noble choice, but she was a little too young to make it.

Still, they lived together for nine whole months, peaceably and maturely, before David came. It was a reasonable achievement for both of them. They did not discuss marriage. The thirteen years since his divorce were the majority of Mary Jo's life, carrying her back into the hazy recesses of childhood. To Robert, however, they were a snap of the fingers, and he had that nerve-edged, skin-stripped sensitivity on the subject that follows burnt-out passion. He would not marry again, and he knew it.

Once only, one extraordinary occasion, was the subject raised between them, and then only by accident, like rubbish on a miscast fishing line. It was not his finest hour. He had taken her to dinner at a friend's home in Sayville on the mainland. An old friend, a family friend, not one from the theater or writing or any of his later worlds. They drank cocktails under arbors of mildewed pink roses on the lawn. Robert's host, a man called Zerega, kept saying, "Lousy junk, scrub. Mildewed scrub," and shaking a wan, prickly branch, "Your father, now, he wouldn't look at a thing like that. Your father. There was a man who knew roses. Flowers. Any green thing." Robert introduced Mary Jo as his fiancée.

The guests were all older people, people that were wealthy, now, the women in hand-painted silk shirts, and silver jewelry, artistic, Indian stuff. They talked still with heavy, ungrammatical accents, some even foreign-born, Italian and Polish, and Brooklyn Irish. Mary Jo thought, if she closed her eyes she'd be somewhere else, somewhere with beer cans and barbecues. But the rose arbors remained, and the handsome silk shirts, wherever she turned. The men looked at her in her black jersey sheath, her one dress, a little too tight, and seemed to nudge mental elbows in each other's ribs. She was partly amused and partly angered, and afterward said, "It's a lie. I'm not your fiancée."

"They wouldn't understand anything else," Robert said, unperturbed. She did not fully believe him and wondered then how he looked upon her. She felt sullied, like the day Matthew Gittelson came to stay.

She had remembered the evening long afterward with complex distaste. They had called him Bob, Bob Zolenski, and no one talked about writing. She was accustomed to city parties or beach-house parties where she would lean on his arm, quietly beautiful and much admired, always the youngest and prettiest of the women, and hear him praised. No one praised him there that night, no one much noticed him, and though he seemed happy enough, she was not. He was Robert Zolan the writer, not Bob Zolenski the rose-grower's son. That night, for the first time, Mary Jo took the married woman's prerogative and chose not to make love.

They did not return to the Zerega house in Sayville. If Robert found the sacrifice of his friends harsh, he did not say.

The next invitation gathered dust on a windowsill and was swept out with the dead moths. Mary Jo did not care. They were one narrow slice of his social life, and she after all had given up every scrap of hers.

A weekend or two in the autumn, she had tried to maintain a remnant of it. One afternoon Chrissie came, cadging a lift in a friend's speedboat, and she made coffee and they sat, a little stiffly, at Robert Zolan's table and talked. Robert wandered from his typewriter to the kitchen, cut half an apple, poured cold coffee down the sink, opened the door for the cats, fidgeted and looked sour, much in the way he had looked when the same black cats had quite unexpectedly brought home a tabby striped companion. Robert did not put it out, on that occasion, but he did not give it milk, either. It left eventually, and so did Chrissie, and neither came back.

"You were kind of rude."

"I was not. Anyhow, it's my house." Mary Jo realized later he had accorded Chrissie the same level of attention her father had maintained for visiting classmates; being not his children, he was not interested. Her father had not liked children beyond his own, and Robert did not particularly care for post-adolescent girls. She should perhaps have been glad, considering it protected her from the need of jealousy. But she felt instead it reflected on herself.

"You don't like Chrissie."

"I don't dislike her. I just don't think about her."

"She's just like me; she's the closest friend I ever had."

"She's not like you at all. She's immature and childish. She's a spoiled brat."

"You don't know her. How can you say?"

He seemed unwilling to speak. "She reminds me of my daughter," he said at last.

Mary Jo was a little shattered by that and said eventually, nervously, "Don't you like your daughter?"

"Of course I do. She's my daughter, I love her." He realized himself it was an odd way to describe someone he saw so rarely, and said, "Oh, forget it, Mary Jo. Please."

But Mary Jo could not forget it at all, and finally said, "Am I like your daughter?"

Robert put down the folded pages of the *Times* that he had been feinting behind throughout the conversation. He looked old and angry and finally said, "What do you want from me? I thought we were happy."

She could not answer, and she never asked Chrissie again, jealous of her suddenly, sensing that to be hated for resembling a wayward daughter was more intimate than being loved in the place of a wayward wife.

The boys came also, Jeff and Marvin and Steve, on another totally different, equally disruptive weekend. They arrived uninvited, which did not please Robert. They arrived in jeans, with swimsuits underneath, even though it was only mild late October, and the ocean was growly and cold. Still they wanted to lie on the beach and listen to transistors, and they wanted Mary Jo to come with them. Suddenly, she wanted to do just that, very much. They were nothing to her, never lovers, barely friends, but they were young. She asked Robert if he would come too, and the look he gave her over the curling edge of the script emerging from his typewriter jolted her into a hearty new awareness. She could not be young, not that young, if she were to be as well his mistress. Oddly, he did not say anything like that, any word of jealousy. He said only, "I'm working," and she was aware that her answer to that was so crucial that it would affect even where she slept that night.

She never had to answer. One of the boys, probably Steve, who had an arch, clever way of doing the most wrong thing he could fathom in any social scene, flicked on his transistor radio, from silence to full volume with one quick bold finger. Music, a love song of the era, bellied up to the dry wood rafters. Robert leaped up from his desk, spilling coffee over both cats, and emerged from his workroom flanked by angry stained fur.

"Get the fuck out," he said.

There was silence, the boys gathering their gear hastily,

only Steve making something of a slow show of it. In the doorway he stopped, with the same sullen boldness, and said, "You coming, Mary Jo?" She wavered, longing for something, a faint something, like the dead-leaf scent mingling with the hot salt of summer, on the air. Not them, not longing for them, but still knowing it was important and knowing as well that if she went out the door to the beach—that most simple act—she could never return. She had only once before played with such high stakes, and that time she hadn't even known the wheel was spinning.

"No. Thanks. I don't feel like swimming. Or anything."

They shrugged. "See you." But they would not, she was certain. She heard them go, sneakered feet padding the board-walk, their voices, and the music of youth retreating on the cooling air. She was throughout that nineteenth winter conscious again and again of that severance from the young. She had gone back into the house and found Robert wiping the cats with paper toweling. Through the south window the music still came, "I need you, I need you, I nee-eed you."

Robert gently mopped the second cat from its nose to its tail, the toweling coming away coffee-colored. When he spoke he was still looking at the small animal that had forgotten the reason for the stroking and had begun to enjoy it. "I need you, I need you, I nee-eed you," Robert half sang. Then he looked up to her with his fine, startling eyes, the peculiar bushing brows half raised, smiling. "That's not what love's about, Mary Jo. Honest to God it's not."

"They won't come back," she said, painfully certain. And wrong. Two months later Robert's dear old friend, the television actor Paul Botvin, greeted them at a New York Christmas party with his eyes full of the hopeless delight of middle-aged love. "I've found the most marvelous boy. Last autumn on the beach. The most marvelous, courageous boy. But you must be terribly gentle with him. He's a soldier of fortune, you see, and he's only just back from Vietnam. They do find it terribly hard to adjust. Dear, courageous child."

"Chickens come home to roost," Robert said sadly, in his mother's car driving home. But it was winter then, and the beach was cold, inhospitable, and empty. Work, and love, were without distractions. It was their best time, and Mary Jo thought life was perfect, shut away in the wind-sifting house in the clear bright days of January, the black cats book-ending the Franklin stove. It was like being under siege to the twin seas and the snow, when the clouds rolled down from the north. Robert, if not she, knew the frailty of love forged in sieges.

Mary Jo did not. By the time David came, she had forgotten the Shack and all her friends, too. She had even forgotten her family, as much as she ever could. She had forgotten too their age gap, and all its accompanying sexual stumbling blocks, aside from an occasional wistfulness. Just rarely, she would stand and see herself and Robert, in the dust-flecked wavy mirror by the workroom door, as they made ready for bed. She creamy-brown, glossy and perfect, and behind her Robert's bony pale awkwardness; she would feel then a physical waste of her beauty. It was a thought she held un-worthy, that she would turn from in shame. That David Wardlaw, on the day they met, had looked at her romantically was an amusing bit of flattery shut from her mind with the same honorable intention.

Flattery, however, can be addictive. Mary Jo found her-self subtly urged to go back for more. She made her image available: washed and brushed her beautiful hair in front of him, and did those pretty bits of grooming that are at once intimate and yet publicly acceptable. She was in the beginning even more intimate than that, more intimate than later, treat-ing him like family, wandering from the shower in her loosely tied bathrobe.

But gradually she grew vain and would no longer appear in the old blue terry-cloth thing. The vanity took a malicious turn occasionally and she would parade about in Robert's shirt, thigh length over brown bare legs. It was a teasing game, proclaiming in the same breath: I'm experienced, I'm spoken for. It was not unlike wearing the Columbia sweatshirt for Robert.

She began to talk a lot to him, about his life in England, his school and his home, and to tease him in a tantalizing, sisterly way about his girlfriends. It was a limited subject for David; he had literally none. But she misunderstood, taking embarrassed reticence for haughtiness, and was inexplicably hurt. Hurt was an involvement of its own, and it challenged her to further intimacies, to regain her lost status as emotional superior. By mid-July, when she went to the city with David and Steve Deutsch, those intimacies had uneasily entangled them both.

The paint-peeling screen door stood open that day, with Mary Jo hovering on the sill.

"Be sure and lock up when you come in," Robert said, looking over the rims of his glasses. He looked at his watch as he said it, as if it were already two in the morning. He looked so much like her father, not his face but his gestures, that she was prickly with annoyance.

"Who's going to break in here?" she said.

"Just lock up when you come in." He began typing, letter by letter. He had the typewriter on the kitchen table, where the west wind blew through the torn screen. Mary Jo was certain he was inventing things to type. Mary Jo closed the door with herself again inside.

"What's the matter?"

"Nothing. I forgot something." She came across to the table and lifted her canvas satchel onto it, and began dipping into it and laying things on the worktable beside the typewriter. She laid out her contact-lens case, the bottle of pink solution, her large, round-eyed sunglasses, her pack of Winstons and matches and her wallet, an oddly girlish pink thing, left over from high school. It was all she carried, with a small amount of money (she would rely on the boys to pay for her drinks), and one week in four, a package of Tampax. No makeup, no handkerchief, no compact, no mirror. Robert, watching her, had a sudden painful nostalgia for girls of his youth, with those secret, innocent treasures, parceled away within patent leather bags. Mary Jo put everything back then without any change.

"I guess I'd better go," she said. Steve and David were already waiting by the bay jetty, with Steve's sixteen-foot powerboat their transport to Sayville and the train.

"So go."

"You mad, Robert?"

"Why should I be mad?" She saw then that beside the typewriter was a stack of papers, a thick wad of a letter, handwritten, with the seal of the University of Edinburgh on top. He was writing a letter, a reply to Victoria.

"About tonight."

"What?" He looked dim, his mind on something else, and his left hand tickling the ears of one of the cats, by rote. It rubbed and purred, thinking it had all his attention.

"About me and David, going to the city."

He still looked blank, and then he took off his glasses and laid them down, face down on the paper, and pulled her satchel toward him. He reached in and found the cigarette pack with no difficulty and drew it out. Mary Jo watched, startled, as he sought out a cigarette, and went back to the satchel in pursuit of matches. Robert had quit smoking four years ago. It seemed he had weak lungs.

"You're not going to smoke."

He got suddenly outrageously angry, pushing the cat away, lighting the cigarette, and shoving both pack and matches back into her satchel. "I'll do what I please," he said. "You're not going to tell me. And my twenty-year-old daughter"—he shoved the stack of handwriting aside—"who hasn't the sense not to . . . my twenty-year-old daughter is not going to tell me what to write."

He hesitated over the word "write" and Mary Jo thought somehow it was a late choice, and another word, a new word, belonged there. The writing thing was an old argument between father and daughter, and this was the first inkling she had that there was now, rather suddenly, a new one. "Damn fool bitch," he said then, quietly. He looked up. "It's not her, you know. You know that, don't you? It's Philippa and that stuffed shirt she married."

"You've always said he's a good man."

"Sure. In front of David. What should I say? Your step-father's a jerk?"

"If you think so. Why don't you be honest?" She was petulant, not understanding his anger, and feeling terribly distant from him. "Grown-ups are never honest," she said.

Robert drew on the cigarette and smiled to himself, watching the cat finding itself a new, temporary security on a window ledge. He wondered then about the situation he'd gotten himself in, where lover and father made awkward combination, wondering for the first time how long his own temporary security could last. He decided to answer as lover, not father. "Honesty is the prize weapon of the smug, my dear. Should I send him back full of my complaints, like they send him here all primed up with theirs?"

"It would serve them right."

"Sure it would. But does a seventeen-year-old kid really need his mess of a broken family playing darts over his head? That's the point, Mary Jo. Getting even is for children."

"Okay," she said a little shakily. "Okay, but I'll tell you something. If you want him to respect you, you'd better put your side of it to him. He's listened to their side all his life, and pretty soon he'll be just like Victoria. I know. I talk to him."

"I talk to him, too," Robert said.

"Yeah, sure. But with me, he listens." She regretted it upon saying it, but it was true. David and his father were bound by blood, but she and David by generation. It had of late become a tie truer than patriotism.

"You'd better go," said Robert.

"So. I'm going." She stood then. He did not stop her. She wanted very much to be stopped, but he did not stop her. Outside in the sun, running down the boardwalks to catch up with the boys, she felt suddenly, extraordinarily free, a physical near-hysteria mounting like nervous laughter in her throat.

The freedom remained like an airy new coat, all the way across the bay in the bouncing, skittering speedboat, where she sat between the two boys, sun-brown and giggly, swinging her long legs. On the long, hot afternoon train ride from Sayville to Penn Station she talked elaborately with both of them, about politics, and war and pacifism. They spiced their conversation with intelligent references, or rather she and David did, but by the end of the journey it had descended into side-taking argument, full of name calling—Pinko and Red, Do-gooder, and Bircher and Hawk—between herself and Steve Deutsch. Every now and then they stopped to explain to a bewildered David what the names meant, and went on, each of them conscious that David's allegiance was the prize to be won.

Steve had experience on his side and said again and again, "Those people aren't like us. I know, I've been there. They don't care about life the way we do." Mary Jo found it appalling, but had no evidence to hold against his. But she had another private weapon, and used it, slipping into flirtation to hold David's attention. It worked very well. But she still considered herself playing a role, condescending from womanly maturity to flirt with Robert's son, and that only for a noble cause.

Their destination was a playground in Harlem where Steve would work at the job Paul Botvin had found him, technician and roustabout to the mobile Shakespeare Theater. When they arrived it was early evening, and the big trailer truck was already there, and the stage under construction. Around it, and hemmed in by the double-height chain-link fencing of the ground, were newly constructed rows of bleacher seats. Mary Jo and David climbed to the top, and Steve slouched off, ill-humoredly, to work.

"It's *Macbeth*," said Mary Jo.

"I love it," said David. "All the sword fights, splendid stuff. I played Lady Macbeth at school."

"*Lady* Macbeth?"

"You know, the sleepwalking . . ." He stopped. "We were *only* boys, you know."

"Oh, yeah."

They watched Steve and four companions wrestle great coils of black cable off the trunk and unravel them in the direction of the distant generator. There was a sign, an electric sign, on the chain-link fence. It gave the hour six-thirty, and the temperature ninety-eight degrees. Small black children clattered up and down the softening asphalt on bicycles, rattling sticks against the fence. David pulled out a pack of American cigarettes and lit one.

"Robert'll kill you," Mary Jo said.

"For what?"

"Smoking."

David shrugged. "I'm not a child, you know. I'm not, Mary Jo." He stretched out full length on the bleachers, covering several rows with his length, his cotton shirt, too short, as all his shirts seemed to be, pulled out of his belted trousers. His skin was brown from the sun, tight, and lightly fuzzed with hair. Mary Jo felt so close to him, so intimate, that she could actually touch that intimate skin without remorse; or she could if it were not for Robert.

Suddenly she was annoyed at Robert and wished to complain. She thought and said, then, "I hope this isn't going to be late. It's a long play, and we'll be back late."

"So."

"Robert. He gets annoyed."

"We won't be late, I'm sure," David said, as consolation, but it was not what she wanted.

"He's always complaining about time," she said. "He can't stand it if I'm late, you know?"

"My stepfather's like that," said David, forgetting for an instant that it was not her parent but her lover she was lamenting.

"What does it matter?" Mary Jo went on, biting at the grainy resistance of a lock of her salt-stiff hair. It crunched satisfyingly between her small teeth. "He keeps looking at his watch. It drives me crazy sometimes."

"I guess it's something that happens when you get old," said David. Mary Jo stopped, lips parted about the strand of hair. She pulled it away, and sat up straighter, glancing nervously across the scattering of playing children.

"He's not old, David. Robert isn't old."

David said nothing. Another word would bring him in contact with the vast awkwardness of himself and Mary Jo: that she made love with her body, a body that he coveted, to the man who had fathered him. They hadn't any answers for that kind of thing at St. Vincent's in York.

"Let's have something to drink," he said. They went off down the murky sun-shivery street, Mary Jo a little afraid, not used to black people, relying on David to protect her. It was unfair, he being unaware of any danger. They found a Coke machine and came back with cold, sweating bottles, drinking through sticky bobbing straws.

When they got back, the bleachers had filled with a growing crowd of black teenagers, boys in cut-off T-shirts, and girls in frilled, hip-hugger trousers, in pinks and bright greens, with shiny patent belts skimming below brown navels. The crowd was hot and noisy and alien, speaking in throaty, thick, indistinguishable accents, full of white-teethed raucous laughter and a complexity of private humor. David and Mary Jo climbed higher up the bleachers to the empty top, and during the play leaned together for security in the dark.

Afterward, they had over an hour to wait. The lighted clock said twelve o'clock and one hundred and two degrees. Wild children rode bicycles beneath the bleachers, waving imaginary swords and shouting, "Mac-beth! Mac-beth!" Mary Jo and David had another Coke and watched Steve and his friends put the play back into its truck. In the dark corners of the playground dark men stood with paper bags, drinking and arguing through the night.

"My stepfather should see this," David said.

"This? Why?"

"He thinks America is so bloody marvelous."

"He does?" Mary Jo said, quite amazed.

"Oh, not Americans. Not like father and his friends. But America. The government. Free enterprise and all that. He ought to see this." Then he shrugged and said, "No. It would hardly matter. You see, he'd say it was just because they were Negro. Different. You know, like Steve says about the Vietnamese."

"That's awful," Mary Jo said vehemently. "Steve makes me sick. Those poor people out there, the children and babies." She spoke as if children and babies were another species. "But it won't go on," she said hurriedly. "President Kennedy won't let it."

"President Kennedy is four square behind it," said David.

"How would you know?" Mary Jo demanded, offended.

"My stepfather says so. He's in Parliament. He said Kennedy comes to Macmillan for advice, only he doesn't listen to it when he gets it." David did not add that the Kennedy most famous in Wardlaw circles was the older Kennedy, familiarly known as "that Fascist bastard, Joe."

Mary Jo said, "I don't care what your dumb stepfather thinks. He's the best President we've ever had. It's the first time I can remember when politics wasn't always about stuffy fat men with bald heads. You can keep your stodgy old Macmillan."

David laughed and said they were not likely to. Then he

added casually, "Steve's right, you know." Mary Jo put down her empty Coke bottle with a clunk on the wooden bench. "Oriental people do have a different view of life. More casual. They are different."

"How would you know?" she demanded again.

"My grandfather was in India, as a boy. He's told me. You know, they throw babies on rubbish heaps. They're not like us, not Christian or anything."

"Big deal. Look what the Christians do. Madame Nhu is a Christian. *I'm* not Christian, either, if that's what Christian means, burning innocent monks."

"Nobody's burning monks," David said with a dismissive wave of his hand. "They're suicides. It's part of their religion, anyway. Gets them to Nirvana or somewhere." His voice had gone harder, more British, and he'd begun to lean toward dogmatic aristocratic authority, as his stepfather would in debate. "You know, Steve really is right. You're the sort of person that plays right into their hands."

"Whose hands?" Mary Jo said, bewildered. "The monk's?"

"The Communists'."

Mary Jo threw up her own hands and turned away. "God, they've really gotten to you."

"I don't think so. I know Communists, Mary Jo. My stepfather has introduced me to several. They have no morals. They're not like us. They don't care about anything but winning. No honor, no decency. I tell you if we don't stop them now in Vietnam, the way the British stopped them in Malaya, there will be no stopping them at all in another ten years." David lit another cigarette and leaned back, waiting for reply, as Andrew Wardlaw would do with his cigar as the gentlemen tossed politics around with the port.

But Mary Jo did not fight. Politics to her was always a matter not of facts but of emotion, a tight little club in which she and her friends reassured each other of the rightness of their heretical beliefs. Her lip trembled. She was tired and hated his sureness, hated losing, but lacked the strength or the knowledge to win.

"What I can't understand is father," said David then. "Of all the people arguing pacifism. When his war started, his knickers were in such a twist just to get in there, he didn't even wait for the rest of his country. Now he's a bloody Quaker or something."

"Maybe that's it," said Mary Jo. "Maybe that's just it. He knows what war is like. No wonder he's against it. No wonder he hates it."

"Hates it? Balls. They loved it, all of them. They never bloody shut up about it."

"Robert doesn't talk about the war," Mary Jo said quickly. "He doesn't, David. He never talks about it."

"Balls," said David again. "They all do. My stepfather. He goes on about it like it were yesterday. Besides, they don't have to talk about it. It's always there, that's the damnable thing. You can never win with any of them. They can always go back to the war. Nothing we can ever say or do comes up to it. They've always got the last word on courage, or fortitude, or keeping their damned chins up. I always feel like a child when Andrew talks about the war. Worse than that, like a backward child, retarded, who never is going to grow up. I can go to school, and Cambridge, and make the cricket eleven. Jolly super. Andrew went ashore with Lovat on D day. Marching. Probably in bloody evening dress." He stubbed out the cigarette against the gray painted wood. Steve had finished work below them and was talking to a bearded black man, their near hands on each other's shoulders, beer bottles in the far ones. David looked grim and older, and Mary Jo wanted to put her arms around his neck.

"We'd better go," he said.

Mary Jo said, to be comforting, "Robert isn't like that. He never talks about it. I wish he would, you know, it's kind of exciting. But he doesn't."

"Bloody marvelous. Then I can't even imagine he's lying."

Mary Jo shook her hair back, wishing to get to some other, more sure and intimate ground. "I don't know," she said casually, "it's all so long ago anyhow. No one here seems to care much about it any more. All my parents ever talk about is the Depression. How awful it was and how much nicer they were because they had it." She laughed nervously. "I suppose that's our famous American materialism."

"Thank God for that," David said. "In Britain it's always the war. They count time from it like B.C. and A.D. Only everything before nineteen forty is always better, more honest, less dear." He put on Andrew's voice, " 'Before the war, you know, you could buy a damned fine motorcar for three and sixpence.' " He laughed, and she laughed, too. They leaned together, joined by a siege against unchangeable time. "The damned thing is I'm never certain whether to laugh at him or, and that's what's strange, simply to give up trying. If our whole world is second-rate, why try to make anything of it at all?" He shrugged and stood up, waving halfheartedly to Steve in the stifling, arc-lit heat. "What's Britain got left worth fighting for, anyhow?"

"That's it," Mary Jo said, suddenly urgent and angry. "That's it."

"What?"

"You're going to Vietnam to prove something to your stepfather, and Robert, and all the old people. And that's just what they want. You're doing just what they want. Getting killed, probably, for all those bald old men."

"Oh, really," he said. "How apallingly melodramatic."

She was crushed, but then she saw he was twitchy and uncertain about the mouth. He was standing three steps down, their eyes level.

"David."

"What?" He was wary.

"David. Would you kiss me?"

He stepped sideways. "Good God, Mary Jo—I don't know what to do."

"I'm not that much older than you. I'm not, you know."

"Steve will see," David said, and turned away. But Steve had vanished.

He could taste the Coke on her mouth still, and her salty upper lip. She did all the tightening, the drawing near, and the funny forceful things with her tongue. He did very little because he had never kissed a girl before in his life. The arc lights switched out, and the July blackness came down thick as black wool.

They both slept in the train home, exhausted by the emptiness of unspent passion. The nothing that had happened between them dominated every day and night that followed.

Mary Jo grew sharp and bitchy, bewildering Robert and David alike, going off every morning to swim by herself, coming back haughty as if she hated them both. Sleeping beside Robert became a stiff, formal misery.

"What's the matter?"

"Nothing."

"No, come on. What's the matter?"

"Oh, leave me *alone*, Robert."

"All right, then." She could hear the hurt in his voice and was intensely surprised, her own estimate of her importance to him much lower. She put her arms around the damp skin of his shoulders and forearms, lying behind him in the rumpled bed. She knew it would end in sex. Because she could not make the passion rise any other way, nor bear another passionless rocking about the hot bed, she pretended he was David.

After, he said, sitting on the edge of the bed and lighting a cigarette, "What got into you? That was terrific." There was the tiniest note of startled pride in his voice.

She cried. Robert put on his silk dressing gown and made coffee, quietly so they would not wake David in the too-near next room. She watched him move about the sandy-floored kitchen, the cats rubbing his bare legs, and giving up eventually. His feet were white and awkward. He always wore sandals, even on the beach. His hands were long and deft, never hedging a gesture. He looked marvelous in clothes, winning the highest flattery from any garment, and slightly unbalanced out of them. He brought her coffee and sat beside her on the bed and told her a long story about a play he was in once, in York, where everyone, the entire cast, completely forgot the second act. She loved him so much. David was nothing; a child.

The next day, yesterday, she swam again, alone, but peaceful, thinking about neither, which was best. She showered, still in her swimsuit, to save rinsing it, and she forgot to lock the door. It rattled suddenly, surprising her into silence, and then swung open and the white light flooded in.

"Oh, terribly sorry." It was David, full of gauche embarrassment. He had his towel around his waist, like a skirt. He blundered backward, but she said calmly, laughing at him from the darkness, "It's all right. I've got my suit on. See?" She smiled. He was a child, she a woman. It could not matter. "Come on in. Save some water. Robert will be delighted." Robert was not there to be delighted, though. Robert was at the Pines, with the laundry. David hesitated. She held the door for him, and he came in. He turned his back to unwrap the towel.

The shower door closed on them both, and the gray light filtered in slowly from above, through chinks in the roof. The water was a tepid, slack trickle, like weak rain, its scope so narrow that they must share the same board to both get wet.

"Have a good swim?" Mary Jo said. They were face to face, six inches apart, dripping with water. It was necessary to say something.

"Yes, smashing." David looked at the wet, sandy top of her head and groping in his repertoire, added, "Awfully nice day."

"Yeah." Mary Jo was shampooing her long hair and white puffs of soap ran down her neck and breasts, her swimsuit top damming a little lake between them, and slid, cascading over bare skin, all the way to the deck. He was watching them. She shook her head and soap covered him, an alarming intimacy.

"I think I'm clean," said David, stepping back.

"Oh, let me do your hair, it's gritty." He shook his head, very slightly, but she was insistent, already bending his neck down so she could reach. She scrubbed expertly at the wet, salty tangle. His hair was blond, and curly, not at all like his father's—she was used to washing that—but his body was patterned on Robert's, the same long neck, and wide bony shoulders, the same flatness of the buttocks, and unexpected width of the hip bones. But he was fit and tanned, supple and young. Robert, perhaps, as Robert was once, long ago, when she was barely born, the body time had cheated her of. She scrubbed fiercely at the roots of his hair.

"Excuse me," David said, suddenly urgent.

"Wait a moment, I'm not done."

"No, please, I must." He turned away, his back to her. Reaching for his towel.

"You got soap in your eyes?"

He shook his head, backing away, the towel held before him. She started to laugh, her wet hand over her wet mouth. She was still laughing when he, still clutching the towel, stopped retreating and bolted forward instead.

"Mary Jo. Mary Jo, I love you." She could not stop laughing, feeling again the free hysteria she'd felt that day on the boardwalk.

"Please stop," he said angrily. "You began it, anyway. You wanted me to kiss you." He sounded to her like a small boy complaining about a revision of sporting rules. Then he grabbed hold of her, terribly roughly, clumsily, like he must hold terribly tight or it would not work. He tried to kiss her, but wet and soapy, she slipped from his grasp.

"Cut it out, David."

"I have to. I love you." She had to wrestle him again and was regretting a lot of things, like not locking the door, and the foolish idea of the shower. He finally got his mouth over hers. She kept giggling and half fighting, and then it got terribly silly with a lot of tickling on her part, and determined wrestling on his. Then suddenly he stopped. He looked stunned, and stepped back.

"Oh." He stepped back further, still shielding the front of his swimsuit, but the reason for that was lessening, under the shock of shame. "Oh, Mary Jo. I'm terribly sorry. Do forgive me. Please."

There was a long silence. Mary Jo turned the shower off, but the overused pump whined and whistled, blending with the low rumbling of the half-buried generator beneath the deck. Then she, realizing he meant to leave, desired him passionately.

She closed the distance between them, clasping first his hands, then his arms, then his shoulders. She began kissing him, and her hands became terribly familiar on his body, peeling down his swimsuit, seeking the rising member he was trying so hard to conceal.

"What are you doing? Surely you can't."

"Come on, David, come on."

She took his hand and guided it all over her body. It was stiff and unresponsive, the fingers lifting away in shyness and remorse. She held them folded under hers on her breasts, and arched her back. Then impulsively she untied the top string of her bikini. It fell away, hanging about her waist, two wet, seaweedy triangles. David looked for two seconds at the white, untanned skin, and then turned away, and pulled away.

"Hadn't we better lock the door?" he said.

Mary Jo stopped, aware of herself half-naked with David Wardlaw. It was enough to switch passion off like a light. It almost did. She started to say "No, no," to the whole thing, but David, thinking she meant only the door, turned back to her and with tentative wonder explored her breasts, and even kissed one shyly. She was at once so excited she would do anything, and had to do it at once.

She thrust his hand down her wet swimsuit, into the seaweedy hair. He did not know what to do. Impatient, she pulled the suit down around her thighs, gasping.

"Shall I take it off?" David said. He was nervously rolling down the top of his brown swim trunks.

"Oh, anything. Come on, David." He stepped out of them, pushing them away with his foot, trying not to look at her, or his own swelling self. The floor was wet and sandy, and the sour smell of rotting wood was rising in the heat to engulf them. David looked foolish in his embarrassed, half-concealed eagerness, the guest at a surprise party that was no real surprise. Desire and disgust battled briefly. She put her hands around his unembarrassed penis.

"Mary Jo. Surely you—what are you doing?"

"Oh, what the hell do you think?" she moaned, bending her legs, awkward with the wet suit about her thighs, too hurried to wriggle out of it. She mounted onto him, rather than he on her, guiding him into her, fighting the resistance of her own fresh-washed body. Within, it was wet with warm need. He slipped in easily, and she sighed.

"Oh, my God," said David. Then there wasn't any time for discussion. Mary Jo clasped his soapy buttocks and thudded her thighs against his, standing on tiptoes, and hurting her back, wriggling from one foot to the other with excitement. She came so quickly that his virgin ill-control was no problem. It was a terribly solitary coupling, she lost in frantic need, he in private discovery, too quick to be satisfying, too violent to avoid the inevitable violent sorrow afterward.

She slipped away, panting, her breasts trembling with her heartbeat, and leaned against the shower wall. It felt gritty against her back. David was leaning on the other wall, naked, shining with water and soap and her own salty wetness. His mouth was half open. She noticed the beginning of his yet unshaven moustache, dibbled with sweat. Her green swimsuit was yet about her thighs. With faint disgust she wiggled from it, and dropped it, a damp heap on the sandy floor. Her top still hung about her middle, and a stubborn crude brown strip of seaweed yet remained pasted on the white skin above one nipple. Her body was, in her own eyes, obscene.

"You're so beautiful. I love you, Mary Jo," David panted.

She was sore from his unpracticed attentions, and her back ached. She put a hand to her maidenhair. He reached to touch her, with both hands, and drew her near to him. She realized she must be smiling because he was grinning so foolishly back. "Oh, David," she said, and it came out amazingly like praise.

The footsteps came then with the sureness of purpose that only an owner has in his own house.

"Mary Jo?"

"Oh, *God*."

"David? Mary Jo?"

"It's father," David cried, standing up straight, staring at her with astounded innocence. He scrabbled on the floor for his swimsuit, abandoned that, and reached for his towel. In his confusion he wound it into a knot and could not get it to cover the only part of himself he deemed important. Mary Jo did nothing but listen as the footsteps strode across the decking with the ring of sure doom.

"Hey, Mary Jo? I'm back." The voice was purely conversational. "You in the shower? Hey, listen, I asked Paul and he says he'll come . . ." The slatted door flung open before his casual broad hand.

Lock the door, Mary Jo.

White light glared. Robert glared.

"Jesus H. Christ," he said.

VIII

"Oh, dear God," said Paul Botvin. "It's Mrs. Miniver." He looked around the roof deck for reaction and got none, partly because of those who had heard him only Robert could possibly understand, and partly because he had broken a silence everyone else was as pleased to maintain. The air had thickened with it, as the sky itself had, paling from blue to gray. Out over the mainland thunderheads traced fat curves and hummocks, blotting out the exhausted yellow sun.

Philippa Wardlaw's hair had something of the same lighting of gray and yellow. Its smoothly cultured waves descended from their multiple gazes in small, halted jerks as she made her way, carefully, step by step down the narrow stair. They were all clustered above, waiting their turn to follow, and the stairway had achieved the aspect of a stage with its demand upon their attention. Paul shrugged, unnoticed still, and turning quickly to David, said, "Of course, I only saw it on television."

David had no idea what he was talking about and, less polite than usual, simply ignored him. Then Paul said, persistent for his attention, "It was a perfectly awful film, actually," and David, driven at last into speech, said simply, "Quite," which was his standard answer to Paul, anyhow, whom he never really understood.

Philippa stepped with quick gratitude off the last step and strode off across the deck as Robert followed her down, trailed at once by Paul, and David, and eventually by Steve Deutsch, who shrugged himself off the rickety roof railing where he had balanced throughout, watching Mrs. Wardlaw go through her greetings.

"Robert, it's utterly charming," she said now. She was walking about the gray wood deck with its clutter of folding beach chairs and salty towels. Her arms were half-outstretched in a subtle half-embrace, either of the scene itself or, more distantly, of Robert. She was doing her Country House Guest scene. He had seen it before, again and again, in the last postwar year of their marriage, when he'd been dragged by Hallsworth manners from one claustrophobic Yorkshire weekend to another. He was highly annoyed that she would turn that act on him.

Her breeziness swept the deck as she strode about, clear to the south side, admiring one foolish thing after another; his homemade table with the one short leg, the old hand pump for when the generator collapsed, the intruding spikes of wild holly and sassafras brushing against the windows. She cast bright smiles on all, and the breeziness swept her own tired face as well, erasing lines, surmounting smudged lipstick.

Greetings were such subtle agony. Robert ordinarily loved them, that is, those that did not so directly involve himself. He loved them so much that at times, when work was a bore and he was restless for the anonymous human contact that stimulated thought, he would go skidding off in his little dinghy, down to the Pines and meet the ferry. Not anybody on the ferry, but the ferry itself. He would stand, sometimes with a drink, sometimes with nothing, at the edge of the dock below the hotel watching the boat come in and the crowds coming to claim its cargo of visitors. Then he would watch them greet.

It was such a marvel of mundane drama: people arriving who shouldn't have; people not arriving who should. People arriving single who should have arrived in pairs, and in pairs who should have been single. And all the halt, elaborate language of hello, the posturings of arms and hips, the inventive variety of hand-waves. Planned meetings were rather like formal weddings, among the few occasions for which people had time to prepare their lines. Robert found, though, that conversation, like lovemaking, was for the most of humanity better ad-libbed.

The British, however, were different. He was never sure if they ad-libbed at all, or if indeed their immense structure of custom enabled them to present an old, tried, true line from an endlessly diverse prewritten script, for every occasion. Philippa was never lost for words.

She had been at her most reasonable: breezy, bright, and reasonable. She was always at her most powerful when reasonable, and most breezy bright when most in deadly earnest. From the first look at her face, calm and rimmed by pearl earrings and necklace, he had raised every lance for the joust to come.

Her greeting had been a masterpiece. He was sure she had managed to embrace and kiss him without ever actually touching. Her lips whisked by his cheek, her arms enfolded his shoulders with air, her hands skimmed by the fabric of his shirt. She was all warmth, behind glass. The way she had said, "Indeed," in response to Steve Deutsch's insulting little "Hi!" As if with no difficulty she could, with another word, topple him off his arrogant perch. The way she shook hands with Paul, at a double arm's length. (Gentlemen in silver medallions, beware.) And the way she greeted her, *their*, son.

"Hello, Daves." Again the cheek-whisking kiss, and how sweetly she had smiled, and how subtly slipped his pathetic reach for an embrace.

That had surprised Robert. He had seen her do that often enough with Victoria, even as a small child, and was never sure whether it was because she was of the same sex, and physical contact therefore risky, or because she had not been wanted.

David, however, had been wanted, uniquely so, even though at the time of his conception his father had not. She had never before eluded David's grasp.

Now as she eyed up Robert's peeling screen door, half over her shoulder, preparing to turn and make her actual assault on his house, he was reminded of yet one more country weekend; at Greenshaws, that one, and a significant weekend at that—the last weekend of their marriage. Nineteen fifty, autumn. They were, of course, already divorced by then, but in those two days the true spiritual severance was made; born, like Victoria, at Greenshaws Hall, and sister to the legal severance that had come after the birth of David.

It was a cold, gray weekend, and on its gray Saturday afternoon, after lunch, and before the stifling coziness of the Greenshaws afternoon tea, Philippa was practicing jumps. She was in fact following a great weekend country tradition, filling in the time between meals with outdoor activity, preferably something brutally bracing involving animals. Training, Robert imagined, for the more delicate anthropoid savageries awaiting them, later, in the drawing room. She was driving a brute of an Irish mare at a three-bar, thrice-refused gate.

She had already taken a dreadful, bone-thudding fall, and both she and the beast were covered with dust. Robert was watching from the paddock fence, as was a younger Andrew Wardlaw, also a house guest that weekend, whom he had met for the first time that morning. Victoria was scuffing about kicking at nettles and ignoring everybody, particularly her visitant father and her mother on the mare's back. She was the only one present who seemed rock-solid unconcerned about the whole business. Robert hoped it was simply because she, a sturdy if slightly vicious little horsewoman at age seven herself, saw no cause for concern. He hoped it wasn't just that she didn't care.

David cared. But he was only four, afraid of horses, and hiding in the stable, crying, though not only because of Philippa's riding. Occasionally he would appear at the shadowy stone-arch doorway and sniffle loudly, but no one paid any notice.

Andrew Wardlaw leaned on the paddock fence, his walking stick under his arm and his brown moustache twitching, saying, "My dear, I do really think you'd be wise . . ." Philippa ignored him, licking her bloody lip with the tip of her tongue, concentrating solely on animal and fence, as if the moving of one over the other would change the weary world. "Come, come, up we go, up we go," she murmured, coaxing half a ton of equine recalcitrance like an ounce of Persian kitten. "Upsie girlies, upsie girlies." Her jaw a forward thrust, and the crop clutched in white fingers; her voice as sweet as a child's.

Upsie girlies, upsie girlies, Robert thought with a slow, quiet smile growing against his will. He put a hand over his mouth, pretending to stroke his beard like a professor. Philippa turned, faced the doorway, and then suddenly refused the fence, bolting for the southern railing instead. She leaned on it, and peered oceanwards.

"Really a most charming aspect, Robert." She half turned to him, and to the sky, gauging directions. "Is it south-facing?" Her smile was quick and sure.

Robert smiled back and said a little theatrically, "Philippa, my love, the whole *island* is south-facing. There are times in summer when I think it's south-facing in all four directions."

"You'll get the sun, then," she said, unperturbed, still laying the old County groundwork.

"Occasionally," Robert said sourly, then added with a burst of frustration, "You'll be amazed to hear that we really don't think about it that much. I mean, there are countries where it really doesn't rain twenty-four hours a day. And nobody talks about it when it does."

"I'm glad you get the sun, Robert," she said.

"Philippa, *everybody* gets the sun."

"No, dear. Even in the tropics, some definitely more than

others." The subject was closed. With another quick smile, Philippa, nodding her "May I?" went inside. Robert felt washed, exhausted by her, as if he had lain in the same cherished sun all afternoon.

He did not wish to rush about, find a place for her suitcase, or her ridiculous tweed jacket. Nor resurrect the aging meal, nor find drinks for everyone. For a moment, he wanted someone, mother, or wife, who would do everything for him, and wondered where Mary Jo was. It hardly mattered; these were his responsibilities, not hers, as it was his house, not hers, or even theirs. Mary Jo did some cleaning, true, and made the beds, as if indeed she were the daily David had once imagined. But Robert cooked, Robert made drinks, Robert maintained the face of the house turned open to the world. At times, he was considerably more bachelor father than adult lover.

He stood bemused now in his own living room, with Philippa's jacket hanging from his half-extended arm, like he were a coat hook. In the end, he simply laid it across a chair, and then a strange thing happened. David, who had not hung up so much as a shoelace all summer, went solemnly to the closet in the workroom, and came back with a wooden hanger on which he hung the jacket, and bending the hook sideways, suspended it from the door.

Robert, seeing it there, was jarred by an ancient memory, and unable to place it, fiddled about with the suitcase, taxing his mind toward it. When he looked up, the suitcase at last harbored behind the cold Franklin stove, he saw that Paul had filled the wife's role and was pouring drinks. He went to the table and picked up a pack of cigarettes that Steve Deutsch had dropped beside his oriental madonna. He lit one, filling time with action, and realizing that among Paul's row of gin and tonics would be one for himself, and that he had already had enough. He couldn't find the effort to say "Not for me," any more than he could resist the easy old comfort of the smoke. Once more he thought longingly of winter, winter past, or winter yet to come, without people or complications, and with the discipline of work to keep him straight. He realized suddenly that the forecasted winter of his mind was one of total solitude.

Mary Jo came in then, as if in answer to his unconscious mental dismissal of her. She was dressed in clean, pale jeans and an old white shirt of his own, still bearing the creases of folding. She did not look at him, or at anyone, falling perfectly into the mood and manner of the small crowded room in which no one was looking at anyone. Philippa Wardlaw, her arms folded, fingers toying with the crepe elbows of her blouse, was looking out the window at the graying bay with politely admiring eyes. David was looking at one of the cats, curled in a wicker chair, stirring it up with fingers along its curled spine so it would justify his rapt attention with some action. Paul was looking at his assembly line of gin glasses, dropping ice into the whole row in one gesture, with a slender, artistic hand. Steve Deutsch was looking at a Marvel comic, and Robert was looking at his feet.

If you don't learn to look somewhere other than the floor ...

"Ice and lemon, Mrs. Wardlaw?" said Paul.

"Oh, please."

Paul extended the glass and smiled, his favorite, British-style smile, with the whimsical downturned corners. He'd been rather good once in *Present Laughter*—in summer stock, of course. Philippa met the smile with one of her own. "Oh, splendid," she said, sipping the tall drink.

"Terribly nice on a hot day, what?" said Paul.

"I'll say," Philippa said at once. "You're the actor, aren't you?"

"In my small way."

Philippa laughed. "I dare say a bit more than that. Robert's mentioned you from time to time."

"Has he?" Paul said, shyly pleased.

"Oh, very much so. Robert used to act, too, you know. Years ago, of course. In the past."

You might as well be a street sweeper.

"Did you?" said Steve Deutsch suddenly.

"Come on, you know that," Robert said sourly, but realized at once the accusation was possibly false, and said, "Yeah, well, I did. Years ago, before the beginning of time."

Philippa laughed. "No, really," she said. "He was quite good, you know."

"Thanks very much," said Robert, taking his drink. She did not hear his sarcasm, but went on to say, "He played leads, always, at Bridlington. He was very much the star. All the shopgirls used to queue up to see him leave the stage door."

"Oh, Robert," said Paul, suddenly laughing. "You've never said." He sounded quite entranced. "A matinee idol, no less."

"Philippa tends to be a bit extravagant," he said. "There really weren't any shopgirls lining up."

"There was one," said Philippa at once, and even after eighteen years her voice was surprisingly harsh. Robert was sadly flattered. He needed flattery just now, he needed it very much. But for her sake he'd have done without it. He said slowly, as he offered Philippa a chair with accustomed grace, "Philippa always had a higher opinion of my charms than I deserved." He smiled. "She was loyal to a fault." She took the offered seat and smiled gently, and said, "Oh, never a fault. Loyalty's never possibly a fault." Then she turned around briskly to her son, sitting with American ease on the floor. "I'm just assuming you're all packed, David. Our train leaves at ten." Robert heard the riding crop crack, like thin thunder, on a distant flank.

David whirled about and looked at him wide-eyed, like the distant child David in the stable doorway with half-accusing eyes that demanded he do something, stop something, stop everything that was happening. Robert finished half of his drink in two gulps, got up, walked to the kitchen and said, "A.M. or P.M., Philippa?"

"Come again?"

"Your train. Tonight or tomorrow."

"Tomorrow, of course. Certainly there's hardly time . . ."

She turned her wrist and looked somewhere in the direction of her arm for an instant.

"You're staying the night, then?"

"Well, Robert, I simply imagined."

"Fine. Fine." He was not looking at her, but reheating the cold meal, and feeling, rather than seeing, her miss her stride. Outside there was a distant thud of real thunder, more like a sonic boom than anything, an imitation of art by nature. Before she could round again on David, Robert said quickly, "Philippa, be a darling, and do the seating. I've forgotten all about it." It was the first he had thought of a seating plan in years, accustomed, once back in America, to following his mother's style, though granted with the addition of candles and silver, and seat all with a careless, help-yourselves hand.

"David, are you packed?" Philippa said more firmly.

"It's just six, the perfect number," Robert said.

"The time?"

"No, the table. Hurry up, everything's ready."

"David?"

"There *are* other trains," Robert said sharply, annoyed at his failure to deflect her.

Philippa half stepped toward the table, instinctively cooperative. "I'm sorry, Robert, but I don't wish to be late. And that is an appalling railway. I thought it was nationalization that destroyed railways, but you people seem to have managed to do it in the private sector." She sniffed slightly and began mentally sorting chairs and people in her head.

"We have other railroads," he said. "It's not our best."

"Thank God for that," she said, not listening. "Robert, this table's impossible. There are too many men." She stood waiting a moment in clear annoyance, as if he could instantly do something about the balance of sexes in the room.

"I wouldn't worry about it," said Paul without expression.

Robert was tossing the salad and grinning to himself within his beard. His unorthodox coupling of guests was at the moment a nasty toy, like a plastic fly to be dropped in Philippa's drink. He did not help, but said to Paul, "Shaw said that the British never care what they do as long as they pronounce it properly. One *could* add that they don't care either who they dine with, as long as they're seated properly. Attila to the right of Ghengis Khan, and oh no, my dear, you can't put Vlad the Impaler next to Richard the Third. They're fourth cousins twice removed, *and* on the wrong side of the blanket, at that."

"Charming," said Philippa. Then with a quick gesture of the side of her hand, she reined in his guests, installing them about the table. Robert found his own mistress suddenly on his right, and Stephen Deutsch on his left. Down table of them were Paul and David and, at the foot of the table, facing him serenely was Philippa. "You don't mind, my dear," she said to Mary Jo. "But Robert does seem to have commandeered me as hostess."

Mary Jo looked very blank and said eventually, "It's all right." She did not care where she sat, and formal tables were unknown to her. Mockery, however, she was familiar with, and she was not sure that she was not being mocked.

"Anyway," Philippa said, smoothing her skirt and seating herself gracefully, "I have afforded you the place of honor. Which is correct, isn't it, Robert?"

He set the tureen of rice on the table, followed it by the open dish of stroganoff. He carefully ladled sour cream in sculptured swirls across the steaming surface, and watched them melt. "Let me go check Debrett's," he said.

"Of course it's correct," she answered at once. "Unless naturally there is a bride of six months present—there isn't a bride of under six months . . .?" Her clear gray eyes flicked sideways to Mary Jo, and then alarmingly down the table to Steve. "No, I don't suppose there is."

She lifted her fork ceremoniously. "Looks jolly splendid, anyway, Robert," she said. "Bon appétit, everyone." She took one bite. "You can pack after supper, Daves," she said.

"Nor," said Robert, "do they care where the *hell* they're going, as long as the goddamned trains run on time."

October, 1945

Bridlington, Yorkshire

"Come back, Hitler, where are you when we need you?"

"That was Mussolini," said Philippa.

"Hitler did it, too."

"Hitler did it. Of course, Hitler did it. But Mussolini was famous for it. There's a difference. That was also in perfectly rotten taste."

"So what do you expect from a bum Yank?"

"Don't be self-pitying. And I really *must* go now. Daddy will be furious if I miss another train."

"It wasn't your fault. They didn't run it," he said.

She looked up with her fresh, clear-eyed look of amazement. "It doesn't matter, Robert. Daddy never thinks anything's my fault, anyhow. It's your fault, always. I'm doing this for you, Robert. I wish you'd come to appreciate that. I'm doing this for you."

"Dammit, Philippa, I'm not some kid courting you anymore. I'm your husband. I don't *have* to please your father, you know. There isn't anything he can do about us." Even as he said it, he was aware how ridiculous it was. Harold Hallsworth could do a great deal about them; he could do everything about them. Not because he had any legal force. He did not. But he had something stronger; he had his daughter on his side. And that his daughter was Robert's wife was seeming to count for less and less with each day that passed.

Philippa was in a foul mood. She had been in a foul mood all day, and since he only saw her one day a week at most, the impact was that much greater. There were reasons. It started with the weather, which, even for October on the northeast coast, was vile. Wet fog clamped down on the moorlands, through which the train passed, making the journey a great tedium of rain-dribbled windows, moving through a corridor of stubble fields bordered in walls of gray. Victoria had gotten bored at once, bored too with the ancient rag doll she had dragged along, and the cloth purse her grandmother had sewn. She spent the journey dropping one and then the other on the grimy floor, and disrupting the crowded compartment with wails until Philippa bent and retrieved it.

The significance of her regular visits to Bridlington was somewhat lost on the child, anyhow, and the purpose of seeing daddy was submerged by the interest of seeing the seaside, and being taken out for a fish-and-chips lunch (after a solemn promise that grandmama would not be told).

But it had rained, and she was yet too young to quite understand that the seaside was not either reliable or instantly creatable, it being rather a subtle balance of place and weather that only existed in its desired form if the sun shone. When Philippa stepped off the train, she was already repeating steadily, "*Now* go and see sand, mummy. *Now*." When Robert gathered her up and held her high over his head beneath the glassed-in girders of the station, she only cried and said, "No. No. Go and see sand *now*," and began to wail for Philippa. Robert handed her over with a weary shrug. She was so like her mother in her eagerness to be gone from him. Philippa's first comment upon stepping off the train into his hesitant arms was always, "I've got to make the four-forty [or three thirty-seven, and once, infuriatingly, the one forty-three] back. Daddy will be waiting." Thus Harold Hallsworth, even at the distance of forty miles, was able to shut the door on their hours together before it was open a crack.

But since the visit was, in theory at least, for Victoria's benefit, and since there was absolutely nothing to do with her in Robert's tiny bed-sit in the St. Leonard's, they took her to the beach, as requested. Gray clouds lay heavy over gray water. The Flamborough cliffs were blotted out, and from their strip of North Beach, below the great Victorian stone seawalls, even the harbor was mist-shrouded. Rain fell steadily and the wind was rising. Lone trawlers crept one by one into shelter. The sand was as wet from rain as the sea. Victoria sat down in it at once, and soaked her plaid woolen dress. Philippa yanked her to her feet with such vehemence that Robert protested.

"You won't be riding home with her moaning she's wet," Philippa snapped.

"No, I won't, will I?" Robert returned at once, the words laden with all his anger about the whole arrangement. Victoria watched from a distance, prodding the cold brown sand with her homemade wooden spade. For no apparent reason the image of her parents, two tall people in dark wet raincoats standing face to face, leaning toward each other with mouths twisting in whispered argument, was intensely frightening. She began to cry.

"Oh, for *God's* sake," Philippa cried, and Victoria knew it was all her fault.

She was right, too. She was the reason, if not directly, still in some way, for every moment of argument between them. Argument, that art at which they were now masters, had really begun in the first, unborn months of her existence. Pregnancy had changed Philippa more than Robert, at the time, could imagine a person could be changed, except by catastrophe. She was like a bomb victim, shell-shocked and bereaved, over this gift of life that neither of them had done anything to avoid.

"But you must have wanted to be pregnant. We didn't do anything," he had said on the day he found her crying at their kitchen table, the results of her medical exam and the forms of her discharge from the WAAF on the table.

"It's not happening to you," she had cried, and there was nothing he could say that would change that. Nor anything he could do that would convince Philippa that even with her pregnant, and honorably retired from the war effort, the war would continue to be won, and their own small partnership in it would continue as well. It was as if at that moment the aspect of life that was a splendid game, a play stylishly acted, must end. "All the fun is finished," she had said. "It will never just be you and I again."

Afterwards, long afterwards, he began to realize that from the time of her pregnancy Philippa lost the ability to live for the present. She was tied to the future now, the time beyond the great adventure, and unfortunately for him Robert had only really existed for her as a part of the great adventure.

He had worried about her. She was tired and depressed, and he wanted her somewhere quiet, and safe, where she could sleep, and tend herself, and eat well, and not dash for shelter in the night. Most ironically, it was he, not she, who decided her confinement was best spent at Greenshaws.

Confinement it was, too, in every sense of the word. They welcomed her back with wide arms and reproachful eyes, welcoming no doubt her green ration book as well. Then something very strange happened. Robert never understood what it was about carrying a child that could make a woman, even a woman like Philippa, so rebellious and untrammeled, become again like a child herself. He had noticed it even the last days at Lime Street. Suddenly there was no more bravado, real or false. Her face went white at every sound, and she leaped up to run at an explosion so muffled and distant that but weeks before she would not have broken the stride of conversation for it. She clung to him tearfully when he left the flat, and flung herself into his arms upon his return, with such desperation he imagined she'd been waiting by the door all day. Which, for all the work she'd done about the place, was entirely possible.

When it came time for her to board her train for the north, he left her at King's Cross with a sort of muffled relief. He told himself it was only because now he could relax and get down to the job at hand: Philippa safe, and he himself free of concern. The first night he went out alone, met some friends, got a little drunk, remembered Mike, which he hadn't done for years, and came home (he had moved back onto the base) with a feeling of inexplicable exhilaration.

His exhilaration left him when the first of Philippa's letters arrived. He read it twice, and then a third time, looking back and forth from its neat, round schoolgirlish hand to the picture of Philippa in uniform he kept by his locker. The black-and-white smile alert, witty, a little sardonic, mocked the words on the page. They did not seem part of the same person. But more letters arrived, dutifully, three times a week at first, later less often. Within two months, the vivacious, courageous young person who was his wife became a weekly two-page letter, recounting in the same regressive hand that Mums was well, and Daddy was well, and Bumble was well, and Ruffles was very well, eagerly awaiting his birthday and the Forces, and Dinky was well, doing active service on the farm, and Harry was not well, having been drowned at sea.

She rarely mentioned the war beyond the incidental details of its effect on country life. Nor did she often mention her pregnancy.

When Victoria was born, he was given compassionate leave, and spent a disjointed two days of travel and tension, centering on a couple of hours with Philippa, barricaded with pillows and cups of tea and plates of toast, in her lofty bedroom at Greenshaws, with a minute, mostly silent Victoria nestled lostly in the cherrywood Greenshaws cradle. He slept in another bedroom down so many long corridors that had he wanted to find Philippa in the night, even for a cup of cocoa, he never could.

It was a terrible occasion, only his third visit to Greenshaws Hall, and one of the worst. It was, of course, only in that winter of Philippa's pregnancy that he had, at last, been welcomed, if that word could be used for the grudged opening of doors it involved, to Greenshaws Hall. The doors were four-hundred-year-old oak, surrounded by sandbags and overgrown climbing roses, flailing unpruned spikes against unpainted windows. By late nineteen forty-three the absence of gardeners, handymen, cooks, maids, all the underlings who had kept Yorkshire country houses alive, was beginning to show.

It wasn't just bananas they'd got none of that day. Austerity baths trickled into vast copper tubs. Austerity meals mocked the grandeur of the table. Austerity fires flickered like small, resentful eyes in immense grates. Austerity tea revealed through its watery depths the ironical splendor of the china. They had, of course, the best excuse imaginable, the excuse that covered everything, from the shortage of matches to the heap of matchwood one might unfortunately find at the address of one's erstwhile host: there's a war on, you know. For all that, Robert could not convince himself that that was the reason. The coldness of the house, its rigid unkindness, was not really the result of shortages of food and fuel, but of shortage of a more basic commodity called compassion.

For Robert, glad on the Monday morning to be out of the place, away from the oppressive echoes of its corridors, and damp silences of its rooms, away from his stalwart in-laws in their tweeds and Wellington boots, and even away from the sniffly young mother on the third floor who was his wife, it was the darkest weekend of the year. It was winter, anyhow, dark in reality most of the time, the darkness of the blacked-out streets aggravated by the long nights and by the simple fact that everyone was fed up to the teeth with the war. It had all been going on just a bit too long for something that did not appear anywhere near to be ending. They were tired. They were tired of large dangers and small petty nuisances, like never seeing where you were going at night, and having to queue for the smallest, most ordinary items, and not being able to buy them anyhow because if the money was there, the coupons probably were not. Robert's firstborn daughter was entering the world of the British Establishment with her bum swaddled in an old tea cloth. Everything about them, even diapers and potties, were either unobtainable or worn and shabby and used.

Romance and glamour had long since died away. Anyhow, what was romantic and glamorous when there were two of you was often inappropriate when there were three. Robert had the first faint regrets about marriage that weekend. Not because he did not love his wife but because he had been presented with the first real strains of putting love into practice in ordinary life. Or rather, an extraordinary life, heavily loaded with tension and deprivation. After four years of active warfare, they both simply lacked the strength.

The following day he was flying again, and almost glad to be back with that straightforward simplicity of survival. He was not, anyhow, any longer involved in active combat. He had been transferred some months earlier to photo reconnaissance, which trained him in photography and provided him with a high-altitude Spit armed only with cameras. But it was essentially safer work, away from the centers of aerial combat. Whether his posting had simply filled some mysterious need of the brass, or whether it contained some hidden judgment on his abilities or apparent mental state, he did not know. He was quietly thankful. Heroics were long over; he had honestly done his bit and he wanted very much, at the time, anyhow, to stay alive.

On the Tuesday after his daughter was born, he almost did not stay alive. It was a routine mission photographing the beaches of northern France. In a dim way he was aware, as they all were, that it must have something to do with the somehow wistful future invasion, but he did not think much about it. He simply did his job, and in the midst of it stumbled onto a vagrant band of Focke-Wulfs returning from some aborted effort, who turned frustrated intentions squarely, with a healthy burst of machine-gun fire, on him. Without guns, and on his own, he followed the only course open and fled for home. The gods and clouds were kind, providing him with cover and an eventual escape, physically unscathed, but not without a few mental scars. The worst was that he knew, so clearly, up there with a determined death pursuing him, that that, for the woman he loved, was the best solution. Without any self-pity he could see it was the one way of winning the approval of the Hallsworth household. Dead, he would be enfolded in honored family memory. Alive, he would be forever a thorn in their flesh.

He refrained from self-pity because he was so plainly glad to be alive, even with his wife distant and changed, and his little family held prisoner by choice at Greenshaws. Being alive, he had long since learned, was very much an end in itself. The ugliness of the day passed, but not the harshness of his relations with Philippa and her family. When Victoria was a year old, fed up with rare weekends together, and hopeless nights with Philippa prissy and shy in her girlhood bed, and the baby forever wailing interruption, he suggested they once again take a flat.

Now it was Philippa who opposed. She had grown comfortable once more in the familiarities of home, a home still able to supply much practical comfort, if not luxury. Besides, the war was promising an early end after the long-awaited D-Day invasion; they were, she insisted, as well to sit tight and make a fresh start when all was over.

All was not over, however, for a disappointingly long time to come. In the course of that last year, with nerves and tempers worn as ragged as everyone's curtains, Robert first conceived the idea that his marriage would not last. He did not conceive the manner of its ending; that came as much as a surprise to him as to anyone. He did not desire its ending, but he knew it would end. It was a knowledge he later forgot, in the first heady weeks after V-E Day, when everyone felt the need to cash in on promises made.

Before that, a time came after a particularly stormy weekend when he had ended sleeping on a couch in the drawing room, and having to rise at dawn lest Philippa's parents discover, and capitalize upon, the rift, when he felt, too, that should one of the V-2s bumbling their clattering obscenity across the spring skies choose to stray as far as Yorkshire, and the cold slate roofs of Greenshaws Hall, it might provide a neat solution. It never happened. Hitler had not the range, anyhow, any more than Robert had really that desire. Death was not at anyone's beckoning, and was not reasonable anyhow. It parted friends and lovers, and left together many bound only by duty. But that was how far two people who had once considered each other's existence the only foundation of their own had come. It was a long way from a far-off, sun-splashed, barbed-wire-tangled beach.

In the end, they came farther still, right through the war, and out on the other side, into the peculiar disappointments of victory. And back, too, as thoughtless fate would have it, to the same memoried beach, with cold, rainy reality and a small fractious daughter to smother even the remembrance of romance.

Robert thought themselves not unlike this small child who, having waited and anticipated for hours her arrival at the seaside, now stood bewildered and disappointed amidst empty stretches of sullen wet sand. So had they waited and anticipated for years the coming of peace, investing that day, the mysterious large day, After The War, with a bounty of hope. But when it came in the end, so little came with it. After the one marvelous outburst of joy at V-E Day it all came so quietly, so that even by V-J Day the idea of victory was somehow jaded. So little had actually changed. Granted danger had gone, and that was no small thing, but so too had excitement and camaraderie.

Almost at once as the newscasters, whose dependable voices had carried them through the war, slipped back into anonymity, each person slipped back into the normal selfish purpose of his own life. It was all at once so quick and so slow. The brave, familial grandeur passed so quickly. It was the petty nuisances that remained. There was still rationing, still shortages, some worse than ever now, still queueing, and it still rained all the time, even over the white cliffs of Dover. There were still meals to make out of limited supplies and in ancient cooking utensils. There was still work to do, if you could find it, but one's own work now, without the comforting shelter of the armed forces. There were decisions to be made, and households to be founded, and precious little material to start with. Into that world, and still to Robert a foreign world, he and Philippa emerged, no longer newlyweds but young parents, and not either so very young any longer. Robert was twenty-five and about to make the start in life most people make in their teens.

He was not alone, but that was not a comfort in a world looking for work. He was, however, still talented, and for a little while, still lucky. So on that day in October nineteen forty-five he had again the thing that once he had considered more important than anything in life—a job in the theater. He was working, and working at his trade. What more could he ask? A lot, actually. Better parts, but with hope that would come; better wages, but those might come as well. His wife and daughter at home with him: a far more subtle issue. With logic, all three would follow in a kind of progression. The Norman Players of Bridlington, as grateful as he was for their employment of him, were not surely the crowning point of his career. But it was a start, or rather, a restart. Bridlington to-day, London tomorrow, no doubt, and no doubt in London there would be better roles than the statutory American army officers he had been playing so far. His accent, of course, was a double-edged tool; it won him parts by default at times, but he had to struggle uphill against it for others. He was not without the skill to disguise it, but he had not the natural range of British voices to present as did his native-born compatriots. And American army officers were going to provide a very short career in a Britain fed up with wartime entertainment. Fed up, too, with something else, surprisingly; fed up with Noel Coward and Terence Rattigan, and all the light, brittle voices of cultured comedy. Something had happened during the war, something to do with class. The same something that had gratefully thanked Mr. Churchill and then booted him and his Tory compatriots out of office had crept even into the theater. Britain had gotten used to the sound of other voices, working voices, and learned to respect them as comrades' voices: the cockney and Birmingham and north of England and Welsh voices whose owners had flown and fought and barricaded and sheltered beside each other through six years of war. And more significantly, the owners of those voices had learned their own worth, and acknowledging it wanted now to see it honored a little, even on the stage. They liked themselves a little more, and wanted to see themselves up there, and not just watch from the sidelines again.

Robert stepped back into the theater he had left in the thirties and found it crowded with a vigorous new humanity. Indeed, his own humanity, people born and raised in the English equivalents of the places he'd come from. The theater had metamorphosed, but then, quite ironically, so had he. He had, through his marriage and six years of unwished-for social climbing, quite accidentally outclassed himself. He had become part of an old order just in time to join in its fall.

"Mr. Zolan, please, a little weight on that line. The man has returned from six years in the bag and found his wife in the sack with someone else. This is a *serious* play, Mr. Zolan. Not a farce." How many, many times he would hear that line about how many serious plays, before he abandoned the theater altogether. Not just here, but later, too, in New York. He had come home after six years indeed, and found his mistress, the theater, in bed with a bunch of draft-dodging slackers. Of the seven male members of the Norman Players, four had somehow remained outside the army throughout the duration. They were his age, all of them, near-abouts, and they treated him as a newcomer. Fair enough, they had had six whole years longer to establish their careers. It was the sort of irony that one finds amusing if it is not one's own career being destroyed. And one's own family breaking up for want of income, or a decent place to stay.

Discharged in early August, Robert set about at once with

enthusiasm preparing for the resumption of his family's life, assuming naturally that Philippa's long stay at Greenshaws would end with the war. By late August he had already found he was wrong. By early September he was beginning to feel like the medieval knight who, having slain the dragon, returns to find that the princess has raised the drawbridge, boarded up the tower door, and cut her hair for good measure. "As soon as you have work," was the first point of delay. When he had work, it was followed by "after we've found a flat." He found a flat in a staid, Victorian brick house on Marshall Avenue and moved in. Philippa came down with her mother, who surveyed it as if it were a child's house of cards, and then decreed it was too small, too damp, and probably too dirty. Philippa, after what Robert was certain was a wistful hesitation, agreed. It was not for her sake, she made clear, but for Victoria's.

"You can't bring a child into this sort of bohemian squalor," Mrs. Hallsworth said firmly, and so unfairly that Robert protested with anger. It was not squalor. But it was small, and a larger flat was agreed upon. Flats, any size, were hard to find. Everyone else was looking for them, too, and furnishings were unobtainable, or at least extravagantly expensive. Robert actually did find another flat, which he doubted he could afford, but by that time, Philippa had settled on London. It was obvious. His real career lay in London. As soon as he had found an agent and his agent had begun to find him work, they would move to London. In the meantime, Victoria was so much better off at Greenshaws, with its gardens and ponies, surely he could understand.

Robert gave up the flat and moved into the St. Leonard's boarding house, into a tiny third-floor room with an old marble-topped washstand and a mirrored dressing table blotting out the daylight in the window. It was perfectly sufficient for a bachelor, Mrs. Pledger, the landlady, decreed. Robert was in no position to disagree.

It was to that place, once a week, that Philippa Zolenski

came down from the drafty splendor of Greenshaws Hall to see her husband. She came also on occasional evenings alone, went to the Pavilion to see the show, applauded politely, and walked home with him through the rain. There in the little room, she was again his wife, in his bed, willingly and lovingly, without the creaking bedboards of home for a distraction. But there was never the zest of their early days; something had gone with the sirens and ack-ack and aircraft overhead. If security had been a casualty of war, then passion might prove to be a casualty of peace. Or perhaps it was simply motherhood that wrought the change. Robert came to realize that Philippa was an actress in her own right, that more dangerous kind of romantic player who sees life as a succession of roles. When she had met him, she was playing a part, the role of well-bred bohemian rebel. Wartime bride was another role. Peacetime mother yet another, and when she had at last accepted that role, she cast herself into it with fervor, wiping out every trait in her character that did not suit it. The rebellious young woman he had met vanished beneath the flowered chintz of convention. Her parents were both delighted at the way she had, at last, settled down.

They turned their efforts then squarely on Robert.

"Daddy would like to see you," Philippa said when they were done arguing about Victoria's wet dress.

"He knows where I live," Robert said, sourly, kicking a large white stone across a stretch of pebbles. Victoria had found a tide pool and was hovering at its edge, yearning to be in the cold water, held back by the thread of her mother's voice.

"Let her be," Robert said.

"We've been through that. You know daddy doesn't like leaving Greenshaws just now. There's so much to be done."

"So what do you expect? I can't leave here, I'm either rehearsing or playing or learning lines. I do work, too, you know. Even if daddy doesn't think so."

"Of course you work. Of course, Robert. Daddy thinks

very well of your work. Only he does feel he'd like to see you a little more secure."

"He'd like to see *you* a little more secure. He'd like to see me secure in hell most like."

Philippa walked off without a word and sat down on a bulwark and looked out to sea. She sat there with her lips tightly together, and her eyes distant, until Robert came and sat beside her. He said, as always the first to speak or apologize, "All right, what does he want?"

"It's only a sort of part-time arrangement. Quite a decent position, actually, Robert, and it would hardly take much of your time, a day or two a week, the occasional director's meeting. It's a very good firm. London based. You'd have time in between to do whatever you please. Surely, Robert, it's the ideal arrangement. We'd be able to afford a flat, consider a school for Victoria."

"She's barely *three*," Robert said. He lifted a shell and hurled it skimming angrily across wet waves. "She's a baby."

"She's growing up, Robert. And she's growing up hardly knowing her father."

"Whose fault is that?"

"Yours, Robert," she said, "for pursuing this obsession with the theater, without a thought for anyone." She untied her silk square and shook out her hair in unthinking anger. The beauty of it as always captured him and made him long to touch it. He made some excuse about a wind-tangled strand and reached to stroke it. She slipped away, like an unwilling cat, bending her neck lightly free.

Robert leaned back with his hands on the damp woolen knees of his trousers. They were purple trousers, quite the fashionable thing, and he had been quite driven to buy them with a silly adolescent urge springing up out of six years of uniformity. They were silly, and foolish, and he had wanted them like a kid. He had justified spending the money by remembering something Anna Beinhart had said, long ago, about the dime-store girl for whom he was always to dress. He said slowly, "Philippa, I've never been obsessed with the theater. But it has always been my profession; it was my profession when you met me, and when you married me. You knew that much about me, what I was going to do for a living. If you didn't like it, you didn't have to marry me. You've got no right to ask me to leave it now."

"Robert," she cried in well-mocked dismay, "such drama." Then she said, practically, "Look, ducky, no one's asking you to leave anything, we're only thinking to make things easier. Daddy is simply frantic to help, and I say if you'd just let him, just take one of his little offers, then he'll be happy and we'll be happy. We'll have our flat, and you'll have plenty of spare time . . ."

"To join the local amateurs," said Robert.

"Of course not," she cried, her dismay as authentic as ever.

"Philippa, there's something you must realize. It's something that people outside the arts never understand, I suppose, because they don't understand how arts are created, but it really is work." He waved away her eager protest. "I know, you'll say you know, and I'm not looking for sympathy. But it is work. It takes wits and energy and a great deal of physical strength. And time. Oh, so much time. And even more than that, it takes commitment. You know I'm forever meeting people who can watch two hours' worth of the culmination of six weeks' work, and then say, oh, jolly splendid, I'm in theater, too. And you know what they mean? They mean they once played a bit part for the amateurs, in some god-awful production they had six months to prepare. And they think it's the same goddamn thing. We break our asses up there, and they think we're a bunch of show-offs having fun and getting paid for it. Jesus, Philippa, can I make you understand, if not your father, that I haven't time to be a company director, banker, farm manager, God alone knows what else he's offered. I'm busy. I'm employed. I'm working. Even if I'm not earning fucking Hallsworth money."

She glared quickly across to Victoria, who was swinging

from a barnacled upright of the bulwark, just out of earshot. "That's quite enough of that," she said in a whisper.

Robert stared in amazement and then laid both hands flat on his knees and laughed aloud, a cold, forced laugh. "Well, Jesus Christ, if that doesn't take first prize. Look, you." He whipped about and grasped her by the shoulders, digging his nails into the slippery cloth of her raincoat so she'd not get free. "Look, you, Lady Muck, just once I'm going to say this. I was here, you know, all along, right through the war and the good old days when we were still married people, and I remember a certain young WAAF who'd kick her bloomers off, spread her legs and shout, 'I say, flyboy, how about a good poke?' "

"Robert!" she whispered again. "Please. The child."

"It's true," he shouted, the wind and rain taking his words, and he shouted louder, "It's damned fucking true."

"Shut up."

"I'll shut up when you say it's true, damn it."

He was beginning to enjoy himself and stood up, dragging her up with him; stood up on the bulwark and dragged her up onto the wet, slippery wood as well. "Is it true?" He was laughing.

Suddenly she began to laugh as well, and he saw the chintz mantle slip. He grasped his chance at once and kissed her on her still prim mouth. The primness resisted him for a moment, and then she kissed back, her mouth cold with rain. He swung her about and they stumbled and fell and tumbled into the sand. Victoria looked up with delighted surprise spreading across her solemn pale face. She hesitated by her tide pool, and then ran across the beach opening her arms and giggling, and was gathered into the heap of wet arms and legs in the sand.

"Oh, Robert, do stop, how shocking of you," Philippa cried, but she couldn't tame her voice back into refinement. Robert kissed her again and she said, "Oh, God, I wish we could go to bed."

Victoria stopped in her romping on Robert's legs, and looked up, suddenly disappointed. "Not go to bed, mummy. Vicky not go to bed." She clung to Robert worriedly. He rose and lifted her and helped Philippa to her feet. "No, pet," he said at last. "No bed for Vicky." She giggled aloud with delighted relief.

Philippa said, "I must go, really, Rob. I daren't miss that damnable train. Daddy will go into a tailspin if I do."

He could hear by the way she said it, the soft, tired annoyance in her voice, that she had subtly crossed a boundary and was momentarily on his side. Again he reached for his moment, and said, "Come on, Phil, we'll go up to the Royal and telephone him. Tell him you'll make a later train; I'll take you to dinner, proper dinner, on plates, no newspaper, how about it?"

"You can't afford it."

"I'll afford it. That's my problem. Come on, we'll phone him now." He had his arm under her wet, raincoated sleeve. Her hair was blowing damply over his face, and Vicky was galloping about the sand like a foal. He saw his little family, and his future, taking form before his eyes. It was all there, a phone call away, a handful of hours, but a beginning. Philippa smiled and took a hesitant step up the beach that once she had run down with heart-stirring freedom. Then she stopped and shook her head.

"No. I can't. It will be dark. He can't bear coming out in the dark."

"Oh, why not," Robert cried, disappointed to the point of fury. "There's no blackout any more. It's only a couple of miles, anyhow."

"I know. I know. But he's got used to it, during the war. He never comes out at night. Mother complains, but you know daddy. Besides, he likes to economize and do the shops when he collects us from the train. He gets his tobacco, and the newspaper, and he'll have waited, you know, one journey instead of two, petrol and all."

"For God's sake, he's got his basic ration again, like everyone else, and I'm sure he never uses half of it. He never goes anywhere."

She laughed a little, tying on her silk scarf. "No, actually, even at the worst, he always had petrol to spare, he was so cautious. I rather think he imagined Jerry coming and him driving us all up to Scotland or something." She laughed again and kissed his cheek lightly. "No dice, Robert. I must go." She made her brightest smile and he turned away. "Oh, don't be angry, I'll come early next week. I promise. And as soon as you're in London, we'll all be together."

At the foot of the stone promenade he turned and looked once back at the stormy gray sea. The fog had never lifted, and the Flamborough cliffs kept their white beauty to themselves. He said, "I'm not going to London, Phil." Before she could express the astonishment on her face, he said it again. "I'm not. I'm not going to London."

"You're going to stay here, Robert? With your talent? You're going to play bit parts for a set of provincial hacks?"

"I'm playing leads," he said mildly.

"It's still the provinces. The *far* provinces."

"And what do you, or Harry Hallsworth, King of the Philistines, know about talent?" He said it cruelly, the first time he had ever struck at her innocent artistic pretensions. "Oh, forget it, Phil," he added at once. "Anyhow, it doesn't matter. I'm not going to London, but I'm not staying here, either, if that eases your snobbish little soul. I'm going back to the States."

He hadn't meant to tell her yet, or that way, or maybe at all, hoping a marvelous piece of fortune would save him from the need to, but she had made him terribly angry.

He would not discuss it further, and after her initial astonishment they walked in silence to the St. Leonard's, gathered Vicky's little pack of homemade toys, and walked in another silence to the train. Robert stopped at the railway newsagent and confectionery and splurged half of October's personal points on a large bag of peppermint creams, and handed them to the child, only to have Philippa remove them from her small hand, place the bag in her handbag, and return a single sweet to Vicky.

"Oh, let her have them. It's the only treat she's had all day."

"Nonsense. She's had the trip, and they'll last for weeks. No point using up the whole ration. She'll get two a day. It's far more sensible."

Robert nodded, weary with sensibleness, remembering his own mother, even in the hard days before the *Diana* had won their fortune, splurging foolishly on a whole sack of oranges, or jelly beans, or candy corn, for himself and Dolores. Weeks would go by between, but the memory of crawling beneath the porch into his Place with a huge crinkly paper bag, bottomless with candy, lasted till this day. He wondered if Philippa had ever had such days in her childhood amongst the great oak-paneled corridors of Greenshaws Hall. But perhaps it was the war that had pinched her so, perhaps it had pinched them all, and all of them, even himself, would take a long time recovering, skimping and scraping and refusing to spend, or ever to throw anything away. In the railway station he saw two children dressed in neat pinafores of recycled blackout cloth. The spirit of forty-six, he thought, as the train and his wife and daughter rolled smokily away.

On the way home, Robert went out of his way to buy cigarettes, and indulged himself angrily with a pack of Passing Clouds. He ended down by the harbor and stood looking a long time at the rain-shrouded trawlers languishing on the mud flats of low tide. The site of the bombed-out café in which he had nearly died so many years ago was so absorbed by wartime changes that he could no longer locate it. He walked out to the end of the North Pier, stood with his back to the wet wind, and lit one of his Passing Clouds. The wind whipped his hair over his face, and he stared through the black wet flicking ends at the lights of the town coming on. Behind him a shy young voice with a strong Yorkshire accent said, "Spare another one?" He turned quickly, surprised in his aloneness. She was standing in a raincoat, soft and indulgently feminine with its full skirts blowing, and her loose dark hair blowing in curling tangles about her face. For a moment, she made him think of the day he met Philippa, not many feet from the spot where they both stood. She was not like Philippa, not at all. What she was like was the pair of girls, anonymous WAAFs, with whom Philippa had gone to swim, those two girls he had walked away from without another glance.

She was not one of them, of course. She was years younger. Her name was Rhoda. And he did not walk away at all.

Instead, he drew out another of his expensive cigarettes and handed it to her with the smallest of smiles. He was assessing her with his eyes, as quickly as he could without staring. He decided on the basis of a few seconds' glance that she was not a tart, as he had momentarily assumed. She was pretty enough, as pretty as north of England girls get, he decided; that is, north of England ordinary girls, not Hallsworth country girls. She was dark haired and dark eyed, with a creamy skin that would in years become sallow. But not yet. Her face was rather too pointed about the nose, and the chin too recessive, all features that would sharpen with age. By forty-five she would be dumpy and homely like most of the women in the area. It was not a town for beauties. But she was not forty-five, and youth and a friendly smile made the very most of what she'd been given.

Her hair, which was really beautiful, thick and rich, an honest brown, not pretending to black or blond, was disheveled by the wet wind, and its looseness added a charm that each night, with pin curls and papers, she would do her best to destroy. Right now she reached to pat it down, and Robert almost said, no, stop, leave it be. But he said nothing, wanting nothing personal that might lead to flirtation between them. She did not look or act a flirt.

She said, letting him light her cigarette with a match, and leaning over the small flame to shield it, its light against the twilight doing wonders of flattery, "No performance tonight?"

Robert was silent for several seconds, disguising his surprise by blowing out the match, and snapping it between wetted fingers, and sliding it back into the small box. He put the box into his raincoat pocket after a moment's habitual fumbling for the familiar position in his now-vanished RAF tunic. He said, cautiously, "Excuse me, but should I know you?"

She laughed, a bit broadly, an unrefined laugh reminiscent of Maisie Rudd. "No, luv, of course not. It's you everybody knows, isn't it? Not me."

"Do they?" he said with genuine incredulity. Somehow he thought of Anna Beinhart. But she was serious and said with a thin trace of disappointment in her voice, "Oh, don't be coy, please. It's not worthy of you."

Robert looked at her very carefully. He was not sure if he was being complimented or insulted. What he did know was that the conversation was becoming a strain and a challenge. He was tired and he wanted a quiet cigarette. He said, annoyed, "Well, what is supposed to be worthy of me, then?"

"I'm sorry," she said. "I've offended you now, haven't I?" Then she added, "Do you really not know? You see, all the girls at Allan's think you're ever so nice. We all come every week, Mae and Val and Jenny and I." She sounded young, now. "But I'm the worst. I even come in the morning to watch you."

"In the morning?" Robert asked. They did not do anything in the morning. "You mean afternoon. Rehearsals?"

"No, no. Not there. Down here." She waved her hand toward the North Beach below, half engulfed by angry high tide. "When you come and ride, I come and watch."

He reassessed her again, the third time. That had to be true, by the fact that she'd said it. The claims of box-office loyalty were easily made, and unreliable. But to know he rode on the beaches in the morning, she must have indeed come to watch.

"Why?" he said.

"Because I'm a silly fool," she said with a small giggle. "Oh, I do love watching you, the way you go off, jumping all the breakwaters, right into the sea and all. You're so beautiful, you and that smashing horse. Is he yours?"

Robert shook his head slowly, amazed that anyone could see him in so golden a romantic light. "No. I rent him from the stables. Ormond Dance's." She nodded, familiar.

"Sometimes I rode there myself, during the war, when I was at school. Can't afford it now I'm working and living on my own. What's he called?"

"The horse?" Robert said, and then smiled, flicking ash over the stone wall into the wild sea. "I don't know. I never asked him. I call him horse."

She laughed again and said, "Imagine me standing here and talking to you. Mae will never believe. Don't think I'll tell her anyhow. Look—" She seemed to be thinking, and then asked very shyly, "Could you maybe write your name, your auto-graph, here. I've my address book, just here on a blank page." She was rustling in her clip-topped leather bag. He could not avoid noticing its shabbiness as she did, the leather as pale-rubbed as the toes of schoolboy's shoes. She found her little book, leather bound with black print, and he knew it would have been a birthday present from her mother or her girlfriend. She handed it to him carefully, and an instant before he could reach to push it away, apologize and explain that he was not some star of the silver screen, he stopped. Again he thought of Anna Beinhart, and then he solemnly took the book as if it were something he did a dozen times a day and signed his first autograph for his first fan.

"Oh, smashing," she whispered. "Thanks ever so. I think you're just marvelous." She held the book a moment, looking at his name in the dim light, and then slipped it with care into her worn purse. She clicked the catch shut and stepped backward. "Thanks so for everything, and the cigarette, too. I hope you don't think me rude."

"Not at all," Robert said, riding more easily into the role of celebrity. "Perhaps I'll see you again."

"Oh, I hardly think so."

"Why not?"

"I don't go often where your sort—I'm only a working girl." She was still stepping backward into the dusk, as if the dim lights of the town were absorbing her back into anonymity. Suddenly he did not wish to let her go.

"Well, you'll see me here tomorrow, for a start," he said, grinning. "On old what's-his-name. It's my only diversion and I won't be giving it up, even if I've been discovered."

"Oh, no. I couldn't possibly now. Not now I've told you. It would be far too bold." Then she turned about and fled, not running, but walking more quickly than naturally, on her little worn-down heels. As he watched her go, he knew what it was that made her seem familiar, as if he knew her from long ago. She was words taken form, *the girl from the five-and-dime* he had dressed for and played for, the invisible single person in the mass of white faces beyond the curtain. She was Anna's shopgirl come to life, for whom he lived in style. She disappeared beside the row of seaside cafés where the harbor met the town. Robert turned and walked along the waterfront with the North Sea for company until the theater was in view. Empty and stark on Monday night, it watched gloomily out to sea as cold and white as the Flamborough cliffs. He turned his back on it and walked quickly across the street, past the rows of empty boarding houses to the St. Leonard's and his own empty bed.

In the morning, despite her protestations, she was there. He should have realized that once the thought was expressed, it was irresistible. He had invited her, and she was, as he would learn, not a girl to turn down an invitation, no matter where it led. He had, as it turned out, forgotten her. The morning had been hectic. Mrs. Pledger had chosen that morning to announce the need of a rise in her rates from six shillings to seven and six, which he, and the other six people about her lace-covered breakfast table, felt an equal need to protest.

There were, aside from himself, three other members of the cast, and two young schoolteachers, and the table had been cast into great misery over the stretching of pittance wages over the ever-rising costs of the postwar world.

He walked to the stables, adding in his head whether he could continue this particular indulgence, and knowing that his hope of purchasing a motorcar with which he could have easy access to Greenshaws and Philippa was fading. He took out his frustration in a hearty gallop along the beach, wet and flat, exposed by low tide. He got as far as Sewerby and turned back, before the tide turned, and cantered easily homeward, jumping the exposed breakwaters, enjoying the thrill of the wet wind and the bright splashes of water from a straying hoof. It was a rare, bright autumn day, windy and dry, and he rode for pleasure, with natural grace and no training, the way he had learned on borrowed farm horses in his childhood on the island.

He had jumped the bulwark on which she was sitting before he realized it was she. He had recognized the raincoat, wrapped now neatly about her knees, nearly down to her ankles as she sat. She had carefully rolled her beautiful hair into a tight, unbecoming little sausage about her small head. He knew she had worked half the night on it to get it right, and she had done it for him. The pathetic devotion of the useless gesture touched him and he slowed the horse and turned it, and it trotted, with heavy thuds of feet in the wet sand, up to where she sat.

"Hello again," she said with a shy, brimming smile. She looked terribly young in the clear, fresh light, and for a moment he wondered what he was doing. After six years of the sheltered moral novitiate of war, Robert retained yet the conventional scruples of youth, oddly mixed with the responsible restraint of an old man. It was a state that would leave him, in days to come, in short, rude lowerings, like something heavy slipping roughly down a stair. It was as if he was the oldest of all at that point on the Bridlington beach, weighing his future years with such care. As those years came, he would grow younger, and lighter, stripped of almost all such concerns.

All he did that day was take her to a café for a cup of tea. No bombs fell, nor did he fall suddenly, inextricably in love. She did, but that was inevitable in her case; she had arrived at an age when her body demanded a bodily partner and her mind, yet innocent, translated it neatly into a yearning of soul. Put another way, he was to her an equivalent of the geraniums in her mother's window, an essential splash of color against the dull yellow brick walls of home. That night, Robert, alone in his bed-sit, drank tea again, thought of her briefly with what he thought was an older man's indulgent reminiscence, and went back to learning his lines. Had she not been bold enough to make the next move, there would never have been an affair at all.

The next move was a classic: the bold and yet somehow pathetically yearning figure in belted raincoat in the damp yellow light of the stage door, the laughter a little too high in pitch, the voice taut with casualness stretched tight as a drumhead. "I just thought, that is, I was out walking late, and saw the show was ending, all the people leaving and all, thought it'd be a bit of a lark . . ."

"Just who I wanted to see," Robert said, lying out of kindness. She melted into giggles of relief. "I was just going for chips," he said. "Come on along."

He walked easily down the Promenade with Rhoda on his arm. He did not feel guilty. He had only been kind, and had not yet learned that more misery in love is caused by weak kindness than ever by cruelty.

The chip shop on Marshall Avenue was a bright glow out onto the wet night, and the darkness of lace-curtained discreet windows. Every third house was a guest house, and the front rooms, busy in summer with many little white-clothed tables, the guests' dining rooms. Now they were empty, and silent, and the houses like so many stern, hand-folded maiden aunts overseeing the dark street. The family always lived at the back, in kitchens, small-windowed and backing onto brick alleyways, the best of the house reserved for strangers. The cold tidiness repelled Robert and made him think of the Hallsworths, who, in their own distant grand style, still insisted on saving the best of life for some mythical future. The chip shop delighted him, an audacious affront. Rhoda homed to it like the native she was.

In the window was a handmade sign, merely a scrap of cardboard on which the day's choices—a direct reflection of the day's catch from the windy sea two streets away—were scribbled in crayon. Haddock, plaice, cod, whiting, turbot. Chips with each and chips alone, and mushy peas.

"The menu, my dear," Robert said with a flourishing wave toward the window. He was consciously playing the actor for her, knowing full well it was half his attraction.

She said, "Just chips, thanks."

"I'm *paying*, you know," he said gently.

"I know." She nodded shyly, and hesitated. Eventually she ordered the cheapest fish. He doubled the order and added mushy peas, against her protest. From nowhere a remembrance came of a young man, long ago, dining at the Savoy and shuddering at the thought of an extra brandy. He was not sure if he had gone forward, or backward, from that day.

"Do you want to stay or go?" Robert asked.

"Mmm, go," she said. She was drawing in great, hungry whiffs of the scent of food, unabashedly relishing the air. "Don't taste right on plates, does it?"

She was right. It didn't. There was an instantaneous alchemy about the stuff; suddenness was its essence. Fish snatched hours ago from the icy seas, tumbled into hot fat with scarce time for execution, whipped out at once into the nubbly warmth of newsprint, and at once again, without the cold intervention of china or cutlery, by greasy wet fingers to the mouth. Any halt in the process, any break in the headlong speed, and the true nature of the dish was sullenly revealed. A moment's chill turned ambrosia into doughy, greasy fish and potatoes.

"Oh, it's gorgeous," Rhoda moaned, nibbling a crusted tail, crunching down to the bony core. Her hands folded back the newspaper with marvelous ease, a geisha practicing origami. Robert thought she must have spent half her life in chip shops to attain that skill. He still fumbled in a transatlantic way, dropping a chip here, letting the folds of the *Daily Sketch* flutter unseemly in the sea wind. He hadn't her style at all. They walked down to the waterfront, passed the now dark hulk of the theater, and stood listening to the tide creeping in.

When he glanced down to look at her, she was looking up at him, her face framed in a cheap headsquare, like a madonna, her whole being radiating an astounding devotion. She dropped her eyes at once, the unadorned lashes damp in the wet air.

"Let's go down to the water," he said. She nodded, expecting something, and followed down the awkward sand-strewn stone steps. When he took her arm, she leaned to him like a warm dog. Once on the wet sands, shaded by the harbor wall, she stood obediently waiting to be kissed.

That was how it began then, the quiet tide of Rhoda, enfolding him, all of him unquestioned, unreproached, in a warm slack of admiration. When trying to explain it later, he would say it was like coming home. He was on native soil at last, in a foreign country still, but on native soil. Rhoda was, as his mother would say, like us. A workingman's daughter, in other words, and he, of course, a workingman's son. She was the sort of girl his mother had expected him to marry. Not the sort of girl she would approve of, no, Rhoda was what his mother called cheap—an attribute that really had less to do with unsteady morals than with unsteady gait on too high heels, lipstick too dark, and not being Catholic. Besides, there was not a girl his mother would have approved of anywhere. But Rhoda was what she'd expect; Rhoda would have done and, after rows and insults, and a baby or two, been accepted as his wife.

There weren't going to be any babies, of course, nor any wedding. Robert was quite firmly wed to another, a fact he delayed telling Rhoda to save her hurt. When he did finally tell her, she took his long reticence to have been a sign of weakness in the marriage, and hope for her cause. It was a natural if false assumption. What there was going to be was what Robert would call a fling, what Philippa would call adultery, and what Rhoda would call wistfully, "This bloke, when I was very young."

She was very young, full of passion and admiration and waiting for an idol to pour it onto. She was too proud and individual to be satisfied with some shared cinema legend, so she found Robert. The adulation she gave him was of the same variety, and for him, accustomed to years of challenge and rebuff, years of upstream swimming in a social stream full of great rocks of pretension, it was a most refreshing change. A neck long stiffened from years of looking up took comfort in the rare chance to look down. He was buoyant with her praise, a swimmer in an overly salty sea.

The day she met him was invisibly circled on the calendar of Rhoda's life, a day she would recall with a nudge of painful pleasure when she was many years mother to another man's children. Robert, if he thought of it, which he didn't, could not have recalled the date. Nor could he recall the day or hour when his occasional meetings with Rhoda on midweek nights after the show, or late afternoon suppers, became something of import rather than a small bright spot in a dull day, like patting the milk-wagon horse in its red traces, or chatting with the man from whom he bought his paper. One night he dreamed about her, an innocuous dream, but yet surprising to find her wedged into his subconscious.

Gradually, very gradually, he developed a sexual passion for her, and as he did, the plainness of her features subtly gave way to a new, earthy glamour. Her hair most of all intrigued him with its lush brown honest beauty, and the liquid freshness of her eyes and skin. One weekend, when Philippa and Victoria came for their brief visit, he was startled to notice small wrinkled lines about Philippa's eyes; character lines, yet lines nonetheless, and was even more startled to find himself thinking of Rhoda, picturing her rain-wet and smiling in her battered raincoat.

It was the following Thursday afternoon that he first took Rhoda to bed. Thursday, because that was early closing day in Bridlington and Rhoda was released from the velvet shackles of Miss Wilkins's millinery department at Allan's, and afternoon because only in the afternoon, when the pursed mouth of Mrs. Pledger his landlady was expressing her disapproval of the world over tea and crumpets on the Promenade, was he able to spirit any strange guest, male or female, into his room.

The imminent return of that lace-collared Boadicea gave only urgency to their passion. Rhoda proved to be what Robert's children would one day call a technical virgin, and he himself in an unkind moment would label shop-soiled. She'd done enough back-alley investigating through a somewhat neglected wartime childhood to have erased all fears and drama from the act she approached now with such fervor. She tumbled into his bed like a warm and wriggly puppy, begging cheerfully to be loved.

He obliged her, and she obliged him by giving him the most flattering afternoon of his life. Everything he did was wonderful, in Rhoda's happy judgment, and her body dissolved happily into complete concordance with his. Afterward she curled up on his shoulder, with all her thick brown hair massed damply under his chin, and whispered that she loved him and would love him forever. Even half-asleep, he was a little shaken by that, trying hard to dismiss it as emotion of the moment.

He awoke to the sound of seagulls crying and the sea, and for the smallest instant could not recall where he was, his mind leaping over other seascapes of his life to home. The lights of early autumn evening shining through his undrawn curtains brought him back to the St. Leonard's.

"Oh, my God. Mrs. Pledger."

Rhoda woke at once, hand over her mouth, vividly aware of his panic. She began dressing blindly, like she would on a winter morning, in the dark, before work, stockings and garters and step-ins, and slip, all the time watching Robert panic with wide eyes. He was scrambling around the floor looking under heaps of clothing and bedclothes for his watch, not sure yet if Mrs. Pledger's return was the best cause of his panic, or whether the additional threat of imminent curtain call was better. He found his watch, his father's watch, in unseemly shelter beneath his shorts.

Six o'clock, and all was well, or would be if he could get Rhoda out of there undiscovered. She was sitting on the edge of his bed, dressed, hair combed, afraid to talk.

"I'm sorry, Robert," she said at last.

"Not your fault," he said fairly, pulling on his socks and thinking wildly. The ever-present odor of frying fish was getting its evening replenishment, mixing dourly with the reek of turnips in the air. Outside his door he heard the two young schoolteachers giggling on their way to the bathroom. The house was a happy hive of activity. Robert got up from the floor, thought a long moment, and then leaped for his mahogany mirrored wardrobe.

"What's that for?" Rhoda asked.

"You." He was holding out his RAF greatcoat and a trilby hat.

"Oh, never," she cried, but she was giggling with delight and slipping into it. "But my feet, Robert. They'll never do." She waved one in its pretty high-heeled pump at him. He was detachedly aware that her voice, with its long-dragged-out northern vowels, alternated between a delight and an annoyance. He dove for the wardrobe again, and came out with his secondhand leather riding boots, shoving her shoes into his pocket as she pulled them on. Rhoda was suppressing waves of girl's laughter, not sure if his desperation was a play-act or not. It was not. If he was discovered he would lose that room, and an explanation to Philippa would be necessary and impossible, as indeed would be the finding of another.

But Rhoda tripped happily after him down the hall, even chancing a bass hello to one of the schoolteachers. At the top of the stairs, Robert heard the steady, uniquely determined tread of the lady of the house. He glanced quickly back to Rhoda in her greatcoat and boots. One great lock of that splendid brown hair dangled below her earlobe. "Christ," he said, and then caught her elbow and whirled her about, bolted down the landing, and into the bathroom.

"We can never stay here," she said, but he was already levering up the stiff old wooden sash, and stepping out cautiously onto the rain-swept wooden fire escape. At the window Rhoda froze.

"Come on, doll," he said impatiently, "before someone wants the loo, eh?"

"I can't." Her voice was a frail whisper. "Robert, I can't, please." She was holding the window sash, her eyes widening with fear, all play and acting gone. "Please, Robert," she whimpered like a child. Rhoda, it turned out, was mortally frightened of heights. It was, he decided later, her only weakness, but it was real.

"I'll hold your hand."

"No."

"Rhoda, if we go back, we'll be caught. I'll lose my room. I can't afford it."

Rhoda started to cry. "I've always, Robert, all my days, could never climb a fence, a tree. I won't manage, Robert. I'll faint."

"I'll carry you."

"No," she shrieked, diving back, as if he were reaching to drag her out.

"All right, all right, I won't touch you, but be quiet." He stood for a moment looking around. He was three stories up.

Over the slate and tile roofs of the Esplanade he could see the gray sea, and flocks of storm-warned gulls circling. The lights of the Pavilion came on, lighting its pale hulk against the evening. He thought vividly, this can't be happening.

Somewhere inside, Mrs. Pledger's voice could be heard over the din of the dinner gong, "Mr. Zolan, are you coming?"

Rhoda heard it, moaned, closed her eyes, and dashed for the window, crouching and climbing over the sill, awkward in his trailing coat. Her face was white and stained with tears.

They scrambled together down the three wet flights of open plank steps, she trembling and clinging to his arm. At the foot she cried, "Oh, I must sit down. I'm so dizzy, Robert," but he hurried her on down the street and around the corner first. She clung there to a lamppost and was unashamedly sick in the gutter. Robert, filled with remorse, helped her mop up, muttering about the room and its importance, and feeling viciously rotten at heart. Not because of what he had made her do, but because he knew so well that she found the strength to do it only in her devotion to him, a devotion which he did not return.

He did his best to make it up to her. The following Sunday—Philippa had put off her visit until next week, and he hardly cared—he took her to the cinema, and the next Thursday for tea at the Lounge on the Promenade, where he ensconced her in state in a cane-back chair at a little round table feathered in by potted palms, and while the small orchestra played Novello melodies and selections from *The Merry Widow*, he stuffed her full of tea cakes and buttered scones. She wolfed them, like a starved child, apologized, grinned and wolfed some more.

"Oh, aren't I awful," she said, ladling jam onto a crumpet, "I do so love sweet things. Mum said when the war began and we couldn't get sweeties any more, I used to cry for them. Really. Real tears."

Robert tried to smile at that, but it hurt inside, bringing up a dual, complex image of the child Rhoda crying at the empty sweetshop window, and Rhoda his mistress crying on the St. Leonard's fire escape. He half feared that he would learn that her immense fear of heights was birthed in some ghastly wartime experience, but he found in the end it was not so. That, at least, was something private, untouched by war. So much of Rhoda, he was to learn, was the molding of those six threatened, harsh years.

The first, sharpest mold was, of course, her father's loss. He was not killed in the war—something simple which children might understand. Instead he was taken prisoner after Dunkirk, in the bag, as they said, for five whole years. He was in a decent camp, and suffered no terrible deprivation, though much frustration. But for five years his wife and daughter slogged through the war without him, and as the years dragged by, the thought certainly occurred to her mother that she had had a far harder time than the prisoner. Rhoda was eleven when the war began and her father left them. When, nearly six years later, he finally walked back to his own front door, he nodded politely to the young lady he passed at the gate, and went by.

"He didn't know me," Rhoda said to Robert.

"How could he?" Robert replied, feeling a pang of guilt toward this man, fellow combatant, whose daughter he had deflowered.

"I'm his daughter. I mean, surely . . ." Her voice died off, fading into the strains of "Vilia."

Later she said, "It was worse for mum. There he was back again, and you'd have thought all he'd been thinking about for six years was . . ." She caught her breath. "Hardly fair, was it? Her being alone all that time, not playing around either. I suppose you just forget what it's like. Like as not she was just too tired. Anyhow, after the first week, she moved into the spare room, and she's been there ever since. Now he's at the pub all night. She sits home sewing. Like death in there on Sundays. We all sit looking at each other, thinking something nice should happen, because the war's over and it's Sunday.

Nothing ever does. I wonder, Robert, were things really better before? I can't hardly remember. I was just ten and all."

He couldn't remember, either, not having been there before the war, and moreover being utterly too preoccupied with a startling image. One day, one day five years ago, he and Philippa Hallsworth met, flirted, courted, and brushed death in a lost café not many yards from where Rhoda sipped her tea and luxuriated in the naughty pleasure of being in a place beyond her means and style. And on that day Rhoda was here, too, all alone, a twelve-year-old scruffy and fatherless wartime north of England brat. They could have passed in the street, blind to each other, a man and a child. No doubt her mother read out the news of the bombed café from the *Chronicle* and poured broad-voweled sympathy upon them all, and Rhoda would have heard and played with the grim facts in her mind, balancing childish fascination with fear. What amazed him was how quickly the time had passed; he could blink twice and see himself and Mike finding their feet in wartime England; it was yesterday, and a whole third of Rhoda's life. The years of his own life stretched ahead in a length of questioned emptiness; what other frighteningly unimagined changes and people might fill it?

It was that thought, the need to grasp the fast-flying present, that made him buy the car. It was a dark maroon nineteen thirty-eight MG roadster, a marvelous lucky find, and although the pretense of its purchase was increased access to Philippa, in reality it represented more accurately the last burned bridge to Greenshaws Hall. He had had a small amount of money set aside, to which he added each week, for their eventual move to London. There were bound to be expenses, even if he found work immediately. Which was unlikely. He had already traveled down there once to audition and found the expense of rail fare, YMCA accommodation, and an obligatory new suit all a bit devastating, coupled as it was with the traditional "We'll call you" and an empty smile.

They did not call him, of course, nor was anyone likely to,

as he realized more strongly with each week that passed. This new, grimly practical, inflation-pinched Britain had little place for him. His days were numbered by the empty seats at the Pavilion, where their fine little performance of *Private Lives* was going essentially unnoticed. Another year at the most, and America was going to be not just the obvious but the only choice. He was saying farewell, a swan song, and he suddenly determined to go out in style.

"Oh, Robert," Rhoda said, a red fingernail skipping across the subtle purply finish. "Oh, Robert." She just breathed it, fondling the cream leather canopy. "Oh, Robert."

He took her everywhere in it. He picked her up at the corner of Regent Terrace and the Promenade, where she emerged from the front door of Allan's in the midst of its morning-coated staff and tweed-suited matrons, Cinderella in a home-sewn flowered frock. They would drive up out of the town, past the canopies and iron fretwork of Carleton's Bon Marche, out through the narrow streets of the Old Town, and up onto the moors beyond. He would not take her walking in the wet, gray air as he might have done with Philippa. Rhoda was town bred and lacked the country, upper-crust delight in getting thoroughly cold and sodden that the Hallsworths held. Instead he took her to sheltered, hearth-fire-glowing pubs, where they ate hot pies and ploughman's lunches, and drank pints of dark northern ale. One week, they spent Sunday night at one such pub (Robert testily balancing guilt, having hours before dropped Philippa before Greenshaws' sullen oak door, and then driven like a madman back to the coast for his mistress), and on another occasion, when the Norman Players featured a play in which he did not appear, he had a whole week of nights with Rhoda in cozy country beds, followed by morning dashes for town, to deliver her before the doom stroke of nine into the arms of Miss Wilkins, millinery. In between they made love, with ingenuity and sore backs, in the unaccommodating seats of the MG. Robert always felt afterward that its spirit, if not its metal flesh, was with him in the endeavor, and forgave it the lumbago he was certain it had engendered. Rhoda throve on it, enjoying it with girlish rebellious glee.

"Supposing someone stops and looks?" she would shriek. "Oh, Robert, I can't bear it." But she did.

Philippa's reaction to the car had been predictably different, and yet not quite predictable. Granted she showed impatience and annoyance, at least while her parents were present. Afterward she said only, "Really, Robert, you can't have been thinking. Daddy was just beginning to have a small measure of confidence . . ." But then she trailed off, as he drove her, just the two of them, roaring down the narrow, stone-walled lanes, empty of cars and speed limits. He glanced across and saw her in Rhoda's place. She was resting her head back, her eyes closed, her blond hair with its handful of gray strands blowing loose of her silk scarf. She was smiling to herself a smile from years ago. He swore to himself he would not see Rhoda again.

The vow did not last. The occasion never arose again. On future visits Philippa refused to go driving, preferring, she said, to have a good brisk walk. Or else they drove sedately to the village shops, with Victoria bouncing about on Philippa's knee. Philippa obviously had felt the tug of temptation and would not expose herself to it again. Instead, she exposed Robert, all too weak, to his own.

It could not have gone on for long, his dual life, and he knew that from the start. Perhaps he only allowed it to begin because in his own mind the time of his stay in England was rapidly ending. If he had set off six months earlier for his new career in the States, it would have ended most innocently and undiscovered. But instead he hung on, writing yet another letter to Anna Beinhart, annoyed at again not getting a reply. But he waited. It was not like Anna. Perhaps she was on holiday. Or perhaps, in postwar chaos, the letters had gone astray. He waited impatiently for an answer, and while he waited, time caught up with him.

It had to happen eventually. Bridlington was a small, tight-knit community, for all its city size, and the country cousins, like the Hallsworths, had their regular connections. Actually, Mrs. Hallsworth regularly shopped in York and holidayed in Scarborough, but her sister, Philippa's retired schoolteacher aunt, lived yet in Bridlington, took her morning coffee at the Lounge, and her afternoon tea on the Promenade. She went regularly to the Floral Pavilion for concerts, and to the Spa and the Pavilion for plays. She shopped also at Allan's and bought her hats from Miss Wilkins, millinery, and her plain little dark assistant. And one day, having dashed in late for three navy buttons from haberdashery, happened to be in the entrance foyer just at closing time, where the manager in morning coat and striped trousers ushered her graciously out the door. She had taken just three steps down the street when she was brushed roughly from behind, and turned to the apologies of Miss Wilkins's little assistant. "Oh, I'm terribly sorry, oh, do pardon, but I'm in a terrible hurry—oh darling, here I am, here!"

The girl dashed past, still apologizing over the shoulder of her little rabbit-fur-collared suit, and then she leaped into the front seat of a dark maroon MG sports car and flung her arms about the driver. When she was quite done kissing him, Mrs. Hallsworth's sister had a good, clear view of his face.

"It was Robert," she said firmly three days later to Mrs. Hallsworth over tea at Greenshaws Hall. She had regarded the whole event of sufficient significance to travel by bus up to Hovringham to tell her sister in person. Though unmarried, and a schoolteacher, she was neither a prude nor a gossip, and Mrs. Hallsworth had very little reason to doubt the story; very little reason, and precisely no inclination. In due course, Philippa was called in, decently enough to a private audience with her mother, and eventually it was agreed that Harold would not be consulted.

"I hardly think daddy will be of any assistance," was Mrs. Hallsworth's accurate appraisal. Philippa took it all as calmly as everyone expected her to, and when her mother said, equally calmly, "Do you wish to file for divorce, dear?" she replied at once, "Don't be ridiculous, mother. It will just be some stupid little fling." Then she walked out, put on her jodhpurs, chose the worst horse in the stables, got on its back, and drove it for a grueling twelve miles over the wet, windy moor.

The following day she went to see Robert. She went unannounced, not because she hoped to catch him *in flagrante delicto*, but simply because her reason for coming could not be divulged in a letter or a telephone call. She intended to have it out, as she put it, and having it out was inevitably face to face.

She arrived off the eleven o'clock train and took a taxi directly to the St. Leonard's, appearing there utterly unannounced. Robert was in. His morning riding he had abandoned, those funds going instead for the support of the MG and his petrol ration. He had been out late the night before, after the show, with Rhoda, and had only just dressed. He was standing in his stocking feet brushing his hair when there was a small, decisive tap on his door. He said, "Come in," without looking up, expecting Mrs. Pledger wanting the rent.

The door swung open, casting sunlight from the landing window onto his mirror. Through the dust motes he saw a pale, determined young face. Plaster dust, he thought. Chin up, ducky.

"Forgive the intrusion, Robert."

"Intrusion?" he said, laughing. "May I have more such." He turned at once to embrace her, thinking most ironically that she had at last fulfilled his long-stated desire of coming for once without Victoria, just to see him in the old romantic way. She made her little fish slither to the right, avoiding his grasp, not even bending a cool cheek for his kiss, and he knew he was wrong. She glanced at her watch.

"I do know you have rehearsals shortly, and I shan't keep you unnecessarily. I would not have come at all, but a matter of some unpleasantness has unfortunately arisen . . ." She paused and Robert felt he was being read a form letter. She found her place again. "And I feel it is appropriate if we settle this simply, and now."

"Is your father causing trouble?" he said quickly, and uneasily. Her short little laugh ended that thought at once.

"Hardly my father," she said again, with another laugh. She added sharply, "Let's not be coy, Robert, it doesn't suit."

Don't be coy, it's not worthy of you.

At once he understood. The hows and whys and wherefores were as insignificant as they were mysterious. The simple, stupid truth was that the whole stupid thing had, sooner rather than later, come to its logical stupid conclusion. Mice in traps must surely realize that God doesn't give cheese out for nothing.

"Oh, Jesus, Philippa."

"I've found out," she finished for him with a cheerless, sarcastic grin. "Robert, what an appalling little farce. Just look at us. This *stupid* little farce. A shopgirl. A milliner's assistant, from Allan's. A *shop*girl."

"She thinks I'm Adonis," he said.

"Whatever is that meant to mean?"

He shook his head, waving it away, wishing he could wave Philippa, indeed the whole world away, into the dusty sunlight. The whole house was utterly hushed, empty and silent, accentuating their private, isolated misery.

"Can you conceive," Philippa said slowly, "how quite utterly humiliating it was for me? My aunt coming to my mother with some—some *fish*monger's tale. Only it happened to be true. Did it not?" There was really no question in her voice.

"Oh, it did," he said softly. "It did."

"Robert." She turned around, looked out the window, searching the wet tile roofs for words. "Robert, why? Why some foolish little tart? Why her?"

Robert suddenly grew angry, regaining conviction, and said

sharply, "Now wait a minute, madam. Just what makes you so sure you know all about her? She's not a tart. She's not at all. She's a nice little kid."

"Rubbish."

"No, damn it. She's a nice quiet kid. How would you or your damned aunt know?" Then he did not wait for an answer but said roughly, "Never mind. I can guess. She works in a shop. She wears cheap clothes because she can't afford anything else, and maybe she puts her makeup on a bit clumsily because nobody sent her to some smart-ass boarding school . . ."

"Oh, for the love of Christ, Robert." Philippa covered her ears. "Our marriage is falling apart, and all you can think of is your damned middle-class prejudices."

"My prejudices," he shouted. "Mine. What the damned hell about yours? She works in a shop. So she's a tart. Look, madam, I know your line of thinking by now, and your goddamned family's. God, to think people like that poor girl's father fought the war to keep shits like *your* father secure with their fat asses on their fat country seats."

"All right, Robert," Philippa said quietly. "I'm leaving now." Her voice was unexcitable and totally reasonable. "We will discuss this further when you've calmed down. I think my solicitor will be present."

He stopped quite still, looking at her as she neatly pulled her gloves, which she had tentatively taken off, back onto her surprisingly stubby fingers. The plainness of her hands he had always found endearing, a contrast to the grand design of the rest of her. He could not comprehend being forever without her.

"You can't mean that," he said uneasily.

"Why not?" She was still perfectly calm and reasonable. "You have provided me with very solid grounds."

"So that's it," he said sharply.

"That's what?" She was still looking mildly at her fingers in white cloth.

"You know very well, madam. Just that. That's exactly

what you've been waiting for . . . that's just what you wanted, and my God, I have played right into your hands. I bet your father's crowing."

"You're not making sense, Robert," she said, but she was halted in mid-stride to the door, apparently by confusion.

"A divorce. Of course. That's what everyone wants, isn't it? After all, the war's over and you haven't got the Luftwaffe to solve your little problem, so now you need legal means. Well, there you are. The least you could do is say thank you."

He laughed and she shook her head impatiently and said only, "Your delight in melodrama has never impressed me."

"I know," he said at once. "Neither have I ever impressed you. No, that's a lie. I did impress you once, I know, long ago. The way I impress Rhoda now."

"Rhoda?" said Philippa with a faint smile.

"Oh, I do apologize. A terribly lower-class name and all, my *dear* thing. Shall we call her something else, so as not to offend your sensibilities? Edwina, or Diana, or shall we stick to the safe ones? Elizabeth. Oh, no, the royals are terribly middle class, I *have* forgotten. Jane. There's a good one, straight, honest, no-nonsense Anglo-Saxon. Maybe Anne? Katherine?"

"Shut up."

"Ursula? Georgina? Oh, hell, Philippa, I know very well what's eating you. It's Christmas morning, the first Christmas in maybe fourteen years, and you've finally woken up. And all Santa—pardon, Father Christmas—has left in your fucking silk stocking is a bum Jewish actor and a lump of coal. Well, hang on to the coal, sweetheart, they might just ration it yet. But don't bother about me. Where I come from we're a dime a dozen," he added bitterly. "And soon enough there's going to be one more."

There was a long pause, and when Philippa spoke again, the anger he had braced for was not there. Her voice was weak and shaky, almost childish, as it was in the days of her pregnancy.

"Are you taking her with you?" she said.

Robert simply stared, silent, for a long time, torn between enchantment at her romantic naiveté and exasperation at her stupidity. Then exhilaration overrode both. It was neither. It was a measure of her jealousy, and that, a measure of her love. She hovered there in his doorway, suddenly lost in her soft fox fur jacket, and he felt if he could physically grasp her now, in her new, rare fragility, she would at last again be his. He leaned toward her, his forearms extending like tentative feelers of a shy beetle. She faded back and broke the mood, saying sharply, "Where is she?"

She was looking about the tiny room, as if it could conceal her rival somewhere. He shook his head and said, "She doesn't *live* with me, Philippa. She's rarely even here. You know Mrs. Pledger." He started to laugh, clumsily, watching Philippa's face. The visible pain of her imaginings of himself and Rhoda here was startling. He wanted to ease the pain and said impulsively, "She's nothing, Phil. She's a woolly cushion. She's very young and very simple and that's all that there is to her, and all I want from her. It's all just a stupid fling."

He had intended comfort, but she withdrew from it, and from him, more severely, and hurt turned to anger.

"You sod," she said finally. "You lying sod. And what then do you say to her about me? Oh, don't tell me, I could reel it off to you, if I cared, line for line. Bad line for bad line. Like one of those stupid melodramas everyone thinks you're so bloody marvelous in. Dear Robert," she said, with delicate sarcasm, "you've fallen at last into the great actor's trap, haven't you?"

"Oh, leave off my profession for once."

"But it's your *life*, dear," she said, dropping her voice several notes and rolling her eyes upward dramatically. "Isn't it, dear? Wartime hero shares bohemian squalor with shopgirl. Oh, what a lovely part. And beautifully cast. At *last*, my love, a starring role."

She shrugged and turned to go, but he caught the end of her

costly sleeve and jerked her around. "Don't you call me love, you sour bitch," he said. Her eyes opened wide. He still held her sleeve, and she pulled, a small impatient tug. He grasped it harder, turning the edge of the satin lining up with his finger. He said finally, "And don't come waltzing into my damned bed-sit in your bloody fur coat again. You embarrass me."

She looked hard at him, as if unsure she was hearing him right. "I what?" she said.

He felt foolish. It was, after all, not exactly extravagant. Not mink, but plain fox, and old fox, indeed something prewar of her mother's, and cut down. Still Robert had, among the friends and family of home, only known one woman who owned a fur coat, an aunt of his father's, who had married well.

"Did you have to wear that?" he said lamely, at last. Philippa looked at him with something approaching disgust. She said, "I'll turn it inside out and wear the lining, if you prefer."

"Ha. Ha. It probably says Harrods."

"No. It says by personal appointment to Philippa Hallsworth."

"Zolenski."

"*Zolenski*. Of course, Robert. Philippa Hallsworth Zolenski. Surely Robert, we've grown past that ridiculous foolishness of names. Surely *now*."

Robert looked, in a tired half-circle, around the dreary little room, from his unmade bed, to the boarded-up cream-tiled fireplace, to the dusty wardrobe and the pink and gray mock Persian rug. Sunlight picked out flecks of old paint and streaks of seagull excrement on the outside of the window. Limp green curtains hung on either side, and the broken cord of the sash dangled forlornly.

"You know, Phil," he said, "I think we're about past everything." He stood still, his head bowed, waiting for her to leave. Instead, she walked across the room with gentle steps, and sat down on the bed. When he looked up, she was still sitting there, her eyes on him expectantly, her polished kid, brass-clasped handbag at her feet. He thought of Rhoda with her scuffed leather satchel.

"I have to go, Phil," he said.

"Rehearsal?"

"No. No, I mean really go. America. There's nothing for me here. I mean, no work."

"You *are* working," she said urgently. "Surely—you're the best they have."

"It won't last," he said. "*They* won't last. Everything's changed, Phil. People, audiences, the theater. Everything. The truth is, my dear, I'm out of fashion. There's nothing worse, you know, in the arts."

As he said it, the import of it truly reached him for the first time. He had known it was true for a long while, but putting it into words gave it a finality that was sickening. His stomach began to hurt and he felt weak at the knees and went to his one chair with its napless velvet cover and sat down. He could not bear to look at her, in his new weakness.

He heard her get to her feet, and waited for the sound of her hand on the rattly ceramic knob. Her hand came instead to his shoulder. Or rather to the nape of his neck. He looked up, startled, and she lowered herself until she was crouching on the floor, her hand now reaching up, the first two fingers caressing his unshaven cheek. Tears clotted her blond eyelashes. "Oh, Robert," she said. Then she began to kiss him, gently, and then with guilty passion.

He had forgotten the great British love of the underdog.

Between kisses, her voice thick with remorse, she said, "Why, my poor dear, did you not tell me?"

He feared condescension and drew back, saying, "Tell you what?"

"How bad things have become. Oh, Robert, I'm your wife, couldn't you tell me? Did you have—" She paused a bit, swallowed her pride, and said, "Did you have to tell a stranger? Oh, what did I do to you?"

She began to cry again, and he said angrily, "Why, for

Christ's sake, did I have to tell anybody? Wasn't it all pretty obvious? I mean, it's hardly the Ritz, is it?" He gave the room a dismissive, angry turn of his hand.

She sat back on her heels, chastened, looking around the room as if it were her first view of it. "Surely, Robert, it wasn't all you could find. Was it?" she said, uncertainly.

"Do you really think I live in this mess by choice?"

Then his irony turned to exasperation because he saw in her face that she did.

"You know we haven't any money. I haven't any money. You have, and Victoria has, but that's not my money, is it? Well, is it, madam?"

She turned away, then turned shrewdly back and said, "You appear to have enough money to run a motorcar, and hardly an old banger at that, is it? Do you know what mother said? Mother said, 'There's your flat in London, dear,' the day you drove up the drive. And she was right, wasn't she? You never intended to take me to London at all, did you?"

"No, madam. And you never intended coming with me, so we can drop that for a start."

"I did, Robert," she cried, childishly. "I did. That's hardly fair, is it? You never gave me the chance."

Robert got up, went to his wardrobe and pulled out first his jacket, then his dinner jacket, in search of his cigarettes. He found them, wincing at the pale pink packet, but needing the smoke too much to hide them. Philippa watched as he lit up, and he said, nervously, "Want one?"

"I don't smoke," she said sharply. "I never smoke."

"No, of course." He shook his head. "I'm sorry. Not thinking."

"She smokes," said Philippa. "And she likes expensive cigarettes. And you took her out last night, did you not? Dancing, or dining, or some such?"

"No," Robert lied. "I did not."

"And you wore your dinner jacket."

"Look, Miss Sherlock Holmes, I wore my dinner jacket on

stage. If you must know, the young lady is quite content with a brown ale and a pork pie. You see, she understands about being broke. She's been broke all her life. It makes it easier."

"How dare you throw that cheap tart up to me?" Philippa whispered. But Robert would not be drawn into argument. He said only, "She takes me as I am, Philippa. Can't you understand how simply restful that is? Her mother thinks I'm wonderful because I brought her a box of Fry's chocolate creams once."

There was a long silence, and then Philippa said with a voice calm to breaking, "Whose points?"

Robert couldn't think for a moment what she meant, but her eyes, dry now, were going a dangerous glittery blue ice color. Then the calm broke, and she leaped for him and slapped him across the face. "You bastard. You used my daughter's sweets ration for your stupid tart. You sod. You rotten sod."

Suddenly it was immensely funny to Robert, and he was wrestling with Philippa's tough horsewoman's strength and laughing aloud and trying to explain that the sweets were an innocent treasure, an unwanted gift, passed on by an actress in the company. "Oh, Phil, Phil," he said, still struggling with laughter. "Stop it, we're not children any more."

That stopped her, and she let go, and rather curtly apologized, and said, "I am sorry, Robert. This entire thing has been rather stressful, you must understand."

After a long silence, he said, "All right. I do understand. Now you must try also, to understand, just a little. I am going to tell you every truth there is, and some are not nice, but when it is done, you will know where you stand. That's something, I guess." She stood very quiet, listening, as if she were a little afraid of what she would hear.

Robert said, "Yes, I have a mistress. Yes, I indulge her with money I should save for us. Yes, I bought a car so I could have someplace to screw her."

"Robert, please."

"Honesty," he said. "Yes, I'm broke, and I'm scared about work, and I'm leaving Britain to see if, please God, things will be better on the other side. Now. I do not love Rhoda. I do not wish to continue the damned thing one day longer than today. I want you to come to America with me, but I'm not even going to ask, because I know what the answer will be. Later, in time. Eventually. When things are better. I know, I know, I know. What you all mean is, when I'm up to Hallsworth standards, and madam, relax, I never will be.

"This, my dear—" he again encompassed the room with a gesture of resigned distaste—"this is Zolenski standard. This, and going down. Fast."

"Robert, you're being dreadfully unfair. I've never complained about coming here, sleeping here, even, when I can."

"When you can," he said slowly. "It's not very often, is it?"

"I have Victoria to think about," she said, indignantly. "Be reasonable, Robert."

"Yes. And the last time you brought Victoria here, you refused to let her sit on the floor. She might get dirty, you said. I half expected you to tell her to put paper on the seat when she went to the loo. Philippa, this is my home. My own, only home. I'm sorry it isn't good enough for our daughter's blue-blooded little bum, but it's all I have to offer. You've turned down the offer once too many times. And now I've offered it to someone else."

"So you are taking her."

"No, madam, I am going exactly the way I came. Alone."

"You came with Mike," Philippa said detachedly. Then Robert smiled, bemused, and said, "Do you know? I honestly had forgotten. I honestly had."

"Oh, it's such a long time ago," Philippa said. "Isn't it?"

She stood in his window, looking out over the rooftops shining in the sun with the salty dampness of the morning. She could see an edge of the beach where they had met, golden brown, and far away.

"Philippa," he said gently.

She did not answer, but he read responsiveness in the line of her neck and yellow hair, set against the sunlight. "Philippa, faithfulness isn't just about bed, you know." For the first time, he felt older than her in every way. "It's possible to commit adultery with the mind as well, and the soul." And then, for no other reason than the careless freedom of a lost cause, he said, "Come back to me."

And she did. She turned around, smiling, leaning back, elegantly graceful, from the hips, her hands outstretched, palms upward, as to the dearest of old friends. He took them, they kissed. She shrugged from her fur jacket, and he hung it, carefully, on the door. He turned the key in the latch, carefully, lest the sound break something. But she was already sitting on the edge of his bed, removing her shoes. He drew the too-limp green curtains together, as close as they'd come, but a wavery line of sunlight crept through. The room took a green cast, as though it were under the sea.

After their lovemaking, they lay sleepily in the narrow bed, clutched together, their thighs yet making a warm wet joining. The crinkled band of sunlight lit Philippa's hair, an unfocused blur beyond the unfocused tip of Robert's nose. Beyond, where the lines of focus met clearly, he saw the sun dusting her fox jacket, graying the russet to dim amber. It was the last moment of his life lit with gold.

They parted with love, friendship, and hope, vowing together a future in America, or wherever fate took them, but together. Philippa left the bed-sit with Robert, but they parted on the pavement outside, at the edge of the red brick steps to his front door, Robert to go to the Pavilion, and Philippa back to her train, her parents' home, and their daughter. In the formality of the salt-weathered old street, beneath a barren plane tree, she kissed the side of his cheek, a sister's kiss. Then she was gone, walking with swift, graceful steps up the slight hill, away from the sea.

At the corner, she was jarred nearly off her feet by a young woman, hurrying, with a greasy paper full of chips, who barged around the edge of the building without a glance. The chips spilled, and scattered, flinging the scent of vinegar over Philippa. She gasped and leaped back, instinctively brushing a light hand over her fur.

"Oh, miss, I'm sorry. I'm terrible sorry. Here, let me help." Chip-grubby fingers extended plaintively. Philippa took a sharp step back, shaking her head. Any other time she would have been furious. But her body was warm yet, and glowing with rare relaxation, and her mind was, for the first time in years, totally at peace. Besides, the girl was so pathetically plain, and short, and chubby, with her pointed little nose caked with face powder, and her dark red lips mumbling apologies as she rubbed a smudge of grease on her weak little chin.

"Nothing harmed," Philippa said brightly, and even smiled her broad friendly smile. "But what a pity about your lunch. I do hope . . ."

"Oh, never mind me, it's your lovely coat I'm worrying about." But Philippa assured her again, and then turned and recommenced her swift, long-legged walk up the street as the dark-haired girl watched. Something tugged inside her, a hunger that had nothing to do with the lost chips scattered on the pavement. But she shook her head sadly and patted down her rolled dark hair. It wasn't the fur coat, or the expensive suit under it. It was how you were born that made you look like that, with sharp wonderful cheekbones, and a smile as controlled as a dancer's. She crumpled up her newspaper, and dropped it a little guiltily on the pavement. Then she forgot her guilt, and her sorrow at being plain, and dark and ordinary. She had caught a glimpse of a tall figure in an old RAF greatcoat, striding down the street a block ahead. She began to run, and caught him at the stage door of the Pavilion.

"Oy there, have a heart, I'm right puffed out. Who you running away from, anyhow?" she laughed.

She never forgot that day, nor the look on his face when he turned around.

As it was, she only saw him twice more. Once that evening, a long, hopeless, tearful evening, and once more, a yearning outsider's glimpse from the crowd as he left the stage door one night, two weeks later. He left alone, head down, walking quickly to the beloved maroon MG, which taunted her now with its new remoteness. He was as remote himself. And when she learned a month later that he had left the company, she learned through strangers. She read in the paper that he was going to America, and spilled her tea in the staff room at Allan's. He had never even said good-bye.

The truth was, he could not face her, but she could not imagine that. So once again, his weakness wore cruelty's cloak, and wore it far too well.

Robert sailed on the *Queen Mary* in early November, a wet, stormy seasick crossing, at the end of which he set foot in America for the first time in nearly six years. It was a modest, untriumphant return of the warrior, without money, without work, without wife and daughter. There was only one person he really wished to see under those circumstances particularly, and that was Anna Beinhart. But he still had had no reply to his letters, and besides filial duty demanded he report first to his mother on Long Island. Which, steeling himself to face an unpleasant mix of recrimination and smug judgment, he did.

He found her changed. Aged, smaller, mellowed, unrecriminative, grown solider and quieter, with the settling of her new house around her. The change in her, however, was only one change of so many that, apart from the relief one feels on finding an old enemy partially disarmed, he hardly noticed. Everything was changed, the house, which he had left with the gloss of the sap yet on the wood, now absorbed in weathering, and thickened with possessions, strange possessions now outnumbering the old remembered lamps and tables and cupboards of his childhood. The town, too, grown large, and less discriminate, and full of strange faces. Shopkeepers he had known since babyhood had vanished, leaving behind their newly renovated counters, sons and daughters who had been his schoolmates, now catapulted into not-so-young adulthood. Faces he remembered as thin and pimply appeared solid and handsome and successful. Girls who had swished by in dirndl skirts were trouser-clad mothers with small images of themselves in tow. The generations mixed themselves. He kept finding the faces of their parents in his own contemporaries, and the faces of his school friends on their children. Time, which he had somehow illogically imagined to have been packed up with him and taken abroad, had been at work in America, too, after all. But it surprised him, Van Winkle in British flannels and sleeveless pullover, awakened from a troubled sleep.

The war had been here, too, or rather, its shock waves had. When he had left, it was a personal private quest, largely unthought of by all around him. But that had changed, and a lot of faces were not there to be seen, ever again, and a lot of boys had become hard men, having in the end had a much harder war in the Pacific, or the European infantry. He felt a bit of a cheat, lauded all around as a romantic hero, he who had slept in his own bed most nights of the war.

Some changes were eerie and disturbing. His sister Dolores, widowed since nineteen forty-two, had returned to the neighboring town of Patchogue. He hardly knew her. Her face was years older, her hair graying, and she had taken to wearing a lot of makeup. She dressed like a tramp, and his mother did not seem to notice. Robert had missed the family catharsis of grieving, and the husband he recalled as a gawky young groom, stumbling engagingly over the lines of the marriage service, seemed to be forgotten by all. He resented it bitterly, as if he and his brother-in-law had been devoted friends, rather than strangers brought together by the accident of someone else's love. Dolores smoked cigarettes, and was dating a garage owner, and quite openly sleeping with him. His mother, seeing his visible shock, said with a small shrug, "It's not her fault, she's a widow. She deserves something," and would not be drawn out on the subject again.

But apart from its capacity to break human lives, the same on either side of the Atlantic, the war had had an immensely different effect on his two nations. And while it had left Britain tattered, and worn, and impoverished—if unbowed, still bloody enough—it had enriched America. The States were booming, as if the whole idea had been a good thing, the nation spoon-fed by violence on milk and honey. The country was thriving. There was money and action everywhere, and it showed. Spindly gold spiders of new houses rose on every third corner. People dressed well and looked well, and demanded a lot, and soon. The Depression and the bad times that had marked all their childhoods seemed as far away and forgotten as Dolores's buried husband. Robert saw the whole of his life since the end of childhood framed in cataclysm, swept in on the hurricane and out on the war, and now he was back again where everything had begun. And yet, some things had not changed at all: the bay, the shore, the salt air, the intense sea-bound light.

It was the light that struck him first. Even in winter, on the docks in New York, the unique strong light of the New World. The air was colder, the wind Canadian and savage, but the light, the clear icy sunlight of Manhattan in December was stronger than any light he could recall. It was as if he had for six years looked on the world through a glass darkly, the rain-washed, near-polar-angled sun of wet northern Europe, in which everything was grayed by latitude as much as weather, the great climatic brownout of Britain. The light, more than the sprawling accents and the distinctive note of New York taxi horns, told him he was home.

Out on the island the light intensified, a painter's light, rattling through the barren white oak and sassafras. That, the salt smell, the tumbling-down wooden Victorian houses, the vulgar, wide macadam roads, without any consideration of friend or family, were the reasons he stayed.

He went back to Manhattan after a week in search of Anna Beinhart. It should have been a simple matter, of course, but something alarming had occurred. Frustrated with the post, he had rung her number and found it had been disconnected ten months before. She had moved, gone somewhere, and had not told him. He was hurt and he was frightened. She was his only link to work.

He began his search at the logical, indeed the only place, the house on West Eleventh Street, where he had gone so many years ago with a slip of paper in his pocket and the untested confidence of youth. He found the house, feeling a rich wash of nostalgia at the sight of it, tucked into the small, neatly gracious street with yellow-leaved ailanthus trees on either side. He was surprised then to realize that part of the nostalgia was the memories it evoked of London. There were dozens of such streets of small townhouses there, a fact which annoyed him. He had always loved that small corner of New York for what he regarded in innocence as its uniqueness. Philippa would not have looked twice at it, he knew now.

The sight of the house gave him a moment of encouragement, as if its very existence boded well for his cause, until he recalled that here, unlike wartime London, houses tended to stay where you'd left them.

It looked at first so unchanged that he was quite convinced that Anna would be there after all, the letters, the telephone, all somehow a mistake. The iron railings were still black-painted, still a little in need of retouching, and although someone had replaced the missing bar in the basement window grill, the missing brick in the steps still threatened the unwary foot. There were even geraniums in the window, though white ones, and Anna had favored red. But every third house had geraniums. There was a cat, also, but only a small, wary tiger, with wide frightened eyes, which cowered as he approached the green-painted door.

Almost everything was there, trees, and ivy, the small brass plate on the door still read, in engraved, elaborate script, "Theatrical Agent." But something was missing along with the regal gray cats, the red flowers, the incense burner in the shape of an elephant that had sat on the sill. A certain insane glamour was gone. The brass plate had a new name bolted on, in place of Anna's. It said Irving Grossman, in neat, modest print.

Robert rang the bell. There was nothing else to do, and anyhow the fact that Anna's place had been taken by someone in her own trade seemed unlikely to be mere coincidence. He was right in that. The door was answered by a small dark man of middle age, balding and serious faced, with black-rimmed bifocals and a shabby brown tweed jacket over an open-throated shirt. He stared at Robert through the upper part of his eyeglasses and Robert stared back, for a moment, uncertain how to begin. It proved unnecessary.

"Are you looking for Mrs. Beinhart?" he said.

"Yes. Well, I am actually," Robert said, startled. "But how did you know?" Then the man did something really startling.

"Oh, you're the English one," he said.

"I'm what?"

"Anna's English actor."

"I'm not English," Robert said at once, "perhaps you're thinking of someone else." But as he said it he heard his own voice honestly for the first time since his return home, and England echoed through it, albeit dimly, but clear enough to be heard.

"Now, you are going to be a problem," said the man. "The business is jammed with your type. What's happening to the theater in London, anyhow? Plague?" He shook his head, and then grinned to himself, turning back toward the interior of the house. "Come in, come in," he said over his shoulder, as an afterthought, it appeared.

It took Robert fifteen minutes to shake from the man's mind the conviction of his Britishness, and even then he seemed doubtful. Robert broadened his vowels consciously, working hard at speaking his native tongue, but he still felt he was being regarded as an impostor.

"How did you know I was looking for Anna?" he said. Irving Grossman shrugged. He sat down behind the big black oak desk that was filling the space where Anna's dresser full of blue and white china had stood. He said, "Eleven months I've been here, and everyone who comes to the door still looks disappointed. So. I know how a second wife feels, I suppose. I should apologize I am not Anna?" He shrugged and took off his glasses and rubbed his eyebrows. Robert was looking around the room, suppressing hostility. The man was pleasant enough. But he missed the plants, and the cats, and the coffee smell, and the smell of Anna even, a trifle oniony, a cozy old-lady smell.

"Is she dead?" he said.

The man shook his head, grimaced, polished his glasses. "She's in a home," he said. "She's gone a bit cuckoo."

Robert recoiled, drawing himself away from the black oak desk and the crude casualness of the man behind it.

"Anna?" he said, incredulous.

"So? She's eighty-four already."

Robert sat stunned and the man said, picking at a speck on one lens, "She gets every care. Don't worry. I should know," he said with another grimace. "I pay the bills. Those nuns, they know about money, you know, as well as God."

Robert was confusedly sorting a tangle of thoughts and finding one thread free, said suddenly, "Why do you pay the bills?"

"Who else? Whose mother is she?"

"Anna?" Robert said. "Anna is your mother?"

"Uh-huh," he said, flicking the last speck of dust with a monogrammed handkerchief, and replacing the glasses. Robert said, "She never even said she was married . . ." and then paused, awkwardly.

Irving Grossman said, "Ah, but she told you about my half-sister, I bet."

"The girl who died?"

"Oh, she was brilliant, a star," the man said softly, mockingly, and Robert suddenly heard Anna's voice behind his. "Yes, that one. My half-sister. She got appendicitis when I was seven. She was twenty-one. She curled up like a crab and died. Mama, Anna, she never cared about anyone after that. You see, she had *married* my father, and I was legitimate, and neither of us died. I was the bird in hand. Maybe worth more, but the one in the bush is so much more interesting. Still, I am here, still, and she gave me the business, all her stars." Again there was a certain mockery on the word. "Every now and then another one turns up, another waif. And what can I do for you?" he said, with a not ungentle smile.

There were only two things Robert wanted: work, and the address of the place where Anna, cuckoo or otherwise, resided. The second was easy, the first less so. Irving Grossman took him on, with a shrug and a whimsical twist of the eyebrows, rather as participants at a will reading take bequeathed objects of alien taste and doubtful worth. Once again, Robert left the small house on West Eleventh Street with his future in the balance and a slip of paper in his pocket, but this time the balance seemed heavy against him. He walked almost aimlessly across town and turned down lower Fifth Avenue to Washington Square. There, on a park bench with pigeons warily approaching, he drew the paper from his pocket, his gloved hand brushing against a hard metal edge as he did so. He removed a glove and read the address of the nursing home, then put the paper away. He was about to put the glove back on when his fingers, groping in his pocket, found a will of their own, and withdrew the small red car. He removed the other glove and ran his fingers along the wheels, and then childishly ran the car down his sleeve, smiling to himself. The wind came up and squandered leaves about the squirrels. He thought of throwing the car away, or leaving it on the edge of the slide in the playground for some child to find. But he could not do it. It had traveled too far with him to be left, lonely, in the November wind.

He returned it to his pocket and pulled on his gloves, noticing with a pinch of annoyance that one seam was coming undone. His gloves and his shoes were important. He would need warmth and comfort for the winter weeks he knew lay ahead, of walking from appointment to appointment. New gloves, like taxi fares, were receding beyond his reach.

He found the nursing home, an anonymous, dirty-gray-fronted establishment on Twentieth Street, run by Catholic nuns. A tiny woman with bright eyes and delicate lips and hands, her face as gray as her habit, sat behind a reception desk behind the double entrance doors. Dry leaves blew in, around Robert's feet, onto the green-tiled floor. He gave his name and his purpose and requested to see Anna. The thin little nun led him into a waiting room and left him there, he a little uncertain if she had understood him at all. She had not spoken a word.

But he sat, waiting patiently. The room was also green-tiled, marbly tiles, worn to their brown canvas backing at the doorway. The walls were painted green halfway up, divided there by a varnished strip of wood, and painted cream the rest of the way to the high ceiling. It reminded him of the walls of his high school, and also of the hospital in London where Porky Piggott had been sent to grow a new skin.

There was a crucifix, somber and dark, on one wall, and a neat stack of *Life* magazines on a low table. The room was as spotless and lifeless as the little nun. He read a while, an article about the trials in Nuremberg. He found it as hard to imagine that the events it related were part of the same war he had fought in as it was to recall that the solemn symbol on the wall had once been part of his own childhood.

The nun came back and opened the door for him, and he followed her out. Anna's was a long high-ceilinged room with eight beds along the walls, and a small area in the center with an old, dark red carpet and a circle of chairs. Only one chair was occupied, though, and on the outside of the circle two wheelchairs had been drawn up. In each of those, an old woman sat slumped half over on one elbow. Only the occupant of the one proper chair sat up straight in all the room. She was not Anna. She was a tall, thin, long-faced woman, whose cheekbones bespoke an almost Indian aristocracy. Her hair was white and braided round and round her head. Her eyes were pale, translucent blue, and blind. There was a radio on a table beside a pink glass vase of hothouse chrysanthemums. Something stirred deep down in Robert, a fishing line of thought, seeking their Latin name.

He stared at the tall, thin woman in the chair, wishing her to be Anna. She had such dignity, the only dignity in the room. There were three humped old-lady shapes in three of the beds. Beside them visitors sat, conversing with each other, in honor of the humped prone presence.

The gray-faced nun, still silent (was it a vow? Robert thought wildly), walked purposefully to the center ring of chairs. Robert felt queasy. His stomach began to hurt, high up, in the usual place, progressing to his back, up under the shoulder blades. The room smelled of disinfectant and urine. The radio on the table was playing "People Will Say We're in Love." The nun stopped at one slumped old lady in a pink, candlewick dressing gown. Robert nonsensically wished it were the other. Though it made no difference, he would not have known Anna as either.

The nun suddenly smiled, a bright, wide smile showing many crooked blue-white teeth. When she spoke, her voice was touched with a faint Irish accent, and a tremendous warmth. "Well now, Annie, you've a visitor. Are you going to say hello?"

The old lady, still with her back half to Robert, made no response at all, but the nun persisted, "Come on, Annie, it's not time to sleep now, here's a nice gentleman to see you."

She began rocking the wheelchair very slightly back and forth, as Robert had seen Philippa do with Victoria's pram, a comforting, gentle gesture. It made him illogically angry, and he said sharply, "Anna. Her name is Anna. Not Annie." But the nun did not seem to hear.

Nor did Anna. But eventually, in response to the nun's rocking and coaxing, she half raised her head. Robert saw a funny wrinkled old face, toothless puckered mouth, round pink cheeks and chin and nose all folding in about it, as if the face were closing like a flower. Her eyes were mild and mindless, a watery blue-brown, her eyebrows gone as wispy as a child's. There were several black hairs making a little beard on her chin. It was not a face that he could recall having ever seen before. He felt too foolish to ask the nun if she was sure she had the right old lady.

"Hello, Anna," he said, as he would to one of Victoria's dolls held up for a greeting. She nodded her little round head back and forth, the puckered mouth puckered tighter, and released. She looked at the floor, at the nun, then at the arm of her chair. She began to pick at that, finding a loose edge of rubber coating, and peeling at it, absorbed. Robert touched her arm, striving his best to achieve some manner of contact. She ignored him at first, but then reached out, touched his hand, and clasped the fingers. With growing hope he extended them. She studied his hand and then drew it closer. He thought she meant to kiss it, and was fascinated. It reached her mouth and the puckered lips began thirstily to suck. Repelled, he jerked his hand away. The nun said nothing, but he felt a flow of understanding. He shook his head and looked away.

Then Anna grasped his hand again, and stared at him for a long, long while, and then reached up to touch his face. He fought the desire to avoid her hand. But this time she only touched his hair just above one ear, and toyed with it with a face full of puzzlement. Then she spoke for the first, the only time.

"Weiss."

"Anna," Robert said eagerly. "Anna, it's me. Robert Zolenski."

"Weiss," she said again, and then she cried it out loud, "Weiss!" Then quite suddenly she began to cry and carry on, sobbing and making a fuss that stirred the whole ward, so that visitors began to stare. The nun calmed her and Robert was led away and told not to worry. It happened from time to time, and had no meaning.

"The mind is gone," said the nun. "It is only a reflex, the tears. No meaning at all." He was asked, gently, not to return. "It does sometimes upset her to see people. Her son comes. It's really all that's needed. The mind is gone."

Robert nodded, guiltily glad to flee. He turned once, at the door, and looked back. Anna was absorbed in rolling her skirt in a careful sausage up over her naked old knees.

It was a mercifully brief decline, the end of his theatrical career. It began at that moment, as the door of the nursing home shut him out and its gray twilight ladies in. It ended three months later in a small rehearsal room where, through the resigned efforts of Anna's son and heir, he met at last his own spiritual heir, the man to whom he had handed his one true chance.

It was, as unsentimental fate would have it, the day Philippa's letter arrived. It was not her first letter; they were regular and kind, bright stars in his cold, workless weeks, with their handful of lines in her beautiful script and then Victoria's baby scrawl, a picture, always a horse, usually with a stick Victoria upon it, and her name in huge asymmetrical letters. He propped the pictures above the disused fireplace in the small Charles Street apartment where he now stayed, alone. Horse followed horse, steeplechasing along the mantel. He had met the mailman this day as he went out the door, and had tucked the battered-with-sea-transit envelope into his pocket to read after the audition, in triumph or for solace.

There was nothing about the envelope to indicate the letter was in any way different from the others, just as there was nothing about the audition to set it apart as the turning point it was to become. It was a new play preparing for its out-of-town run, entitled *Out of Step*, on a theme Robert was finding recurrent and a little tiresome, a returning soldier's difficulty in readjustment. He had read it without enthusiasm; the characters were stock, the dialogue only partially believable. Halfway through he was resisting a temptation to pencil in changes, something he found himself more and more inclined to do of late.

Like many a performer fed up with the standard of material, he had felt increasingly the urge to write his own. The even more recurrent need for money, however, restrained his creative pen. Dreary it may have been, but somebody had put money behind this play, and that, for the moment, was significant. He studied the appropriate part dutifully and went off to take his chance.

He did not actually recognize the name of the director until he saw it in print. Irving Grossman had mentioned it, but it was the sight of it in cold print, on the black-and-white stenciled sign on the backstage office door that brought recollection. At once he saw it, as if superimposed on the black and white of countless news cuttings trundled across the Atlantic by his mother. Michael Martin, The Man Who Played The Dauphin, his own artistic child.

The child had waxed wise during the war years and had progressed from a triumphant onstage career to his current status of bright hope of modern directing. He did not, however, know his own father. He sat across from Robert with a smooth green metal desk between them, and asked irrelevant questions, and with a bored hand wrote down something, perhaps just his name for some kind of future reference.

Later, as Robert and a nervous young girl read, he lay down physically in the footlights, as if from that position artistic truth would be more readily apparent. He was cool, crisp, flamboyantly handsome, and savagely self-assured, a man with the confidence that comes from years of unquestioned adulation.

"Try that line again, Mr. Zolan. Please." He dragged the words out as if the effort of speech was painful, his sleek brow furrowed up with creative pain. "And no little grin this time, please. This isn't light comedy, you know. This is a serious work." Of course it was. Everything, everything was serious. Somehow, here too, while he and the diminishing survivors among his friends had laughed and joked and grinned their way through six years of war, preserving their sanity with remembrances of gaiety; somehow the world that had not joined them, those who had stayed safely behind, had grown grim and serious and had lost the ability, indeed the desire, to laugh. Robert had beautifully mastered the delicate comic art of the thirties. The dying forties could not have cared less.

Michael Martin did not even bother to say "We'll call you." But then he was an innovator with no time for conventions.

Outside the theater, a blind man with an accordion was playing the "Tennessee Waltz" and swaying in the late February cold. The air was blue and crisp and scented with soot and roasting chestnuts. Robert felt homesick for the coal smoke and vinegar smell of British streets. He dropped a dime in the blind man's cup.

Then he found an Automat and dropped several nickels in slots and collected a warm plate with a flat slice of apple pie and a cup of black coffee. He took them to a corner shelf of a table, a table convincingly designed for one only. He did not wish to talk or even share air space with a stranger's silence. He stirred cream into the coffee and opened Philippa's letter, awkwardly, with his cold hands. He spread it out on the glossy surface of the table, carefully avoiding spots of spilled cream. Then he wrapped his hands about the coffee cup for warmth and began to read.

They were still wrapped there when he finished, and stayed like that. Until he set the cup down, the coffee untouched, got up, and walked out the door. As he turned through the revolving doors he could see the shelf table, where already a Negro man, with that common and bewildered crushed-pride look of an out-of-work veteran, had tentatively commandeered his pie. Philippa's letter remained, delicately ignored by his large, dark hand.

He did not need it for future reference, like Michael Martin seemed to need his name. It only said two things and neither was readily forgettable. Philippa was pregnant and Philippa was seeking a divorce. There was no scribble from Victoria, and no ludicrous horse. There was, however, a small, legally couched note attached. It was from Harold Hallsworth and it advised him, strongly, not to contest. Clipped to it was a discreet Bank of England check. Robert wondered if the Negro veteran would try to cash it.

He walked twenty blocks uptown, along Fifth Avenue to the park, with his gloveless hands jammed into holed pockets, rubbing the salt of its opulence into the old wound of poverty. Then he crossed to Columbus Circle and followed Broadway, leaning toward the river. He left it at Seventy-second and went more purposefully riverward, until he was back on West End Avenue for the first time in seven years. He walked four blocks further, to West Seventy-sixth Street, searching the barren ailanthus trees for a long-vanished spring. It was very thoroughly winter. The yellow leaves of autumn in the gutter were mashed into a muddy slime. Robert remembered the boy with his peashooter envisioning the war on the New Jersey Palisades. He realized with a jolt that the boy would be a man, and might even have entered that far-off war by the time it reached its close. He would be Rhoda's age. New children, unthought of then, played now on the brownstone steps.

His old apartment was occupied, of course. Everything was occupied these days, and vacancy signs barely lasted the time it took to print them. The curtains at the second-floor window were dotted and frilly, exuding a cloying domesticity. He was disappointed. He had unconsciously been searching for the solidity of familiar ground, and found change instead. He thought then that the writer and his wife must be gone, too, because a battered gray baby stroller stood outside the basement entrance of their garden apartment. Then he came closer and saw the children on the steps more clearly and knew that they had not.

They were a boy and a girl. The girl at the toddling stage

and the boy about the age of Victoria. There had been change here, too, but the kind that involved not a taking up of roots, but a digging in. Each of the children had the dark blue eyes and the black hair of the writer's wife. The boy had a touch of her Slavonic cheekbones, and the girl, though a plain-faced, straight-haired creature, the same frail white skin. He was hurt by a remote jealousy. He had never imagined that they would have children.

He stood across the street looking at the house and the children until he was aware of them aware of him, whispering and shoving each other. He crossed the street then, pushing his hat back to show his face, and smiled to reassure them. Good city children, they shrank visibly away. He said hello, and asked their names and got a silence and then a hasty session of whispering amongst themselves. The girl, tugging her brother's sweater by its border of knitted spruce trees, was attempting to beat a retreat. Robert hiked up his gray over-coat and searched about in his trouser pocket for coins. He found a dime, decided quickly he could not spare more, and offered it to the children.

"You'll have to split it."

"We're not allowed," the boy said reasonably. He had a broad mouth, with small neat white teeth. He smiled when Robert spoke, and taking advantage of that weakened defense, Robert slipped the coin into his hesitant hand. The girl punched her brother in the back.

"Get in trouble," she said, ominously. Robert left and walked quickly to Riverside Drive, not looking back until he was nearly at the corner. When he did, he saw the boy and girl on tiptoes by a tall wire trash can, dropping his coin within.

He shrugged. It was not a family for accepting his advances, after all. He went around the block, feeling he mustn't show up again in front of the old house lest he appear a threat, and returned to Broadway, where he sought out Baldwin's bar, a few blocks further along, that he and Mike used to haunt. He was sitting alone over a Budweiser, smoking and nibbling the nuts in the glass dish on the bar counter, when the writer came in.

When Robert saw him, he felt for the first time since coming back to New York that he had found that peculiar notch in the world where he had been in nineteen thirty-nine, which he had been looking for since his return. The writer, unique among all things about him, had not changed one iota. The world, the war, the turbulence of time, even apparently fatherhood, had bumbled impotently over his big round shoulders and gone their way, leaving him untouched. He seemed to be wearing the same black and red woodsman's jacket, the same black beret, though neither seemed to have worn. He was not young in nineteen thirty-nine, years and years older than his black-haired wife, and he was not young now, but he did not seem really any older than before. His fluff of hair on either side of the beret was perhaps slightly grayer, his gray-green eyes a little more watery with time, or maybe it was just the February wind. He said "Pardner" with a nod to the barman, the way he had always done, in his high-pitched southern accent, and went to the same two square feet of bar. There was an indentation in it that Robert was convinced was from his elbow.

He looked at Robert, and his moustache made a small twitch. "Long time no see," he said.

Robert drank with the Western writer until three in the morning. He had a dim recollection of a brilliantly lit, loudly clattering subway interior, and of flailing about in the winter blackness of the Village, searching for his street, then his house, then his key. He woke up at three the next afternoon, lying fully dressed including his coat on the rug in the bathroom, with the absolutely worst hangover of his life. He roused himself enough to undress and go to bed, and slept until ten at night. So it was only the following morning, when he blearily tidied the floor, that he found in his trousers pocket a piece of paper, a used manila envelope, with, in the writer's vast illegible scrawl, an address.

At first he could not even read it. Later, as recollection began to revive, he remembered more about it, that it was a business address, for instance, and was able to decipher most of it, except for the top line which was smudged inexplicably with ketchup. He became very curious and scraped at the ketchup stain with his penknife, hoping the writing would cling beneath. It did, at least enough for him to read the name. It was the name of a pulp magazine, one of those that cluttered railroad newsstands, and the address below was that of the publisher.

Three months from that date, his first story was in print. It earned him fifty dollars and he blew every penny celebrating with the writer and his wife.

Within another three months, he had enough money left over after food and rent to pay for his fare to Britain, had he wished to go there. He did not wish it. Not even when his son was born. At first, upon receiving Philippa's letter, he had been determined by some means, God knows what, to get back to England, certain that his physical presence would counterbalance that of her father. But he had no money, and too much pride to turn to his only possible source, his yet acerbic mother, and plead for his fare that he might win back the unwilling wife she had never met. But time, the traditional great healer, proved also a great hedger. His own impotence in the situation turned in on itself and rankled into bitterness. Desperate hurt turned to anger, then to vengefulness, at which time he wrote two or three bitter letters, and one very successful pulp love story about a misused and cuckolded veteran. Then, after writing the story and receiving a satisfying check for it, he found that the vengefulness had died away. Ironically, the same medium that now earned him enough to return for his family had he still wished, in reasonable style, managed through emotional diffusion to relieve him of the passions of caring. By the time his son, conceived in a ridiculous romantic fling with his own wife, was born, Robert had found a new love. Not Philippa, nor a substitute Philippa, like Rhoda, not even the theater any longer, but writing. She proved to be the most faithful of all his ladies.

His success was logical. He knew language, and he had an innate sense of the dramatic moment, from years of speaking other people's carefully sculpted words. Now that the words were his own, the quality slipped painfully. He left the world of Shaw and Shakespeare and artist's subtleties for his own world, peopled degradingly enough with the wide-eyed heroines and stern-chinned heroes of pulp fiction. He had little choice: that was what sold. Besides, he rather soon learned he was really not up to much more. He suffered that most painful humiliation, discovering that his imaginative vision outstripped his talent to reproduce what was seen. For a little while he tried to better himself. After his initial success in the pulps, a handful of detective stories, a couple of romances, and one very stock Western, he succumbed to a brief artistic self-fancying and made a fling at the slicks. He failed miserably, bringing himself down to his proper level: his clay feet firmly planted on the ground. There they stayed thereafter. He no longer dreamed of greatness, as briefly he had done on the stage. He knew himself honestly as a good, solid professional hack. It was enough to earn a living, and that was sufficient to satisfy his diminished pride. Whether it would have been sufficient to satisfy the Hallsworths was something he never learned. He had almost no contact with them any longer, after his brief bitter flurry of letters with Philippa. Small notes came, reminding him of children's birthdays, something which, even in the case of his unseen son, he did not actually forget. He was notified that divorce proceedings had begun, and then heard, for nearly three years, nothing more. Nor did he ask. It was not his choice, and not his problem, and if they needed him, they knew where to find him. Actually, his silence was suiting their purpose perfectly as well.

Toward the end of the second year, late in forty-eight,

Robert made two eminently satisfactory moves. One was to shift from the declining pulp magazine market into the rising field of paperback books. The other was the invention of Grant Holland. Like many another creation of the imagination, he was born over a bar counter. On one side of the bar was Robert and an editor friend, Moe Weinstein, who was seeking a good, solid detective series. On the other side of the bar was a long, glittering row of bottles. It was a place that specialized in malt whiskeys, which was why Robert, in his new-found wealth, frequented it. Someone had fortuitously placed the Glen Grant in close alignment with the Advocaat.

"Dutch Grant."

"Sounds like a gangster."

"Glenn Holland."

"A geography lesson."

"Grant Glen?"

"Why don't you call him Budweiser?"

But he became Grant Holland in the end. It was corny, it was trite, it was unlikely. So were the stories. They took off at once, sold with happy vigor, and began quite amazingly to make Robert a rich man.

Four days after the publication of the third, Robert received notice from the Hallsworths that Philippa's divorce had been heard in the High Court in London's Strand. The grounds had been desertion, uncontested, and after three years of preparation it had taken nineteen minutes to reach a conclusion.

Afterward, Harold Hallsworth, feeling magnanimous and pleased with himself, took everybody to the Savoy for tea. As he watched his daughter, in black tailored suit and white blouse (why *did* she choose to dress like a widow for the occasion?), pour tea for her mother and Andrew Wardlaw, he relaxed for the first time in seeming years. He lit a cigar and offered one to Wardlaw, and they both sat in quiet satisfaction puffing Havana smoke into the still air. Philippa smiled politely, stood up, excused herself, and went off to the ladies'.

There, she locked herself in a cubicle and stood for a few seconds with handkerchief lightly to her eyes, so as not to smudge her makeup, and let the few intolerable tears dribble down her cheeks. She unlocked the door, washed delicately, replaced powder and lipstick, blotting her lips on a tissue. She combed her hair, thought briefly about Victoria and David in Bridlington with their great-aunt, and returned to the company at the table. She said, by way of opening, "You are right, of course, Andrew. I simply must find a reliable nanny. This entire day has been a frightful problem, has it not?"

Harold Hallsworth took a great gulp of tea, lest his look of amazement and delight be too obvious. But Philippa saw it. For a moment she smiled a little to herself, and heard in her head him saying, "Quite right, too. Knew from the start the little fool would come around. Only a matter of time." Well, she had come around. It had taken nearly ten years, but she had. What God and Caxton Hall had joined together, Harold Hallsworth had finally managed to put asunder. It had not been easy, and she supposed he deserved his hour of glory. She was tolerant, an older, bruised woman. She had given youth and its rebellions away, in peeling layers, like onion skin. Some to her first child, some to her second, a great deal to her father, over the question of divorce, and most of the rest would go soon enough to the pompous young member of Parliament nibbling shortbread across the table, whom she, three weeks before, had agreed to marry.

Andrew Wardlaw was patient, if nothing else. He had waited, discreetly on the edge of the picture, like a grave-digger at a funeral, for two and a half years. Of course the divorce was underway, but in postwar England that, like almost everything else, took time. There were queues in the courts as well as the food shops, and the Hallsworths soon discovered they were not the only family with a problem. The divorce courts were heavily laden with cases which, although Harold Hallsworth would not choose to admit it, were very like their own. There were other wives deserted by

Yankee husbands, more genuinely than Philippa. Conversely, there were romantic GI brides, returning disillusioned to mother and Mother England at once. And there was as well all the emotional ugliness of the less romantic side of war, prisoners of war, and servicemen returning to cuckoos in their nests, or perhaps more sadly returning changed and aberrant to baffled wives. And most simple of all, and most common, men and women remeeting each other after six years of separate adventure and finding they had little left in common. Amongst them all were a good many, precisely like Philippa, nursing the wounds of the spur of the moment.

Moreover, Harold had made his own delay as well, for, having decided on breaking the marriage, he still stubbornly refused to use the obvious tool at hand, Robert's adultery. Firstly, it would probably have involved dragging the offender back across the Atlantic, and then, if he chose to contest, there would be a courtroom scene of great ugliness, culminating in the crudities of a wrangle over a Bridlington milliner's assistant. Even if they managed to keep it out of the papers, which Harold with his Fleet Street connections was fairly confident of doing, still everyone who mattered a damn would know. Wardlaw had made clear that there was just so much of that sort of thing he could tolerate, considering his position. Harold agreed entirely, and settled then for the lengthy but dignified charge of desertion.

It meant by definition that Robert Zolan would not appear, and that in itself eased Harold Hallsworth's mind of a persistent fear, a fear he was shrewd enough never to admit to in Philippa's presence. That fear was simply of Robert's physical presence. The man seemed to possess some peculiar magnetism regarding his daughter; Harold largely suspected it had to do with the genitals. Whatever, he was not taking the chance of a meeting between them. Even with Zolan at a distance, there had been times when he had found it necessary to put a great deal of pressure on the girl, particularly after one or two of Zolan's letters. And he was quite certain that there were ways in which Philippa's absent husband still held immense power over her. What else would explain her persistent and pig-headed refusal to allow him to put the boy's name down for a decent school? The child was already two; time was running out. Already the best doors were closed. He had totally given up worrying about the girl, Victoria. She was already mixing with the village children more than he would like; that is, mixing without any true sense of appropriate place. It was quite all right being cozy friends with the gardener's daughter at five, as long as one realized that one was meant to eventually take a clearly different path. That was the real purpose of prep schools, Harold was quite positive, a pointing of appropriate direction. For a while Harold thought he would succeed, even over Victoria, but Philippa had grown, if anything, more stubborn since Robert Zolan's return to America. But the boy, David, was after all a boy. The issue was serious in his case, and Harold had no intention of being thwarted. Just get the divorce out of the way, decently and quietly, and the door open for Wardlaw, and then perhaps the thing would take shape. Philippa was not a fool, after all. She was his daughter.

"I'm not a fool, Andrew," Philippa said four weeks later at Greenshaws. "Besides, what precisely do you expect me to do? The man has a right to see his children."

"I don't see why he should come here, though," Andrew Wardlaw said petulantly. "Surely you could arrange a meeting. You know. London or something." He was fiddling nervously with the bit and bridle, and the big gray hunter was slinging its heavy head around with annoyance. Philippa took the bridle from him.

"I'll do it," she said, as she might to Victoria when Vicky was being elaborately stupid about something, on purpose. She suspected that Andrew was afraid of the animal, and it annoyed her. "I can't send them to London alone, for God's sake. They're babies."

"Well, send someone. Send their nanny." Philippa thought,

you can always tell someone who's never had children of their own. It was not comforting, considering. But she was determined to keep everything, absolutely everything, cool and calm for the whole weekend. "No. Quite out of the question. They hardly know her; she's only just arrived. And they don't know him at all." She slipped the bit in between the big wet teeth with a satisfactory clunk. She said, maliciously, "Shall I go with them?"

That at least got Andrew to agree to Robert coming to Greenshaws.

It was Harold, however, who got him to agree to meet Robert at the train at York, for something of the same reason. He was making damned certain his princess stayed in her tower until properly rewed this time. She was not going to be permitted to see the father of her children alone. That he should imagine she might wish to under the circumstances was one measure of the emotional rhinoceros hide that had surrounded him in all his personal relationships. The dotty, fluttery figure of Mrs. Hallsworth, a once beautiful woman, reduced to a pink pudding, was another.

That was how Philippa saw her now, as she watched her mother flustering about the big, slate-floored kitchen of Greenshaws. There was no longer a cook, nor any staff, only a part-time woman who came in from the village, gave everything a perfunctory dusting, prepared the midday meal, and wandered out with the slovenly confidence of one equally happily unemployed and on the dole. Mrs. Hallsworth knew she was just waiting for a chance to quit, and therefore treated her more like a house guest than staff, lest she take offense. Philippa would not have bothered, preferring to do the work herself than fuss with the silly cow. She had little time any longer for her mother's simpering pretenses. Partly because of that, she sat doing nothing, rocking peacefully in the elaborate bentwood rocker by the warmth of the stove. Besides, they could afford proper help if they really wanted. Something, the war perhaps, had simply made them mean. Her father at least had grown fussy and penny-pinching, forever harking back to the grand days Before, when life was lived in the proper way.

"I've had Ellen make up the bed in the old nursery for Robert. That will be better."

"Why not the west guest room?" Philippa said mildly.

"Well, really not, dear. I mean after all."

Philippa rocked again, and raised her feet in Morlands slippers, resting them on the warm back of the oven door. Then she sat up straight suddenly, and said, "Mother, you don't possibly mean . . ." and then shook her head, exasperated.

"Well, you know, dear, I do think . . . After all, what would Andrew Wardlaw imagine?"

"If you put Robert in the guest bedroom next door to mine? Mother, how utterly stupid. How outrageously stupid. For God's sake, Andrew's on the other side anyhow."

"Yes, I know, dear." Mrs. Hallsworth was pinker and damp about the brow under her kerchief. She had been out to the garden an hour ago and had not bothered to remove it. But then the kitchen was vast and cold, like all the house. "And you are engaged, after all," she said, fussing with the chicken she was stuffing.

"I was married to Robert, mother. Married. We did sleep together, you know. Those were not virgin births." She waved angrily toward the window where, beyond the rattling white-painted sash, she could see Victoria and David scuffing feet on the immaculate gravel drive. They looked bored. They were always bored, and the vast scope of Greenshaws meant positively nothing. They much preferred the rather scruffy streets of Bridlington where their great-aunt stayed.

"Philippa, really. What if Andrew heard?"

"Andrew will not hear. Andrew's halfway to York by now, I sincerely hope. And even Andrew might just concede that Robert and I did more than hold hands."

"But that's over now, dear."

"I know that, mother."

Alison Scott Skelton

"And we must remember our places, dear."

"What are you worried about? Jiggery-pokery in the corridors?" Philippa laughed. "Do you honestly think I'm going to hop into bed with my ex-husband, with my two children, you, daddy, and my fiancé all down the corridor? Mother, at times I really wonder what you think of me." She laughed again because, if she wondered, she hardly cared.

"I think you're a very nice girl," said her mother primly. She opened the slow-oven door and put the chicken in. Philippa repressed the wish to say no, the other oven. Or the other sauce, or the other God knows what. Her mother was a spirit-less cook, but women living in their mothers' houses learn to hold their tongues. That at least would soon be ending.

"Did I tell you Andrew signed the lease on Wednesday?"

"Did he? Oh, Philippa, I am pleased. How super for you both. I know you've always wanted a flat in London." She stopped suddenly. Philippa's change of partners still took her a bit by surprise. The old thing about the flat was still from the Robert era.

"Yes," said Philippa. "Haven't I." She said it without irony, not thinking much, dreaming in the narrow band of heat cast out by the stove.

"Of course," she said, "we'll have the Sussex house. And our summers on Arran. Andrew loves Arran." She spoke uneasily. That Scottish, tweedy side of Andrew was most un-nerving, threatening to send them careening off into a heather-and-grouse future she did not desire.

"Yes," her mother said uncertainly. "They say the summers are quite pleasant, really."

"It rains nonstop," said Philippa. "All day, every day. One gets accustomed, or so Andrew says." She began rocking gently, amusing herself. "I do hope Robert's remembered Vicky's birthday," she said.

"Yes," said Mrs. Hallsworth with the same uncertainty, "and with something appropriate this time."

Philippa maintained silence, rocking gently, hoping the

wickery creak of the chair would speak for her. But she could not resist saying, "Vicky loved that bracelet. It was her favorite Christmas present."

Mrs. Hallsworth put her lips together as she rolled pastry, a little tighter for each roll of the wooden pin. At last she said, "Children have no taste, Philippa. It must be taught."

"Pity no one ever taught Robert," Philippa said, with a small sly laugh.

"Yes," Mrs. Hallsworth replied at once. "It is a pity. I will not be drawn into this, Philippa. I don't know quite what's come over you, and I might add that Andrew doesn't, either. You've been frankly impossible. He has no idea why, or what to do."

Philippa only rocked gently, and leaned her head back against the sheepskin cushioning the back of her chair. She was not really seeking argument, only playing, like a bored cat with the tattered corpse of a bird. Andrew, she knew already, would never have any idea why, or what to do, about practically anything. He was one of life's permanent unseated riders, joggling along without stirrups or reins. He was also wealthy, influential, and knew every delicacy of social custom, taught, like taste, from the cradle on. There was not a club, house, or society that would not open its doors to him without questions asked. Schools beckoned from all sides for his future stepchildren. Later they would attend country house parties, entertain in the Victorian splendor of Lamlash House, gather friends from all over the country into a wonderfully secure, silent stratum of success. They would dance eightsomes at the Oban Ball, brush occasionally with royalty, making absolutely nothing of it, of course, and their weddings would gain glossy double spreads in *The Scottish Field*.

Once inside that circle, behind its invisible silent doors, they would need absolutely nothing more. Money would be nice but not necessary. Education would be laudable but secondary. Partners would be provided, and their own children sent forth, shielded and sheltered into the same world. In the staggering uncertainties of postwar Britain, it was still a most amazing security. Philippa was not buying it for herself but for them, those two now romping in the boxwood hedge with the Yorkshire gardener's daughter. The price would not be so high. Andrew was, after all, a decent sort. He would create for her a world of the same grace and dignity in which she had grown up, and as she grew older, her need for that graciousness strengthened. Love simply did not enter the question. "We're rather beyond all that nonsense, old girl, aren't we?" Andrew had said, and seemed rather relieved when she had agreed. Still, he had bought her a valuable and dignified ring, and kissed her in between loud, nervous, champagne-inspired guffaws of laughter. Then, everyone had been watching and cheering him on. When the cheers of their wedding died away, in the lonesomeness of the bedroom, she doubted he'd be up to much. It was a cold and frank decision she was making, the kind that women make only for their children's sake.

She was still sitting there, half asleep in her childhood kitchen full of the warm smells of baking, when Andrew's black Humber drew into the drive. The gravel crunched under it, and her half-dreaming mind suddenly brought up the bright image of a renegade maroon MG. She smiled to herself, and then rose resignedly and stood at the window, her hand, a little nervous, patting down her smoothly cut hair. The black car stopped and two men got out, two strangers, she felt suddenly, a short stolid figure in a dark blue London suit, and a big tall man in a red and black checked wool lumberman's jacket. Robert, whatever is that you're wearing? she thought. She found she was smiling to herself, just at the ridiculous sight he made. The children, her two, and the gardener's daughter, stood staring. She saw Andrew's mouth move as he shouted something which she could not hear through the solid old glass. He waved one hand jerkily, pointing it almost straight up, signaling to the children in his embarrassed overloud way. They stared a moment longer, and then Vicky, small hands outstretched over the four years between them, ran headlong into Robert's arms.

Andrew stood there with his foolish arm slowly lowering, like a sagging marionette. David, with one awed look over his small shoulder, fled after the gardener's daughter into the boxwood hedge.

IX

Late Summer, 1963
Isle of Arran, Scotland

"He gave me the most gorgeous dress," Victoria said. "Red velvet, with lace all down the front, and around the edges, like in my Hans Andersen book. I always fancied myself like Thumbelina. I was forever drawing pictures of girls with long blond hair and dresses like that. Mother never let me wear my hair long. Too messy, of course. No, don't laugh, please."

Hugh shook his head and apologized, looking fondly at her in her overstretched jeans and his own floppy jersey.

"I can't imagine you ever so romantic."

"Oh, but I was. Once. You know what that bastard Wardlaw did? You know?" She shouted almost. She'd had too much red wine, and her pregnancy made her both unstable and unable to hold her drink as before. "He gave it away. He said it wasn't appropriate. He gave it to the gardener's bloody daughter. I hated the cow for years." She paused. "The odd thing is, well, it must have cost father a positive fortune. Couldn't have got the thing at all in Britain, naturally, what with rationing and all. But he brought it from the States. Still, it would have set him back, and he wasn't that rich, yet, I don't imagine. But the odd thing was David. All he brought David, and after all he was seeing him for the first time, all he brought him was one little Dinky car. One. And it was not new, either. It was secondhand, I'm sure. I remember noticing that, you know how children are, for knowing if a thing is new or not. That's all he brought him. Of course, I suppose David scarcely meant anything much to him yet. He was barely three. You know, David maintained for years he wasn't father's son at all."

"Surely not," Hugh said, a little shocked.

"Oh, it was all rubbish, of course. After all, they all say he looks exactly like father, and they're none too pleased, you can imagine. But they weren't even together, you know, when it happened. They were already living apart." She paused a moment and said, "A dirty weekend, I suppose, with each other." She giggled, nervous of her parents' sexuality.

Victoria spooned brown rice out onto the brown pottery dinnerware, for Hugh, herself, and Peter. Peter took his off to a corner of the room and sat down cross-legged and alone on a goatskin rug. Victoria's pregnancy had changed everything, underlining both her and Hugh's coupledom, cocooned within their innocent threesome, and also their mutual advancing age. There would not be another summer on Arran. All three knew, and none had spoken.

"I can't imagine what it's like," he said, "having divorced parents. It must be so bloody schizophrenic."

"How?" Victoria said mildly. She had had divorced parents so long, she could not really recall otherwise.

"Having two sets of parents."

"Well, I haven't that," she said. "I haven't that at all. Wardlaw's not my father," she added with a touch of testy anger. "Wardlaw is not bloody anything. And father isn't married, even."

"I thought he had a mistress," Peter said. Hugh said, "Come, come. Off bounds, don't you think?"

"Vicky said so. Didn't you, Vicks?"

Victoria shrugged. "I think he's got a girlfriend." She was very quiet. She got up and poked at the peat fire, making it worse, not better. She sat heavily, her arms folded across her borrowed jersey, enclosing the lowering bulge of baby. She held her palms flat, feeling the comfort of an interior baby heel, like a passing fish within her.

"He's bloody old for girlfriends," said Peter.

"Lay *off*, won't you," Hugh said, still mild. They were such old good friends, he would not be riled. Besides, he knew that Peter was only picking at the scab of his own new loneliness. He said, to change the subject, "Why *don't* you come with us, then. Cambridge is absolutely super, you know. You'd find something to do. Work at your pottery. You could open one of those little shops or some such."

"Do spare me," Peter said, wincing. He worked his mouth into a narrow fish shape. He had that sort of oddly awkward aristocratic face, rather like the royals, where every feature that could have gone wrong over generations had managed to, and yet, by sheer distinction, remained attractive. Like some old antique, Hugh thought, ghastly ugly to the point of delight. Peter was beginning to go bald at the temples, lengthening that tall smooth brow. He rubbed his hand over the top of his head, flattening the dark brown hair down over the balding points. "I've had rather enough being Aunt Sally here. Don't much want to trade third wheel for fourth wheel, anyhow."

"Fifth," said Victoria. Hugh said, "Rubbish. You've never been a third wheel here." Then he added as an afterthought, "How fifth, old girl?" He smiled then, and thinking he knew, leaned, his face crinkling into pride, and patted her bulging stomach. "Ah. Son and heir."

"No," Vicky said seriously. "David's got a girlfriend. She'll be there, too."

Hugh stopped short, his hand slipping onto her knee instead. "David? Really?"

"Baby brother? A girl?" said Peter. "Dear oh dear, what will mother say?"

"Dear knows," said Victoria, then added, "I dare say she's pleased enough. After all, he will be going to Cambridge, and that's what she wanted. That's what she went over there for, isn't it?"

"But a girl. Baby David? I'm quite flummoxed," said Peter. "I'm flummed all over my ox." He grinned to himself and then added, "Oh, no, don't say she's American? Oh, she's not really, Vicky."

"How should I know," Victoria said. "I only heard about it over the phone. I haven't met her or anything. I suppose she must be, if he met her there, and I guess he must have. Father didn't say. He didn't say anything about her. You know what it costs phoning from there. Just that David would be coming, and his girlfriend, and would we be willing to share a house if he paid."

"Would that someone would make me an offer like that," Peter sighed. "You do fall on your feet, you two. First this place, and now your own house in Cambridge, with roses round the door, no doubt. It's not every lecturer, you know, rates that style."

"Well, come too if you're jealous," Vicky said sharply.

"With some American female braying about the place? Never. God. Poor David. She probably wears a ponytail and bright pink lipstick, and calls him *Dave*. Dave *dear*. American females, may God preserve me."

"Oh, shut up, Peter," Vicky said sourly. She was testy with pregnancy, and tired, and suddenly terribly conscious of the dirt and muck everywhere. "You've damn worn your damn Wellies into the scullery again," she said. "I spent half an hour scrubbing up and my back hurts like hell. What's so wrong with Americans anyhow," she added. "I'm half American."

"Rubbish," Peter said. "It's living there makes you American, not bloodlines. It's only your father, anyhow, and he's hardly ever seen you."

"That's a lie, damn it," Vicky said. She shouted it, jumping to her feet and regretting it, the bulge shifting awkwardly. "I know my father very well. We don't have to see each other. He writes to me every fortnight. He's written for years. Super letters, too. I like his letters better than most books."

"Does he really?" Hugh said. He was leaning over her loom, trying to mend the spar that had broken. She had not woven anything for weeks and seemed in no hurry to begin again. He said then suddenly, "Do you answer?"

"Who do you think I'm always writing to?" she said. "You've seen me."

"I thought your mother."

Vicky shrugged. She paused a long time, then said, "Mother's always there. Why should I write?"

"Why all this defense of dear old papa, anyhow, Vicks?" said Peter. "If he writes letters, it's all he's damn well done. Other than give you a dress once that didn't suit you."

"Well, that's just it, Peter, only I doubt you'd see it. You really are very like old Wardlaw sometimes, you know. I'd watch that pomposity act, if I were you. If you're not careful, it'll turn out genuine and we'll all be stuck with it. Of course it suited me, that dress. It suited *me*. It was them it didn't suit. I was seven. It was the most beautiful thing I'd ever seen. Oh, certainly it was ghastly. You know the sort of thing young fathers think of, all sugar and ribbons. But I was seven. I hadn't learned taste yet." She said it with a light cynicism, as if she spoke consciously another person's lines. "Father got me something he knew I'd love. Mother and Wardlaw and grandfather never ever gave me anything that didn't advance their own cause. Always, the best quality, the best taste, the best dress, the best school, the best university they could squeeze me into. I've rather let them down, there. But it was always their way. The best anything they could squeeze me into, like a gelatin mold, so I'd come out, gleaming and pristine and quivering, for some gawky chinless wonder with a pedigree back to the Conqueror, and no balls at all."

"No balls at all, no balls at all," Peter sang delightedly. "When Vicky gets married, there'll be no balls at all . . ."

"Shut *up*, you sod," Vicky said, on the shaky edge of laughter and pregnancy tears.

"Well," Hugh said smiling to himself, his solid, gentler face twisting with a small grimace, "I've proved myself in that department, haven't I? What does father think of that?"

"He was shattered," Victoria said honestly.

"Shattered? Shattered? The hypocritical sod. Romping around with a teenage mistress, and he's shocked because you're pregnant? How, may I ask, does he justify that?"

"He doesn't have to. I'm his daughter. It's different."

"You don't accept that rubbish, surely," Peter said, stretching his wooly socks to the battered hearth with insolence and disdain.

"Yes. I do." She began to cry, and Hugh moved himself over, and casually put his arms around her, having gotten used to her moods of late. "I do accept it, because he loves me. He's the only one. He's the only one who never expected anything of me. He just loves me. He doesn't care what I do as long as I'm happy, and he's afraid I won't be happy unless I get married properly." She was sobbing and speaking in little bursts between. "And I *know* he cares, because he's the only adult I know who doesn't see me as an investment."

She sobbed louder and said, "I'm such a shit for letting him down."

That was when Hugh realized she really wanted to get married after all. He made two or three small adjustments, mentally, in his finances for the next two years, considering rapidly his really rather good salary as lecturer for the following year; they had snapped him up, with his honors degree. His parents would make a reasonable settlement, and there would be an unknown quantity from the American writer Robert Zolan. He said, "I think we could just fit a quiet ceremony in before going up to Cambridge, don't you?"

There followed a lot of denying, a great deal of concern on

Victoria's part that he might feel trapped. An insistence that he would not, a little cynical laughter there from Peter. Then, as the long empty twilight of Arran's summer drifted by outside to the sound of gulls, they drank homemade wine with increasing gaiety throughout the night. Victoria fell asleep on the goatskin rug. Hugh covered her with his parka and fell asleep beside her.

Peter walked out into the cold northern summer dawn, following on the heels of sunset, like middle age on the heels of youth, and wondered why it was the world over that people who'd stumbled battered and bruised out of the door of marriage were so happily willing to usher others in. He kicked a pile of sheep turds from the doorstep and walked back in, feeling an intruder, a stranger in his own erstwhile home.

"I say," Hugh called from the scullery, "will you have some tea?" He sounded buoyant and adult and terribly pleased. Peter nodded, took an old Woolworth's mug, turning the chipped side away. "You can keep all this rubbish if you want," Hugh said casually. "Since you're staying on."

"Won't you need it?"

"This?" Hugh laughed. "Can you see professors' wives taking tea with Vicky with this? Hardly appropriate, now, is it?"

"No," Peter said, surveying sadly their damp kitchen with its heaps of rough pottery and shabby, fire-blackened pots. The old haybox sat disused in the corner, abandoned since Hugh's turkey stew had gone moldly green one day and threatened ptomaine.

X

"It's simply not appropriate, Robert." Philippa was still turning the wood carving around in her hands, over the neat vertical alignment of silver on her finished plate. "Of course there is nothing intrinsically wrong with the thing. I dare say it would be quite pleasant, in a different, an *entirely* different setting." She set the oriental madonna down then, firmly, in front of her plate. "Only here it clashes with your silver, does nothing for your table linen, and contradicts the mood of your entire setting. Aside from being utterly out of place, there's nothing wrong with it at all."

Robert smiled indulgently, suppressed the surprisingly strong urge to disown the object, and said, "I'm sorry you don't like it. Steve just gave it to me, today."

She was not embarrassed. She said only, "How kind. I'm sure you will eventually find some place for it. Somewhere."

"Well, why not right there," Mary Jo, who had been silent throughout the meal, said suddenly. "Who are you to say where it should go?" Her voice was childishly belligerent.

"I didn't," Philippa said mildly. She sipped from her wine, added as an aside, "The main course was very nice, Robert," and then said, "I only said where it should not go. It should not go with Georgian silver and lead crystal."

"The main course it is, actually," Robert said. "I didn't make anything else."

"Quite right too," Philippa replied at once. "We all eat far too much at dinner, most times, anyway."

"Why shouldn't it go with Georgian silver, and that crystal, whatever it is? Well, why not?" Mary Jo said.

"It's inappropriate," Philippa said mildly. She was watching David watching the girl. He reminded her of her own self, years ago, when her own children were babies, watching, always watching, with hovering hands and tense eyes.

"That's so stupid. It's so conventional. Think how boring everything would be if everybody paid attention to things like that." Mary Jo pushed small bits of rice around her plate, aimlessly, with the sharp edge of her silver knife.

"Think how British," said Robert.

"Oh, come on," Paul said suddenly. "That's a ghastly old cliché. The British aren't conventional at all. And they're hardly boring. They're the greatest eccentrics in the world."

Philippa laughed. "How charming," she said.

Paul raised his glass. He was being uncommonly chivalrous, although it was her nationality rather than her sex he was defending. Philippa said then, "Actually, *that* is the cliché." But before Paul had time to be crushed, she said, "Of course clichés are essential truths. And conventions also. Both only exist because they are firmly rooted in human truths. Of course we have eccentrics. So have other nations. However, other nations confine them to asylums, or browbeat them into submission. No one else seems to have the confidence to let them be."

"It isn't confidence at all," Robert said. "It's detachment. None of you care a damn for anyone any different from yourselves."

"How utterly self-pitying," Philippa said at once.

"I didn't mean me."

"Of course you did. That's utterly American. You're the

most self-conscious nation in the world." She was twirling the wooden madonna around, on its base. "And American artists! One *can* get too much of a good thing."

"Philippa, I don't believe you," Robert said. He had finished eating, and laid his cutlery, crosswise, American style, and said, "How can you make these impossible sweeping judgments? This is a nation of one hundred and eighty million people. They can't possibly all be self-centered, and even if they were you couldn't possibly know."

"If nine-tenths of them are, does it matter?" She patted her lips with her linen napkin, and said, "*Is* there any more of that delightful wine, Robert?"

"It's American."

"Quite right too. I always drink the wine of the country when abroad."

"Your *father* used to say that. Always. It used to make me sick hearing it."

"I can't imagine why," Philippa said mildly, accepting the wine that her own son David poured for her. She said though, a little sharply, aside, "No dear, you don't wrap a tea cloth about it. That's for restaurants. At home you either decant or present the label." Then she turned back to Robert, all wide innocent eyes. "Why?"

"Because it's so sickeningly condescending."

"How, Robert, just how, is it condescending of me to drink your wine, in your country. I happen to like it, incidentally."

"Balls."

"Robert?"

"I said balls, and you heard me say balls. You're slumming. You're mucking in with the peasants. Oh *do* try this charming little Spanish wine we picked up in Minorca. Quite naive, actually, but it has a certain earthy enthusiasm. Rather like the natives." He turned the vowels narrow for effect.

"Your English accent is appalling, Robert. Surely you could do better once."

He rode right over that, though it had its effect and his voice began to rise. "You goddamn all think the whole goddamn world is beneath you."

"I am quite certain you have never heard my father say that. Or myself."

"You don't have to say it. You think it. And we all *know* you think it, and that is all it takes. If you'd ever have the nerve to say it we'd all tell you where to get off. But you just think it, damn it."

"Robert, that is really rather appallingly paranoid."

"Paranoid?" He half stood up, as if to get something, and couldn't remember what. He sat down again, conscious of Mary Jo watching him, now, with a trembling lower lip. She had probably never seen him really angry, he realized, and it was frightening her. He was sorry, but not enough to control himself. "Of course it's paranoid. We're all paranoid, and self-centered, and self-pitying. But we make fucking good wine." He slammed the table with his fist, and the candles jiggled and the wooden madonna fell over on its face.

"Shit," he said, to himself.

Philippa picked the madonna up and lifted it in her hands. Paul stood up behind her and began clearing away plates. Mary Jo unfolded her fingers from her clutched napkin and laid it reluctantly down. When she spoke her voice was weak and thin, but she was trying to be very brusque and hard and said, "Why in God's name did you two get married?" She shrugged as she said it.

"Why?" Philippa said, smiling a little, and turning the madonna around. "Well why ever not? We were *very* much in love."

There was a long awkward pause, while everyone waited for Robert to do or say something, which he did not. Then Paul resumed clearing plates, and scraping them discreetly into a plastic garbage pail, at the kitchen sink, and David, who had not spoken since his chastisement over the wine, said suddenly, "It's from Vietnam, mother. It's handmade by a hill tribesman. Stephen brought it home from the war."

"What war?" said Philippa. She kept turning it in her hands, in the silence that followed.

"Mother," David said, pained, "there's a war going on in Vietnam. *Surely*, mother."

"Haven't you *heard* of Vietnam in Britain?" Mary Jo said, with disbelieving scorn.

"Of course I've heard of Vietnam," Philippa said at once.

"But the *war*," Mary Jo said. "You must have heard of the war."

Philippa said, looking from Mary Jo to David and to Stephen, "Naturally I've heard of Vietnam. The French were forever in a dreadful muddle there. It's hardly anything new, after all. And I hardly think you'd call it a war. It's an insurrection, surely."

"People are killing people," Mary Jo said. Her face still mirrored amazement, mixed with pleasure at discovering Philippa in what appeared to be rank stupidity.

"People often do, my dear."

"I think you're disgusting," said Mary Jo.

"And I think you're naive, dear. But let's not call names, shall we?" Mary Jo opened her mouth, but found herself wordless. "That's a good girl," said Philippa. Then she turned the statue over in her hands, ran her manicured but unpolished nail over the bottom of the base, and said, "It's not handmade of course, Daves."

"Of course it is," he said at once. "Stephen made this sketch and took it to a Montagnard tribesman and he . . ."

"It's lathe-turned."

"It's what?" said Robert, interested.

"It's lathe-turned. Machine-produced. Finished by hand of course, but machine-produced. Do you see?"

She offered the base of it toward the table, and traced the small splintered hole in the exact center of the base. "That will be where it sat on the lathe. If you study the shape you will notice it's very symmetrical. A good eighty percent of the work could be done on the lathe, and then the finished shaping, naturally, by hand. But it would save an immense amount of time, and they could produce them much faster."

"But it's not mass-produced at all, mother. It's unique. Stephen made his sketch."

"I don't doubt it," Philippa said, as she set the statue down. "But it had nothing to do with this."

"Steve?" David said, uncertainly.

Steve tapped his fork along the rim of his plate as if he were not hearing, and then eventually raised it, balanced it across his thumb, and shrugged, his one drooping eyelid half-rising with cynical inquisitiveness. "What the fuck do I care?" he said.

Paul said quickly, "Please, Stephen." But Philippa smiled brightly and said, "That appears to settle that, then." She turned to Robert, as if she would speak of something else, but David, still a little confused, asked, "Come now, mother. How would you know a thing like that? Woodworking. That's not a woman's thing, anyhow."

"How very conventional," said Philippa. "Actually it was a woman who told me. During the war. A young woman I knew doing war work. She learned a lot about lathes. We all learned all sorts of things, you know." She smiled as if she doubted he'd believe her.

"Who was that?" said Robert, curious.

"Maisie Rudd. She was a lathe operator."

"Who?"

"Maisie. Oh, you know. Mike's little piece."

"Oh," Robert leaned back in his chair, thinking. "Oh yes, of course. I'd forgotten her name."

"What does she do now?" Mary Jo said sharply. "Build tractors for the revolution?"

"No, dear," Philippa said mildly. "She's dead, actually." Mary Jo seemed a little surprised and she added, "People do get killed in wars." She said then to Robert, who had risen to make coffee, "Did you ever contact Mike's family? I recall you'd meant once to go to Canada."

Robert counted spoonfuls of coffee grounds into the stained percolator basket. He said, eventually, reluctantly, "No. I didn't. I don't know. I meant to, but, well, his aunt was rather old, and she hardly seemed interested, and when I asked about his parents she seemed kind of surprised. Like I'd come six weeks late to a party or something and everything was all over. *All* over. You know, it was all an awfully long time ago, by the time I got home."

"Who was Mike?" said David.

"A friend of daddy's," Philippa said with the remote calm reserved for events beyond children's concern. "He was killed in the war."

"Sounds like everybody you knew was killed in the war," Mary Jo said, trying again to be brisk and cynically adult. Philippa did not smile. She said quietly, "A great many were," and then she added, rather more to herself than anyone, "It wasn't really a very pleasant time."

"Oh come now, mother," David said. "How can you say that? You all loved it. You must have loved it. You never stop going on about it. It was the best time of your lives, and you lapped it up. Admit it."

But Philippa did not admit anything. Instead, she said to Robert only, "Do you remember that time you took me to the Savoy, and that dreadful chap, the naval officer, you know, turned up, and ordered huge brandies on your round?"

"Oh God, don't I. Archie, wasn't it? It wasn't brandies, though, it was something else."

"Dear knows. But wasn't he awful?" Philippa began to giggle. "Actually, you handled him frightfully well, as I recall."

"Thank you." Robert grinned, trying to be sarcastic but rather pleased. "Do you ever hear from him?"

"Well, yes, actually," Philippa said. "Actually, he stays not far from us in London. And I ran into him, now where was it, I think some charity do, recently. He married that Scrymgeour-Haig woman, silly fool. Leads a dreadful life. He tried to corner me at a house party not long ago and I practically had to call Andrew to set the hounds on him. Quite incorrigible, old Archie."

David thought Robert might be angry about all that, but he laughed instead. "Never gives up, does he. More coffee, Phil?" he said. She shook her head, and then Robert forgot about coffee, and Paul had to get up to offer it to the rest of his guests. Robert still had his eyes on Philippa, and seemed to be searching for something else to say. "Do you ever hear from that girl who came to our wedding? You know, the Wren, that Irish one?"

"Oh no. Never. You know how it was, after the war. People went their own ways again."

"Of course," Robert said, without irony. Then he added quickly, "Hey Phil, do you remember that dreadful wedding cake? I'd forgotten all about it, until just this moment. Do you remember?"

She began to laugh and said, "Cake! You're rather flattering it, aren't you? Wasn't it ridiculous? You'd have thought they'd have found *some*thing decent. I swear it was just dried egg and sawdust."

"But the cover," Robert said, "that fake thing on top."

"Oh yes," Philippa said. "But that was just for effect."

"What kind of cake was it?" Mary Jo said sharply. "What's so funny about a cake?"

Robert started to explain, "Well, there wasn't anything for making cakes, and sugar icings were practically treasonous, so they'd make these cardboard . . ."

"Porky Piggott tried to eat it," Philippa shrieked. "Don't you recall?" Robert, when he had finished recalling, and laughing with Philippa about it, tried to continue his explanation of wartime baking, but Mary Jo, offended by the interruption, went sour-faced and refused to listen. So he said instead, "Did you ever hear any more about Porky?"

Philippa shook her head, a small, restrained gesture, but said at the same time, "He was really in a dreadful mess. After that infection, it just went on and on, and the last I heard, oh, some time after you left, he was still at home. He never married or anything. I know they did marvels with plastic surgery, but, God knows, it would take a saint of a woman to wake up to that every morning." She stroked down her hair, thoughtfully, and looked away.

"Helluva nice guy," said Robert.

"Isn't war wonderful," said Mary Jo, but they were not listening to her, and neither she nor anyone was quite able to break into the web of reminiscence about the table. She tried though. She said, "You ought to put people like that on exhibit, show people what wars do."

"What a charming idea," said Philippa.

"You can get the same result smoking in bed," Robert said at once. "Besides, Porky knew what could happen. He was there by choice."

"Bullshit," Mary Jo said. But it was ignored. Philippa smiled at Robert, and said quite suddenly, "It was a funny little wedding, wasn't it?"

Robert nodded. Mary Jo twisted her thick blond hair into a rope and drew it over one shoulder. David sat watching her, thinking of the way it had looked wet from the sea and the shower, and was flooded with hot embarrassment, sure everyone could read his thoughts. He looked down at his coffee cup and turned it around. Mary Jo said, "Nobody ever chooses to go to war. It's all those fat bald men in power, manipulating innocent kids."

"Oh, we were hardly innocent," Philippa said, smiling to herself.

"Well, maybe it was different for you and Robert," Mary Jo conceded. "It was your country, and you had ideals. I mean, Robert, you were a Jew, after all, fighting Hitler. All right."

Robert only shook his head and said, "I never thought of that, at the time. I didn't think of myself as a Jew anyhow."

"Rubbish," said Philippa sharply. "You never let anyone forget."

But he insisted again, "No, Phil. That was never the way it

was. I never thought of myself as a Jew. Not then. Now, maybe different."

"But you went to fight Hitler. You must have," Mary Jo said urgently.

"My dear," said Robert, "can you possibly believe none of that entered into it? You see, we didn't know then. Oh, we knew, a little. But we had no idea what was happening. No real idea."

"So why did you go then?" Mary Jo said querulously. "For glory?"

"For Britain," David said suddenly. "And why not?"

"Why not indeed," Robert sighed.

Philippa said, "Oh, I'm glad we had some effect, after all."

Robert paused, uncertain, and finally said slowly, "You've had plenty of that. Surely you know that."

"Sometimes I really did wonder," she said. Then she added, "Do you remember how the sirens went during our wedding?"

"Could I forget?"

"What did you do?" David said. "All run for shelter, in the middle of it?"

"Of course not," Philippa said. "We just ignored it. Of course."

"But it was terribly bad luck," said Robert. "Everyone knew of course. It was terribly bad luck."

"So we all laughed very loud, and talked, and tried to drown it out."

"But we all heard it anyhow," said Robert.

"And that silly Irish girl, the Wren, remember how she started to cry? Just then, because of the luck, and the siren."

"Well, she was Irish."

"And Catholic," said Philippa. "She thought marriages should last forever, you see. And the sirens meant . . ."

"I thought marriages should last forever too," Robert said.

"Rubbish," said Philippa.

"Why not? I was Catholic too."

"Rubbish," she said again. "We weren't married in church and you weren't Catholic at all."

"I was. Besides, it's the intention that counts. Even at Caxton Hall. I meant it to be forever."

"Well, so did I, dear," she said at once.

"Then why the heck did you two ever get divorced," Mary Jo said, with a sour jealous twist of her soft young mouth. Robert smiled and shrugged, and Philippa just kept looking down the table, her eyes meeting his, that wide strong mouth turning gently up at the corners.

"Forever," she said finally, "was so conveniently short in nineteen forty."

"I think that's beautiful," Paul said, suddenly, from the window.

"What's beautiful?" Mary Jo cut in, angrily.

"The two of them, getting married like that, in London, with all that danger all around. It's so romantic. It's beautiful." Mary Jo stood up. David found her painfully lovely with the slight tremble of her lip, and the anger lighting her clear bright eyes.

"Oh, is it?" she said. "What the frigging hell would you know about romance, you big pansy? And if it's so romantic as all that, why don't you let Steve go back to Vietnam and get killed. *And* David. If war's so frigging romantic and beautiful. You hypocrite. All your damned poetry, and lamenting. The truth is you get a big sexual kick out of it, as long as it's at a distance. You all do. As long as it's far away, or long ago. And you"—she turned to Philippa—"with all your bragging and remembering back to the good old days, and how terrific you all were; do you know what you've done? You've got your own son so thoroughly bullshitted that he's going to Vietnam with Steve. Only it isn't a war. It's only an insurrection. A colonial incident. Isn't it? So I guess he won't get killed." She stalked away and Philippa did not look at her.

Instead she turned to Robert and said evenly, "What is this?"

"Baloney," he said.

"It's not, father," said David.

"You shut up," Robert said, without turning. "It's nothing, Phil. This is the first I've heard of it."

"I was waiting till mother came to tell you. I'm going to join up. With Steve."

"Oh Stephen, *please*," Paul whimpered.

Philippa stood up and left the table. She was still looking at Robert, stepping back one step, and then another, and then half tripping over one of the cats that had crept illicitly in. She gave it an angry shove with the side of her foot. "Robert," she said slowly. "Is this what's been going on? Is this why David is staying on?"

"I told you. It's news to me. And it's baloney."

"This, instead of Cambridge. You must be desperate."

"Philippa, you can't believe—"

"I can believe practically anything where you and my family are concerned."

"I'm not sending my own son to get himself killed."

"Father, I *wish* to go. I wish to fight for what I believe in."

"You're too young to believe in anything. Just shut up."

"*You* did."

"I did nothing. Now look." He thought carefully and then said, "David, whatever he's saying, was not staying because of that. It's nothing to do with the marines, or freedom, or anything . . . political. He was staying because of something personal."

"You mean to say he's staying because he loves you more than me," said Philippa, at once.

"No," Stephen Deutsch said suddenly, pushing his fair hair off his face. "What Robert *means* to say is that David is staying because David fucked Mary Jo in the shower yesterday."

"Right," said Robert, standing as he said it. "Right. I'm sorry, Paul, I'm sorry. I'm sorry." He spoke in a rising crescendo, so that the last "I'm sorry" was a full shout, and by that time he had actually reached Stephen. "Right," he said again.

"God believe me, Paul, I'm doing you a favor." He had Stephen by the collar and the bunched-up back of his shirt, and he had the impetus of four strides across the room. Stephen teetered, and muttered, "Fuck, man," but Robert was already swinging him around, and then, with a last thought for his screen door, he let go. He hadn't used so much strength in years. The cats scattered, and Stephen hurtled, arms spinning, flustered curses flying, into the battered screen. It crashed open, breaking at its hinges, and there was a wild shout as Stephen continued right on and over the edge of the deck, with a splintering of ancient timber and a great deal of crashing of shrubbery. Robert had only a moment's remorse, and that for his battered old screen.

"You might have killed him," Paul cried. He ran outside, through the screen, half hung on its hinges. But there was a crashing, snapping sound of someone struggling away through the scrub.

"I should be so lucky," said Robert, at last.

Then he turned to the table, snatched up the wooden statue and hurled it, with a great joyous crashing, through the window glass. Mary Jo shrieked, terrified.

"And you can take Our Lady of the Malaria Swamp with you!" he shouted to the hot August night.

After a short while, Paul came in, brushing his face and not looking at anyone. Philippa stood up, clutched Mary Jo by the arm, and said, "Robert, the ladies shall retire."

Mary Jo struggled, but found Philippa's grip remarkably solid. Mary Jo turned around over her shoulder, but neither David nor Robert was looking at her. She said, desperately, "Robert?" He still did not look at her and she said, still fighting to get free, "I'm sorry, Robert. I'm sorry. I said I was sorry."

Robert had gone to the kitchen cupboard, where he kept drinks, and was peering into it, shifting bottles with dull annoying clinks. "Robert?" Mary Jo said, her voice a little whiny, on the high edge near tears. He found what he wanted and stood up, still with his back to her, and made quite a slow business of finding precisely the right small glasses.

He said, as he did so, "One day, sweetheart, you are going to learn that, beyond the confessional, that word really does not work all that well. There just aren't any instant absolutions out in the real world. Now be a good kid and go with your hostess. The gentlemen"—he looked over his shoulder at David and Paul, and then resumed filling the three glasses—"such as they are, are about to have their port."

He turned then, and lifted the three full glasses on a small tin tray, and set them, with flourish, on the table, where the wooden madonna had stood.

"You're a big shit, Robert," Mary Jo shouted and then crumpled into tears.

"Gentlemen," said Robert, "the Queen."

Up on the roof deck Philippa settled herself comfortably on the old wooden bench by the railing. She untied, and retied, the crepe bow on her Jenner's blouse. She straightened the back of her skirt, smoothing the tailored vent, and carefully crossed her legs, and then recrossed them the other way to conceal the run in her stocking. She did it quite instinctively. The girl, Mary Jo, was curled up on the roof deck, just at the edge of the staircase, her knees drawn up and her arms wrapped around her legs, and her face against her knees. The masses of dark yellow hair tumbled all over, a messy outline in the darkness. Philippa could tell by the small gasping sounds that she was crying very freely, but she could not really see more than a shape. She waited patiently for the crying to finish. She was accustomed to this kind of performance from Victoria. Sometimes for an important reason, sometimes for no reason at all. Eventually she said, "Are you cold? I'll get my jacket if you like." But the night was not cold, even the wind blowing off the ocean was hot. Thunder rolled over the distant light-starred mainland.

"Oh leave me alone," Mary Jo said in reply. Philippa shrugged. That was usually standard with Victoria as well. In another moment, if the pattern held, the head would rise, and the accusations would begin; against Robert, David, herself, anyone but the young selfish center of it all.

Philippa closed her eyes, and leaned back, and began counting to ten. At eight Mary Jo raised her head, glared at the shadowy figure at the railing, and said, "Now you know what kind of a bastard he is, don't you?"

"Who," Philippa said, "Robert?" Her voice was mild.

"Of course not. David." She began to sob, "The bastard. The stinking bastard. Telling Stephen. And it was his idea anyhow. Oh you won't believe that, your darling little son, will you, but it's true."

"I'll be the first to believe that any seventeen-year-old boy might be interested in sex, dear, if that's what you mean."

That brought Mary Jo up short and she straightened one leg out and looked up curiously. "Aren't you angry?" she said. Philippa shrugged slightly, delicately, and said, "There's hardly any value in being angry at this point, is there? Sorry, perhaps. Good God, it's certainly not a very pleasant situation. But what's done is done."

"Is that all you can say?" Mary Jo asked, with scorn.

"Now what, dear, are you expecting? Do you want me to get into a flaming temper and shout and scream at you? Will that help? It strikes me that there are really quite enough people in flaming tempers around here already."

"God," Mary Jo said. "Haven't you any feelings at all?"

Philippa smiled to herself and said, "I doubt it. Not as you define them, anyway."

"No wonder Robert divorced you," Mary Jo said.

"Oh indeed," Philippa replied at once. "Only I divorced Robert, as I recall. It had nothing to do with 'feelings' as you call it, anyhow. Those are the easy sides of marriage, actually.

It may astound you to hear it but Robert and I were really rather pleasant together in bed." She smiled because Mary Jo turned her eyes away. "Oh come dear, where did you think David came from, hmm? But no, that wasn't it. No, it was money, and children, and education, and how one sets the dinner table, and who one invites to sit at it, and every other small thing like that. That's what makes marriage difficult, not those few minutes in the night."

"I don't agree," Mary Jo said calmly, at once.

"Of course not. How old are you, twenty? Twenty-two? Sex is the only line of communication at that age. But later it changes."

"No," Mary Jo said again. "I know already. It's always the only thing. Oh, Robert and I argue about millions of things, but really it's only one. He's . . ." She began again to cry. "I don't know why I'm saying this . . . he's not very good . . . or I'm not. Honest, I don't know which. But it's not very pleasant at all, in bed. It's rotten, actually. But I love him. Only he's so old sometimes. Not always. But sometimes. I just need someone young, not to love, just for a good fuck, and then I'd be glad to go back to Robert."

"It's rather a bit much to ask, don't you think?"

"Of course. It's hopeless. Oh Mrs. Wardlaw. I don't know what to do. I am sorry, honest I am. But why should I always have to go to bed with someone who doesn't excite me?" Philippa was silent a long time, and then she said, "No doubt you excite Robert."

"I guess so. I mean, I guess I must. I am pretty, I know. I mean, I can say that without being vain, can't I?"

"Of course. That's only honest. But it won't always be, you know, dear. Oh, you'll never be old, or even middle-aged, while Robert's around, I know. You're safe enough there. But suppose you married David?"

"Mrs. Wardlaw, honest, it was just a . . ."

"Just a stupid fling." Philippa laughed softly. "Oh yes dear, I know all about those. Stupid maybe, but there's never

a fling without a string, dear. Suppose, just suppose. David
is, well, David is actually younger than you. Three, four
years, am I right?"

Mary Jo nodded. She was so used to being the youngest
in every gathering that it came as a bit of a shock.

"Well, now, just think. Just for a moment. Think twenty
years. You'll be, what, forty?" Mary Jo nodded again. "And
David, well, David will be thirty-seven. A little young yet;
try thirty years. Some marriages do actually last that long,
even today. You'll be fifty. Older than I am, actually. Oh, I'm
well preserved, I know, but hardly ravishing, am I?"

"You're . . . you're very nice looking," Mary Jo said
nervously.

"Oh yes. And I'm sure you'll be too. But Robert isn't
chasing me into bed, is he? Nor is he chasing any other forty-
five-year old. He's chasing you. Do you know, dear, that the
little girl David would leave you for is probably not yet born.
But she will be. She will be."

Mary Jo laughed, at first, as she was accustomed to do, when
presented with an unheard-of situation. It was an embarrassed,
high nervous laugh, ending in a little choked giggle. Then she
grew indignant and said, "What a rotten thing to say. You
really are a bitch. You really are."

"Perhaps," said Philippa, unmoved. "But hardly for that.
It's the truth, after all, and I didn't invent the truth. There's
nothing I can do about it, and nothing you can either. So
you might as well accept it. Men have more time than we do,
much more time. They've time for two whole lifetimes; two
wives, two families, one after the other. We do not. Oh,
surely, you can have a young lover when you are young. But
you can be as sure that he will be twice the man he was,
when you are but half the woman you were. Or you can play
safe, as you are doing, and have all the secure flattery of an
older man, some other, older woman's erstwhile companion,
more than likely. But do not complain if after a while he wants
his slippers and pipe, and you must fetch them."

"Oh really," Mary Jo said. "Robert's not like *that*."

"Then why are you crying?"

Mary Jo shook her head, and Philippa said for her, "Because he is not David?" Mary Jo shook her head again, and Philippa smiled in the darkness, and said, "I can remember when he was." Then her voice hardened and she said briskly, "So then, we can either rail against God because of the unfairness of it all, or we can cut our losses, be provident, and create a life for ourselves that is separate, a life that includes neither husband nor children, for that must carry us in the end."

Mary Jo drew back in haughty young disdain. She sat up straighter, and finally said, "If that's all I could see in life, I'd probably kill myself." Philippa laughed out loud, a ringing laugh, rather delighted, and said, still laughing, "Oh come now. Surely it's not that bad."

Mary Jo could frankly not understand the laughter, but it still annoyed her intensely. She said, "I haven't the slightest idea why Robert ever married you. You're the stiffest, stuffiest, coldest, most unromantic person I've ever met."

Philippa nodded calmly. "I suppose I probably am. And tell me, is Robert so romantic then?"

"Well, yes. I mean, he's a hell of a lot more than you are."

"I doubt that, actually, but we'll assume it's true for the moment. He certainly was once. But then, so was I. Oh yes, I was really. We both were. Very, very romantic. You must understand though, romanticism is a solo act, my dear, a one-man show. For all that romantics are forever proclaiming their ever-so-desperate need to find a like spirit, they are, actually, repelled by like spirits. There is nothing that drives a romantic into cynicism faster than the company of another romantic. So do be careful, dear. There's only one of you can be the butterfly. Someone, always, must be the grub." She finished speaking and opened her handbag and retrieved a comb. "Excuse me," she said before she began, thoughtfully, to comb her hair.

"Mrs. Wardlaw?" Mary Jo asked, uncertain of her attention. Philippa made a small sound of acknowledgment, which was largely lost in a rumble of thunder. She looked up, about the cloudy dark sky, lit from beneath, in the distance, by the lights of Long Island. "Will it storm?" Philippa said.

Mary Jo did not even answer that. It stormed more nights than not at this sultry time of the year, though mostly the thunderheads kept themselves over the mainland, as if hooked onto the lights. She said, "You remarried. Why did you remarry, if you're so cynical about love?"

Philippa laughed and then said, "Precisely." But she did not mean that as an explanation. She said after a while, "I had a great many good reasons, none of which you could yet understand. In spite of what you might feel, you don't really know so very much about life, just because you've been to bed with a man." Then she put the comb away and said, "My son David has an excellent future. He also has at least four more years of education to complete before he can commence that future. If you wish to continue a relationship with him it must be discreet, undemanding, and cooperative. And there must be no pregnancies. Do you understand me?"

"Mrs. Wardlaw, this is ridiculous. David and I; we haven't any plans or anything. We just. We just . . ."

"Fucked," said Philippa Wardlaw. Mary Jo opened her mouth wide and said nothing. Then she burst out, "We haven't done anything *serious*, Mrs. Wardlaw. We aren't getting married or anything."

Philippa sighed and said, "I'd like to imagine not, my dear, but he's obviously besotted with you, and I suspect you return his affections, as they say. And if you remain together any length of time, no doubt you'll marry. You're too young to have the sense not to. Everyone seems to need to try it once, anyhow."

"What are you talking about?" Mary Jo shouted. "I've never thought of marrying David." She was aware, as she said it, of the lie. She had thought of doing almost everything with David. "Anyhow, I live with Robert."

There was a long silence, and then a slight pitying laugh. "You silly little fool. How long, precisely, do you imagine that's to continue, after tonight?"

"What do you mean?"

"My dear, you don't seriously consider that he'll allow you to remain?" Philippa laughed again, in amazement at the girl's incredible naive innocence.

"Shut the damned door," Robert's voice shouted from below. Slowly, Mary Jo began again to cry, new, serious, adult tears, her short-breathed sobs interspersed with the sound of footsteps on the stair.

"Is this then the withdrawing room?" said Paul, in his best British accent, as he reached the roof.

"Oh, Jesus," Mary Jo moaned. "Not now."

But Philippa said, cheerfully, "Do join us," as if they had been discussing nothing of note.

Paul had brought the kerosene lamp, and his face was lit by it, from below, and shadowy in all the wrong places. He set it on the deck and pulled over one of the canvas chairs that were folded against the roof railing and set it up, awkwardly, beside the lamp, so that he faced Philippa and Mary Jo, who had retreated to the railing and was looking over it pointedly, at nothing. "*Am* I interrupting?" said Paul.

"Not at all," Philippa said. She could see Mary Jo's hands tighten on the railing with the stress of silence. Fine. She could think a bit, something she apparently did far too little of, anyway.

"Oh thank goodness," Paul said, trying for lightness. "Sometimes it's rather useful being neither fish nor fowl. It's positively dreadful down there. And I hate port, anyhow. And they're both getting drunk. I was clearly *de trop*, I will tell you. Robert is positively raging. Positively. Silently, but raging, if you understand."

"I understand," said Philippa.

"Oh, this is terrible," said Paul.

"Will you shut up?" said Mary Jo.

"I'm sorry," said Paul, elaborately unsorry. "I am sorry, I am sure. Shall I leave?"

"No. No," said Philippa, still mild. "Come sit down, Mary Jo." Mary Jo did, welcoming, without realizing it, any voice of authority.

Paul's face was stretched too firmly into his brittle, handsome smile. It did not surprise Philippa at all when he began, quite without warning, to cry. She looked up quickly to Mary Jo, temporarily dry-eyed, and said, "I suppose you'd better lend him your handkerchief, dear."

"I haven't got one," she said. Philippa nodded, knowingly. Victoria never had a handkerchief either, or any of the other equipment women had always needed. Victoria never carried a handbag, and she carried her money in her jeans pocket like a man. She said she felt freer that way. Philippa was intrigued with that equation of freedom and ill-preparedness. She slipped her fingers into her own neatly arranged possessions within her alligator bag and brought out a large, unused, pristinely folded linen square. "Why do you carry that if you never use it?" was Victoria's retaliation. Now she had an answer. In case I run into a middle-aged homosexual having a nervous breakdown. She wondered what Victoria would say to that.

Paul rejected the handkerchief. "Oh please, I'm not a child."

Philippa shrugged and returned the linen square to its place. The bag clicked shut, sounding sharp. The air was yet still, and silent between the nearing rolls of thunder. "Would you care to talk about it?" Philippa asked, rather gently.

"There's nothing to talk about," Paul said at once. Philippa shrugged again and, as earlier, began silently counting to ten. At seven, Paul said, "That bastard. That selfish bastard."

Philippa leaned her head to one side, and took a guess. "Stephen?"

"No. Not Stephen." Paul jerked his head away so that she could not see his face clearly, in the light of the lamp.

She tried again. "Not David, surely."

"Not the *boy*." Paul recoiled, shocked. "I'd never say such a thing about the boy."

"Well, Robert certainly appears to be charming his friends tonight," she concluded then, and to Mary Jo said, "Is it always like this here?"

"Friends," Paul squeaked. "Friends? *Robert* does not have friends."

"I see," said Philippa, reserving judgment.

"Robert is a writer. *Writers* do not have friends."

"I see," Philippa said again, nodding wisely, as if grateful for a valuable piece of knowledge. "He just entertains passing strangers, then?"

"Oh, he entertains. Robert is very entertaining. He entertains all the time. He never stops, and he's oh so terribly thrilled to see practically anybody. And then the moment he turns his back he forgets about them, completely. Robert doesn't give parties. He directs plays. Then he gets bored and sends everybody home, and writes it all down and gets rich. He's a vulture. A scavenger. A vampire bat."

"Then why do you come?" Mary Jo said, sharply, her head coming up with an angry jerk. "You're here all the time. Why do you come?"

Paul sniffed and wouldn't answer at first. Then he blurted out, "Because I get lonely. Besides, he comes to me at the Pines. Why shouldn't I come here?" He paused and added slowly, "He gets lonely too."

"He's got me," Mary Jo said, indignant.

"Men need men," Philippa comforted.

"*He's* not a man," she returned at once, with scorn. "What are you saying?" she demanded of Paul. "Come on, you big self-centered perv. What does Robert need from you?" Her scorn was touched with just an edge of nerves.

Paul withdrew, leaning away from her, at an angle, and crossing his long legs. His white costume glowed softly in the dim light of the kerosene lamp. The wind had begun to pick up, and the flame flickered within its sheltering chimney. Paul reached to shelter it with his hand, and then thought better, finding the air above the chimney too hot. He said quietly, resigned, "Oh nothing your bourgeois little prejudices might fathom. And not friendship either. No. None of the blood-sucking variety, *lam*preys and mosquitoes, none of them have friends. He comes for company, I suppose, a little stimulation, fangs in the intellectual jugular."

"I do think you're being rather harsh," Philippa said mildly, watching Mary Jo, who had risen and was scuffing sneakered feet around the gravelly corners of the asphalted roof.

"To Robert?" Paul said. "Oh, don't worry, he won't care. He hasn't any real feelings. Not about people. He'll sit and listen politely, but all the while he's carrying on a conversation in his head with a bunch of strangers, any one of whom, being self-created, is more interesting and more complaisant than you are. Once I completely left the room, completely left it, and he didn't even notice I was gone."

"Maybe he was just holding his breath in case you came back," Mary Jo said, without turning around from the railing.

"Oh don't be a jealous little bitch," Paul returned, his voice going high and nasal. "It's nothing to do with sex, you know. It's just age. Different sexes we can accommodate. Different ages are more difficult. All of us, all of us, my dear, need a dose of our own kind, occasionally. And you should know, considering." His voice had gone sly and Mary Jo dropped out of the conversation, at once.

"I didn't mean Robert," Philippa said, as if Mary Jo had not spoken at all, "I meant yourself. You're harsh on yourself." Paul shrugged, and she could see his grimace of acute self-awareness.

"No, my dear. I'm honest. It's about all I've got left, but I'm honest." Then he paused and said, "I'm sorry I'm being so rotten about Robert. I keep forgetting about you. You and he, I mean. Anyway, that's not it. It isn't Robert." He turned his face away, and she could see the corners of his eyes were squinting shut.

"No?" she said calmly.

"He's going away," Paul whispered. She knew he meant the boy Stephen. She also knew, from long experience with Victoria, that at this point a catalogue of Stephen's obvious faults, as a measure of the lightness of his loss, would do no good at all. So she said brightly, instead, "Frankly, I can't get used to Robert the Writer. It was Robert the Actor I knew, after all. I've not yet grown accustomed to the change."

"Of course, it was a dreadful mistake, you know," Paul confided, his eyes open again. She was pleased to have avoided another tearful scene, and pursued that. "I don't know. How?"

"You should never have allowed him to leave the theater. Never. It was a dreadful mistake."

"I'm afraid I was not responsible. It had nothing whatever to do with me, you know. I was thousands of miles away, and he neglected to consult me."

"But it's been the absolute destruction of him. Absolute," said Paul, nodding wisely.

"A rather successful destruction, for all that, surely," said Philippa. "I have it on fairly good evidence that he's doing quite all right."

"Oh yes," Paul said, leaning back, his hands folded across his knees. "Oh yes. In a material sense, of course. A great success. But artistically he's utterly ruined."

"Oh. Artistically." Philippa smiled to herself, thinking suddenly of Bridlington, and the room in the St. Leonard's, and Rhoda. "Artistically," she said again. "I suppose that *is* a consideration."

"A consider*ation*. It's everything." He paused smugly and then said, "Oh, I will admit, of course, that writing is truly creative, in a way that acting will never be, but you can see what it's done to him. He's so embittered."

"All the way to the bank," Mary Jo said from the railing. Paul completely ignored her.

"Naturally enough. I mean, to have spoken the words of so many *great* writers, all those years. There's a kind of artistic cannibalism; one speaks other writers' words and eventually *absorbs* them into the streams of one's own thought. And *then*. To be left, with all that vanished, and just the cold comfort of a typewriter, and for words, the mediocrity of your own. Oh, it's devastating, dear. Devastating."

"Then why doesn't he write something decent?" Philippa said, at once.

"Why doesn't Paul act in something decent?" Mary Jo interrupted. " 'Queen for a Day,' maybe?" Paul was quiet and calm, and said, "Who's going to buy it?"

"I gathered money was not the object," said Philippa.

"Money, my dear, is the medium of communication. Art that does not communicate is dead. Silent. Like the proverbial tree falling in the forest. Money proves ears are attended."

"It's not silent," said Philippa.

"What?"

"The tree. God hears it."

Paul was quiet for a long while. Then he said, wearily, "Oh no dear. No Berkeleyan loopholes, please. To be honest, I can't wait for the applause of God. It's rather long in coming." He was again silent for a long time, in which the wind came up, gustily, the thunder rolled, louder, along the long lighted strip of the mainland, and Mary Jo, bored as always with conversations about other people, got up from where she had settled by the railing and padded down the stairs without a good-bye. A stronger gust blew out the lamp.

Paul said slowly, from the new darkness, "I used to have a dream. I still have it, sometimes. I used to have it a lot. When I was doing more legit stuff. I'd be on stage, at the end of something marvelous, and very dramatic; one light, just on me, and I'd know I'd done so well. And then there would be silence. Like before the very best kind of applause, that marvelous silence. Only, in the dream, the applause didn't come. And the silence remained, and I just sat there for a long time, and then the house lights came up, and I saw the reason for the silence. There wasn't any audience. There never was. There was never any audience at all." He began then to cry, really cry, and Philippa moved closer and put her practiced arms about him.

"I'm so scared," he said. "Everyone's leaving. Stephen. David. Everyone. I don't want to be alone. I'm so scared."

"You'll hardly be alone," she said. "I'm sure you have many friends." She remembered David then, in the hospital at York, and it worried her. "Robert is your friend, I'm sure, and if you just calm down a little, and think about it, I'm sure you'll think of others."

"Robert doesn't care about me. Robert doesn't care about anybody, or anything, other than his work. Writers are only happy or sad in relation to work. Tell them World War *Three* has started, and they'll just smile their self-satisfied smile, as long as the work's going well. And if it's not, then nothing, nothing, not wives, not lovers, not children, and certainly not friends, can reach them. Do you know what's eating him now? Not you, not David, and not that silly bitch. He hasn't worked all summer and he only exists in relation to work. I could die tomorrow, and if he thought of a good line at my funeral, he'd think it was a good day."

Philippa started to laugh, in spite of herself, and he jerked away from her arms. But she reenfolded him, conscious of him only in the sense of a well of despair, like any saddened child of her own.

"I don't want to be alone," he said again, between sobs. "You can't understand. I've been alone all my life."

"It's quite possible," said Philippa, "to be every bit as much alone within a marriage." She paused, and thought, and then said, "When you have children, you learn the difference between the replaceable and the irreplaceable. After that, you're never really a materialist. With thwarted love, you learn the difference between the obtainable and the truly unobtainable. Both knowledges give their own tremendous freedom. One from things, the other from desires. Those are two of the foundations of human happiness. The other is the ability to be alone. You aren't likely to have the first, I know, but the second you've obviously experienced. I suggest now, you concentrate on the third."

"I can't bear it."

"You'll have to. Buck up now; being a fairly good hermit isn't so bad. I'm one. Count yourself lucky. You won't have to share your cave with a middle-aged Scottish bombast in a pinstriped suit." She giggled softly.

Paul smiled, and said, "I think you're quite marvelous. I really do. Robert was an absolute fool. An absolute fool."

"Yes," Philippa said, sighing. "And so was I. I still love him, you know."

"I know," Paul said shyly. "So do I."

"I still love her," Robert said.

"Even after yesterday?" David held his port glass, half empty, clutched between his two big hands. He swallowed hard, even mentioning yesterday. It was the biggest day since creation. His father started to laugh, a big roomy laugh, with a lot of drink in it.

At last he said, "I didn't mean Mary Jo. I meant your mother. If you must know, I'd forgotten about yesterday. I am a little drunk."

"Father," said David, not quite comprehending what had been said, being a little drunk himself. "Father, how did Stephen find out?"

"Simple. Paul told him."

"How did *Paul* find out?" David asked again, more bewildered. Robert poured himself more port, as if he were thinking of something else, and then, looking up a little startled, rubbed his beard, and said, "Oh, *I* told Paul. I thought you realized."

"Why did you do that? Why ever did you tell anyone?"

"For Christ's sake, kid, it wasn't that important. Anyhow,

if you must know, I had to talk to someone. It did hurt a bit. I'm not a saint, you know. Not yet."

"But Paul's your friend. Why'd he do such a perfectly rotten thing; spill the whole thing out like that."

"Because he's in love," said Robert. "People in love don't have friends; they're like nations at war, they have allies or enemies. He was jealous of you, over Stephen, and wanted to prove you were straight, so Stephen would lay off and come home to the fold."

"I feel sick," said David.

"Sick? You're seventeen. Wait until you're my age to feel sick."

"No. I mean it. The port." But he sat at the table swaying back and forth, saying nothing.

"You're going home with your mother," said Robert. David's face went slightly yellowy-green. He pushed his glass away. "I'm not," he said.

"Oh yes you are."

"I'm going to join up. With Stephen. I am." He was speaking in small bursts because any longer use of his voice brought nausea. "Can we talk about it tomorrow?" he pleaded.

"Tomorrow you'll be on the plane."

"But father, I thought you wanted me. I thought you wanted me to stay. I swear, I won't go near Mary Jo."

Robert drank from his glass, turned it around and set it down by the candelabra. Wax had dripped, green, onto the table linen. He picked at it, with his long forefinger. "If I thought for one minute that you would do that, simply stay, you could have Mary Jo on a silver platter. You're not going to Vietnam."

"I want to, father. I feel it's right."

"What precisely do you know about it?"

"What Stephen has told me. And what I know. You should understand. You fought for your beliefs. You had your war. This is ours."

"You're planning on making the world safe for democracy?"

"Why are you laughing at me, damn it?" David had to hold his hand over his mouth, until he burped, uncomfortably.

"Because you're an ass. David, do you know why I went to war?"

"Of course I know."

"You don't know at all. Do you want to know? I went to war because I was scared. I was scared of what was happening in my life. I had been offered a chance in the theater. A very special chance. It was going to be the making or the breaking of me. Only it was going to be the breaking because I wasn't good enough. It was too good for me. And I knew it. So I went and joined the RAF because I was scared shitless of failing. It was the stupidest thing I ever did in my life. And it was absolutely typical. I was terrified out of my little wits all through the war. The moment I got my kite in the air, the only thing I could think of was a way of making it unserviceable, so I could come home with my ass intact.

"And you know what I did when I was really, really scared? After I helped my best friend get killed? I married your mother, because she was ten times the person I was, and she wasn't ever scared of anything. I needed her courage, and damn it to hell, I took it. I took it. And then I cheated on her and broke her, and sent her scuttling off to marry that idiot we call your stepfather." Robert gulped down the rest of his port, reached for the bottle, found it empty, and felt he could cry. He wanted so much to keep getting drunker and drunker. David was watching him with those cool, unmoved English eyes, like Philippa, twenty-five years ago, in the hospital, after the bombed café.

"Then I ran off to America, because I was scared to keep trying in Britain, and then I left the stage, because I met up with the truth one day, and the truth was I wasn't worth a damn. Now I spend my days writing stupid stories for stupid people, and everybody says I'm wasting myself. The fuck I am. I'm right where I belong."

David was sitting absolutely straight, his face expressionless. Behind the disdain in his eyes was pity. And behind that a certain gentle detachment. He was thinking quite unreasonably of St. Vincent's School, on a clear autumn English day, and the cricket ground. It all seemed hazed with a soft glow. Nostalgia for it crept in under the veil of port wine, like the first word of a long lie.

"Oh really, father, the stories are quite all right. I rather enjoy them myself." He smiled patiently. "If you don't mind, I think I'd like some air." He stood up, smiled again at his father slouching drunkenly in his chair, behind the guttering candles. Then he walked out, managing to control his unsteady gait, and quietly closed the door. He met Mary Jo on the deck, silently took her hand, and they began to walk, hand in hand, down the boardwalk to the ocean beach.

Robert stood at the doorway, watching. They passed out of the lights of the window, but in a few moments a flash of distant lightning brightened the whole sky, and showed the two figures mounting the boardwalk. Even in that light, even through the screen, he fancied he could read, in the set of the strong young shoulders, David's utter disdain.

He went back into the room and picked up one of his two cats, the shy, remorseful one that liked his company, and sat down in the wicker armchair with it. It was black and white, exactly like the other, with carefully marked paws and throat, and a whiteness beneath its belly, like an otter. It alone had one ungraceful mark, though, a smear of white on its lip that gave the look of a permanent sneer. But it was not sneering; unlike its exquisitely marked sister who had no time for anyone, it was a loving creature. He called it the "not entirely beautiful," after something Paul had said, about Yeats and the nature of love.

He held the cat, stroking it thoughtfully, and said, his voice slurred by port, "So what then, if the goose ate the grain? What was he losing? So he was a farmer anyhow. And now he had a fat goose. A nice fat goose. Why not?" The cat circled on his knees, curled round and round, and covered its white lip with its tail. Robert leaned back in his armchair with the thundery wind blowing in, and they both went to sleep.

It was not the storm that woke him. He was so accustomed to those that he would sleep through lightning striking all about the house, though David, all through the summer, rose and drank tea, sitting nervous on the edge of his bed, unable to sleep through even mild thunder, after the peace of English nights. And the storm tonight was yet far off, though the lightning reflecting from one sea to another was so frequent that the house was flickering with its distant presence, like a failing neon sign.

What had wakened him was a voice, David's voice, speaking into his sleep. He opened his eyes. The room was dark, except for the flashes of lightning. The candles had burned out. Robert switched the light on beside his chair. David's face appeared, in the fresh glare, as pale as if it had been dusted with flour. "Mother's gone," he said. "Mother's not here."

Robert sat up straight, and stood up, confused remembrance mixing with the sound of sea, wind, and thunder. Mary Jo was standing behind David, sheltering behind him. "I think she took the dinghy," she said. "Paul said she just got up and left, like she was mad or something. She left her suitcase, and her jacket. But the boat keys are gone. I suppose she's gone to the Pines."

Robert jumped up and brushed by them both, and pushed open his broken door. Outside the wind was like hot breath, strong, and unsated yet by rain. Thunder rolled repeatedly. "Father?" David called. Robert did not answer. He was running down his boardwalk, ducking under the low sassafras trees. He was not the least bit worried about Philippa's handling the dinghy. Philippa could handle a ten-meter racing yacht. But even Philippa needed more than the teacup of gasoline in the fuel tank.

He heard the sputtering of the engine when he reached the bayfront walk, but he still had a hundred yards to go. He ran faster, panting, and out of breath, feeling foolish and unfit. He could hear the engine still, when he reached his jetty, and then a flash of lightning lit the water, around the little dinghy with its whirl of white foam behind, and Philippa, calmly confident, her braceleted hand guiding the tiller.

"You stupid bitch," Robert shouted.

"Hush," Philippa called back, "you'll wake your neighbors."

"Screw my neighbors."

"I'm going to the hotel," she shouted. "Good night."

"There's not enough gas."

"Then I'll row, dear. Be a pet and bring my things tomorrow."

"Philippa, there's no gas. You'll damn well capsize without power. It's going to storm like hell."

"My dear, I'll bloody swim before I spend a night in that house full of lunatics. Don't forget my coat. It's on your door. And tell David I'll meet him at the airport. Ten o'clock. Tuesday. Idlewild." She waved one hand, paused, and then called in remembered mockery, "Scramble."

She revved the little outboard, and the dinghy took off, skipping like a light shell, into the stormy night.

"Dumb bitch," Robert shouted to the empty whiteness of her wake. "*Stupid* dumb bitch." Then he ran back to the sandy shore and the long flat fiberglass hull of the Sunfish. He raised the mast, cursing, in the darkness, and then drew up the sail, and cleated it tight. It began to flap at once, reminding him of the severity of the rising wind. Of course he hadn't a hope of catching her until she ran out of fuel. But then he'd have to catch her fast.

He dragged the flat hull down the seaweed bank and into the shallow water, and then waded out with it until the water was up to his thighs. He jumped aboard then, flipping the centerboard half in, and snapping the rudder down into place. The fitting was worn, half-broken, and it caught only soggily, but he hadn't time to fool with it. The sail came around over his head, and he tucked his sodden sneakers into the little cockpit, leaned back against the low railing and took up the slack sheet. The little boat caught the wind at once and slipped at a gaily quickening pace across the dark bay flats, waving its aluminum mast reassuringly toward the lightning-crossed skies. "*Damn* dumb stupid bitch," he said.

He hoped briefly that Philippa would make the logical mistake, stay too close inshore, and run aground. It would cost him a prop pin, but it would be worth it. However, either instinct or memory of the route Mary Jo had taken kept her wisely offshore, on a course more northerly than westerly. He followed with difficulty, trailing the foamy wake of the boat, and more effectively, the sputter of the engine, clear enough in the night, even over the sound of the growing storm.

The wind was erratic, gusty, and unpredictable, shifting about behind his sail, so that he ran alternately downwind and across it. Then it would drop entirely, leaving him fetching about hopelessly with flapping sail until it rose with gusty suddenness and half turned the little craft over before he could let out the sheet. It was in one such mock calm, with the nylon sail luffing frantically, that he heard the engine noise sputter and stop. The rain came then, as if on signal, blotting out visibility in every direction and soaking through the few bits of his clothing remaining dry.

A quarter of a mile to the east a great tree of lightning came down onto a channel marker pole, lighting up the whole of the bay around him and the outline of the island behind. He was a mile out, Philippa, in her powerless dinghy even further. He was aware suddenly that he was no longer the slightest bit drunk. He was sitting in the middle of the bay, in the middle of the best thunderstorm of the year, on a sheet of fiberglass topped with a lightning rod. It was absurdly comical and absurdly dangerous. He brought the nose of the little boat around, and headed north, out into the storm.

He could see nothing, and was only guessing, and as he cleared the lee and the wind rose, whitecaps began breaking over the smooth sleek bow. He grew terrified, not for himself but for Philippa. If lightning didn't strike him, his little craft could sail happily to the mainland and back, providing he maintained the strength to hold it in line and right it when it, almost inevitably, capsized. It was utterly unsinkable, though surprisingly tiring to manage, like a half-broken horse, slamming along the wave crests. But his little power dinghy was as seaworthy as the proverbial bathtub it rather resembled. It was made for clamming and lazy summer fishing, and shore-hugging journeys for the laundry. "Stupid bitch should have known that. She damn well would have known that." That annoyed him most of all. Not her foolishness but her perennial reckless courage. She would ride anything, sail anything, dare anything, always three steps ahead of him, for all the time he'd known her.

When the next lightning flash lit up the half-swamped dinghy, suddenly surprisingly close, Philippa was calmly kneeling in the bow, in her tweed skirt, her Jenner's blouse, and her nylon stockings, bailing energetically with her alligator handbag. He brought the silent Sunfish to within ten yards before she saw him.

"There's a coffee can under the seat," he called. "It'll hold more." She looked up, registered no amazement in gesture, though he could not see her face, until the next blue-white flash.

"Why, Robert. This *is* a pleasant surprise."

"Philippa, I'll break your bloody neck."

The wind took the tops off the nearest two waves and drenched them both. "I'll come alongside, and you'll have to hop on. Carefully, or you'll turn it over." She nodded but did not hurry. Instead she emptied most of the water from her handbag and set it carefully under the seat. Then she uncoiled the bow rope, handed it to Robert, and prepared to abandon ship. But she stopped, then, and sat on the pitching seat of the dinghy, and began to struggle with something in the darkness.

"What are you doing?" he shouted. "I'm going to capsize in a moment."

"One minute, please." The lightning flared again. He was left with an afterimage, glaring red in the darkness, of Philippa, shoes off, neatly rolling down her stockings to her ankles.

"For the love of Pete," he shouted. "The war's over, Phil. I'll buy you a bloody crate of stockings. Will you get on the boat?"

She hesitated, said something he couldn't hear, then climbed onto the pitching gunwale, leaned over, took his outstretched hand, and stepped onto the edge of the Sunfish. "Get flat," he shouted, but she hesitated one second too long, and the mast wavered frantically, the wind caught under the tip of the unmanaged sail, and the boom jibed wildly, flipping the little craft in an instant, and tossing them both into the bay. Robert broke surface under the sail, fought with it frantically, freed himself in the darkness, and shouted Philippa's name. His fear must have sounded in his voice, because her own was so elaborately calm.

"Just fine, ducks. What do we do now?" She was holding on to the low edge of the dinghy, now but inches above the tossing waves. Robert held the mast of the Sunfish before it could drift away, and panted, "Hold on, I'll right her," and swam laboriously around and clambered aboard the centerboard until the mast and sail swung up, dripping, toward the sky.

"Righto," said Philippa's voice, "I'm on the other side, up you get." He scrambled aboard, gathering up the flapping sheet and catching the wildly swinging tiller. Philippa hoisted herself up beside him. With expert ease she rolled her skirt up over her thighs. "Beg pardon, dear, but it's rather awkward," she said. "Now what do I do?"

Robert sighed. He would love to say, sit still, I'll do everything, but there was little point. "Would you like to take the sheet?" he said.

"Right you are." She scrambled into position, and took over the little sail with just the right light tension, scooping up the wind with ease. "What a smashing little craft," she said.

Robert caught up the dinghy bow rope and the Sunfish slowed as if sea-anchored, and then struggled gamely forward.

"Shall we just have a little sail, then, before we go home?" he said wearily.

"Oh Robert." Philippa paused, tightening the sheet. "I am terribly sorry. How utterly foolish of me. I honestly did not believe you, about the petrol. I thought you were being awkward, or I'd never have gone. Are you terribly wet?"

"Don't patronize me," he shouted. "Of course I'm wet. Of course you're wet. Let's just get home, before we drown."

"Rubbish," Philippa said. "We're hardly likely to drown in this dinky piece of water. You could almost walk across. Come now, no dramatics."

"If it's six feet deep it's still over your head," said Robert.

"Nobody drowns within spitting distance of shore, Robert." Philippa jerked the sail in for emphasis, and Robert swung the tiller around, and it came off in his hand.

"Jesus," he said.

"What now, dear?" Philippa was looking landward, at the rain-smeared lights. "Bring her bow around, Robert, she'll lose way."

"I've no tiller," he shouted. He struggled with the hinged clamp, but it was no use. It had come free, screws and all, in his hand. He'd always known it would, one day.

"Robert, she's going to jibe, bring her around."

She did jibe then, with vehemence, backed by a healthy easterly gust. In an instant they were both in the sea. Philippa broke water beside him, struggling for breath, shouting angrily, "Robert, I'm too old for this nonsense."

So was he. He was tired and wet and very cold. The swim around the bow that he had completed easily a few minutes ago was far harder the second time. When he reached the centerboard he clasped it with two hands, and held on, trying to rest. "Phil?" he called.

She was a while in answering. When she did, her own tiredness sounded in her voice. "I'm all right, Robert," she said. "I'll come around and help." He did not answer, conserving his breath, and waited until she had struggled around the stern of the little boat. She also clasped the centerboard.

"Just lean on it," he said, quietly, between breaths.

"Are you all right, Robert?"

"I'm tired. I'm all right."

"What do we do when we get her up? What about the tiller?"

"It's gone. It's broken anyway."

Philippa thought a moment and said, "Right now. We'll right her, and I'll use the centerboard to steer. Like an oar. It will do."

"She'll just skid sideways."

"We'll manage. Come on ducks. Up and at them."

Robert grinned in the darkness. He pulled himself up on the centerboard and the Sunfish righted. It took most of his strength to get himself aboard again, and the rest of it to drag Philippa after him. He sat astride the little boat, with his wet sneakers dangling. "I'm going to take these off," he said, but suddenly was too tired. He knew if they flipped it again, he'd never have the strength to get back on, anyhow. He saw the dinghy, at a distance, swamped, and floating away. It did not seem to matter very much. Perhaps it would come ashore. Philippa handed him the sheet.

"Come now, love," she said, her breath short and shivery. "Pull her in lightly, and I'll steer." She lifted the centerboard free and aligned it with the stern. The little boat began to sail, painfully forward, sliding as much to the west under the easterly wind, and wallowing awkwardly on the waves.

"No use Phil, we're making no headway."

"Of course we are," she said bluntly, and he realized suddenly that she was using the same well of emotion that had carried them all through the war, that arch refusal to recognize an obvious sure defeat. This time, however, it did not work.

The Sunfish slid sideways, and a sudden cracking gust caught it. Robert let out sail as fast as he could, but it jammed somewhere, just for an instant, and the little boat went over like a drowning butterfly. He scrambled upwards, against the rearing hull, as Philippa pitched into the water. But it did no good, and for a third time he felt the black salt water closing over him. He broke surface so slowly that he doubted he ever would.

Philippa was searching for him in the wet darkness. He caught the edge of the capsized hull, and her hand, at once.

"Robert?" she said weakly.

"That's it," he said.

"Robert?"

"That's damned it," he said again. He closed his eyes for a moment, absurdly wanting to sleep. "It's so silly. Damn the bastard. It's so inane."

"Robert? Who?" Philippa's voice had the uneasy delicacy of one addressing the unbalanced.

"God," said Robert, and before she could speak, he said, easing his weight in the water, and adjusting his slipping hold on the wet handrailing, "The bastard could have done this properly twenty-five years ago, if he really wanted. So why the hell now?"

"Come on, dear," said Philippa, her voice thinning with strain. "We'll just get her up again."

"I can't," Robert said angrily, "I'm just too tired. Can you?" It was a rhetorical challenge.

"Of course I can," Philippa said, but he knew she knew she couldn't. He said, between fighting the slapping waves against his face, "Just because that worked against Hitler doesn't mean it will work forever."

"Robert, stop jabbering nonsense, and let's get on with it."

Robert tried to get his arm over the narrow tiller end of the boat, failed, and slipped back into the water. He said, between waves, "The hurricane, the bombs, the Luftwaffe. Everything. And now I'm going to drown in this polluted puddle half a mile from my own house. What's he playing at?"

"Robert, this is ridiculous. How could I face everyone? You and I out here. How could I face *any*one?"

He laughed, choking more than laughing, and managed to croak out, "It's worth it. It's worth it. Just to see Wardlaw's face at the funeral. You'll be dead, Philippa, you won't ever have to face anybody again." He began to laugh slightly insanely, and lost half his hold on the boat.

Philippa caught his sleeve and said fiercely, "I don't think any of your flyboy bravado is the slightest bit funny, Robert Zolenski. We're almost grandparents. We can't just giggle ourselves to death playing silly buggers out here."

"If you must know, my dear, I'm scared out of my wits."

She gasped softly, and said, in an alien voice, "Actually, so am I."

There was a silence in which Robert struggled once more to right the drifting boat, and giving up, they both tried to swim it toward the dim lights.

"I think we're drifting out," Philippa said.

"I can't tell."

"Please don't let go," she said, clutching at his hand. But he did let go, and let go of the boat as well.

"Philippa," he said in response to her shouting his name. "Philippa, do you love me?" There was an odd wistfulness in his voice, which she took to be an acceptance of death. She called his name once more, losing sight of him in the dark, and shouted then, "Yes Robert, I love you. I love you."

"Good," he said, "I love you too. Now try putting your feet down. I'm standing."

Very slowly, Philippa let go of the drifting boat with one hand, and felt fearfully into the cold salt depths with one still-stockinged toe. When she had bent her leg nearly vertical, the toe brushed gently against a soft curve of sand, as comforting as a pillow. She lowered the other foot, and straightened, buoyant, in water up to her neck, but standing. In the growing grayness of dawn she could just make out Robert, taller, shoulder deep in water, watching.

"Sandbar," he said. "There are lots of them. Honest."

"You sod," she shouted. "You effing sod. You knew. You knew. Hurricanes, bombs, Luftwaffe. All your ungodly impossible dramatics, while I made an ass of myself. You knew all along."

"I didn't, Phil. I really didn't." But he knew, already, like the truth about Rhoda, this was something she would never believe. So he began to laugh, then righted the boat, and lowered the sail, and caught hold of the aluminum-tipped prow and began plodding through the water, still cautiously, toward the beach. It followed him like a dog, and Philippa, her hand reluctantly connected to his by its fiberglass length between them, followed too.

She would not speak until they reached the shore. Then she stopped, on the seaweedy old bayfront, scrubby and unromantic, and slowly lowered the rolled hem of her soaking skirt. She straightened her blouse, and roughly knotted the dripping bow, for convenience. Then she straightened her back, with a wince that betrayed the age that her athletic, graceful body denied. She smiled suddenly, in the gray wet light, and held out her hand, "Game, set, and match, my dear. Frightfully well played."

He stood with his mouth open for a long time, and then took her tough broad fingers in his own. They were not beautiful, still, but dear with familiarity. He shook her hand solemnly, and then turned his fingers the other way, and linked them around hers. Hand in hand they walked up the beach to the first wooden boardwalk. They had drifted over two and a half miles, and were at the eastern edge of the Pines. Paul's house stood starkly unlit in the gray dawn, on his ocean-facing dune, a few hundred yards away. When they reached it, Robert was thankful to find it locked. That would mean Stephen had not come here, but found refuge in some den of thieves of his own.

"How will we get in?" said Philippa.

"It's worth a quarter of a million, and there are two Picassos on the walls. And the key is under the mat."

"Doesn't he worry?"

"I don't think he cares." Robert let them in, and went about switching on the beautiful subtle lighting. He pulled his soaking jersey over his head and dropped it on the floor. He started to apologize, then shrugged, and grinned slowly, and said, instead, "Bags I the shower, old girl."

XI

Mid-November, 1963
Cambridge

"Of course they didn't," said Victoria, settling in her rocker while Hugh struggled with kindling and coal on the hearth. "Of course they didn't. It's unimaginable. Give me that towel, love," she said to Mary Jo.

Mary Jo handed her the towel from off the tall wooden drying rack full of diapers and small white nightgowns. Victoria flung it, folded, over her shoulder, with a growing expertise, and slung the baby up on it with a satisfactory burbling hiccup. She patted its back noncommittally. "Where's David?" she said.

"Walking the sitter home," Hugh said, lighting the corner of his heap of crumpled *Times* and split sticks. The flame flared, yellow and heatless, and smoke coiled up the sooty chimney. Victoria drew her chair closer, with the baby still balanced on her shoulder. "It's only unimaginable," Hugh said then, "because they're your parents." He smiled slightly, his older, wise smile, crinkling the smooth young corners of his mouth. The firelight fluttered on his spaniel hair, and he settled cross-legged by the slate hearth. "Here, let me have him," he said, and Victoria handed the light woolly bundle across. "He's dribbly," said Hugh, wiping the small wet mouth with an edge of the baby's shawl.

"Use this," said Vicky, and tossed the towel to him. Hugh was absorbed in studying the near transparent skin of his baby's eyelids. "He's growing lashes," he said, startled.

"What do you expect?" said Mary Jo.

"I thought he was going to be a lizard." Hugh rocked back, leaning against the wall, glad the long drive was over, warm, and immensely content. Victoria fastened her nursing bra, tucked fresh cotton into it, and said, "That's a relief. I was puddles of milk, all the way back from London. Breast feeding's a bloody bother sometimes."

"You're not to stop," said Hugh sharply.

"I shan't," she said. "It's still a bother, though."

"Next time we'll take him with us. I don't know why we didn't."

Victoria made a small sound of disbelieving disgust, while she buttoned her blouse up, and pulled her sweater down again. "Well, I know why we didn't," she said. "And so do you, if you're honest. Wardlaw's why we didn't." She mimicked her mother's voice and said, " 'I do think, dear, if you leave Tristram at home, you'll be far more relaxed. Find a good reliable sitter and then you'll really be able to *enjoy* yourself.' " Enjoy myself! Two hours past milking time and no sign of the dairyman. Screw."

"Come on, Vicks, we were hardly that late."

"*Bloody* Wardlaw. He's so afraid it'll do something. God knows, fart, or puke on him. Like it was an evil spell, and then maybe he'd turn into something. A raging fairy, I daresay. As if he wasn't one already."

"Vicky," Hugh said, reproving, but gently, still rocking the baby in his steady young arms. "You really mustn't. Whatever you think of him, he's still your mother's husband. A little respect, I think, don't you."

"Why should she respect him if she can't stand him?" said

Mary Jo, rising to answer David's jangling ring on the doorbell.

"Because it's only appropriate," said Hugh.

"I'm not bloody respecting anyone who can't stand my baby."

"Not *your* baby, love. Any baby. He's just, I don't know, squeamish. He'll get over it. Just wait." He stood up and took the baby to its crib and returned, stretching and yawning. "I don't think he's such a bad sort really, Vicks," he said. "I rather like him. Serves a damn decent port, anyhow."

"I wouldn't know," said Vicky, pointedly. Hugh laughed. She was still smarting over having been asked by her mother to retire with the ladies, after dinner.

"Nobody, Hugh, nobody does that any longer. It is so appallingly dated."

"I couldn't believe it," Mary Jo said, her voice hitting that nasal pitch that always made Hugh ever so slightly wince. "I just couldn't believe it. I thought that went out with the Dark Ages."

"Wardlaw belongs to the Dark Ages," said Vicky.

"Actually," Hugh said, "I rather enjoyed it."

"So did I," David said, entering the room and dropping his coat comfortably on the rush matting of the floor. "I say, Hugh, what did you think of old MacKenzie?"

"The old colonel?" Hugh laughed secretively, and said with a winking nod to David, "It was all balls, I'm sure. He was shooting a line. Of course everyone knows the Arabs are frightfully frisky, but really."

"He swore he saw it happen. And he was there, in the Gulf."

"Rubbish, anyhow," said Hugh. "Jolly super story though, eh what?"

"Go make me some coffee, please, Hugh," Victoria said coldly, "I'm fagged out." She and Mary Jo exchanged a sour glance as the two men went laughing to the kitchen. They returned with a tray and four mugs of weak instant coffee, swimming in milk, and a plate of cookies.

"How cozy," Hugh said, settling by the fire again, but he was only half mocking.

"Makes me think of Wardlaw," said Vicky, "Every night, every damned night. 'Time for my Horlicks, dear. Like a bicky, dear? Has Mitzy had her walkies? Must lock up now. Always like to be locked up by ten.' Good God, how does mother stand it? How does she stand it?"

"Maybe she doesn't," said Hugh. There was a silence, and Vicky said in a small voice, "What do you mean?"

Hugh shrugged. Then he looked up and said, "Well, David, what do *you* think of the famous night on Fire Island?"

David was so taken aback that he swallowed half his milky coffee in one gulp and choked and spluttered, and had to run to the kitchen for a length of paper towel.

"You all right?" said Mary Jo. He nodded, still gasping.

"We were only just discussing it," Hugh said mildly. "In a purely academic sense. Vicky thought it was all totally above-board, and no doubt she was right. I was just curious, what you thought. From what I heard it was all a bit peculiar, the pair of them arriving at ten A.M. in someone else's clothes."

"They'd *been* in the water," David said, recovering. "The boat had capsized. From what I heard I think they were jolly lucky not to have drowned."

"But what were they doing out there, David?" Mary Jo said. "It was such an awful night. Robert never went out in bad weather on that thing, or in the dinghy. He was always kind of cautious, a little scared, I guess."

"Dear knows," said David, shrugging. "I suppose mother took one of her whims. She can be quite appallingly willful, you know. The old girl has a frightful lot of spirit."

The baby cried and Vicky got up, but Hugh waved her back to her chair, and went himself, to settle it. Vicky curled up, snug and well tended, her hands about her coffee mug. Mary Jo sat alone by the hearth, nibbling a cookie and staring into the fire. She said slowly, "You know what I think, David? You know what I think. I think he made love to her at Paul's house. I think he did."

"Never," David said.

"Oh surely not," said Vicky. "It's quite unthinkable. Indecent practically. Anyhow, they're a bit old for that, don't you think?"

"No, come on, listen," said Mary Jo suddenly, urgently. "I know it's kind of hard for you to imagine, because they're your parents. But you see, I've seen them, Robert, I mean, from another side. I think he was just so hurt and so jealous, because of what I'd done, you know"—she shrugged a small embarrassed defiance—"with David, that he had to get back at me, somehow. Anyhow. And he did."

"Well, God, Mary Jo," said Vicky, "what about my mother? Do you think she'd, well, let him?" She paused for breath, and her hand was a little trembly on her coffee mug.

"Maybe to get back at Wardlaw," said David, slowly. "Besides, she's really rather fond of father. You know she still keeps things. Funny things. She still keeps her wedding ring. You know, her first one. I've seen it in her jewel case, when I was little. I took it out once, to look at, and she got quite upset. And she's got other things. Silly things. A champagne cork, well, that could have been more recent, but I can't see her being that sort of sentimental over Andrew. And a bar of soap. Just a bar of soap. She told me once it was from during the war. Soap was hard to get or something, and he got her a whole bar and she just kept it."

"Mother's so funny about soap," Vicky said suddenly. "They've got so much money, but she still saves all the little scraps of soap, from the guest bedrooms even, and puts them in a little jar."

Hugh shrugged, and said, "My mother has this extraordinary thing about butter. She saves all the papers and uses them to grease tins, or scrapes them and puts *that* in a little jar."

"Good God," said Vicky, "we'd best not ever get them together again. Suppose they get their little jars mixed." She laughed, delightedly, and leaned back in her rocker, stretching her feet to the fire. " 'Spare the coal, Vicky,' " she said suddenly in Andrew's bass, " 'that's half a scuttleful just this evening.' Oh, God, to live like that, all cramped up like crabs."

"That's just the war," said David slowly. "And all that sentimental rubbish, mother and all, that's just the war too. I suppose it wasn't because she particularly loved father so much.
It was just because they shared the war when they were young
and they're all so frightfully reminiscent about it."

"Reminiscent enough to hop in the sack for old times' sake?"
said Hugh with a grin. He was what Andrew Wardlaw would
call a "stirrer," although Andrew Wardlaw was something of
a stirrer himself.

"No," David said firmly, not angrily, but with confidence.
"Not father."

"How are you so sure?" Mary Jo said. "I think I know him
better than you do."

"Quite frankly," said David, "I feel I know him very well.
And quite frankly again"—his voice changed subtly, turned
older, with the slightest tinge of scorn—"I think he lacks the
guts."

"How so?" said Hugh.

"He's a coward. He's always been a coward, all his life.
He's spent his whole life running away from one failure after
another. Failing, and running away, that's the whole pattern
of his life."

"I honestly don't think," said Hugh mildly, "that anyone
who flew fighters in the Battle of Britain can be called a
coward."

"Why not?" David returned, a little angry at being reminded
of that. "Why not? Anyhow, that's all balls about the Battle
of Britain. He was hardly in it. He missed most of it anyhow.
Broke his ankle up in Yorkshire. You know, the day he met
mother, you've heard that story."

"He still flew fighters," said Vicky uncertainly.

"Of course he did. But it doesn't make him all that much of
a hero. I happen to know he only got into the war because he
was running away from something. Something in his career.
Some part he was frightened to play because he was going to
make a mess of it. And he was pretty terrified all through the

war, and only married mother so he'd have someone to come home to, someone to hold his hand."

"Steady on," said Hugh, "that's a bit harsh."

"It's true," said David. "And then he ran away from his marriage, *and* from the theater. Took up writing that rubbish instead. He's spent his whole life hiding from the slightest hint of a challenge."

"How would you know all that?" said Vicky uncertainly.

"He told me," said David, his scorn grown large and triumphant. "That same appalling night when you're all imagining him playing the great lover. He was too damned drunk for that, for a start, by the way. He told me the whole gorgeous story of his life."

Vicky was quiet for a long time. She picked at the hem of her tweed skirt and smoothed her nylons. She was wishing they'd never gone to dinner at her mother's London flat, and never gotten home so late, and tired, and never gotten into this conversation. She'd have to be up at six for the early feed. She started to rise, but felt too weary and softly warm and said, instead, "You liked those books once, David. You loved them. You read them day and night."

"*When* I was a child," said David. "Please. Of course I did. I thought they were bloody marvelous. I thought father was bloody marvelous, too, but I didn't know him then. I was all for being just exactly like him. I was even convinced I wanted to go off, like he did, and fight someone else's war, for freedom and all that rot. Let's face it, father could lay it on pretty thick about the good old days, couldn't he?"

"He only mentioned it once," said Mary Jo.

"What?" David was ready to argue.

"The war."

"She's right," said Victoria, "father does not talk about it."

"But we all know it's there, damn," said David, "don't we? They've bloody drummed it into our subconscious all our lives."

"All he said was, 'It wasn't very special really, that time. It was only that we were young,' " said Mary Jo. "That's all he said."

"*My* father said, 'We just lived for tomorrow,' " Hugh said suddenly. He stood up and found the fireguard, and set it in front of his new fire that had only now become warm. "Which is strange, because now they all seem to live for yesterday. Come on, mother, time for bed."

Vicky looked up, narrowed her eyes suddenly with an odd unease. Then she stood, tiredly, and said, "Yes, of course. What about you?" she added to Mary Jo and David.

"Oh, we'll just sit up, I think," Mary Jo said. She had settled in front of the fire, and removed the fireguard again. "And sleep late in the morning." David moved to the phonograph and put a Beatles record on to play. He leaned back his handsome blond head and swayed to the music. Vicky fought a surge of resentment at their freedom and gathered an armful of diapers from the rack.

"*Try* not to wake Tristram when you come up the stairs," she said at last. They never did actually, but she had, in some way, to voice her small discontent.

When she and her husband had gone, David settled on the floor and Mary Jo lay down with her head on his knee. He put his arm around her body, letting his fingers drift at will. "Are you going in early?" David said.

"No. Not till ten; Peter knew I'd be out late." David resented this Peter, Vicky and Hugh's friend, who had settled in Cambridge and opened an antique shop, where Mary Jo now worked. He was older, and terribly self-assured, and always chose the cleverest wines at dinner.

"He certainly makes it easy for you," he said, also needing to voice a small discontent. "I rather think he fancies you."

"That's crazy," said Mary Jo, a little too quickly. "Wasn't that a dreadful party."

"I rather enjoyed it." David stiffened, his hand stopped halfway up her sweater. "By the way, why don't you get some decent clothes? This was hardly appropriate, you know." He gestured to her short, above-the-knee corduroy skirt, over her lacy black tights.

"What's wrong with it?" she demanded, sitting up.

"Nothing. Nothing, for kicking about the shop, or whatever. But, really, dear, once the season's underway, there are going to be more parties. One does have to dress, actually, for some of them. One can't go to the May Ball in one's jeans."

Mary Jo sat up and pushed her thick hair out of her face. She stared at David with utter amazement. Finally she said, "Do you realize that in all the time I knew him, your father, your own father, never once objected to the way I dressed. And he's twenty-six years older than you. What's happening to you?"

David withdrew into himself, and wrapped his arms about himself, as always when his father was mentioned. Then he regained composure, straightened his ascot, and said, "I'm quite sure he didn't, old girl." Then he added, his voice brittle with scorn, "But then, what the hell would he know? He's an American."

Mid-November, 1963

London

"She's an American, dear," Philippa said patiently. "That's simply the way they speak." She was sitting up against her pillows, checking the following day's appointments in her large leather-bound diary while Andrew prepared for bed. "You will have to see about that painting yourself," she said, "I have Red Cross in the morning, and the hospital trust in the afternoon."

"Bother," said Andrew softly. He was standing in shoes

and black socks and garters and white shirt, carefully adjusting his trousers on the trouser press. "Can't you possibly cancel? I did so want your opinion."

"Yes, and you'd promptly ignore it. Go on now, you'll either have it or not, according to your own wishes. So have it." She knew she would not like the painting. It would be valuable, another thing to be insured and carefully protected, and it would be dreary, dull, and in impeccably unquestionable taste. She said then, closing the diary, "To be perfectly frank, I thought Mary Jo behaved rather well, tonight."

"She behaved appallingly," said Andrew. "Let's face it, the girl has absolutely not a grain of sense. Going on that way to MacKenzie about the blacks in America. What in hell interest would that be to him, eh? Bored the pants off the poor sod, when she wasn't positively enraging him."

"He did rather start it. 'Black men begin at Calais' is hardly an acceptable postwar philosophy. Of course the poor girl was rather off track, raving on about racism, but how was she supposed to know what he meant?"

"Perfectly clear what he meant. Black men do begin at Calais. I've no time for the Froggies, myself."

"Yes," said Philippa, without spirit. She leaned over the heavy brocade bedcover, and laid the diary on the bedside table, with her reading glasses and the *Times* crossword puzzle. Andrew took his shirt off and fussed about a while in net undershirt and shorts, still wearing his shoes. Then he found his pajama jacket, buttoned it up carefully, starting from the bottom, and sat, removing his shoes and methodically placing a wooden last in each. He set them aside, removed his shorts with his back to the bed, and stepped into the pajama bottoms. They were striped, vertically, blue and paler blue. He tucked the jacket in and pulled the trousers up well over his waist and tied the cord. Philippa had not watched, the while. Instead she had let her eyes examine each of the Dutch oils on the walls, the white picture molding, the high molded-plaster ceiling with its elaborate center rose. When Andrew was actually in bed, beside her, with his half-eyeglasses on the bridge of his nose, and his collar buttoned up to the graying stubble of his hair, she turned to face him.

"I'll just read a bit, old girl. Can't sleep otherwise."

"Of course," she said, slipping down the bed, and pushing one of her two pillows to the floor. Andrew waited a moment, sighed slightly, then got up, walked around the bed, picked it up, and laid it on the pink velvet armchair in the corner of the room. He returned to bed and Philippa, lips firmly set, refused to acknowledge the entire small act.

He settled again, but laid down his book and said, "Damn it all, we will have to do something."

Philippa did not wish to answer. She had been on the edge of sleep, thinking about the party, the golden warmth of fire and candlelight in their beautiful dining room. Not quite the Sussex dining room. (She had never forgiven him that loss, the lovely brick inglenook with its ancient black oak benches.) Nor even the stern gray dramatics of the dining hall of Lamlash House. But beautiful. Not beautiful just now, of course; rather a chaos of dirty china and silver and smudged half-full port glasses amidst overflowing ashtrays, pungent with the smell of cigars. Still, that was Jean's affair, not hers. She could never thank Andrew enough for finding Jean. The woman was an absolute marvel.

"What will we have to do something about?" she asked, quietly, turning on her side, gentling toward her husband.

"That appalling female. Terrifying woman. She'll jeopardize David's entire future. Where can he take her, will you tell me, the way she talks and the way she dresses? Did you see the length of that skirt?"

"How could I miss?" said Philippa mildly. "They're all wearing them. It's only the fashion."

"Vicky doesn't."

"Vicky has no taste, dear. No fashion sense. She never has had."

"Damned sensible of her, if that's the fashion. Always thought the girl had a good head on her shoulders."

Philippa opened her eyes wide, staring at the Regency patterned wallpaper. Finally she said, lightly, "Once she came around."

"Indeed," Andrew said, not breaking stride. "And she has. Always knew she would. Quite a decent chap, actually, Hugh. Did I tell you I met his father, Thursday, at my club? Grand fellow, the best. Had a chat about the boy; he thought to put his name down for his old school. Quite all right with me actually. How about you?"

Philippa sighed and said nothing. She was enjoying the unquestioning pleasure of her first grandchild, a warm damp bundle of gratification. She did not wish already to imagine him with blazer and tie and scuffed sore knees.

"*He* didn't think much of the name, either," Andrew said with some satisfaction. "Bit sissy, what?" Philippa still said nothing, and he added, "But he's quite a likable little chap really."

"Who?"

"The baby. Tristram. Where was he anyhow?"

"Home. In Cambridge. With a sitter."

"Oh. Hm. Why didn't they bring the little chap along? Would have liked to see him." Philippa smiled to the Regency wallpaper. She knew he was only saying that now because it was too late; he was safe. She took it at its true value, and made no reply.

"Mary Jo's a great help to Vicks, you know," she said instead. "With the baby. And they get on rather well, I gather. With a few differences."

"I've no objection to her being there, Philippa. You know that. As a sort of mother's help, even. Jolly well. But this relationship with David is going to have to stop, you know. Certainly before it goes any further. I don't suppose they go to bed." He cut the end of the sentence short, with a question, which she was meant to answer with reassurance or condemnation. She gave silence, and he said, "Frankly, my opinion of the silly woman's morals is not very high."

Philippa wondered what his opinion might be if he knew the

whole story of Mary Jo's origins, something there had been a broad conspiracy to conceal from him. Eventually she said only, ambiguously, "Well, they are rather young."

"Quite." Then Andrew decided to make light and said playfully, "Well, he's a healthy young man, and I suppose he'll soon enough be feeling the need of a good poke." As always when he dealt with sexual matters his voice was schoolboyish and forced. "And it may as well be little Yankee Doodle. As long as he keeps the thing in its appropriate place. Nothing serious, or permanent, or anything."

"I wouldn't imagine for a moment it will be permanent," she said, "even if they married."

"They mustn't marry," Andrew said angrily. "They shan't marry. I'll see to that. Besides, I don't think it's a topic one should treat so lightly. You know how I feel about divorce."

"Yes," she said quietly, turning sideways from him, again, in the bed. "I know."

Andrew Wardlaw was quiet for a long while. Then he leaned forward, removed his bifocals, and placed them in their case. He laid his book, a study of the battle of Waterloo, down, with the glasses case marking his place, and turned out the light. He slid down in the bed and lay on his back. She hoped he would turn, before he slept, or else he would snore. He did turn, but toward her, and said, "I'm sorry, old girl, that was rather thoughtless."

"No matter."

He stretched out a shy, boyish hand and found her fingers. His hand was warm, and she allowed him to curl her own up into a ball, and hold it. It was a comforting feeling. He said, "You know, old girl," and then stopped.

She whispered, "What was that?" half asleep, and thought he would not continue.

But after a while he said, "You know when you were in America, I had this terribly silly, I don't know, sort of a fear."

"Fear?"

"About Robert. I was afraid. I was afraid you'd, well, go a

bit, get into a bit of a spin about him. Again. I know it was absolutely ridiculous and all, but I was really quite afraid. Jealous, really, I suppose."

"Andrew. What nonsense."

"I know, I know. Ridiculous of me, but I couldn't get it out of my mind."

She sighed and said patiently, "You know that Robert and I drive each other up the pole. And always have. Ten minutes in each other's company and we've both completely lost the rag. It's not very pleasant. You've seen us together," she added. "We simply cannot get on."

"Of course," he said, "I know. Only. Only sometimes"—his voice went very tentative and shy—"sometimes it all seems rather exciting. I'm just a bit jealous, I suppose."

"Of the way we fight? Don't be ridiculous. It would absolutely appall you."

"Yes. Naturally. Oh damn it all, Philippa, I never should have said anything. Pardon me, do. I imagine it's just the old animal thing about one's mate."

Philippa smiled in the darkness, trying to think of Andrew in relation to anything animal at all. "Surely you know me better than that. You know me so well."

"Oh yes. I do know you so well." He was silent for a long time with his hand gripped around her fingers. She sensed his other hand move toward her, and for a moment quite surprisedly imagined he was going to attempt to make love to her. He did not, though. The first hand tightened suddenly, as if he were in the midst of a sudden spasm of pain. He blurted out, "Did he make love to you, Philippa?"

"Andrew!"

"I'm sorry. I'm terribly sorry. How appalling of me."

"It's quite unthinkable, Andrew."

"Yes, of course."

"Unthinkable."

"Quite."

He rolled over, then, with his back to her, and after a long while she turned, and gently put her arms about his shoulders from behind. She rested her face between his boyish sharp shoulder blades, comforted by the familiar smell of him, vaguely sweet and unsexual, like a small child. "Do you want?" he whispered dutifully.

"No. No. Far too late."

"I suppose," he said, with an equally dutiful try at disappointment. "Early rise tomorrow. Good night, old girl."

Philippa closed her eyes, half dreaming, finding in her vision suddenly an empty stretch of beach, sand, golden sand, and the sea, and something, something she could not make out, tangled and black, between her and the fresh blue water. She stretched her mind toward it, and then failed, not remembering clearly what, or where, the place might be. She curled closer to Andrew, marvelously peaceful, without the exhausting potential of passion. The rain rattled against the tall old sash, washing the London street without, an old, unchanging, and familiar sound.

Safe as houses, she thought. Safe as houses. And quiet, quiet as the grave.

Mid-November, 1963
Fire Island Pines

"You can't stay out there alone, Robert. You can't. It's not even safe. There's not a soul about. You'll get, God knows, *cabin* fever out there alone in the winter. The place is an absolute mausoleum."

"I like it."

"You can't *like* it. You might survive it. You might put up with it. But you can't like it." Paul shook his head and waved his arms so that the cashmere sweater looped by its tied sleeves about his neck came loose and dropped to the concrete dock. "I won't allow it," he said suddenly. "I'll insist you come back to the mainland." He waited a minute and said shrewdly, "I'll tell your mother you're ill." It was his final weapon.

"I'm not ill. And my mother would only think it served me right if I was."

"Of course she would. And she'll make your life an absolute misery," he said, triumphant, picking up his sweater.

Robert said, "Over four miles of open water, even *my* mother won't manage that. She hasn't got a boat and she can't even swim." Then he looked off at the distant outline of the mainland and said, "Do me a favor and don't tell her."

"She will wonder what's happened to you, you know. When she phones your apartment in the city in the middle of January."

"I don't have an apartment in the city."

"Oh, you've not. Oh, Robert. You've not given up the lease."

"Why not? I don't need it. I'm not going back to it. I live here now."

Paul walked away to the edge of the dock and stared at the empty place in the water where the ferry would be shortly. It was the last week of service and there was no one else waiting yet, on the landing that in high summer was packed with weekenders. "So you're really going to just cut yourself off from the whole world. All your friends. Everyone who cares for you"—his voice was slightly shaky—"all because of that dumb stupid bitch treating you like . . ."

"Because of *who*?" Robert said, with a curious uncertainty.

"Mary Jo of course. Leaving you."

Robert began to laugh, setting down Paul's third suitcase with the other two. "You're not serious," he said at last. "You don't honestly think . . ."

"Well, why else are you staying away out here alone?"

"Do you honestly think I'm becoming a hermit? Thwarted in love. Brokenhearted over Mary Jo. Good Lord, I thought you knew me better than that."

"Was it because of Philippa, then?" said Paul suddenly.

"Philippa. Whatever could Philippa have to do . . . can you not realize that I'm staying simply because I like it."

"*Last* winter was bad enough. But Mary *Jo's* gone."

"I've noticed."

"You'll be all alone," Paul insisted.

"But I like to be alone."

"I see." Paul nodded stiffly and began fussing with his suede satchel, looking for nothing.

"Oh c'mon. You know what I mean. Of course I like being with people. I just like being alone too. Anyhow, I've got the cats."

"I hate cats."

"I know," Robert said patiently, "but you haven't got them. I've got them."

Paul nodded and walked away to the end of the pier. It was a brisk cold day, smelling of winter, a cold shifty north wind sending ripples across the empty Pines harbor and blowing little waves of sand in eddies on the boardwalks. The sky was utterly empty and clear, blue from horizon to horizon. The mainland was gaining its winter gray.

Paul came back suddenly, walking deliberately, eyes down. He walked right up to Robert and said, "I wish you would find someone else. Honestly. Someone nice to settle down with. You know, I've found someone myself." His voice dropped shyly. "I've found the most marvelous boy. He's rather young, of course, but terribly nice. Rather like David. To look at, I mean. He's just eighteen actually, and terribly sweet. Charles. He'll be meeting me, at Sayville."

"Another soldier of fortune?" Robert said with a wry smile.

"Oh no. Oh not at all. He's a pacifist actually. A conscientious objector." He said hurriedly, "Of course it takes tremendous courage, you know, to stand up for something you believe in."

"Of course," said Robert. He paused and added, "Here she comes." There was a white smudge developing between the mainland gray and the island.

"Robert?"

"Yes."

"Will you come across with me? Just for the evening. I'll take you to dinner. At the Foster House. Lobster." He paused a moment and looked away. "I'll send Charles away. Somewhere."

"No. Thank you. But no."

Paul nodded, unsurprised, and tied his sweater back on, and adjusted the silver medallion on his black turtleneck. The ferry drew nearer. He said cautiously, "Do you ever hear from Philippa?"

"All the time. Actually, she said to remember her to you. To 'that splendid chap, Paul,' was what she said."

"Oh, do tell. Really?" He was terribly pleased. "I thought she was absolutely marvelous, Robert. I really did." Robert looked off again at the ferry drawing nearer; the *Island Princess*, the small fast light one.

He said, "Oh she is, she is." He paused and then said quite suddenly, "Do you know that once there was a time, during the war, when we were so close, so very close, that I thought I would know if she were killed. I'd just know. And I'd crash. On purpose. I'd crash my plane."

Paul was a little embarrassed. He looked away, and then allowed a decent interval and said, "Did you ever, oh you know, Robert, did you ever think of getting back together, you and she?"

"Never. It's unimaginable," said Robert, at once.

"Of course." Paul was quiet, as if he had overstepped. "And David? How is he getting on?"

"Fine. Settling down at Cambridge. Doing quite well, I believe."

"And Victoria?"

"Happily married. And a mother. I'm a grandfather. Didn't I tell you?"

"Robert, you didn't." Paul's voice was subtly hurt.

"I'm terribly sorry. I was sure I had. I was working so hard at the time. Look, I am sorry. I hadn't seen much of you."

"I suppose you told the cats," said Paul. He untied the cashmere sweater and pulled it over his head. He said eventually, having distilled hurt to anger, "Well, anyhow, at least it's legitimate. It didn't look like it was going to be, for a while."

"I wouldn't have cared," Robert said lightly, "I'd almost prefer it. Now she's so snugly in the fold I doubt I'll ever hear much from her again."

"So. She's seen the light. Don't complain."

"Yeah, I suppose so. Most rebels do, eventually," Robert said slowly, "even if it's only the fuse on the bomb held by their offspring. The rebellions of youth we relinquish for our children. Philippa did. Now Vicky's done too."

"What about you, grandpa?"

"Is your birthday before or after mine?" Robert said with a small smile.

"*I'm* not living like Robinson Crusoe all winter, in blue jeans and a Columbia sweatshirt." Robert looked down at the faded, cracked lettering, and shrugged.

"I suppose Mary Jo is still *with* David?" Paul said sharply, as the ferry slowed in the harbor mouth, settling down, with the cold water slapping angrily about it. "And not run off and left him too."

"Oh, she's with him. She's with him." He was smiling so broadly that Paul said, "I really don't understand you. Isn't it even the littlest bit humiliating?"

"It's massively humiliating," he said mildly. "But we'll treat that as penance. Paul, she didn't exactly leave. I sent her. I even paid for her plane ticket."

"Did you *want* her to go?"

"She *had* to go. She's my fighter cover, don't you see? An escort for David. As long as she's with him, and God willing it will be a long, long time, he's mine. He's unacceptable. She's unacceptable. Inappropriate. She won't do." He turned his voice expertly narrow. " 'My God, old man, the girl's an absolute albatross.' I've hung the American flag about his neck. Hands across the sea, and all that rot. Screw Wardlaw. Screw Hallsworth. Screw the Queen. Gentlemen"—he picked up Paul's suitcase—"your ferry."

Paul shook his hand at the edge of the dock. His blue eyes went dreamily wistful. "I'll worry about you," he said.

"That's very kind. And unnecessary." Robert was used to Paul's farewells. "I can't wait," he said.

"Why not?"

"Got to feed the cats."

"You're a hopeless bastard."

"That's right." He smiled, waved, and turned away.

But he stopped as Paul climbed up the stairs to the roof deck. Robert was leaning familiarly over something at the bow of the boat when Paul, once more out in the cold open sun, called down from above, "Thanksgiving dinner? The Foster House. Turkey?"

"If I'm not busy."

"What's going to happen in November?"

"Nothing. Okay. Thanksgiving." Paul smiled to himself, nodded, and made a brisk little British-army-style salute. He settled himself on the top deck, with his suitcases in an open square about his feet, secure in the emptiness.

Robert turned back to the faded planking at the bow of the ferry. *Fire Island Princess* was painted in bold black letters. Under them, coated in forty years' layers of paint, but still visible in little raised ridges, like the spars of a ship lost in sand, were the old, old letters, *Diana*. Five round bullet holes, crusted with filling paint, circled the name, an irregular corona.

Robert patted the side of the boat and walked away. He went inland for a while, over the boardwalks, and walked out to the eastern end of the Pines, toward Water Island. Then he followed the old inland sand track, the Burma Road, down among the dunes, enjoying the sun, hot, in that sheltered place, away from the wind. Eventually he got tired of slipping and sliding in sand and beach grass and turned toward the ocean strand. On the top of a deserted dune, just before the fall away to the smooth, ocean-pounded beach, he stood, invigorated by the wind and solitude, and looked back across the bay side of the island. He always felt a marauder on the ocean beach. The bay beach was his, the old island, the island of his childhood, where the summer shacks stood and the smugglers came and went. That was his island, from the days when it belonged to men like Stan Zolenski and no one ever came there who acted in plays, and no one had ever heard of Picasso.

Far out on the bay, the ferry bounced to its winter harbor. He watched it, remembering the surge of its power under his childhood's feet. "Cheerio, old girl," he called. "Ta-ta and all that . . ."